Ben and Sarah,

I hope you really enjoy this book. But I didn't write it to entertain. My prayer is that, it will, in a sense, be a 443 page parable, that will cause people to better understand 1 Pet. 2:18-23. Years ago, I made it my life's verses.

Ben, it's so wonderful to watch the Lord answer the prayer I prayed over you when I first held you!

Stay steadfast!

Papa

Michael Green
(official autograph)

Heaven Comes Later

Michael Green

CROSSBOOKS

CrossBooks™
A Division of LifeWay
1663 Liberty Drive
Bloomington, IN 47403
www.crossbooks.com
Phone: 1-866-879-0502

© 2013 Michael Green. All rights reserved.

No part of this book may be reproduced, stored in a retrieval system, or transmitted by any means without the written permission of the author.

First published by CrossBooks 2/18/2013

ISBN: 978-1-4627-2457-4 (sc)
ISBN: 978-1-4627-2459-8 (hc)
ISBN: 978-1-4627-2458-1 (e)

Library of Congress Control Number: 2013900351

Scripture quotations are from The Holy Bible, English Standard Version® (ESV®), copyright © 2001 by Crossway, a publishing ministry of Good News Publishers. Used by permission. All rights reserved.

Printed in the United States of America

This book is printed on acid-free paper.

Any people depicted in stock imagery provided by Thinkstock are models, and such images are being used for illustrative purposes only.

Certain stock imagery © Thinkstock.

Because of the dynamic nature of the Internet, any web addresses or links contained in this book may have changed since publication and may no longer be valid. The views expressed in this work are solely those of the author and do not necessarily reflect the views of the publisher, and the publisher hereby disclaims any responsibility for them.

List of Main Characters

Luke Martin	Plantation owner
Sally Martin	Luke's wife
Frank Martin	Luke's son
Mabin	Luke's slave; close friend

Luke's other slaves
    Toby   Joshua
    Zekiel   Gideon
    Tal and Sadie   Hope
    Mahta   Otis
    Ambrose   Dinah
    Clara   Washington
    Richard   Sondabay
    Deanna – 10 year-old girl
    Russell - Deanna's 1 yr. old brother

Tom Grant, plantation owner	Luke's neighbor
Etta	Tom's house slave

Tom's other slaves
    Abel   Belle
    Big Joe   Maybeth
    Rena

Wally Matkin	Owner of general store
Henry Blackstone	Owner of feed store
Ben and Wilma Statler	Banker and his wife
Sid and Maggie Pennington	Tal and Sadie's former owners
Jeb Dukett	Slave trader
Sheriff Patrick Roily	Town sheriff
Pastor Matthew Davies	Luke's pastor
Al Willis	Friend from church
Ted Willis, Nathan Willis	Al Willis' sons
William and Holly Mance	Gin house designer and his wife
Jerry Ellis	Luke's antagonist
Gregory Ellis, Rascal Ellis	Jerry Ellis' sons
Lenny; Billy Glenn	Community trouble-makers

Preface

Slavery has always been a part of human history, a dark side of all races that cannot be denied. Growing up in the United States of America in the mid-1900s, I learned about the enslavement of blacks by whites and wondered what it felt like to be owned. The concept of people owning people in a land said to be founded on the principles of faith, freedom, and liberty for all presented a double standard that I've struggled with.

As an adult, I have had African American friends and African American employees, and as a pastor, I have performed weddings between black and white couples. It is difficult, if not impossible, for me to imagine myself believing the black man to be anything but fully human. Yet that is how the cruel slave masters justified their wicked treatment of slaves.

The apostle Paul writes in 1 Timothy 6, "Let all who are under a yoke as slaves regard their own masters as worthy of all honor, so that the name of God and the teaching may not be reviled. Those who have believing masters must not be disrespectful on the ground that they are brothers; rather they must serve all the better since those who benefit by their good service are believers and beloved".

I've wondered, *could I do that if I were owned by another man?* I don't think I could, in the power of my own strength, without Christ. Only if I was doing so in obedience to someone greater, whom I loved dearly - that someone being the Lord my Creator.

This is addressed in 1 Peter 2:18-19 "Servants, be subject to your masters with all respect, not only to the good and gentle but also to the unjust. For this is a gracious thing, when mindful of God one endures sorrows while suffering unjustly."

Historians make fleeting comments about there being "a few" slave owners who treated their slaves righteously, but those situations don't make exciting and anger-stirring stories, and so, little has been written about them. I have wondered about those few. Would I be among them?

One morning, I read the apostle Paul's letter to Philemon in the Bible. Later that day, as I went about my work, I believe the Holy Spirit began melding what I'd read in the New Testament with my questions about the human side of slavery, and a story began to form in my mind. That evening, I sat down and began to write.

The creation of this story has been an adventure for me. It took on a life of its own, carrying me along on a journey from a short story into a full-fledged novel! Sometimes I would come to the end of a writing session and think, *So that's where you were going with this*! Although I had a general idea of how it would end, I was frequently surprised at the turn of events and how they developed. Some cultural and historical aspects were researched before including them, and others were confirmed as I continued to study various historical sources and visited the area in which this story was set.

I would like to give a heartfelt thank-you to my dear wife, Laura, and to my family and friends for their encouragement and editorial input on this book. Thanks to Steve McClure for his skillful editing; his insights helped to improve the story. Thank you, also, to artist Karen Hall for her wonderful sketches. They help to make the story come alive.

I am sending him back to you ... that you might have him back forever, no longer as a slave but more than a slave, as a beloved brother – especially to me, but how much more to you, both in the flesh and in the Lord.

The Apostle Paul, in Philemon 1:12, 15-16

Chapter 1

Luke Martin had no intention of buying a slave when he came into town. He just needed a few supplies and a saddle repaired. The cobbler told him it would be finished in a couple of hours, so Luke had some time to kill.

The busy streets of Grantsville, Georgia, offered little shade, and the day was hot and muggy. The only respite from the beating sun was provided by two gigantic, spreading live oak trees near the stables. A couple of benches with backrests had been placed under each of the trees and that was all it took for them to become the central gathering place of the community. Luke sat on one of the benches, crunching an apple while watching Jeb Dukett, the slave trader, as he stood on a makeshift platform beside a shackled adult female slave. Jeb was a good diversion on this lazy day as he tried to convince the small group of men gathered around him that she was just about the best cook and housekeeper that had ever set foot in Grantsville. Once in a while, as Jeb was talking, different men would come up to her and check her teeth, hands, and feet, or even feel her arm and leg muscles for strength as if they were buying livestock to plow their fields.

"I know how hard it is to afford everything you need, gentlemen," Jeb was saying, "but in these modern times, wives are not meant for manual labor. Why, your little woman wouldn't be nearly so tired at the end of the day - and she'll probably even live longer - if you were to gift her with one of my fine house Negroes to relieve her of all that cooking, laundry, scrubbing, and the many other things that shorten her life."

Jeb paused, removed a sweat-stained handkerchief from his back pocket, and smiled, giving them time to think about it while he wiped his brow.

"Whadya say, gentlemen? Do I hear $800? This'n is worth every penny."

"I'll give $250," shouted a grizzled old farmer from the back of the group of onlookers.

Jeb looked as if he was about to have a heart attack. Having perfected his acting skills over the years, his look of being personally offended had become a regular feature.

"Not even close, Harvey! I spend a lot of time finding the very best Negroes for ya'll and here you are makin' fun of me. I won't take less'n $500 for Belle here. She's a real prize. Why, she can even sew! I should know." Jeb looked down and pulled at his shirt. "She put this here button back on this here shirt, she did."

"$260," said someone in the middle of the slowly growing crowd.

"I'll give $285," shouted another.

Jeb's shock shifted to frustration - another look he used regularly. "I ain't got time to mess around. If you don't want to give me a fair price, well, there are more towns down the road and the folks there are much more generous. Now, whadya say?"

A short, well-dressed man raised his hand and said, "$350, Jeb. That's more than fair and you know it."

"I need at least $400 for this fine stock," said Jeb with a determined tone in his voice. "She's worth $500 to your wife, fellas! Now, c'mon," he pleaded.

It was late July, the cotton bolls were blossoming, and the harvest would soon follow. Planters were in need of workers but it was also the time of year when they were the shortest on funds. Until they were paid for their crop, families were holding a little tighter to their pocketbooks. After harvest, there would be plenty of spending on the more pleasurable things, but not today. Today, men were interested in harvest equipment such as field slaves, rather than house servants.

After a little more pleading and cajoling, Jeb dropped his arms to his sides and presented his practiced broken-hearted look.

"Sold, to Tom Grant," he said dejectedly. "The bargain of a lifetime, I tell ya."

Jeb shook his head, then threw up his hands and turned to a man near the stable door. "Bring out the big'un and the boy, will ya, George?"

A large, unshaven man with a cigarette in his mouth nodded and lazily strolled into the stable. Tom Grant filled out some paperwork while another of Jeb's assistants led the slave woman to a nearby fencepost and tied her to it.

When Luke finished his apple, he stood up and walked back across the main thoroughfare to Wally Matkin's general store. The town was busy with people bustling about, carrying out the business of the day. The streets were dry and dusty because there had been no rain for two weeks. The wagon and carriage traffic kept the dust stirred up enough so that a common sight around town was slaves dusting and sweeping inside and outside of the many small businesses.

A bell tinkled as Luke opened the door to Wally's store and stepped inside.

"Back again so soon, Luke? Can I sell you a dress or something?" The voice came from behind a dress rack in the back corner of the store next to a table covered with flowered hats.

Luke smiled as he headed for the candy jars on the front counter.

"Last dress you sold me didn't fit, so I had to give it to my wife. Nope, this time I'll just take another apple and some candy for Frank."

"Last of the big spenders, are you?"

Wally grabbed an apple from a box and then walked around behind the counter.

"Cherry and lemon, same as always?"

"Yup, Frank's favorite."

Wally squinted suspiciously at Luke.

"I suspect the candy is really for you, and Frank gets the apple. I just can't prove it."

He slipped a handful of each flavor into a bag. "Does Sally know about your addiction?"

"To be quite honest, Wally, Frank likes to give some of it to the field slaves once in a while."

Wally shook his head disapprovingly, "Asking for trouble, doing that."

"Maybe." Luke grinned in a knowing sort of way. "Don't think so, though." He tossed a coin onto the counter. "See you Sunday, Wall."

The bell tinkled as he stepped out onto the boardwalk. He pulled his watch from his pocket and checked the time. A little less than an hour and the saddle should be ready.

By the time Luke returned to the stables, the benches under the oak trees had filled up with chattering women whose husbands were 'window shopping' for field slaves. For most of the farmers gathered that day, the slave auction was just a form of entertainment, a social gathering. There were some, however, who would be short of workers for the upcoming harvest and were hoping to find a good deal. Luke was well aware of his need for more workers, but he was one of the few Georgians in the area who had a strong aversion to slavery. He owned a few slaves he had inherited and, he had to admit, needed, but he was not happy about it. Leaning against a tree, he was just waiting for the saddle and trying to stay cool.

The slave on the platform was huge. He wore pants but no shoes or shirt. Jeb wanted to make sure that everyone saw the rippling muscles that could make a lot of money for the lucky winner of the bidding contest that was now under way. Luke noticed that there were quite a few scars on his back and arms. He guessed they were probably put there as reminder that even though he was big and strong, he was not in charge. Standing beside this giant of a man was a young boy clad only in tattered pants that were two sizes too small. He looked to be around 10 or 12, maybe. The two were chained together at the ankle.

The price had slowly climbed until the bidding was narrowed down to Henry Blackstone, owner of the local 'Feed N Seed', and Tom Grant, owner of the plantation next to Luke's place.

Unlike Henry, Tom was in no way an easy man to like. He was

a short, slightly overweight, obnoxious man who looked down on most of the townspeople from the imaginary pedestal on which he had placed himself. The town was named after his great-grandfather Cyrus P. Grant, who had owned a large cotton and tobacco plantation, and also the 'C.P. Grant Shipping Company', which was located to the southeast of Grantsville, in Savannah. Cyrus had been south-eastern Georgia's main access to European buyers, with three cargo ships by which he regularly delivered cotton, tobacco, and other southern-grown products to England and Spain.

Cyrus's son, Charles P. Grant, had sold the shipping company just before his grandson was born, to pay off his huge gambling losses. Charles's son, Chadwick Phillip, was so angry with his father for losing most of what he would have inherited, that he ended the line of "C.P.'s" by naming his son Thomas. Chadwick's bitterness led to a life of drunkenness and gambling.

When Tom's father was killed in a bar fight six years ago, Tom had inherited two things. The first being the plantation, which had dwindled from the original 5,000 acres to a still large 3,200 acres and 30 slaves by the time of his father's death, and the second being his father's anger. There were also two things he had learned from his family's history: never touch alcohol and never gamble.

Luke Martin was a Christian man who also, like Tom, did not believe in drinking alcohol, or in gambling. He did however, indirectly benefit from gambling because he had purchased some of the Grant acreage when it had come up for sale. Tom was convinced that Luke surely must have taken unfair advantage of his father's gambling problems.

Tom was not a 'church-goin'' man and had somehow convinced himself that he was very much superior to those who needed to get up on Sunday morning and go 'sing songs with the women'.

Now, as Luke stood in the shade of the oak tree, he was secretly hoping that Henry would be the top bidder for the two slaves, but that was not how it was to be. As the price inched up to $800, the young boy became tired of standing in the scorching sun. He sat down and leaned against the big slave's leg. Dukett was also tired and soaked in sweat. He had been selling slaves all day and wanted nothing more than to be finished and in the bar drinking a cold beer. Even this minor distraction of the boy setting himself down on the platform angered Jeb and he grabbed the boy by the hair and angrily yanked him to his feet.

Before Jeb had any opportunity to say even a word, the big slave had clasped his hands together and with arms held straight, swung around and planted both fists on the side of Dukett's head. Jeb's feet left the ground as he sailed into the horse corral behind the platform. He bounced off the rear end of a horse and landed face first in a pile of manure.

To the sound of exclamations and a woman's scream, the black giant slowly turned back to look at the crowd. His face turned from rage to defeat. His stunned audience watched as he looked down at his son and cringed as the enormity of his actions began to unfold in his mind. Tears formed in his eyes. His legs and arms were shackled, and there was nowhere to run. There was nothing he could do.

All eyes were on the slave and no one saw Tom Grant pull his gun out of the holster under his jacket. The next thing Luke heard was a loud shot and screams from the ladies sitting under the tree. The slave crumpled dead on the platform. The terrified young boy was frantically trying to escape, but he was still chained to his father.

"Can't have no wild animals livin' in these parts. None of us would be safe! The way I seen it, Jeb's life was in danger."

The speaker was Tom Grant, still holding the gun in his hand. A few onlookers mumbled uneasy affirmations as most of them quickly remembered some place else they were supposed to be. They all understood that a black man striking a white man could not be tolerated, but somewhere deeper inside, most of them knew that what had just happened was wrong.

Two of Dukett's men were helping him to his feet while wiping blood and manure off his face and head. He wasn't quite sure where he was, and it took a couple of minutes for him to remember *who* he was.

Luke watched Tom slip his gun back into his holster. "That oughta prove to you hymn-singers that these savages ain't capable of learnin'! That one couldn't even put two and two together. If I do this, then they do that. You'd think they could learn that much, but no…."

"Shut up, Tom!" Luke interrupted. "You're displaying a similar lack of intelligence!"

Henry Blackstone, and a few others who had hung around, watched as Luke threw his apple to the ground and the two men started toward each other.

"How dare you, Luke Martin! You got no right to compare me to……,"

"Shoot him!" Every head turned in unison toward the voice of Jeb Dukett.

"I said, 'Somebody, shoot him!' " Jeb yelled in his fury.

"He ain't worth two bits without his pa, and his pa tried to kill me! I'm out a lot of money."

Jeb walked toward the frightened young boy who was now whimpering and wildly trying to escape the grasp of the two men who were now holding him.

Luke glanced down the street and saw Sheriff Roily leaning against a post, chewing on a cigar and watching, as if hoping for more entertainment.

Jeb wiped some blood and muck from his quickly swelling face. "Somebody give me a gun and I'll do it myself!"

"One hundred dollars!" someone shouted.

Jeb spun angrily around and shouted at the small group of observers. "I just need to borra it for a minute, not buy it, you idiot!"

"One hundred dollars for the boy," Luke heard his voice, but it took a moment to connect. People were now staring at him.

A smile came across Tom Grant's face and he jumped into the game, "I say $300."

For some reason, Luke couldn't keep his mouth shut. "I'll give $500, Jeb."

Grant looked over at Luke with a smile. "Thought I'd make you pay a little extra, Martin. The boy's too small, and he'd be worthless to me now, after what he saw me do to his pa." He looked back at the boy and chuckled, "You deserve him."

Dukett was just standing there with his mouth open and blood oozing out of his right eye socket. Anger was suddenly overtaken by greed. "Will someone give $800 for this fine boy? Do I hear $800?"

The others looked expectantly at Grant.

"Ha! That's the price of a full-grown one. Martin's the loser this time." He turned and walked away.

The slave trader looked disappointed. "Well, my good man, looks like you bought yourself a worthless, skinny, little black pup. Sold, for $500!"

Chapter 2

It was a long ride back to the farm. Clouds were building in the eastern sky, but a storm had already arrived in Luke's head as he considered the day's events. For a while now, he had been struggling to make owning slaves fit into his Christianity. He wasn't succeeding.

Most of the citizens of Grantsville claimed to be Christian, and at least half of them attended the three churches in town. Three-quarters of the families in the Baptist church, which Luke's family attended, owned two or more slaves.

Luke turned and looked at the quaking boy sitting in the back of the wagon.

"This makes six," he thought. "What happened, Lord? How am I going to explain this to Sal? Why can't I mind my own business? This young fella's too small to make a big difference at harvest. Did I just waste my money?"

"*He's alive, Luke,*" came a thought from somewhere deep inside.

Luke knew who had just placed that thought in his head. He had heard the voice before. He let out a deep sigh. "Yeah, I guess he is at that. You must have a reason, huh?"

He listened, but got no response.

As Luke rode down the tree-lined road toward home, he thought on his situation. He had too much land and not enough men to work it. He didn't believe in owning people, but now owned six men. Well, five men and one boy to be precise. The irony of it all was that he believed God had directed him to make every purchase he'd made, whether land or men.

Unlike most men in the area, Luke's father, Evan Martin, had not been a farmer. He had made his fortune buying and selling furs from trappers and Indians west of the Mississippi River. As the years passed and Evan grew older, he decided to aim toward staying home with the family and taking up farming with his son, Luke.

Luke's parents were both devout Christians who believed it was perfectly fine to own slaves, as long as they were treated well. Luke believed the same until he was twenty years old, when his father had been killed in a wagon rollover while bringing a load of furs home to Grantsville. The slave his father had taken along with him had suffered a broken arm and crushed hand, yet somehow had managed to lift his master's body onto the one horse that was not injured. Weak, and in extreme pain, he made the two day journey leading the horse back to Grantsville. Sadly, just outside of town, the slave encountered the Ellis brothers. They had been drinking. When they saw Evan's body on the horse, they accused the slave of murder and hung him from a nearby tree.

When Sheriff Roily brought the bodies out to the farm, he said the Ellis boys had probably kept the slave from coming back to kill them too, and that they should be grateful.

"Why would he bring the body along with him, if he was coming to cause trouble?" his mother had asked.

The sheriff made it clear there would be no investigation. He offered his condolences and returned to town. Luke and his mom buried his father and their slave side by side on the small hill that overlooks the river.

Nearly two weeks later, the Martins learned a man had ridden into town three days after the hanging and told the sheriff he'd seen a busted up wagonload of furs with a dead horse at the bottom of Coon Hill. When Luke rode out to check on the report, he found his father's wagon and the horse, but the furs were gone. He could see clear evidence of bundles being dragged to the road. The drag marks ended at a set of wagon tracks that were wider than his father's wagon would have made. Luke followed the tracks until they disappeared in the busy streets of Grantsville.

It was then that the seeds of doubt had been planted about the honesty of Sheriff Roily, and about slavery. Now, fourteen years later, Luke was pretty sure that, as a Christian, he shouldn't own other people. So why did he now own six of them?

The lane leading up to the Martin house was lined with eight large oak trees on one side and a long open field of ripening cotton on the other. At the end of the drive, against a background of pine and pecan trees stood a white two-story home. It wasn't small, but not so large as to brag of great wealth, as so many houses did in the South. A large barn was southwest of the house, with several smaller outbuildings lined up to the south of the barn.

Luke scanned the wrap-around covered porch ahead of him, hoping for a glimpse of his wife and son. Near the end of the drive, two legs appeared in the nearest tree as the wagon approached the house. A twelve-year-old boy hung by his hands from a branch, dropped to his feet and then to his seat in a puff of dust. Letting out a whoop, he jumped up and ran to greet his pa.

Frank's father was his hero. When he grew up, Frank wanted to be just like him. To Frank, no one was stronger, kinder, or smarter than his pa. With no brothers or sisters to play with and no close neighbors his age, his world revolved around Luke Martin. As Frank reached the wagon, he was already talking a mile a minute.

"Yer just in time to see my raccoon, Pa! I caught him by the river. What did you bring me? Huh, pa? What did you bring…..?

Frank stopped in mid-sentence as his eyes locked on the small dark face peering over the side of the wagon, his words now frozen in his half-open mouth.

Luke smiled down at his son, "Says his name is Joshua. Hasn't said anything else."

Jumping down from the driver's seat, Luke gave Frank a big hug, but Frank couldn't take his eyes off the terrified new arrival.

"Go get Mabin for me, will you, son? I need him to take care of Joshua here while I go talk to your ma."

Frank took off running up the north-south road to the tobacco field as if shot from a cannon. Luke smiled again as he walked to the back of the wagon and motioned to Joshua.

"Hop on down and stretch your legs, young man. Mabin will be here in a few minutes to get you cleaned up and fed. This is your new home now, so come on down.

The boy was accustomed to obeying 'the massuh' or facing punishment, so he quickly scooted to the end of the wagon and jumped down, then backed away from Luke immediately with fear in his eyes.

"I won't hurt you, Joshua. I bid on you so I could help you. I think you'll come to like it here." Luke paused and looked helplessly at the young lad, then with a sigh he added, "I'm really sorry about your pa."

Suddenly, the dam broke and tears poured down the young boy's face.

Luke's wife, Sally, could never be quite sure when to expect her husband's return from a trip to town. He was rarely earlier, and usually later, than the prediction he would give before leaving. Allowing for his usual timing, Sally had delayed her meal preparations about an hour, hoping to serve her man a hot meal when he finally arrived. But now everything was cooked and ready to set on the table and Luke was not there to eat it. She looked around the kitchen, sighed, and decided to go ahead and call Frank in to eat while the food was still hot. She leaned over the counter and pulled the curtain back to see if Frank was in the yard.

What Sally Martin saw, when she looked out the kitchen window, was the last thing she expected to see. Leaning against the wagon was her six-foot-three husband, with a young, dark-skinned boy held tightly in his arms. And both of them were crying!

When Frank, Mabin, and a young slave named Toby arrived from the fields, three people were sitting on the ground. Luke was explaining the day to his wife as Joshua, still sniffing and sobbing, now sat on Sal's lap. Frank ran quickly to his parents, silently hoping no one was hurt. Mabin and Toby were more hesitant, unsure of what to do. They had never seen the master and his wife sitting in the dirt before. When Luke caught sight of them, he quickly stood, brushed himself off, and wiped his eyes with the back of his hand.

Though it was unspoken, Mabin was considered the foreman among the slaves. At forty years old, he was the oldest slave on the farm and had been with the Martins longer than any of the other slaves. He had played a key role in keeping the farm functioning after Luke's father and the slave died.

Toby was in his early twenties when, out of sheer necessity, Luke purchased him for his size and strength. There was just too much work to be done on the farm and Luke was not keeping up with the field work with the few slaves that had been left to him. When Luke married Sally, his mother moved to Savannah to live with her sister. She left the small farm and three-quarters of the money her husband had in the bank to Luke, and she had taken two of the slaves with her.

"Mabin, Toby. Come on over here and meet Joshua," Luke called in a tone that was meant to put the two slaves at ease. "The boy has had a real hard day. Get him washed up and into some clean clothes. You might have to cut the pant legs shorter on some of those pants we've got in the box in the barn, and maybe the sleeves on one of the shirts. I'll get something that fits him when I get to town next. Sal will send Frank out with some cornbread and beans after we eat."

Luke leaned down and helped Joshua stand up, and then his wife. He nudged Frank by the shoulder and brought the two boys together and then, looking down at Joshua, he said, "Joshua, this is my son, Frank. He needs a work partner that's more his size. I think you'll do just fine."

Frank offered the boy his hand and said, "Hi, Joshua. It's nice to meet you."

Joshua looked at the outstretched hand but seemed confused as to what was expected of him. After an awkward moment, Luke bent down and took Joshua's hand and placed it in Frank's hand. Then he wrapped both boys' hands in his own and began to pump them up and down while smiling and saying, "Hi, Frank. It's nice to meet you, too."

Both boys smiled shyly at each other but didn't say anything. Luke nodded, satisfied with the smiles. "That's a good start," he said. "Now, Joshua, you go with these fellas. They'll get you settled in. Nobody's going to hurt you."

Toby looked a little confused about what to do next, but Mabin caught on quickly. With a smile, he reached out and took Joshua's hand.

"It's okay, boy," he chuckled. "You don' know it yet, but d' Lord take good care o' you. Miz Martin, she sho' do make some tasty cornbread. Come on now, I ain' no snake. I don' bite. Do I, Toby? Too old, anyhow. Lost mos' my teef long time ago," he said, pretending to be toothless.

Luke put his arm around Sally as they watched the three slaves walk off toward the slaves' bunkhouse. Joshua turned and looked back over his shoulder at the Martins and then he looked up at Mabin as he shuffled along at the big man's side. Toby followed along behind silently as Mabin continued on with his verbal attempt at making the boy comfortable. The Martins could still hear his voice faintly in the distance as they went inside for supper.

Chapter 3

The Ogeechee River flows down from the wooded hills in northern Georgia, east of Grantsville. Luke's farm was nearly six miles to the north of town and the small river was the dividing line between Tom Grant's place and his own. Tom's father used to own cropland on both sides of the river. The Martins originally owned nearly 200 acres of woods and only 100 acres of open farmable land along the east side of the river to the north of the Grant property. When the Grant land on the east side of the river, adjacent to the southern border of the Martin property, came up for sale, Luke's father had purchased the entire 450 acres of rich, sandy loam, fully intending to purchase more slaves to work the land. He had not lived long enough to complete his plan.

The cotton bolls had matured and begun to crack and blossom right on time in late August. After a week of light rain, the sun had come out in full force. The crop had been left to dry for a few days. The rain had allowed for everyone to rest up and be in top shape when the picking began. Now, the humidity was dropping a bit, so Luke decided to begin harvesting, as had other planters in the area.

It was midmorning, a week into the harvest. On Grant's side of the river, thirty slaves were bent over picking cotton, while two white field bosses sat in the shade of a wagon keeping an eye on their charges. Across the river six slaves, and Frank, steadily worked their way down the rows.

At noon, all work stopped on both sides of the river, and every inch of shade around the wagons was taken by the resting workers. There was, however, a contrast in the two groups other than the number of slaves. Twenty minutes after the call to lunch, the thirty slaves were back in the fields, while Frank and his fellow workers dozed for another twenty or thirty minutes. This was no small irritant to Tom Grant and his field bosses. Tom feared discontent and possibly rebellion among his slaves. He knew they were aware of the differences on the other side of the river, and he was convinced that Luke allowed such laziness just to cause him trouble.

Frank was the only picker on either side of the river who received wages. Fifty cents a day was good money for a twelve year-old boy. But the rule was that it was to be deposited in Ben Statler's bank, collecting interest until he was old enough to go to college.

Joshua worked alongside Mabin and helped him fill his sacks. Frank worked the row next to Joshua, and had his own sack to fill. He enjoyed having someone around who was closer to his age and size. Frank had a healthy imagination and loved telling stories about wild Indians or talking animals. Joshua had never had any schooling and, therefore, had a difficult time discerning truth from fiction, taking most of what Frank said to be true. He had never worked around a white boy before and was surprised at how much white children seemed to know. The older men were not as conversational as they worked. Sometimes they hummed or sang songs, but as the day wore on and the heat grew more oppressive, the weight of the cotton sacks hanging on their shoulders continued to increase until even the singing stopped.

When the sacks were full, they were dragged to large baskets at the end of the field. The baskets were stomped down until they could hold no more cotton, and then loaded onto a horse-drawn wagon. By late afternoon, Frank was to take the wagon to the gin, where he would help his father and mother gin the cotton and fill new sacks with clean cotton. At dusk, Frank would drive the wagon back to the field, and the slaves would load whatever cotton had been picked into the wagon for Frank to take back to the barn in case of rain during the night. The next day, he would take the wagon back to the field and join the pickers until the wagon was full, and then return to the gin.

Across the river came the sound of a whip slapping across the back of one of the pickers. Frank and Joshua cringed and looked over their shoulders to see what was happening on the other side. The five adults continued picking as if nothing had happened, but deep inside, all seven were counting their blessings.

Mabin stood up, stretched his arms and arched his back. The day was hotter than usual and he noticed that Joshua wasn't accomplishing much.

"Boy, d' wagon' full, so why don' you go on back to d' gin with Frank 'n hep him unload."

Joshua let out a whoop that didn't go unnoticed across the river. The two boys suddenly found an extra bit of energy and ran to the wagon.

"Maybe Pa will let us go down to the river for a swim, once the wagon is unloaded," said Frank, as he drew the wagon up to the gin house. "Climb in the back, Josh, and we'll push these baskets out.

As they worked to empty the wagon, Josh grew thoughtful.

"D' day I come here, your pa say d' Lord had a reason fo me here."

Frank stood up and wiped his forehead. "Pa, he don't really like slaves."

A surprised look came across Joshua's face and Frank quickly continued, "I mean the idea of owning 'em. Pa says slavery ain't a good thing, but there ain't enough workers without 'em. He says we don't have enough people to work all our land, so he rotates fields each year, leavin' some of it to lie fallow. I don't know what fallow means but some of the land is just laying there doin' it."

Frank and Josh both worked together to push the last basket of cotton to the back of the wagon and onto the platform of the gin house.

"I heard Pa tell Mama that the Lord told him to buy the 150 acres he got from Mr. Pennington on the south end of our place along the river, just beyond the part he got from Mr. Grant."

Frank arched his back and stretched. "Mama says Pa sure better be hearin' right, cause we already got too much land. She says she's prayin' for more workers."

"Well, dey gots us, don'they?" asked Josh.

"Nope; not if we go swimming!" Frank yelled as he ran into the barn to find his pa.

Joshua smiled and ran after him.

"Where dem boys, Massuh?" Toby asked, surprised to see Luke jumping down from the wagon.

"They seemed to think they would work harder tomorrow if they went swimming today."

"Maybe so," Toby smiled. "I hear it do feel good on a hot day."

Toby started lifting a basket into the wagon as Luke turned to greet Mabin and the others. All of a sudden, they heard angry shouting and the cracking of whips across the river. Luke looked through the spaces in the trees that lined the river to see both field bosses whipping and kicking a slave who had apparently collapsed in the heat. Grant's other field slaves had looks of fear mixed with determination as they began to pick faster.

Luke paused and looked back at the five men on his side of the river.

"Toby, why don't all of you go upriver and make sure the boys are having a good time. I hear it feels mighty good at the end of a hot day."

Toby looked doubtful. "Massuh, dey's a whol' lot o' cotton to pick 'n we ain't d' biggest group o' pickers in Georgia, you know."

Luke glanced back across the river. "Well, the boys seem to think it will help them work harder. Let's call this an experiment and see if it has the same effect on grownups. Make sure you all go up to the swimmin' hole where the boys are, so nobody else can see you."

Toby called the other four over to the wagon and they quickly loaded the remaining baskets. Luke stood and watched the five black men head to the swimming hole, laughing and talking as they went.

Across the river, the two nosy field bosses watched in anger. Unfortunately, the trees had been cleared almost to the rivers edge many years earlier making it easy to see what was going on, on the other side. However, the thirty slaves showed no sign of noticing anything at all as they continued to work.

Luke drove the partially filled wagon back to the gin house where Sally was working at ginning cotton.

"Lord?" he said, looking to the sky, "What am I doing? Toby's right. I need more help, and here I am sending what little help I do have off to the swimming hole.

"*Visit Ben tomorrow!*" came a thought from within.

Chapter 4

"May I help you, Mr. Martin?"

Luke smiled as he approached the counter in the empty lobby of the bank. "Hello, Harry. Is Ben in?" he asked the bank teller.

"Yes, I believe he is, and he has no more appointments for the day. As a matter of fact, just this morning he said he needed to discuss a matter with you."

Harry led Luke around the counter and down a short hallway to a door with large black print on the glass reading, 'Ben Statler – President – Georgia 1st Bank'

The teller knocked lightly and a voice inside called, "What is it, Harry?"

Harry opened the door slightly.

"I won't be able to see any one else today, Harry. I'll be going out to the Martin farm to talk to Luke."

Harry smiled, "Mr. Martin is here to see *you*, Mr. Statler. Perhaps he can save you a trip."

Ben's eyebrows raised as he swung his swivel chair around and, smiling, stood to his feet.

"Well, perhaps he can at that. Come on in, Luke," said Ben in a loud voice.

Harry opened the door wide and motioned for Luke to enter. The teller closed the door behind him leaving the two men to their business.

"How's it going out at your place, Luke?" Ben had come around his desk to shake Luke's hand. "I was going to drop by to discuss an idea I had."

Luke sat down in a thickly padded chair. "I felt like the Lord was urging me to come to town today to see you. Maybe he *did* want to save you the trip."

Ben sat down in the matching chair across from Luke and shook his head. "I sure do wish I could hear from him like you seem to. But then again, maybe I did hear from him, this time."

Luke sat back in the chair. "Don't sell yourself short, Ben. My father told me you were hearing the Lord way back when you and him were both still kids, even though neither of you were very good at sitting still in church."

"Speaking of church," Ben interrupted. "I was talking to Sid Pennington after church Sunday and he told me that he and Maggie are heading west soon to try his hand at mining, with his two brothers. It seems they have a pretty good claim and they invited Sid to join them."

Ben paused and looked at Luke, trying to decide how best to say what was on his mind.

"Go on, Ben." Luke squinted his eyes suspiciously, "Somehow, I suspect this might involve me."

"Well, I was kinda surprised when you bought the hundred and fifty acres from Sid a few months ago. Do you remember me trying to talk you out of it?"

Luke nodded his head with a grin.

Ben leaned forward slightly with an air of excitement. "You didn't have enough help to work the land you had, but you said you felt you were supposed to buy it. You said….,"

"The Lord told me to!" interrupted Luke.

Ben nodded. "That's right. That is what you said. And Luke, being your banker, I happen to know your father left you setting pretty well, financially. But you're not using your money well. You have all that choice river valley soil and you have to leave half of it unplanted! If you had more workers, you could put all of that ground to good use."

"We've been over all of this before, Ben," Luke sent an irritated look to his friend, but the bank president didn't seem to notice.

Ben held up his hand, "Stay with me for a minute." He stood up and began walking slowly around his office. "Sid will have no trouble selling his place. But he is dead set against splitting up Tal and Sadie."

Luke stood quickly and held out both hands in protest. "Hold on, Ben! You know what I think about owning slaves! I didn't come in here with any intention of buying more slaves! I'm not even sure it's Christian."

Ben smiled at his friend. "I know, I know. Now listen to me. You and Sid and I are all Christians. We even go to the same church. You don't feel right about owning slaves and Sid doesn't feel right about separating a man and his wife. He's had two offers to buy Tal, and Sam Gault said he's interested in buying Sadie but so far, nobody's interested in buying them both."

"Can't do it, Ben!" Luke stood up, turned, and walked to the door. "I know you mean well, but I just can't."

"All I ask is that you think it over. Will you do that much?" Ben opened the door for Luke.

Luke frowned and grunted as he walked out the door and walked down the hall.

With a sly smile on his face, Ben said, "See ya Sunday, Luke."

Luke almost slammed the door of the bank as he stepped outside. He couldn't remember being more frustrated. He needed the manpower but he didn't believe in owning people, and that didn't make much sense either, because he owned six of them.

Grumbling to himself, he turned to go to Wally's Market to buy some candy for Frank. Walking down the boardwalk toward him were Tom Grant's two field bosses. When they recognized who he was, they stopped and stood side by side, blocking his path.

"Excuse me, fellas," Luke said as he tried to get by.

"There's *no* excuse for troublemakers," said one of them, with a defiant look.

"I don't want any trouble," Luke replied. "Excuse me, please."

The two men glared at him for a moment.

"You don't want no trouble?" asked the one named, Del.

"No, I don't," Luke answered, holding eye contact.

"Then stop treating your nigras like they was white!"

Then they tipped their hats politely, and smiled mockingly at Luke as they stepped aside to let him pass.

"What was that all about?" Luke wondered as he stepped into Wally's store. The small bell tinkled, announcing his arrival. Wally was busy showing Tom Grant some of the latest seed catalogs. Both heads turned to the sound of the little bell.

"Be with you in a minute, Luke," said Wally, turning back to Tom. But Tom didn't notice Wally. His angry eyes were boring into Luke. "I don't know why you let your slaves lay around where mine can see 'em," Tom growled. He grabbed a catalog and threw it across the store. "Just who do you think you are, Luke Martin? How dare you try to stir up rebellion in my slaves! You got the laziest bunch of field slaves I ever seen. You got no business ownin' nigras, Martin, and if trouble starts with any of my nigras, I'll hold you personally accountable. Do you hear me!?"

Tom's face was beet red and Luke thought he saw a little steam coming out of his ears, but he wasn't sure.

"Why Tom, how could I be causing your slaves to rebel? I have never met a single one of them. You must be thinking of someone else."

Tom looked as if his head was about to explode. "I'm warning you! Don't say I didn't warn you! You know very well that my boys see everything you do in that field, and so do my nigras!"

The bell tinkled as Tom opened the door and slammed it shut as he left. Luke and Wally were suddenly alone, staring at the door.

"What ...?" Wally looked quizzically at Luke.

"I think it had something to do with going swimming but I'm not sure," Luke said, in pretended puzzlement.

"Huh?" Wally looked back at the door.

"Never mind, Wall. I came to pick up a little candy and ask you if you know of anyone looking for work. I'm lookin' to hire a couple of fellas to help get through this harvest."

Wally shook his head. "I don't know of anybody right now but you might check with Ben Statler at the bank. He'd know if someone was behind on a payment and needed work." Wally handed the bag of candy to Luke.

"Actually, I was just talking to Ben. That's the main reason I came to town." said Luke as he handed Wally the money.

"Well, did he know of anyone?"

"I forgot to ask him. Thanks for the candy."

"You forgot to ask him?"

"Yeah, Wally, I came all the way to town to ask him and I forgot! Okay?" Luke felt embarrassed and convicted. "I gotta go. Uh, I'll see you Sunday."

The bell tinkled as Luke opened the door.

"Don't you go giving Tom Grant's pickers any candy, do you hear?"

"Why, Wall? Don't you think that would cheer Tom up some?"

Wally frowned as Luke closed the door behind him. "Didn't know ole Tom knew how to swim," he mumbled to himself as he shook his head and began dusting the shelves behind the counter.

There was a knock on the bank president's door.

"What is it, Harry?" asked Ben through the closed door, as he continued jotting down figures in his ledger.

The door opened, and in stepped Luke Martin.

Ben looked up and lay down his pen. "Back so soon, Luke?" he asked in feigned surprise.

"You win, Ben, but how on earth am I going to explain it to Sally?"

"She'll thank you for doing it, Luke." The banker leaned back in his chair with his hands locked together behind his head. "That was a tired woman you brought to church Sunday, and your harvest has only just begun. She'll thank you, I promise."

A smile came across his face and he placed his hands on the edge of his desk, pushed his chair back and stood up. "Let's go see Sid right now, before you change your mind." He grabbed his hat off the hook by the door and headed down the hall. Luke paused for a moment as if having a change of heart. Then he let out a big sigh and looked to the ceiling, hoping someone would stop him. But instead, he heard Ben's voice calling from somewhere down the hall. "It's the right thing to do, Luke. Now, c'mon!"

Chapter 5

Sally sat on the porch humming as she sewed curtains for Tal and Sadie's new home. She watched as her husband and Mabin unloaded lumber for Tal and Sadie's home from the two wagons. She could hear the high voices of Frank and Joshua out in the field as they laughed at something one of the field slaves must have said while they all worked at picking the cotton. Sally paused for a moment to look up at the fluffy white clouds floating along at their own lazy pace across the dark blue sky. She listened to the birds singing as they went about their day, and to the laughter in the fields, the sound of boards being stacked, and the muffled voices of men, discussing the matters of the day.

Everything was good today.

Eventually, she returned to her sewing. But the smile was still there, and soon the humming resumed.

"She seem happy today, Massuh," Mabin commented as he grabbed some boards.

Luke nodded, "She does at that. How could I have been so blind, Mabin? She's been doing the work of two women for years. Never complaining! Ben saw her need. You saw it. Everyone saw how tired she was, except me!"

"De Lord saw it, Massuh, and he send you to town. You done what he say to do." Mabin stacked the lumber on a pile. "Mos' men, they don't do what He say. Miz Sally, she knows what she got. She got a man who obeys d' Lord."

Luke wiped the beads of sweat from his forehead as he sat down on the stack of lumber. Mabin stood politely by and waited patiently.

"Have a seat, Mabin."

"Yes, Massuh," Mabin sat down.

Luke turned his head and looked at Mabin eye to eye.

"You're not a slave in my eyes, Mabin."

"Massuh?" Mabin looked a bit puzzled.

"You're a friend. You and Ben Statler are the best friends I have."

"Yes, Massuh," Mabin looked at the ground. Both were quiet a moment. "Mos' folk don't abide dis' kind o' talk. You da Massuh. What you sayin', mus' stay tween us."

Still looking down, Mabin allowed a slight smile to cross his mouth, "To da worl', you da Massuh. To da Lord 'n us, you's sumthin' else."

Luke put his hand on Mabin's shoulder, "Sorry it has to be that way. It's been over twenty-five years since a slave named Turner and his followers killed some fifty or sixty white men, women and even children and babies. But people remember it as if it happened yesterday. Most southern whites are living as if another slave revolt is right around the corner, and yet they continue to treat their slaves in ways that make revolt more and more desirable."

Mabin turned and looked at Luke but said nothing.

Luke became curious as to what Mabin might be thinking. "What?" he finally asked.

"More to it den how a man's treated, I think," Mabin nodded thoughtfully to himself and then added, "But, most black folk don' have it so good as here, suh. Don' git me wrong."

"What are you thinking, Mabin?" Luke asked, curiously.

Mabin again nodded his head. "We are friends, I agree, but…" He paused, turned and looked out over the farm. "You know sumthin' I don'."

He stopped talking and waited.

Luke put his hand on Mabin's shoulder and urged him to continue.

"Go ahead, Mabin. What is it?

Sadly, but kindly, Mabin asked, "What' it like, to *own* a friend?"

Luke felt as if the ground had dropped out from under him. He was frozen in place until his hand finally fell limply from Mabin's shoulder.

"Mos' slaves don' have it so good, suh," Mabin reiterated.

"No, they don't," Luke replied as he weakly rose to his feet. "But yes, there's one more step I need to take, and quite frankly, I have been afraid to take it."

Sally looked up from her sewing and watched the two men walking slowly back to the wagon. Shortly she turned back to her work and began humming another hymn.

The following day, Frank and Joshua were standing side by side looking down at a big X that Mabin had marked in the dirt. Each of the boys had a shovel in his hand.

"S'pose we'd best get started," said Frank, as he began to dig.

"What's your pa mean by sayin' 'Don' start no volcanoes or nothin'?" Joshua asked as he joined in the digging.

"You know what a volcano is, don't you?" asked Frank.

"Don' know as much as you, Frank. You go to school; I don't."

"Well, a volcano is a mountain," Frank began.

"A mountain!?" Joshua looked incredulously at Frank. "How we gonna start a mountain? Dis just gonna be a small pile o' dirt."

Frank kept digging, "I was taught in school that the earth is probably a big round ball and the middle of the ball is made of boiling hot stuff. Now if it finds a way out, like a crack or hole in the ground or something like that, the stuff shoots into the air like a fountain and then piles up, cools off and gets hard, and slowly becomes a mountain."

The boys continued to dig while Joshua thought about this new information.

"So how deep we gotta dig before we pop out on the other side of d' worl'?"

"Don't matter," replied Frank. "We'll hit hot liquid before then."

Joshua leaned down and felt the bottom of the hole with his hand. "I say we dig real careful like, 'n if d' dirt starts getting hot we quit 'n go tell your pa."

"Probably won't get that deep, but I'm with you. Won't hurt to keep an eye on it, just to be safe."

Frank threw another shovelful of dirt out of the hole.

"How they know we's walkin' around on a big ball anyway?" Joshua looked skeptical.

"I guess someone must have walked all of the way around it or something. How should I know? I think my teacher said it was someone named Sir Newton, or something like that." Frank threw more dirt out of the hole.

"An you believe that?" exclaimed Joshua in amazement. "How'd he keep from fallin' off o' the bottom?"

"Gravity."

"Gravity? What's gravity?"

Frank stopped shoveling and thought for a moment.

"I think Sir Newton said that's what kept him from fallin' off."

Luke and Sally stood on the porch of the newly completed building and watched the boys dig. Sally put her arm around Luke's waist. "The boys sure do work well together.

Luke nodded, "Yes, they make a good team. They'll easily have that hole dug by dark. It won't take any time at all in the morning for us to frame it up."

The two walked together, hand in hand, to the main house.

"Luke, I've been thinking," Sally glanced up at him and then ahead again as they walked. "I think it would work best if Sadie and I took shifts on the gin, the housework, and the cooking. Maybe half a day each on the gin, while the other works in the house. Frank and Joshua can load the ginned cotton in the sacks and take some turns cranking the gin to give us a break. Tal can help pick the fields and you could be wherever you're needed."

Luke was quiet for a few steps. "Sounds as if you've been giving this a great deal of thought."

Sally nodded, "I've been thinking about this for years, Luke. It's like a dream come true; an answer to my prayers."

Luke winced. A mixture of embarrassment and relief swept through him. He looked to the sky and mouthed the words "thank you". It did not go unnoticed by his wife.

As they arrived at the steps to the front porch Luke said, "I'll fetch 'em tomorrow and we can put your plan into action. Meanwhile, I'd better get back to work at the gin. We've gotten behind while building their place. I'm afraid we'll lose some of the east field crop if we don't get a move on."

"Ring the bell when lunch is ready." He added, "The boys will be starving by then."

Chapter 6

Luke arrived with Tal and Sadie near noontime. Sid Pennington and his wife followed behind in their carriage. Sally came from the gin to greet them, hurriedly straightening her hair and wiping the sweat from her forehead.

When Luke pulled to a stop, Tal and Sadie climbed out of the back of the wagon and stood quietly, waiting for instructions. Sid pulled the carriage up alongside the wagon. He hopped out and went around to the other side to help his wife.

"Hi, Sal," greeted Luke, "I've invited Sid and Maggie for lunch. I thought they might help Tal and Sadie to get settled."

Sally looked nervously over at the Penningtons, and then back to Luke.

"That's nice of you, Luke, and I'm sure Maggie can help Sadie get settled in, but I've been out at the gin all morning and have no meal prepared."

"Perfect!" exclaimed Maggie Pennington, "You can show Sadie around the kitchen while the three of us rustle up some grub." She took Sally by one hand and Sadie by the other and hurried them up the steps and into the kitchen.

"She'll do better out west than I will," Sid commented as the screen door slammed shut behind the ladies. "She's a 'take charge' kinda gal. Ain't nothing she can't handle!"

He clapped his hands together and looked around. "Show us where you're bunkin' them, Luke, and we'll unload their things. They don't have much, but I am so grateful they get to keep each other.

They've been married two years now. They met at my place. Tal here is twenty-five years old, and Sadie is somewhere near the same. She's not sure exactly."

Sid motioned for Tal to follow, "C'mon boy, grab your bags and follow us."

As the three men walked around the back of the horse stable, Sid and Tal came to a halt.

"Whooee!" exclaimed Sid. "Looks brand new! And look over there, Tal. A brand new outhouse, to boot!"

"It's brand new, alright," Luke laughed. "Finished the house a couple of days ago." He pointed to the new shack. "This here is only one room but it is 14 foot by 24 foot, with a small loft. And the outhouse got finished this very morning! Four foot by three foot. It's never even been set in!"

"How many'll be in this'n?" asked Sid, matter-of-factly, nodding toward the shanty.

"Just the two of them, Sid," said Luke. "It doesn't seem right, having single folk living in the same room with married folk."

"No, I don't reckon it is," said Sid, looking back at Tal, whose eyes were about to pop out of his head. "Looks like you struck gold, boy! C'mon now, let's see what you got inside."

The room was furnished with a table, two chairs, some shelves, a small wood burning stove for heat, and a platform built into the corner with a used, but not in too bad condition, double-wide straw mattress and some blankets. A lantern hung from a nail at the center of a ceiling beam, and built into the wall above the table was a window, adorned with newly sewn curtains.

The young black man stood still in the doorway staring, taking it all in while Sid walked around oohing and aahing. Luke noticed that Tal's eyes were watery, and he became concerned.

"Is something wrong, Tal?" Luke asked.

Sid spun around, "Huh? Oh, no! Nothing's wrong, Martin. Tal here just moved into a mansion. There's a smile on each one of them tears if you look close. You see, I couldn't afford to give them their own place. They've been living in a building about twice this size, with only a blanket between them and five others. Only one outhouse, too. I haven't made much money the last few years because the ground is about worn out. My place was too small to leave some of it unplanted each year. That hundred fifty acres you bought was the best I had, but, it's good you're lettin' it sit awhile.

Sid walked over and took Tal by the elbow and led him into the room.

"Am I right, boy? Are you okay?

"It's real good, Massuh. Sadie ain't never had a window before.

Tal walked over and set the two bags on the bed. He turned to Luke and suddenly smiled, "I'll work hard for you, Massuh. You'll be glad we come."

The dinner bell rang in the distance.

"I'm counting on it, Tal, but for now, get settled in a bit. I'll send Sadie out with some food and you can have your first meal in your new home. C'mon, Sid, let's go eat."

Luke and Sid opened the kitchen door and entered the warm, well-lit kitchen. Maggie was placing a steaming hot pot on the table and talking a mile a minute. Sally handed Sadie a cloth covered basket and smiled at the men as she led Sadie to the door.

"I'll be right back, Luke. You all go ahead and have a seat at the table. Maggie will serve you up."

Sally paused at the door and looked first to Sid, and then to Maggie, "I think maybe Sid has a few things he'll be wanting to tell you, Luke. Come with me, Sadie. I'll show you where you'll be staying."

Sid glanced at Maggie and let out a big sigh.

Luke lifted the lid from the pot of stew and took a healthy sniff.

"I've got an idea," he said. "Let's all dish up and then, Sid, you can talk between bites.

When the bowls were filled and all were seated, Luke pressed Sid, "Now, what is it that Sally thinks that you think I should know?"

Sid relaxed a little and grinned sheepishly, "Well you see, uh," he paused, but only for a second, "I sinned, Luke." He took a bite and chewed slowly as he seemed to be reconsidering what he had just said. "Well, at least my pappy said it was a sin." Sid took another bite.

Maggie gave a threatening look Sid's way, as she spread butter on a biscuit. "Luke didn't really mean between every bite, Sid. He meant, 'We eat, you talk!' Now quit beating around the bush and get on with it!"

Sid acted as if he hadn't heard her, but eventually continued.

"My pappy said it could be the ruin of the south if people began doing it. He said the slaves would get all kinds of big ideas and start thinkin' they were more than they are." Sid lifted a biscuit to his mouth.

"Sid!"

The biscuit was quickly returned to the plate. He continued, "For years now, them folks up north been complaining about slavery. Do you remember the preacher that come through a couple years ago, Luke?"

Sid didn't give Luke time to stop chewing and answer. "He preached a mighty powerful sermon about Christ setting captives free. Then he asked if that meant Jesus believed in slavery. Remember, Luke?"

Luke's mouth was full but he managed to grunt and nod. Sid started to lift a spoon full of stew, but thought better of it as he glanced at Maggie.

"Billy Glenn, Tom Grant, the Ellis boys, and a few others run that pastor out of town real fast, they did."

Sid took a quick bite, carefully avoiding his wife's frown.

"I never forgot it, Sid," said Luke. "I still think about it. I think about it a lot. Slavery has bothered me for years, even before that preacher came. Pastor Davies isn't so bold as that fella was, but he feels the same."

"Word up north is that folks want to stop it." Sid bit into a carrot. "The anti-slavery crowd is really stirring up a ruckus in some places."

"Is that what Sal thinks you wanted to tell me?" Luke put his fork down and leaned forward on his elbows. "Sid," Luke paused, "did you...?"

"Set 'em free?" interrupted Sid. "No, of course not. I wouldn't sell you something I didn't own. But I've been thinkin' about what it would be like when and if slavery were abolished. That's what the Quakers up north are pushing for, you know, and the idea is catching on. People in places like Philadelphia are getting real vocal about it, and the Massachusetts Anti-Slavery Society holds yearly conventions."

Sally walked in and quietly washed her hands in the bowl of water on the counter. Without turning around, she asked, "Well, Luke, what do you think about Tal and Sadie knowing how to read?"

Drying her hands with a towel, Sally turned to the table and was met with looks of shock. She froze. "Uh, oh. Maybe I spoke out of place. I thought......"

Luke's look of surprise turned to a look of revelation as he turned back to Sid, "Why, you old coot!"

Sid, with a halfway embarrassed smile, raised his eyes to Luke.

"Pappy'd say I sinned." Sid leaned back in his chair and drank from his glass of lemonade, his eyes on Luke, measuring his reaction.

"Bet he would've, at that," Luke mumbled, as he attempted to process this unexpected information.

"Probably would've disowned me, too." Sid smiled, "He couldn't read half as well as Tal can."

Luke smiled slightly, "You seem quite happy with yourself."

"I guess I sorta' am. Pappy said it couldn't be done. He said the good Lord gave the white man all the brains so's we could rule the earth. But even as a child, I wasn't quite sure he was right. I remember wondering how slaves could talk if they didn't have any brains. Turns out the black people have lots of brains. It was my pappy that was in short supply."

"Could be trouble, if certain people found out," Luke said. "It goes against those ugly slave codes."

"I feel kinda bad about that part, Luke. But Tal and Sadie know to keep quiet. It could be trouble for them too, and they understand that."

Sally had seated herself between Luke and Maggie. Both of the ladies listened with interest as the men talked. All four understood the seriousness of the conversation. They remembered the winter after the traveling preacher had been run out of town, when one of Slim Wilkins' slaves showed up dead on the front porch of the church. Both arms and both legs had been broken, and an English reader and Bible had been placed neatly on the slave's chest.

"Why did you take such a risk, Sid?" Sally interrupted the two men. "And why didn't you tell us before Luke bought them?"

"My nigras have been around so long I kinda took a shine to them. I asked myself what they would do with freedom if slavery became illegal." Sid smiled, "I thought I'd give them a little advantage, that's all. I also thought it was important for them to be able to read the Bible. When I started their schooling, I had no idea we would soon be heading west. Thaddeus, Tal, and Sadie just seemed like family to us."

Sid looked at the ceiling, "Sorry, Pappy."

"All that time each night learning together, also resulted in Tal and Sadie getting married."

"Thadeus can read too?" Luke asked.

"Yup, but I'm taking Thaddeus with me. He seems to have a real head for numbers too, and that should be useful to us. I plan on handing him his freedom papers as soon as we step into a 'free' state."

Luke straightened up in his chair. "Numbers? How did he..? Did you teach them arithmetic too??"

"All three of them!" Sid said proudly. "Pappy said it couldn't be done. I guess I should have told you, Luke, but I didn't want to scare you off. Ben said you'd be the one to treat them best and we knew we couldn't take them all with us."

Sid paused, slumped in his chair, and gave a sigh. "I guess the only right thing to do is give you your money back if you don't want em."

All eyes were on Luke. He looked at each one, and then put his head in his hands.

"*Is this you, Lord*?" Luke silently asked. "*What's going on? Would you please let me in on your plan? I don't know what to do!*"

Sid became uncomfortable in the silence. "I'm sure sorry, Luke. I shouldn't have done it to you." He slowly shoved his chair back and stood up. "I'll go get Tal and Sadie and take them home."

As Sid turned and walked to the door, Maggie and Sally looked uncomfortably at each other and then both slowly stood and turned to go help Sid break the bad news to Tal and Sadie. As Sid pushed open the screen door, Luke raised his head and said, "No, Sid, they stay."

All heads turned to look at Luke.

"Something's going on that I don't know about. Tal and Sadie fit the pattern." He paused. "I didn't plan on buying Zekiel, but Mr. Clark needed the money for his wife's doctor bills. I didn't plan on buying Joshua. I was just waiting to get my saddle fixed. And then I went to town looking for some temporary help with the cotton harvest and now I wind up owning Tal and Sadie so that they won't be split up. The more uncomfortable I get about owning slaves, the more slaves I own."

Sid hesitated a moment. "It appears to me that the nigras' time in history for being slaves might be coming to an end. That's why I taught 'em reading, writing, and arithmetic."

Sally and Maggie began removing things from the table as Sid stood looking out of a kitchen window.

"Could it be that the time for owning slaves is already over, but not everyone knows it yet?" Sally asked.

"Maybe it never was the right time in God's eyes," Luke remained seated at the table. "Maybe most things were supposed to be different, but men messed it all up, and now we can't fix the mess we made, without Jesus' help."

Sid was suddenly a little tense. "Me and Maggie are just as Christian as you are and we felt fine about owning slaves! The good book says masters are supposed to give their slaves what's right and fair, and we did that! We did it 'cause you and me are slaves too, Luke, and I know my master, the Lord, has treated me good."

Luke nodded. "All I'm saying is that I don't think there would be slavery, if right at the beginning, man hadn't decided he knew better than God. I'm uncomfortable with owning people, and I don't know what to do about it. I believe you were led of God when you decided to teach them. I'm still waiting to hear what it is He wants of Sally and me. You're probably ahead of both of us, Sid.

"That's right," Sally added. "When God has a plan, He uses each person in a different way. If we are each obedient to what we hear, then God will bring it all together."

Sid and Maggie both relaxed.

"What you've done with Tal and Sadie seems right to me, Sid," said Luke. "Not legal, but right just the same. What frustrates me is not knowing how Sal and I fit in. You were obedient even at great risk to your own family. I used to feel the same way as you do, and I was as Christian then as I am now. Now the Lord seems to be changing my thinking." Luke leaned back in his chair and threw up his hands, "But why?"

Sid and Maggie smiled at each other and Maggie nodded.

"We haven't been exactly straight with you two," Sid said with a smile. "We can't tell you any details right now, but the reason we're heading west has to do with helping to fight this injustice. The less you know right now, the better. But your response has brought us great peace about choosing you to help us."

Chapter 7

"I been doin' some thinkin', Sadie." Tal took the teapot off the woodstove, poured a cup of tea for each of them, and sat down across from his wife at the table. "Mr. and Mrs. Martin have been real good to us since we've been here. It seems to me that they don't have enough field workers and ginners to handle larger crops. We need to work real hard and make them glad we're here."

Sadie nodded. "I overheard Miz Martin say she don't know why Massuh Martin bought so much land when he can't keep up with what's already planted."

Unknown to Tal and Sadie, Mabin had come to the door with a bag of corn meal over his shoulder and was about to knock when he overheard the conversation inside. He was mildly ashamed of himself as curiosity got the best of him. Mabin lowered the bag of meal and listened. He couldn't believe what he heard.

Tal was getting excited. "I was reading in that book Massuh Pennington was teaching us from. They spoke of new ideas like the cotton gin that changed farming in the South. Massuh Martin even has a small gin! Well, I got some ideas of my own. Nothin' fancy, mind you, but I read about raising peanuts, tobacco, cotton, and even more chickens. If things was timed right, Massuh could have more steady money all year."

Sadie looked worried. "Black folk ain't supposed to have ideas. Remember, Mr. Pennington told us to always be careful about our learning."

Suddenly Mabin heard the voices of Frank and Joshua coming

from the stable. He quickly threw the bag of meal over his shoulder and knocked on the door. The boys came around the corner of the shack just as Tal opened the door.

"Lo, Tal," Mabin greeted Tal innocently. "I got some grub here from d' massuh. He say we is to come by d' barn in d' morning an each take a hen. He been movin' all dem' chicks to dat pen and needs d' room. He say dey ain't layin' so good no more, anyways."

Mabin looked down at the two boys as they stopped to listen in on the adult conversation they had stumbled upon.

"You young chicks best be gettin' yourselves ready, cuz we ol' roosters'l soon be ready for d' soup pot too," said Mabin with a smile.

Frank thoughtfully shook his head for a moment, then said, "Mr. Mabin, it seems to me that you could ruin a perfectly good pot of soup!"

Mabin chuckled, bending down to put his hands on his knees.

"I was thinkin' da same thing, Massuh Frank. I hopes everyone else agrees wid you 'n me. I shore do!"

"C'mon, Josh," Frank said, grabbing Joshua's arm. "Let's go see if Mama will let us have a slice of pie before we have to go to bed."

Joshua let Frank lead him off to the main house but his mind was still trying to picture Mabin in a pot of soup.

As the boys left, Mabin turned his attention back to Tal and Sadie, and studied them thoughtfully. Maybe there was more to this young couple than he previously thought.

"Mr. Mabin?"

Mabin suddenly realized he was making them uncomfortable. "Did the massuh say anything else, Mabin?" asked Tal.

"Oh, uh, yeah, he did," Mabin quickly answered. "He say to get your chicken first thing sun-up, cuz we has to get goin' right quick an finish pickin d' back field by dark.

"Thank you, Mr. Mabin," said Sadie with a smile. "We'd best be getting some sleep, then. Thank you for the corn meal."

"It was Massuh Martin dat sent it, ma'am." Mabin hesitated, then continued, "We all glad you come when you did. Da Lord knew we was needin' more help." Then he added, "The Lord done *you* good, too, lettin' you come here, you know."

"We can see that's true, Mabin," agreed Tal.

As Mabin was leaving, he overheard Tal lower his voice and say, "The good book says the Lord makes all things work out for good for those that love Him."

"He sure does, at that," Sadie quietly agreed, as they turned to go into the shack.

Mabin spun around and asked curiously, "How you know da good book say dat?"

The couple stopped at the doorway and slowly turned. Tal glanced nervously at Sadie. "Uh, Massuh Pennington tol' us what it said, that's all."

Mabin thought for a moment about what he had heard earlier.

"Wished I knew more what da good book say. Massuh and Miz Martin tell us some, and my mama prayed for me when I was little. She say da Lord don' know no difference 'tween black 'n white, but I don' bleve he's blind."

"God isn't blind, Mabin," Sadie said. "Truth is, his eyes are better than any black folks *or* white folks. He sees past color. He sees deep into the man. Don't matter if the man's purple.

"Now, how you know all dis stuff?" Mabin blurted out.

"We just hear things, Mabin, but we best be going on in now and gettin' our rest," said Tal as he hurried Sadie inside and closed the door.

Mabin turned and walked toward the men's shanty. His mind was racing. "I wonder if Massuh Luke knows," he mumbled to himself.

"Sadie, we have to be more careful," Tal said as they lay in bed in the dark. "Massuh Pennington said our learnin' is for if we ever live free. You say he tol' em, but we don't know how Massuh Martin feels about it. We could be in trouble if anybody else finds out."

Sadie lay silently, mulling it over. Finally, she said, "But Massuh Martin and the missus treats us well."

"Maybe it's cuz they're still trying to decide what to do with us."

"Maybe so, but I feel safe here."

"Everyone is safer, Sadie, if we stay real careful."

Sadie rolled over and put her arm around Tal, "I've never felt so safe. With you, the Martins, and the Lord, what can go wrong?"

"Don't think like that, Sadie!" Tal said sternly. "This isn't heaven! Things *can* go wrong, even here."

Tal took her hand and pulled her close. They lay silently together in the dark.

"Heaven comes later, Sadie."

Chapter 8

It was late September. The weather was cooperating, and Luke was optimistic. The cotton crop was in better shape than most years. Sally and Sadie were becoming close friends as they spent the evenings canning fruits and vegetables. The air was hot and humid and each day's work was hard, but fulfilling. Luke was especially pleased with Toby and Zekiel, his two strongest slaves. It seems that Mabin had asked them which could pick the most cotton in a week, and they gamely accepted the challenge. For five days, they had been doing the work of three men. By the sixth day, Luke felt like he was watching two smooth-running machines.

The last two days, even Joshua and Frank had joined in the spirit of competition, trying to see who would be 'muscle boy of the year'. The boys had never worked harder, and it was catching on. Without any conscious decision by the others, every person, black and white, pushed themselves a little harder. Luke, Sally, and Sadie fell way behind at the gin.

Finally, when it was too dark to pick, Luke went out to the field and called them all in. Saturday night had arrived at last. Bodies ached and feet dragged, but there *were* a few smiles going around as the group of men walked down the dusty road back to the barnyard too tired to talk. It was probably good there was not a full moon, so the neighbors across the river couldn't see the procession. Luke and Mabin walked ahead of the group, arms over each other's shoulders as if they were brothers. Both were smiling. Mabin was very pleased with himself for having challenged Toby and Zekiel, and for how well it had all turned out. The two young boys were second in line, also arm in arm, imitating the two men in front of them. Frank had out-picked Joshua by two bags, Toby proved five bags faster than Zekiel, and the others were pleased with their counts, as well.

Tal brought up the rear, deep in thought. The silhouettes ahead of him were all black. There were no white silhouettes. All of the men looked the same - kind of like family. He knew that, across the river, there was no way a white master would be walking down the road with his back to his slaves. No, the drivers were always in back, always barking orders, always distrustful.

"I must be careful," Tal thought. "I have no idea what the massuh thinks of us being taught readin' and writin'. He ain't said a word."

"Heaven comes later," he whispered as he looked up to the stars. "But it seems you've given us a little glimpse of it right now. I do appreciate it, sir."

"*But I must be careful*," he reminded himself.

There was no picking on Sunday at the Martin place, but by mid-afternoon Luke and Frank decided to catch up with the ginning. They didn't push themselves, but worked steadily while enjoying each other's company.

From the bunkhouses drifted the faint sound of men's voices singing and clapping to a slow rhythmic beat. Sadie was hanging some clothes on a line strung between their shack and a persimmon tree as she hummed along to the men's singing.

Sally was also busy on her day of rest. However, she did not consider it work. Five cherry pies were cooling on the table; they had turned out perfectly. She placed four of them into two picnic baskets and stepped out onto the front porch, a basket in each hand. The sun was low and the air calm. Luke and Frank watched Sal as she approached the bunkhouse and called to the men inside. The singing and clapping stopped. Soon Mabin and Toby respectfully stepped outside. Joshua followed curiously behind, while a couple of others peered out the window. Sally spoke with them for a minute and then handed the basket with two pies to Toby. Next, she took a pie out of the other basket and handed it to Mabin. The men spoke a few words, bowed appreciatively, then turned and took the pies inside. Joshua had a big, white-toothed grin on his face.

As Sally walked across the barnyard to Tal and Sadie's shack, Luke could see the excitement in her face. He smiled proudly as he watched her finding so much joy handing out her blessings.

Sadie met Sally on the porch and called inside to Tal. It took a few minutes before Tal shuffled sleepily out to the porch. When Sally pulled the large pie out of the basket and handed it to him, the drowsiness left him immediately and his eyes got as big as saucers. After chatting a few moments, the young couple thanked her profusely and then Tal, with both hands under the pan, gently carried it into the shack. Sadie followed close behind.

Sally walked over to her own two men, about as happy as she could be. "Sadie told me that Sid and Maggie gave them each a slice of cherry pie on their wedding day. They had never tasted it before or since that day. When I told them the whole pie was theirs, they could hardly believe it! Tal said it was like getting married all over again, only better." Sally laughed and said, "Sadie acted all offended and said something about not letting a pie get all of his attention tonight."

Frank watched as Luke took her hand and said, "I guess pies aren't such small blessings after all."

A serious look came on Sally's face. "Luke, they all worked so hard this week. I wanted them to know it meant something to us."

Luke drew her to him and gave her a big hug. "I'm with you, girl, and I'm bettin' they got the message."

As Luke looked past her to the bunkhouse, he saw Toby and Zekiel sneaking off and disappearing into the trees. He looked concerned and Frank and Sally turned to see what had gotten his attention.

"Sal, I just saw Toby and Zekiel run off, and it looked as if they were taking a whole pie with them."

Sally looked knowingly to the trees and grinned.

"I took three pies to the men. Two were for everyone to share, and one for Toby. I told Toby the third pie was all for him because he worked so hard and won the contest, but it looks as if he plans to share it with his opponent."

Luke looked down admiringly at Sally, "You'll never let me forget why I married you, will you?"

"Hold it! What about me?"

Frank was now standing on a bale of cotton, with his hands on his hips.

"I beat Joshua, you know! Where's *my* pie?"

Sally nodded her head thoughtfully. "I do think I remember seeing another pie on the kitchen table, but I'm not sure," she murmured, as she stared into space.

Suddenly Sally shouted, "First one in the door gets three slices!!" as she turned and ran for the house, with Luke right behind her. Just as her feet reached the first step, Frank shot by both of them and burst through the kitchen door.

True to her word, three slices awaited the winner.

Chapter 9

By Monday noon, two wagons were fully loaded with bales of ginned cotton and headed for Grantsville, with Luke and Frank on one wagon and Toby and Zekiel on the other. They were all grateful to be out of the fields for a few hours because every part of them ached from the previous week's labor.

In town, at the Feed 'n Seed, Luke left Toby and Zekiel to unload the wagons while he took Frank with him to Wally's general store. It was time once again to stock up on flour, beans, potatoes and other supplies. The familiar sound of the bell announced their arrival. Wally glanced their way and acknowledged them with a nod, then returned his attention to the couple at the counter.

Luke noticed Pastor Davies near the back of the store, looking at a pair of overalls. As Frank ran to the counter to check out the jars of candy, Luke started gathering the items on his list. He picked up a jar of honey, studied it for a moment, held it up to the light, and spoke as if he were speaking to the jar. "Looks as if the good pastor is switching careers."

He placed the honey in his bag and picked up a can of beans, pretending to inspect it. He spoke to the can of beans, "Might be for the best. For the life of me, I can't remember a word he preached on Sunday."

Luke heard a chuckle behind him. "I've never seen such a sight before in my life," said the pastor. "The whole Martin family, sound asleep in the front row! Even Sally!"

Luke smiled at the can of beans, and then put it and a few more, into the bag.

"I hope this stays a secret just between *us*, Matthew." Looking over his shoulder, Luke added, "We don't want word getting out about the effect your sermons have on people, now do we?"

"It's too late for that, Luke," Wally had wandered over to join them. "Your snoring took the punch right outa' the good pastor's message. The Martin family fame is spreading far and wide."

The three men had a good laugh.

"Well, I guess we finally figured out a way to help build the church's attendance for you, Matthew."

"That you did," said Pastor Davies, as he wiped his eyes. "You weren't the only ones, though. Old Sam was asleep in the back row, too, but at least he doesn't snore."

"I'll have to work on my snoring problem next Sunday, Matthew, but for now, I'd best go round up an empty wagon to haul Wally's store home in." Luke looked at Wally and handed him the list. "Wall, if you'll ring up these six bags of stuff and the rest of the things on the list, I'll be right back with a wagon." He glanced over to the counter where Frank's nose was pressed up against the glass. "Throw in a couple dozen candy sticks while you're at it, okay?"

Luke opened the door. The little bell tinkled.

"Cherry and lemon?" asked Wally.

"And one grape," Luke said as he walked out the door.

Toby and Zekiel were half finished unloading the second wagon when Tom Grant pulled up with a wagon full of cotton.

"Move them wagons outta my way, boy!" he shouted at Toby. "You got no right to be in my way. Now, git!!"

Toby and Zekiel looked around nervously, hoping to see Master Martin. Not knowing what else to do, they hurried to move both of the wagons. Tom grabbed his horse whip, and as Toby climbed up on the wagon, he reached over and struck him across the back of the neck. Toby hesitated at the sting of the whip. He almost responded, but decided against it. Grant struck him a second time as Toby reached for the reins.

"You're not movin' fast enough, boy! Now, get outta my way!"

He swung the whip a third time but missed Toby as the wagon lurched forward, making plenty of room for Tom's wagon.

Henry Blackstone stepped out of the 'Feed 'n Seed' to see what all the yelling was about, just as Tom took his third swing of the whip. He watched as Tom Grant pulled his wagon up to the dock and ordered the two slaves sitting on the back of his wagon to begin unloading.

Henry glanced over at Toby and saw the reddening stripes on his neck. The problem with the law in Georgia, was that it didn't protect the black man. Slaves were not considered to be fully human, and therefore, protection under the law did not apply to them.

"Tom, you had no call doing that. Luke Martin was in line ahead of you, and I aim to finish with him first!"

Pretending to be surprised, Grant asked, "Luke? That was Luke's wagon? I don't see Martin around anywhere. How was I to know them nigras was his? Oh well, since I'm here, just let me get my load off and I'll be on my way."

Henry hesitated, but then he remembered the vision of the entire worn-out Martin family asleep in church.

"No, Tom. You can keep the wagon here, but I'm going to have those boys bring the rest of Luke's sacks over here before I start counting yours. Luke was here first."

Tom Grant gave him a challenging look, "That's right. All you hymn-singers gotta stick together, dontcha?" He took a step toward Henry.

Henry's face clouded, "There's a better way, Tom. All that anger and bitterness is killing you."

Tom raised the whip, then thought better of it when he saw a couple of ladies walking down the boardwalk toward them.

"Henry, you know nothing about me! If you ever treat me like a second-rate customer again, I'll see to it you only get second-rate customers! You hear me?"

Henry nodded, "All my customers are first-rate, Tom, and that includes you. But I gotta be fair to everybody; not just you." He motioned to Toby and Zekiel to finish unloading the wagon.

"You'd better make it quick! I ain't got all day!" Tom blustered as he turned to leave.

"I could get to you faster, Tom, if you have *your* men help unload Luke's wagon," Henry said.

Tom quickly turned to his two slaves. "You two stay put!" he barked, as he stormed off to the cafe, grumbling as he went.

Luke arrived at the wagons just as Grant left. He was curious as to why his wagons had been moved and why the unloading was not finished. As Toby heaved a bag onto his shoulder, Luke came up beside him.

"Was there a problem, Toby?"

Toby looked straight ahead. "No, suh. No problem."

Luke was puzzled, but decided to let it go. "Well, okay then. I'll take the empty wagon up to Wally's. When you finish here, bring the other wagon up and give me a hand."

"Yes, suh. I will, suh," Toby replied, and walked off to the unloading dock.

Zekiel was coming back for another bag. He seemed tense but didn't say anything. Luke sensed that something wasn't quite right and almost asked Zekiel, but decided against it.

Luke hopped up onto the empty wagon and grabbed the reins. As he snapped the horses into action, Luke glanced back at Henry. A sad look was on his face.

He made a mental note to talk to Henry.

When all of the supplies were loaded, Toby and Zekiel drove the lead wagon through town toward home. Luke and Frank followed. Frank was sucking on a cherry candy stick, and Luke had the grape one in *his* mouth. As they went past the corrals, Luke noticed Toby staring off to his left. Luke followed his gaze, wondering what had gotten his attention.

Jeb Dukett was back in town, and was once again auctioning off slaves. There were five slaves lined up along the fence, each waiting their turn to be sold. Luke noticed that Toby was staring at the last slave in line. She was the only female in the group.

"She's kinda pretty, ain't she, Pa?"

Frank's words surprised Luke. Frank had not only noticed Toby's interest; he'd also noticed how pretty the girl was.

Luke shot a glance at Frank. "*He's growin' up,*" Luke thought to himself. Then he looked at Toby, and back at the girl. She appeared to be around seventeen or eighteen years old. And yes, he had to agree, she *was* pretty. She was also very frightened.

As they continued on through town, Toby finally turned back to watch the road ahead.

Luke felt his anger slowly rising. He not only didn't agree with slavery; he was beginning to hate it. The image of the frightened girl filled his thoughts. He knew what men were capable of, and she had good reason to be afraid. He wondered if Toby was thinking the same thing he was.

Luke was steaming as they left town and headed upriver. Fear was the goal of many slave owners. The only limit to punishment for many slave owners was that it shouldn't permanently damage their property in a way that would hinder their ability to work. It was beyond his understanding how these white men could look upon themselves as superior.

"Could we buy her for Toby, Pa?"

Luke's jaw dropped, and what little was left of the candy stick fell to his feet. He stared in wonder at his young son.

"Well, can we?"

Luke tried to explain. "Frank, I don't like the idea of people being slaves. I've told you that before. I do not like to buy other human beings. And I can't afford to buy all the slaves Jeb brings into town."

"Did you see the look on …?"

"Yes, Frank," Luke interrupted. "I saw the look on Toby's face."

His gaze returned to the wagon ahead. "It doesn't work that way. You don't just go around buying girls for boys, Frank. And besides, they might not even like each other."

They rode along in silence for awhile.

"*Somebody's* gonna' buy her, Pa. And Toby's our friend," Frank mumbled.

Luke gave Frank a thoughtful look. "How old are you? Twenty?"

"I'm twelve years old, and you know it, Pa."

"Well, sometimes you talk like you're twenty."

Luke shouted at Toby to stop the wagons. "Frank, you go on home with Toby and Zekiel. You keep your mouth shut about this, you hear? I may be too late to do anything, so don't say a word - not to anyone!"

Franks face lit up. "I promise, Pa! Not a word. Except, I might say a couple of words to God, if that's okay."

"That would be just fine," said Luke with a smile.

Frank jumped down and ran up to the front wagon. "Pa has to go back to town. Says we're to go on home." He climbed into the back and sat watching his father coax his horses around and head back toward town in a cloud of reddish dust. The two slaves couldn't see the anxious smile on the boy's face as he looked heavenward and said a prayer.

Luke pushed the horses hard all of the way back to town. "I can't believe I'm doing this, Lord," Luke said out loud. "It feels like you've got this big ol' plan and you're not letting me in on it. What if she's already sold?" He thought about that for a minute and then added, "I suppose, if she's sold, then it just wasn't your plan."

As he pulled up to the stables, passersby could hear him carrying on his conversation with his invisible friend.

"I must be crazy! I don't even have a place for her to stay. How can I be sure this is you?"

Approaching the group of people gathered in front of Jeb, he mumbled, "Sally's never going to let me come to town again. This is crazy!"

"What's that you said, Luke?" asked the man standing near him.

Luke glanced over and recognized the town barber. "Never mind, George. I'm just going a little crazy, that's all."

Luke couldn't believe his eyes. There she was, standing next to Jeb. It seemed as if God had timed everything just for him. (Or was it for Toby?)

Jeb Dukett's voice rose over the crowd. "I got $350 for the girl. Do I hear four hundred?"

"I'll give $400, Jeb," Luke called out. The barber looked at him with a surprised smile. "I see what you mean by a little crazy."

Luke frowned back at him, "The Lord and Frank wanted me to do it."

"Do I hear $500?" Jeb shouted hopefully.

George was shocked. "Frank? Luke, that girl's not a day under seventeen. Isn't Frank a little young? And in case you haven't noticed, she's a Negro!"

"Do I hear $500?"

"Frank thinks one of our workers needs some motivation."

"Sold, to Luke Martin for $400!" Miraculously, the bidding had stopped as soon as Luke made his original bid.

"Well, Luke, it looks like you just acquired some motivation," said George.

Jeb shoved the girl aside and apologized to the crowd for not having any more merchandise, assuring them he would be back in a month or so.

Luke signed the paper that Jeb handed him and headed over to the bank to get the money. The bank had closed and Harry, the bank teller, had gone home for the day. But a light was shining in Ben's office window, so Luke banged loudly on the front door until Ben came out to see what the ruckus was all about. Because they were such close friends, Luke was treated to some very personal banking that evening. Ben chuckled through the whole transaction, making comments about people who say they're going on a diet as soon as the next meal is over. Luke suffered through his friend's pleasure, fully aware of how it looked.

When he returned to the corral, the crowd was gone and the girl was tied to a fence post as if she was just another horse in the stable. It was obvious she'd been crying. She stiffened when she saw him approaching and pressed her back against the fence. He read the fear in her eyes but he also saw a trace of defiance.

"*She's a fighter,*" he told himself. "*She'll run if she gets the chance.*"

Luke saw Jeb and one of his men come out of a nearby barn. "Sun's going down, Martin. Let's get this finished so's I can get me some food and some sleep."

Luke handed him the money and Jeb signed the paper he had given Luke earlier.

"I don't know how you can sleep at night, Dukett."

"I sleep just fine." Jeb looked up from the paper and smiled, "I figure I'm doing you all a favor - for a fee, of course. You couldn't get your harvest in if you didn't have slaves."

Luke sighed, "All the same, I'm praying for the day that slavery comes to an end." He nodded toward the girl, "These people don't deserve this."

"People?" Jeb raised his voice, "You were there when I got this scar on the side of my head! They ain't people!" he yelled. "They're wild animals!"

Luke just stood there looking unimpressed, and Jeb calmed down a little. "Most can be tamed, but you gotta always be careful with 'em, Martin, same as with any wild animal."

Jeb suddenly lowered his voice and pointed to the young girl. "She's a pretty one, ain't she? Looks can fool ya, Martin. She ain't been tamed yet." He turned and looked squarely at Luke, "She still thinks there's hope!"

Jeb smiled, and walked away.

The sun was sitting on the horizon of pines that lined Grantsville, and the town seemed deserted. The girl didn't move a muscle, as if hoping to blend in with her surroundings. She kept her eyes glued on Luke. He walked up to within a few feet and studied her, as if trying to read her thoughts. She didn't move.

"My name is Mr. Martin." He paused, "What's your name?" She remained silent and motionless. "If I take these ropes off, you gonna run?" Her eyes glanced quickly to the left and right, then back to him. But she remained frozen.

"She's never been sold before."
Luke knew who was speaking those thoughts.
"Tell her you know me, Luke."

Luke relaxed. He thought for a minute. "You heard what Jeb told me. He said you still think that there's hope." He watched for a response, but got none.

"Good for you!" He shook his head but kept his eyes on her, "Never! Don't ever, give up hoping!"

No movement, only a tear.

Luke dropped to his knees and began to cut the ropes off of her ankles. "Have you ever heard of someone named Jesus?" he asked. He didn't look up, but kept cutting. "Do you know what a Christian is?"

The ropes fell away and he stood to his feet. He was surprised to see a look of curiosity mixed with suspicion on her face.

Luke nodded, "That's what I am. That's what my family is. We're Christians. Now, I know some pretty rough people call themselves Christians, but that's not the way it should be."

Luke began to cut the ropes that bound her wrists to the fence. He spoke calmly, "I know him. I know Jesus. You may think I'm nuts, but I even believe he talks to me. And I believe he's telling me that you know him too."

Luke paused in his cutting and looked her in the eye. "You know Jesus, don't you?"

The girl's eyes filled with tears. She nodded her head and then looked down to the ground. "Yes, suh, I know him."

A surge of relief swept over him. "Is he telling you not to run?"

He could see that she was thinking things over, and then her body relaxed as she nodded. "Yes, suh, he is."

Luke finished cutting the ropes and they fell away. "That's good. That's real good. Now, what's your name?"

"Girl," she said quietly, still looking down.

Luke's eyebrows raised, "That's not a name."

"Massuh say it's good enough."

Luke sighed, and then he took the girl by the arm to walk her to the wagon. "We gotta get moving. It'll be dark before we get home."

Girl hesitated.

"C'mon," Luke nudged her. "You're safe now. We can't just stand here all night. My wife is wondering what's keeping me." Girl looked nervous, but walked to the wagon with Luke.

"Hop on up there, now. There's room between the sacks and boxes." He let go of her arm and walked around to the side of the wagon and climbed up. He turned around in the seat and saw that she was still standing at the back of the wagon, with a doubtful look on her face. "Girl, the safest place for you in this whole world right now is here with me. If you decide to run, there's folks around here that won't treat you good at all, and that's a sad fact. I'm going home, with or without you. I have family waiting." He turned around and picked up the reins. Girl quickly jumped onto the wagon as it began to roll forward. It wasn't until he was at the edge of town that he glanced back to see if she was on board. He turned back around and urged the horses on home. With a frown he mumbled, "That makes nine, Lord. How am I going to explain this to Sal?"

Chapter 10

It was very dark when Luke saw the welcoming lights in the windows of his house. Mabin had lit the yard lamps and came from around the corral with a lantern in each hand as Luke stopped in front of the barn.

"Ben 'spectin' you, Massuh. I'll get two o' d' men to unload d' wagon. You go on inside 'n git some of dat food I bin smellin."

As Luke climbed down, Mabin handed him a lantern and then he set the other lantern on the back of the wagon. He called out toward the slaves' shack and two dark figures came out of the shadows into the torchlight. Luke looked to the house and then back at Mabin.

"Uh, Mabin? I kinda went on another spendin' spree."

"Yes, Massuh," Mabin quickly responded. "I find a place to put everthin'. You go on inside and get some nice hot food."

Luke smiled, "I'm not sure you...."

Mabin had turned to the two slaves standing ready to help. To the older of the two he said, "Gideon, you 'n Toby take all d' potatoes to the cellar, rest to d' barn. We'll put the horses to bed, and den sort out everthin' else.

The two men stood staring into the wagon between the bags of rice and potatoes. "C'mon now, dey's lots to do. You boys look like you seen a ......" Mabin stopped mid-sentence as he caught sight of what held their attention. ".......girl!" Mabin quickly glanced at Luke and then back at the girl, and then back at Luke.

Luke simply shrugged and held his hands out face up, to Mabin.

At that moment Frank was running down the steps to his father.

"Did you get her, Pa? Did you get her?" He ran up to his father and stopped as he noticed the shocked looks on the faces of the three black men.

Suddenly he gave out a whoop. "Ya got her, didn't ya, Pa? Ya got her!" he yelled, jumping up and down in excitement.

"Calm down, boy," Luke said, putting his hand on Frank's shoulder. "You're gonna wake up the whole state of Georgia." He grinned at Mabin, "I don't think we can just put her in with the rest of the stuff in the barn, Mabin."

"Now, what have you gone and done, Luke Martin?" Sally's voice surprised them all. No one had seen her approach in the ruckus.

"I guess I spent a little more than I planned," Luke answered sheepishly.

Sally walked around to the back of the wagon to see what held the men's attention. "I don't believe this. Can't any of you see how frightened she is? You're all just standing around chatting and staring, as if she can't hear a word you're saying! Don't you men have any sense at all? Toby! You and Gideon get those sacks out of the way right now! Mabin, help her get down from there!"

The men snapped into action, bumping into each other as they all rushed to obey. Toby and Gideon both grabbed the same bag of rice and pulled it so hard they found themselves sitting on the ground with the huge bag laying in their laps. As they scrambled to their feet, both men reached down for the sack of rice and bumped heads.

"Stop, fore somone gets hurt!" Mabin had a knowing look of humor on his face.

Toby and Gideon brushed themselves off and looked at Mabin.

"Gideon, you take d' rice. Toby, don't you move!" Mabin acted serious. As Gideon heaved the bag onto his shoulder and headed to the barn, Mabin said, "Okay, Toby, reach up slowly fo' dat sack o spuds, den take it to d' cellar."

Toby looked embarrassed but did as he was told. Frank was standing behind his father, trying to stop laughing.

Mabin stepped up to the end of the wagon and reached out his hand, "Can I help you down, ma'am?"

Girl stayed wedged between the remaining bags. Mabin began

to look flustered, as he once again urged her to get out of the wagon. "C'mon now, you can't just live in d' wagon, now can ya?"

Girl looked around and saw heads peeking around the side of the barn. She saw Joshua looking from behind a big pile of cotton. Tal and Sadie were standing at their front door with a lantern in hand. She tried to disappear into the supplies. As Mabin looked helplessly at Luke, Sally realized what was frightening the young girl. She walked out into the middle of the barnyard with her hands on her hips and spoke firmly to the curious gathering.

"Everyone go back to your beds! Right now! You'll all get to meet her in the morning."

There was a flurry of activity, and soon nobody was in sight except the Martins and Mabin, who was standing uncertainly off to the side.

Recognizing his dilemma, Luke said, "Mabin, you go on to bed, and tell Toby and Gideon they can finish unloading in the morning."

Mabin looked very relieved, "Yes, suh. Thank you, suh." He tipped his hat to Sally and scurried off.

All three Martins quickly gathered at the back of the wagon. Luke motioned with his hand. "C'mon down, girl. Nobody's going to hurt you. Everyone was surprised and curious, that's all. They're good people."

Sally smiled at girl reassuringly, "I've got some food on the table. Are you hungry?"

Girl looked questioningly at Luke.

Instantly he realized his mistake. "Oh, yeah," he stammered, clearing his throat. "This is my wife Sally, and my son Frank. Sal's a great cook and I need you to climb down outta there 'cause I'm starving and I can smell the food from clear out here." He motioned again for her to climb down.

This time she obeyed and got out of the wagon.

In the light of the lantern, Sally could see her clearly. "My goodness, girl, you're so young. What's your name?" asked Sally.

"Name's Girl, ma'am," Girl said, without looking up.

"What I mean is, what is the name your mama and papa gave you?"

"Don't know no mama and papa, ma'am."

A sad look came over Sally, "How old are you?"

"Don't know, ma'am."

Sally looked questioningly up at Luke. Luke took charge. "Let's go eat. Once you taste Sal's cooking, you'll be glad you didn't run." Luke put his arm around Sally's waist and walked to the house. Frank took Girl's wrist and began pulling her along. She hesitatingly followed his lead.

"It was my idea to buy you," Frank said gleefully. "Nobody knew 'cept me 'n pa. Well, God knew, but he kept our secret. He didn't even tell *me* that it was for sure. He sure is good at keeping things a secret til it happens. Kinda like having Christmas every day. God knew Joshua was comin' but he kept it a secret; then suddenly, blam! There he was! I had a best friend."

As they neared the steps to the porch, Frank let go of her, ran up the steps and spun around. He was surprised to see that she had stopped. Girl was looking past him to the screen door that had just closed. Fear had returned.

Frank looked puzzled, "What's the matter? Ain't ya hungry?"

Girl looked back at Frank, "I can't go in massuh's house."

Frank tried to reassure her, "Sure you can. That's where the food is." He smiled and started down the steps with his hand out to lead her up. Girl quickly backed away and Frank stopped half-way down.

"No, suh. Bad things happen in massuh's house. I don' go in massuh's house!"

"Don't be silly, now," Frank took another step down. "I can't think of one bad thing ever happening at our dinner table. Not ever!"

"It's okay, Frank," Sally had come out to see what was keeping them and had overheard the end of the conversation. "You go on inside and tell your dad that the ladies are having a lamplight picnic out here. Help him bring the food out, and then you go in and eat."

"But, Ma...."

"Do as I say, Frank. It's way past your bedtime, and I'd like some time to get to know our new friend."

"Shucks," Frank pouted, as he went back up the stairs. "Seems like I'm gettin kicked out of my own idea."

Sally turned her attention to Girl and descended to the bottom step. "Come on over to the steps where there's more light and have a seat. You don't have to go inside if you don't want to."

"Yes'm," Girl walked forward and stood.

Sally sat down. "Please sit down beside me so I don't have to look up at you while we talk."

Girl slowly sat down. Sally took Girl's chin in her hand and gently turned the girls face toward her own, "It's different here."

They looked at each other for a moment.

"Luke says you know Jesus."

"Yes'm."

Sally smiled and put her hands in her own lap. "He knows you, too. And he knows your name, and it's *not* Girl."

Did she see a flicker of hope on the poorly lit face?

"You're safe here." Sally put her hands on Girl's two shoulders and smiled reassuringly, "You're finally safe."

The screened door slammed and both women looked up. Frank came out on the porch, carrying another lantern and a table setting for two. He proceeded to set the table that was on the porch, and hung the lantern on a hook above it. Luke brought out two pots, while Frank ran back in and came out with some bread and butter.

The girls watched from below as the two men came to the edge of the steps and took a deep bow. "It's all yours, ladies," said Luke. Turning, they went inside and closed the door behind them.

Sally stood up, reaching down to the girl, "I told you it was different here." She paused, and smiled, "Shall we eat?"

With a shy smile, Girl stood and accepted Sally's hand, "Yes'm."

They walked up the steps together.

Chapter 11

Frank beat the rooster out of bed the next morning. In seconds, he was fully dressed and sliding down the banister, landing with a crash at the bottom.

Luke groaned.

The screen door slammed.

Sally groaned.

They both pulled their pillows up over their heads. It had been a late night of talking after settling the girl into the barn loft. The memories of last night's events slowly crept back into their foggy heads. When the rooster crowed right below their open, second floor window, they both groaned in unison. Sally eased herself up to sit on the edge of the bed. The aroma of fresh coffee drifted through the room and Sally sniffed the air, letting out a sigh, "I don't know how Sadie does it."

"Ummph," Luke groaned from under his pillow.

Standing, Sally asked, "Want me to bring you a cup of coffee?"

She heard a faint mumbling coming from under the pillow.

Sally smiled, "Sorry, but I don't smell any bacon cooking, only coffee. If you ever want to smell bacon again we have to find time to do some butchering, and we can't do the butchering until the cotton is picked."

At that moment Sally leaped on top of Luke jabbing her fingers into his sides, right below the ribs as she yelled out, "And we can't pick the cotton if everyone stays in bed all day!"

Luke gave a shout and flew out of the bed. They both landed in a heap on the floor, but Sally would not let go of his ticklish spot. They tumbled across the floor yelling and laughing until they bumped into the dresser. The wash basin and full water pitcher came crashing down on top of them.

The sounds of shocked screams and shattering pottery that came from the master's bedroom could be heard across the barnyard. Chickens scurried in all directions and then, there was silence.

Heads peeked out of windows, doorways, and from around corners.

Frank came bursting out from the barn with Joshua right behind him. The boys ran as fast as they could to the house. They thundered up the steps into the kitchen, bumping into Sadie and almost knocking her over. "What happened, Sadie? Are you all right? Why did you scream? Did you see a ghost? Did you see a mouse? Was it a robber?"

All the commotion upstairs, and both boys talking at once, flustered Sadie. She tried to calm the boys down and regain her composure. Suddenly, the three of them heard the bedroom door shut, and they all looked to the top of the stairway in silence.

Slowly and calmly, Luke and Sally descended the stairs, still soaking wet, and walked to the kitchen table as if nothing at all had happened. Luke politely pulled out a chair and offered it to Sally. She accepted it and sat down.

"Thank you, dear."

Luke helped her slide her chair in and then stood behind her and put his hands on her shoulders. They both looked at their speechless audience.

"Good morning, everyone," said Sally, with a straight face.

As if no one had heard her speak, everyone remained silent and continued to stare at the wet couple. Luke moved over to his chair and sat down.

"What's for breakfast, Sadie? The coffee smells great! I think we'll both have a cup," he said calmly.

At the sound of her name Sadie came to life and quickly rushed to the stove. Frank and Joshua looked at each other and then back at the soggy display at the kitchen table.

Sadie became a flurry of activity, grabbing bowls, spoons, and some butter knives.

"I got some biscuits and oatmeal ready for you, suh. The coffee's hot and d' milk's cold. I could cook up some flapjacks for you o' some grits if you wish, o' some cornbread........" Suddenly in mid-sentence, she spun around looking bewildered. "Don' you two know you're still in your nightclothes? You both drippin' wet! An Massuh Martin, you have a big ol' bump, an a cut right square in the middle o' yo fohead!"

Sally continued the act, "Frank and Joshua? Have you boys had your morning baths?"

Again, the two boys gave each other puzzled looks and then looked back at Sally. "No, ma'am," they said in unison.

"But Mama, it's only Tuesday!" protested Frank.

Luke looked thoughtful for a second. "Hmm, so it is. Well, your mama and I took a bath this morning; I guess we forgot it was only Tuesday."

Sally couldn't keep a straight face any longer and began to giggle, and that got Luke going. "I guess we forgot to heat the water, too," he said, as they both broke into full laughter.

"That ain't all you forgot!" said Sadie, still a little flustered. "You forgot that folks don' come to the breakfast table in their nightclothes and soakin' wet, upsettin' all the other folks! An did you know you's bleedin' in the head?"

The room broke out in loud laughter and the curious gathering outside relaxed.

Mabin shook his head and smiled, "Guess we best be gettin' back to our breakfast. Don't know fo' sure, but things seems okay, I guess."

The others nodded and the gathering broke up, a few of them glancing over their shoulders as they left.

About twenty minutes later, Sadie came out of the main house and went home to have breakfast with Tal and get ready for the day's work. It didn't go unnoticed that soon there was laughter coming from Tal and Sadie's house. Tal would be answering lots of questions in the fields that day.

Across the river, the workers and their drivers would hear the laughter.

"Mama, where's the girl?" asked Frank, as he finished cleaning his place at the table. "Joshua and I looked all over for her."

"Oh, my goodness! In all of the commotion, I forgot all about her!"

Sally quickly excused herself and hurried to the barn. She went inside and stopped at the ladder that went up to the hayloft.

"Girl, are you awake? It's time to get up now and eat a little breakfast."

There was no response in the loft, so Sally climbed up the ladder and peeked over. The blankets that had been spread out on the hay had been slept in, but the girl was not there now. As her eyes scanned the loft, Sally noticed a slight movement at the back corner of the loft under the straw. She frowned and climbed the rest of the way up and went over by the mound of straw and sat down.

"Anyone under there?"

There was a long silence. "Yes'm," came the eventual reply.

"Well, it's a beautiful day and I'd like to show you around and introduce you to the rest of the people that live here." She moved some of the straw so she could see the girls face. To her surprise, it was stained with tears.

"I hear d' screamin' in d' big house," Girl cried. "Ain't a beautiful day. It'sa bad day," she whimpered.

Sally immediately understood and became concerned. "Oh, my dear girl, it's not what you think! The screams you heard? That was Master Martin and myself."

Girl looked up at Sally, "You hurt, ma'am? Did he hurt you?"

Sally gave an understanding smile and spoke encouragingly. "We're both fine. Well, he does have a big bump on his head, but he's fine. Do you remember what I told you last night that it was different here?"

"Yes'm," Girl answered curiously.

"Well, have I got a story to tell you! It all started out with a little innocent tickling....."

Mabin, Toby, and Joshua came into the barn to fetch the horses and hook them up to the wagons. As they worked with the harnesses, they looked up to the loft where they heard quiet female voices and occasional giggling. Mabin smiled at Toby and shook his head as he continued working.

As they led the horses out of the barn, Toby said "Seen dat girl in town, Mabin. What she doin here?"

"Don' know, Toby. Don' know. Massuh Luke's jus' bein' Massuh Luke, that's all," said Mabin, and then he chuckled. "She sure were fine lookin' in the dark last night," he chuckled again and glanced slyly over at Toby. Toby knew exactly what Mabin was remembering.

"That was Gideon's fault!" said Toby, acting offended. "How'd I know he had hol' on d' same bag I had a hol' on?"

Mabin nodded thoughtfully, "You right, you know. Din't neither of you even see d' bag til it was settin' on top o' you! You was both watchin' sumthin', or someone, else."

Mabin couldn't keep it in. He burst out laughing at last night's memories. Toby looked flustered and Joshua, who had walked up to them, snickered.

Toby stopped in his tracks, pointed back at the main house and said to Joshua, "You go on, boy! Get back to d' house and tell Massuh d' wagons is ready to go!"

Joshua snickered again. "Yessuh, Toby, I'm a goin'," he said, running off toward the house.

The two men hitched the horses to the wagon as Toby said, "I don' like looking foolish in front o' Miz Sally and Massuh Luke."

Mabin cinched the straps tight, "Don' think it the Martins you' worried about."

"Ugh!" Toby threw up his hands and walked away. "There ain't goin' be no peace fo' me t'day, I kin tell! Lord, help me! Looord, help me!"

Mabin smiled at Toby's back and mumbled under his breath, "Maybe he is, Toby. Jus' maybe, he is."

Chapter 12

By noon on Wednesday, two wagons were once again rolling toward town. Mabin and Toby were in the lead wagon, and Luke and Zekiel followed behind. Sitting beside Luke, Zekiel was careful to remain quiet and not disturb the master. There seemed to be a dark cloud forming over Luke's head as he silently fought back the anger that had, once again, come over him.

Earlier, while loading the wagons with cotton for the trip to town, Luke had noticed the two whip gashes on the back of Toby's neck. It had taken a while, but Luke finally got the whole story out of Toby and Zekiel. Now, as he drove to town, he was furious at Tom Grant. He also repeatedly chastised himself for not even noticing Toby's wounds from Monday afternoon.

Toby and Mabin rode quietly in the lead wagon, both reviewing in their own minds the events of the morning. Toby had been working near Luke, loading the wagons and preparing for the trip. Toby had bent over to pick up a sack of cotton when Luke noticed a red stripe on Toby's neck. He leaned over and pulled Toby's shirt collar down and saw the second whip mark. Both marks showed the beginnings of infection. Toby had let go of the sack and stood up.

"Who did this to you, Toby?" Luke asked with an intensity Toby had never seen before. "It's nothin, suh. I be fine."

"Tell me what happened, Toby!" Luke was trying hard to control himself.

"It was an accident, suh," Toby was getting nervous.

"Zekiel! Get over here!" Luke yelled loud enough to make Zekiel run quickly from the corral where he was working.

Sally and Sadie stepped out onto the porch to see what Luke was shouting about. Girl watched from behind the pecan tree at the corner of the barn.

It took a few minutes, but when Luke finally got the whole story out of the two young men he shouted for everyone to gather where he was standing. He angrily kicked the wheel of the wagon while he waited impatiently for them all to arrive.

Eleven people hesitantly formed a half circle around the raging bull. Girl arrived last and stood slightly behind Sally. Frank and Joshua stood side by side, eyes round in amazement. Not one person standing there had ever seen Luke in such a condition.

"Every one of you, listen up! Do you hear me?"

They all nodded. "Yessuh, we hears you," Mabin said.

"Good! Now get this clear in your heads! Are you all listening?" He was trying not to shout, but it was barely working. They all nodded while Mabin said again, "Yessuh. We hears you, suh."

Luke reached up and grabbed the whip off of the wagon and held it up. A couple of the slaves stepped back a step.

"Do you see this?"

All heads nodded again, "Yessuh, we sees it," Mabin said.

Then Luke looked Toby right in the eyes and spoke slowly and deliberately, "This was made for animals! None of you are animals!"

"NOT ONE OF YOU!" he shouted.

Luke paused for a minute. You could have heard a pin drop. He was visibly shaking. Then a sudden change came over him.

He turned and walked over to Joshua. For some reason, he was calm now.

"Joshua, the day I met you, a man called you and your pa animals. Joshua, that was a lie from the pit of hell. Do you understand me?"

Joshua's eyes grew large as he looked up at the big man. "Yessuh. I do, suh."

"But do you *believe* me, Joshua?" Luke was still intensely serious.

Joshua's eyes relaxed a little. "I bleve you. Yessuh."

Luke turned and walked over to the young girl clinging, tightly now, to his wife's hand.

"Two days ago, you heard a man say that you were an untamed animal. Do you remember that?"

"I do, suh," She looked sadly up at him and she heard Jeb's cruel words echo in her mind.

Luke bent down to her eye level and put his hands on his knees, "Well, young lady, that man is a liar!"

"He sho' is, suh!" Girl replied firmly.

Luke's eyebrows went up, surprised at her response. Then in his own mind he heard Jeb's words echo in the distance. *"She ain't been tamed yet,"* Jeb had said. *"She still thinks there's hope."*

Luke stood up, turned and walked to the center of the circle. He was about to say something when suddenly a dazed look crossed his face and he stopped. It looked as if he was listening to something, or someone. Then Luke turned back around and looked at the girl.

Sally immediately discerned revelation in her husband's eyes. She knew it would be good, so she gave a gentle squeeze to Girl's hand.

Luke walked back to her, "Fascinating!"

He stared at her for a moment. "Jeb knew your name, but he didn't know that he knew it!"

"Suh?" Girl responded.

"You know Jesus, and Jesus knows you. And he knows your name!" Luke looked almost as excited as Frank did on Christmas morning.

"He just told me your name. I know he did! Your name is Hope! That's what he's always called you. From the day you were born, your name has been Hope. That's what your mama named you!"

Luke couldn't help it. He stood still, arched his back and raised his hands to the sky. "I knew it!" he exclaimed. "I knew you knew her!" Then he walked off to the house, completely forgetting there was anyone else around - and forgetting what it was he was going to say to them next. He was too busy talking to the Lord.

For a minute, the gathering was silent; then Sally smiled and looked down at the girl by her side.

"Well, Hope, I suggest you come help Sadie and me get these men some lunch so they can be on their way and we can get to the ginning this afternoon."

Hope was beaming as she looked up at Sal.

Toby was thinking she was twice as pretty as yesterday. "Hope," he said to himself and nodded his head. "I like it."

The group was left up in the air as to what they should do next. They had not been dismissed. So, as the three women walked to the house, Mabin took charge. "Well, since there ain't enough animals to do all the work, I s'pose we *people* best be gettin to it. C'mon now, I hears cotton callin'. Let's have things all loaded up when Massuh Martin remembers what he was doin 'n where he was goin."

When Luke left home, he had felt pretty good. But Sally had always said he reminded her of the apostle Peter, in the Bible. Peter could be hearing from God one minute, and letting circumstances control him the next minute. Now, as Luke sat in the wagon staring at the bandages on the back of Toby's neck, the anger had resurfaced.

"Who did Tom Grant think he was?" Luke thought to himself. He pictured himself tying Tom to a tree in the center of town and painting him black. He could see himself standing in front of a large crowd shouting, *"Do I hear 5 cents? Who will give me 5 cents?"*

"Nobody'd give a plug nickel for him," Luke said absently.

"Suh?" Zekiel asked curiously.

Luke came out of his mental fog and realized that he had spoken out loud. "Uh, nothin', Zekiel. Just thinkin, that's all."

"Yessuh, jus' thinkin'," Zekiel repeated.

The wagons rattled on down the road. Toby finally broke the silence in the second wagon, "Mabin, how you figure Massuh Martin knowed her name is Hope?"

"He heard d' Lord tell him so, dat's how," Mabin said, matter-of-factly.

"I din't hear nothin'. You hear sumthin'?"

"Nope," Mabin said, "Didn't hear nothin'." Then he added, "Massuh Martin knows what God's voice sound like."

Toby glanced over at Mabin, "You ever hear his voice?"

"Not sure."

Toby looked down the road ahead. "I ain't sure, neither." He paused, wondering if Mabin would laugh at him if he continued, "Maybe once."

That got Mabin's attention; he turned to Toby, "Yeah? What he sound like?"

"Ain't sure. Don' knows it had a sound. But when dat man use d' whip on me, I'z gonna grab it 'n use it back on 'im. Den I hear, "Don' do it, Toby!" But dere weren't no one else aroun'."

Mabin thought on it for a while, then said, "Maybe it was Zekiel."

"Nope. I know Zekiel's voice. Wern't him."

The two rode on in silence.

As the wagons rolled up to Henry's loading dock, Luke gave out instructions and the men went to work unloading the wagons. Luke's eyes searched up and down the street, but Tom Grant was nowhere to be seen.

"Howdy, Luke," Henry approached with clipboard in hand. "You brought these in just in time. There's a ship leaving Savannah in four days and this'll just about finish the load I'm sending out today."

"Had a real good week, Henry, but I can't expect them to keep up a pace like that. I took on another worker two days ago, but I could use a couple more."

Henry nodded, "Seems to be the story around here these days. Jerry Ellis was in here this morning complaining about lazy slaves and not enough daylight hours. If you ask me, it's not his slaves that's lazy; it's his two boys."

"Have you seen Tom Grant in town today, Henry?" Luke interrupted. There was an edge to his voice as his eyes fell on Toby.

Henry glanced at Luke, and then followed his gaze to the bandages on Toby's neck.

"No, I haven't. But I did mention his altercation with your boy Toby to Sheriff Roily. All he did was shrug and say you should keep a better eye on your property."

When Luke stiffened, Henry took his arm and pulled him out of earshot.

"You gotta be careful, Luke. I heard your name mentioned last night down at the cafe. Billy Glenn and one of the Ellis boys were saying you'd be siding up with the northerners if they come down here to free the slaves. Some others were agreeing with them, saying you treat your blacks like they were white. Folks are getting pretty worked up about the rumors coming down from Boston. There was great relief when Douglas beat that anti-slavery, Lincoln fellow running for the Senate, but the Boston papers say some folks are urging Lincoln to run for president, next year." Luke pulled his arm away from Henry. "So what am I supposed to do, Henry? Smile at Grant and say, "Thank you, Tom, for beating my slaves. You do it so much better than I do. Come on over any time you want and knock 'em around a little?"

Henry looked around to see who was listening, "Keep your voice down, Luke! You can't do any good in jail, or dead. Now calm down, will ya?"

Luke looked puzzled, "What are you talking about?"

"I'm just saying people are getting pretty angry - maybe scared is a better word. They don't think too kindly of white people siding with negroes. You go hittin Tom Grant and you know the sheriff would be more likely to side with him than you."

"The sheriff has to uphold the law, Henry. That's his job."

"You're forgetting the Supreme Court decided negroes are not citizens and therefore have no say in a court of law."

Henry looked around again and then said in a hushed voice, "Billy Glenn bragged about needing to send a message to the nigra lovers in Boston a few days ago. Yesterday morning one of the deckhands that come up here from that Boston ship I'm sending this load out on, was found tied to a lamp post in front of the cafe. He was beat up pretty bad. Had a note tied across his face that said, 'SLAVERY FOREVER!"

"So, is Sheriff Roily looking for Billy?" Luke asked.

Henry shook his head."Nope. George told me that the sheriff said that since no one saw it happen, then there was nothing he could do. Case closed."

Luke's shoulders sagged and he let out a big sigh, "Thanks for the warning, Henry. I guess I'd better think this thing through a little more."

"One more thing, Luke," Henry added. "I don't think Tom is all that dangerous. As long as I've known him he has been angry at his father and grandfather for losing so much of what he considers his birthright. You happen to be a stark reminder of what he's lost as he watches you farm the land that he feels should still be his. And he's also been angry at God since his wife died in that storm. But there are others I think are truly dangerous. Billy Glenn, or the Ellis family, could kill a man for looking at them wrong. They're just looking for excuses. Don't give them any, Luke."

"Are you kidding me, Henry? Tom killed Joshua's father right in front of the whole town!"

"I guess I was meaning he wouldn't hurt white folks. Billy Glenn, Sam Kane, the Ellis family – well, they wouldn't think twice, even if it was your own wife or son! Those people are dangerous to anyone who gets in their way."

Luke was getting frustrated with Henry. "There is no difference between white people and black people, Henry! Tom killed a human being!" His voice had gotten louder as he spoke and Henry looked around nervously. Again he took Luke's arm and tried to pull him into his office.

"We either talk inside, or this conversation is over and you can load your cotton back on those wagons and take it all the way to Savannah!"

Luke followed Henry into his office, "I'm sorry, Henry. It's just that....."

"Stop talking and listen to me!" Henry interrupted as he slammed the door shut.

"You don't get it, do you? Where have you been, Luke? I'm not just talking about a few hotheads in Grantsville. The whole South is a powder keg. Eighty percent of the people walking these streets are afraid of losing their whole way of life. Who would bring in their crops? Who would do their planting the next season? These white people don't even know how to do their own laundry!

The door opened and one of Henry's slaves brought in some boxes and set them against a wall.

"Thank you, Gabriel," Henry said, as the man straightened up. "Tell the others to help unload Mr. Martin's wagons. Oh, and I want no interruptions for awhile."

"Yes, Massuh Henry. I'll tell em."

"Thank you, Gabriel," said Henry, as the slave quickly left the office. He pointed to the door while looking at Luke.

"I've got four of those, Luke! And five years ago I did not agree with you at all. Back then I thought blacks were sub-human, not really full-blown people. But you and Pastor Davies went to work on me. I tried it your way. I talked to them. I asked them questions about themselves, and I found out they feel, and think - and yes, they even pray!"

Henry walked over to his desk and sat down. He opened a drawer, pulled out his Bible, and placed it on the desk.

"Pastor Davies started showing me some things in this book that got me to thinking. Did you know that you can be a Christian most of your life and still not know everything in this book, even if you've read every single word?"

Luke nodded. "As a matter of fact, Henry ...."

"Stop talking and listen to me. I ain't finished."

"Sorry, Henry," Luke rolled his eyes and leaned against the wall, and settled in.

Henry cleared his throat, "Now, as I was saying, I've read what the Bible says about slaves and their masters, but for some reason I thought God was talking about the slaves back in Egypt, Rome, Greece, and places like that. Ain't it strange how you can think God is talking to everyone but you?"

"Yeah, it is. I remember once ...."

"I'm not finished yet, Luke!"

"Sorry."

"Shush!"

"Now, where was I? Oh, yeah. Well, Pastor Davies showed me where the Bible says that a black man who believes in Jesus is as Christian as I am. And get this: it even says that he and I are brothers! Five years ago I would have punched Matthew right in the mouth for saying something like that! But it's in there - 1 Timothy 6."

Henry stood up and walked to the window and looked out at the busy town. "The pastor plays it careful. He waited three years, until he knew I was ready to hear that."

Henry turned and looked at Luke, "You don't play it careful, Luke! You're gonna get someone hurt, or maybe killed. You keep letting your emotions lead you around like a dog on a leash."

Luke nodded thoughtfully, his eyes on the floor. He kept quiet.

"Gabriel and I are brothers, Luke."

Luke looked up in surprise. Henry nodded, "That's right. He's a believer every bit as much as I am. We pray together every Sunday morning before sun-up. Some other times, too, at night. But we play it careful. No one knows about this but Matthew, and now you. Sometimes Matthew even joins us, when it's *real* dark."

Henry looked back out the window. "If you don't guard what I just told you, you could get me hurt. Or Gabriel. Some folks don't much care for the idea of blacks and whites worshipping together."

After Henry was silent for a few moments, Luke stepped away from the wall, preparing to leave. "You're right, Henry. One minute I'm listening to God, and the next minute I'm listening to myself."

Henry was still looking out the window. "Well, now's your chance to start playing it careful, Luke. Your wagons are unloaded, and another customer is in need of my services."

Henry went to the door and held it open for Luke. Luke stepped out into the sunshine and saw Tom Grant standing in his fully loaded wagon, yelling at Mabin, Toby, and Zekiel for being in his way again.

A rush of anger swept over Luke and he took a large breath, and clenched his fists. Mabin caught his eye for a moment and shook his head ever so slightly. Luke stood there, in his own private turmoil, struggling with his flesh. At last, he let the air out of his lungs and looked back at Henry, standing in the doorway. Then he looked up at the sky. Nodding to himself, he unclenched his fists, and walked over to his very vocal neighbor.

"Afternoon, Tom. Is there a problem?" Luke couldn't bring himself to smile, but at least he remained civil.

"Just who do you think you are, leaving empty wagons at the dock?" Tom raged. "I'm a very busy man, and Henry there, he's got a business to run! Now get them wagons outta here!"

Luke tried to sound concerned. "Tom, I was just holding your place until you got here. I'm sorry if there was any inconvenience. I know you're a busy man; I was only trying to help. Maybe someday you can return the favor. C'mon boys, we did our job for Tom. Now let's be gettin' on."

Tom Grant was now flustered, as well as angry. He looked over at Henry. "Did you hear that? Martin thinks he was doing me a favor. He thinks he was holding a place for me!"

Henry gave him an interested look, and shrugged.

Tom continued as he looked after the two retreating wagons, "He can't be that dumb, can he, Henry?"

Henry stepped forward, shaking his head and grinning, "No, Tom. Nobody's *that* dumb. Now, let's get your wagon unloaded, shall we?"

Chapter 13

Later that afternoon, the four men arrived home with two wagon loads of lumber that they had picked up after leaving the "Feed 'n Seed". To Luke's surprise, three horses were tied to the corral fence. He recognized the pastor's horse, but not the others.

Luke instructed the men to stack the lumber next to Tal's and Sadie's building, then went to the house to greet Matthew Davies. But the pastor wasn't there, and neither was Sally. Luke checked in the kitchen, and Sadie told him that as far as she knew, Sally and Hope were out in back of the barn ginning cotton.

"Do we have company, Sadie?"

"I don't know nothin bout that, Massuh. I been in this kitchen all morning. Nobody been through here 'cept Miz Martin."

"Thanks, Sadie. I'll go check it out with Sal."

Luke rounded the corner of the barn and looked into the gin house, fully expecting to see Sally and the visitors. But all he saw was Hope, cranking away at the gin, while Sally fed the cotton into it. No one else was in sight. Puzzled, he walked up to Sal. Smiling, she gave him a big kiss on the cheek, then continued feeding the gin.

"Uh, Sal?"

"Yes, dear?" she responded as she kept working.

Luke thought he saw a slight smile flit across her face, but only for a moment.

"Would you happen to know anything about three horses tied up out front of the barn?"

"Horses?" she asked with a look of innocence. "What horses?" Then she appeared to have suddenly remembered something. "Oh, yes. Horses. Those belong to Pastor Davies, Deacon Willis, and his son, Teddy." She went back to work, acting as if the conversation was finished.

Normally, Luke would probably have attacked his wife and tickled the information out of her right there in front of Hope, the chickens, and anyone else who happened to be watching. But after his conversation with Henry, Luke was in a slightly more serious mood.

"So, did they need a place to park their horses for the day, or did the horses just wander in and tie themselves up?"

Sally kept working, but she knew when not to overdo it. "Closer to the first part. They needed a place to park their horses for the day, because they are all out in the field, picking cotton."

"Are you kidding me, Sal?" Luke asked, trying to decide if she was serious or playing around with him.

She arched her back, and twisted to get the kinks out, "Couldn't be more serious. I'll trade you places for a while, Hope."

Hope kept cranking for a few seconds before she realized Sally was talking to her. She smiled shyly at Sally and stood up. "That's my name," she said, and Luke detected some pride in her voice.

"It sure is! A beautiful name. A God-given name," Luke said gently. He stood back as the two girls switched places. Hope seemed comfortable with Sally but he recognized a "not so sure," reaction to himself. He understood she would need more time.

Sally returned to the original subject. "Pastor Davies showed up in some brand new coveralls right after you left for town, saying he was in need of some physical exercise to help him lose some weight. He asked if we would do him the favor of letting him pick some cotton to help him get in shape."

She looked at him to see his reaction, and then continued, "Just a few minutes after the pastor showed up, Deacon Willis and his son Teddy rode in. He said my snoring in church was a might distracting, so he and Teddy were here to help solve that problem. I protested, of course, but when Frank took the wagon out to the field they hopped on. What was I to do, drag them off?"

Suddenly a look of dismay came over Sally. "Oh my!" Both of her hands flew to her mouth. She stood up quickly and dusted herself off.

"Luke! Grab the crank and start turning!" She spun around, "Hope! He's a harmless old man. Won't hurt a flea! I forgot to tell Sadie to prepare enough food for three hungry guests!"

Sally's last words trailed after her as she raced around the corral and barn to the house.

Hope looked doubtful as she stood with an armload of cotton, unexpectedly alone with the 'Massuh'.

Luke shrugged after a few seconds of silence. "It's true," he nodded, "I don't even hurt fleas." And with that, he bent over and started cranking the gin. Soon after, Hope hesitantly resumed her work.

They worked quietly together for a few minutes, and then Luke asked, "When did the men show up?"

"Soon after ya'll left, suh." She made sure not to look at him.

Luke kept cranking, "They're good people."

Hope began silently stuffing the clean cotton into empty sacks. Luke stood up and began moving the empty baskets around to make room for the load that would soon be arriving from the field. The sun had just gone down.

He was surprised when Hope asked him, "You don' hurt fleas?"

He turned around to see her looking at him curiously. He nodded and gave a pretended nervous glance in the direction Sally had gone.

"Sally doesn't know it, but between you and me, I *have* hurt a few fleas, but it wasn't on purpose. Honest."

Hope's mouth curved upwards slightly when she decided he wasn't serious.

"This is just between you and me, right?" he asked hopefully.

Hope nodded uncertainly, "Yes, Massuh." Then she went back to work. She gave him one last glance as she asked herself if this white man was for real.

Sally, Mabin, Toby, and Zekiel all arrived at the gin house as the wagon arrived from the field.

Sally took charge of the situation. "Hope, you can go wash up at the pump before the rest of the men get here.

"Yes, ma'am," Hope brushed the dust and cotton off of her very tattered old dress and left quietly as Sally turned to address the men.

"Now, Luke, please make sure our guests stay for supper. Tell them I'd be terribly upset if I couldn't feed them for all their hard work."

Before Luke had time to respond, Sally turned to the three black men, "Okay you three, get your barn chores finished while Hope is cleaning up. And by the way, she'll be living in the loft until you get her place built. She's still new, and nervous, so spread the word to the others that, if you don't know where she is, bang real loud on the barn door and listen extra careful for an answer before you go in."

There were three "Yes, ma'am's."

Sally nodded her head approvingly, then noticed Luke standing nearby, studying her with his hands in his pockets. She suddenly became self-conscious and cleared her throat. "Well, um," she fidgeted and cleared her throat again, "I guess I'll go help Sadie finish up." She straightened her apron as she hurried back to the kitchen, wondering if she was being too protective. She relaxed a little when she heard Luke saying, "Sounds like she means it, fellas. Give the girl some space."

The wagon rattled up next to the barn as Toby and Zekiel hurried off to do their chores. "Howdy, Luke!" said Deacon Willis as he and his son hopped down off the seat. The deacon reached out and shook Luke's hand. "We found all this white stuff out there messing up your field," he said, pointing to the load of cotton. "Teddy, me, and the pastor thought we'd help your boys clean it up."

"Well, that's mighty thoughtful of you, Al." Luke turned curiously to Teddy. "Do you and your dad just go around cleaning up messy fields, Ted?"

"Oh no, sir! Only yours! Pa says yours is the messiest he's ever seen."

Luke chuckled, "I really do appreciate the help. Sally's hoping you'll all stay and help clean up the mess of food in the kitchen before you go."

Teddy looked at his dad who nodded his head and said, "We're always glad to help out where help is needed. The pastor here says he's helped clean up some mighty fine-tasting messes in that kitchen of yours."

The rest of the field crew arrived and unloaded the wagon in no time at all. Then the slaves went to their shanty to prepare biscuits and gravy and sing a while, before they went to sleep. Mabin was careful to relay Sally's message about certain places being off limits at certain times.

"Have you ever thought of opening a cafe, Sally?" Pastor Davies asked as he buttered a hot cheese biscuit. "You and Sadie could change the attitude of the whole South if you could somehow get your cookin' into all of those grumpy bellies."

Sally smiled as she slipped a large platter of perfectly cooked steaks in front of Luke. "Well, thank you, Pastor. You're welcome to come out and work on your attitude any time you think it's necessary."

Al Willis chuckled and said something about the Martin's food bill going through the roof.

After they all had a good laugh, Teddy spoke up, "Mr. Martin, I've never worked around slaves before, but I sure did enjoy being out there today. I admit I was kinda nervous when Pa suggested it. I guess it was a new experience for them, too. We all started out real quiet but Pastor Davies didn't let that last long. They finally warmed up to the idea of us being there and we had a good time."

"That's good to hear, Teddy. They're a great bunch of guys," Luke said as he poured himself a glass of water.

"They sure are," agreed the pastor.

Luke passed the potatoes and began cutting his steak. For a minute, the only sound at the table was the tapping of knives and forks on plates of food as weary friends ate a meal together.

"You didn't just help me and Sal today," Luke finally said. "You helped everyone on this farm. We're real short of hands for this harvest. Each person has to give 110% from dawn to dusk most days.

The good book mentions showing our faith by our deeds. Well, you fellas showed your faith today!"

"Well, sir, if it's okay with you, I'd like to come back tomorrow," said Teddy. He looked across the table at his father, who nodded in agreement.

"That's right, Luke. The three of us talked it over and are planning on working the rest of the week. We can't have Matthew putting you folks to sleep again on Sunday morning, now can we? His preaching requires the listener to be well rested. As you can see, he'll even do field work if it helps protect his reputation."

"Al's right, you know," agreed the pastor as he wiped his chin with his napkin. "And along with guarding my reputation, I need to break in these coveralls. I may need to use them full time if people keep falling asleep during the service."

"Well, what about us? Our reputation is ruined forever!" Sally said, acting properly offended. "What do I have to do to put an end to this scandal?" She stood up, stuck her nose in the air, and in a pretend huff went to the stove to fetch the coffee pot.

"Fried chicken tomorrow evening?" Matthew hinted.

"Deal!" Sally answered, so quickly that everyone broke out laughing.

"Count us in," said Al. "Good thing I've got seven children. All of the work will still get done at home, and Marge won't mind if Teddy and I slip over here to help you clean up the mess in your kitchen."

"Mess? What mess?" Sally looked around her kitchen in puzzlement.

"The real reason Ma lets us come over here," Teddy piped in, "is so she don't have to put up with so much guff at home."

"What's guff mean, Pa?" asked Frank.

"Orneriness!" interrupted Pastor Davies. "Al is just plain ornery."

Luke could feel the Lord giving him a real big hug through his friends. "Well, I can't say that I don't need the help. You fellas are a blessing." He was more grateful than he let on. "Maybe you could help Mabin and me build Hope's home tomorrow."

Pastor Davies looked more than a little disappointed. "Al and Teddy are the carpenters, Luke. I was kinda hoping I could try out my sermon on your fellas while I was out in the field picking with them."

"What mess?" Sally asked again in confusion.

"Why, the mess o' chicken, of course!" Al held his arm in front of his face as Sally picked up a cheese biscuit from the table and threw it at him. "Just trying to help, that's all," he said, wearing a self-satisfied smile as he picked up the biscuit and casually began to spread butter on it.

Sally looked at her son and tipped her head toward Al, "That Frank, is guff!"

Luke rolled his eyes, shook his head, and took a sip of coffee.

"That would be fine, Matthew. The men would enjoy having you, and Hope would probably sleep better if she knew *real* carpenters had built her house."

The pastor turned serious at the mention of Hope. "I was surprised to see her. How long have you had her?"

"She's been here for two days," Frank chimed in loud and proud. "We bought her for Toby! Isn't she pretty?"

Eyebrows raised all around the table.

"Uh, Frank?" said Luke, as he shifted uncomfortably. "You can't go around saying that. Toby and Hope might not hit it off. We don't just go around deciding who gets who. Granted, some planters do exactly that, but we don't. If word got back to either of them, they would be extremely embarrassed."

"I'm sorry, Pa. I forgot. I'll keep quiet from now on."

Some eyebrows were still raised, so Sally intervened, "If you're finished, Frank, you may be excused to go play until I call you for bed."

"Okay, Mama," he said enthusiastically, as he scooted out his chair. Standing up, he looked at Teddy and blurted out proudly, "It was my idea!"

"Frank!"

"Yes, Mama," he yelled behind him as he ran out the door.

Sally looked helplessly at Luke.

Al chuckled and said, "This has been a very interesting evening. I hate to see it end. But Teddy and I had best be getting on home.

We'll come with our tools as soon as we finish our chores in the morning."

Teddy tipped his head politely toward Sally, "Lookin forward to tomorrow, ma'am. The food was great. G'night, now." Then he turned and followed his father out the door.

"Nice young man," Pastor Davies remarked, as he remained in his chair holding his cup with both hands and sipping his coffee. He wasn't in a hurry to leave. He had plenty of time for visiting since his wife had died of sickness three years earlier. The Martins had always treated him like family, and they seemed to understand that his house was sometimes too quiet these days.

Luke reached for the coffee pot and refilled all three cups. Sally looked out the door to check on Frank, and then joined the men again at the table.

"You have quite a boy there, too," Matthew continued, with his eyes on his warm steaming cup. "Seems to care about Toby a bit." He looked across the table at Luke and smiled, "Shows some insight, too."

Luke nodded and smiled sheepishly. "I have to admit, things went pretty much the way Frank told it. We both noticed Toby looking at the girl Jeb was selling. Frank got the picture before I did. It was pretty clear Toby was interested. Then Frank asked if I would buy her for Toby. It seemed like a crazy idea for about a mile. Then I felt as if the Lord was using Frank to push me to do it. So I went back, and bought her!"

Matthew grinned widely, "Like I said, you've got quite a boy there."

Sally looked from her cup to the door and then at her pastor. "I know why they wanted to buy Hope. But I'm not sure it's right to try to interfere, to get them together."

Matthew set his cup down and got serious. "There's no way my daughter was interested in David. He started teaching at the school the year before she graduated, but she hardly knew him. He went to the community church on the other side of town, so their paths rarely crossed during the next couple of years.

"I got to know him through various church connections. The children from our church, including your son, all seemed to like him a great deal as a teacher. I came to the opinion that David would be a good husband for Missy, so I interfered. If I saw David go into Wally's Market, then I would ask Missy to run an errand there for me. I invited David over to our house to discuss a situation at the school and then asked him to join Missy and me for supper. When I was sure David was going to the same function as I was, I would ask Missy to accompany me."

"I didn't make their love happen, but I did help give it every chance. Is there someplace in the Bible that says that's a sin?" He looked at Sally making it clear he expected a response.

She sat in her chair, quietly registering what Matthew said. Luke watched her curiously. He realized by the familiar look on her face, that she had reached a conclusion and a plan was forming.

Finally, she placed both hands flat on the table and rose to leave. "Thank you, Pastor. If you gentlemen will excuse me, I have a dress to make!"

Mathew looked extremely perplexed. "I hope I haven't offended her, Luke."

"Nope, you did just fine, Matthew. Just fine."

Chapter 14

Luke and Sally had decided that the new building should be a mirror image of Tal and Sadie's house, joined with theirs at the back, as Sally felt Hope would be more comfortable near another woman. It would be a little big for one person, but Luke didn't want a perpetual building project should the 'Toby plan' work out, or the Lord direct them toward more female slaves.

Arriving from town the next morning, the pastor once again suggested that if Luke really needed another man on the building project Toby would probably be more useful than himself in that type of work, and he could be considered Toby's replacement in the field.

For some reason, Sally liked the idea.

At lunchtime, Pastor Davies joined the slaves sitting in the shade of a wagon out in the field, eating bread and cheese and smoked fish, as they taught him the correct way to sing spirituals. Back at the farmyard, Sally sent Hope out with a basket of rolls, sausage, and fruit for the men who were building her new home.

After their lunch break, the men worked on into the afternoon in the sweltering heat and were grateful when Hope was sent back out to serve large cups of lemonade. Luke knew exactly what was going on and was the only one that noticed Toby trip over a board while watching Hope as she walked back to the house.

Close to sunset, the last wall was stood in place as the men and boys were coming in from the field. As everyone gathered at the pump to wash up, the smell of fried chicken filled the air. Noses were sniffing and eyes were drifting toward the main house.

"Sorry, guys," Luke apologized. "We're trying to bribe our guests into coming back tomorrow. We didn't mean to torture you with the smell."

Tal was quick to speak up. "That's fine, Massuh. We was bein' filled up with the things of the Lord all day. Now we can stand here and enjoy the smell of fryin' chicken for our dessert."

The pastor nodded as he washed his hands. "That's right, Luke. These boys were wonderful listeners, and not one of them fell asleep! They taught me a few things about singing, too."

"Remember our deal with Sally, Pastor," Deacon Willis interjected. "We can't talk about them sleeping any more."

"I haven't had my chicken yet, Al. But I do admit it's going to be a real challenge to let 'em off the hook."

"We'll let Sally decide your punishment if you slip up after tonight, Matthew," Luke said. "I'm thinking I might offer a whole fried chicken to the first guy to fall asleep out in the field tomorrow while you're talkin.'"

"I can do it, easy!" offered Joshua eagerly.

Frank nudged his friend, "Pa was just kidding, Josh. Besides, you couldn't eat a whole fried chicken anyway."

"I could, too!" Joshua challenged.

"Could not!"

"Could too!"

"All right, you boys," Luke interrupted. "The way you two eat, either of you could probably finish off a whole chicken and still have room for a slice of pie."

Mabin chuckled and added, "Two slices, prob'ly! C'mon, young Joshua. Let's go see what we can cook up for these hungry men."

The group was breaking up when they heard Sadie call from the steps of the Martin house. She held up a basket in her hand and was walking toward them.

"Wait up there, Mr. Mabin! Miz Sally sent me with these two dozen hard-boiled eggs and a nice hot loaf of fresh bread to keep ya'all from coveting that fried chicken in there."

That brought a few hallelujahs and some hand-clapping as Sadie handed the basket over to Mabin who bowed and said, "You ladies just made my job a whol' lot easier."

"Not mine," said Tal. "Now I have to decide whether to eat Sadie's cookin' or sneak over to try Mabin's cookin' and some boiled eggs."

Sadie acted indignant. "It's already been decided! You're eating with me! Now get on home, you hear? I declare! You want these folks to think I don't feed ya good? Hmmph!"

Tal pretended defeat as he let his shoulders sag and followed Sadie to their shack. "Guess I'll be sleeping on the floor tonight," he said, loud enough for all to hear. "Ya'll enjoy your supper."

Frank always enjoyed the evening meal, especially when there were guests to make it more interesting. Tonight was no different. He didn't say much, but he soaked in every word of the adult conversation.

There was talk of farms, church, and food. But eventually the conversation turned to the division that was growing between the northern states and the southern states, owning slaves, not owning them, treating them nice, or keeping them down and afraid.

Frank realized that he often forgot that the black men and women here on the farm were his father's slaves. He was immensely proud of the way his father treated these people. His father considered them his friends. The difference was very clear to Frank because of what he saw across the river. Tired black men being stripped of their clothes and given twenty lashes just because the two drivers wanted a little bit of entertainment on a dull day. Only one hundred feet or so divided laughter and sadness. Frank was often tempted to call across and invite Mr. Grant's slaves to come over and live with him on the Martin farm. In the past, a bridge had stood between the two fields, but Chadwick Grant had it torn down when he sold the land to Luke. Frank wished it was still there. If it were, he would have liked to take lemon and cherry candy sticks over to the workers.

Frank thought he heard pine logs popping as they burned in the fireplace – but the sound had come from outside. All heads turned. Luke went to the screen door and listened, as everyone at the table also listened. After a moment of quiet, Luke turned back to the group, only to hear another pop, then another, and then silence.

"Frank, stay with your mother," Luke commanded, as he grabbed his coon rifle and a lantern. "I'll go take a look around."

"We'll come with you, Luke," said the pastor, as the three guests joined him on the porch.

The barn and trees were silhouetted against the darkening sky as the four men stood on the porch watching and listening. Only a couple of torches were burning in the farmyard, but Luke could see his men moving around in the lantern light shining out the open bunk house door. The men were talking among themselves.

"Everyone all right over there?" Luke called out.

"Yessuh, we al'right," Mabin responded. "Think we heard some shootin', though."

Luke and his three friends had walked half the distance to Mabin when a dark figure ran up behind them, seemingly out of nowhere. The pastor let out an involuntary shriek, scaring the daylights out of the other three men.

"I'm sorry, suh, didn't mean to scare you none. I thought you seen me coming." Tal was visibly distraught over the response of the four men. "I heard some shootin' over at Town Road an I come runnin'. Really, I *didn't* mean to scare you."

Pastor Davies tried to put him at ease while everyone else took a deep breath and regained their composure.

Luke took charge, "Probably coon hunters, but let's do a head count, just to be sure. Tal, do you know where Sadie and Hope are?"

"Sadie's home under the bed, suh, and Miz Hope done gone to the barn right after eatin'. She said she needed to rest."

Luke nodded, "Toby, you go check on Hope."

He then turned to Mabin, "Is everyone else accounted for? Anyone been wandering tonight?"

"We all here, suh."

"Okay then, everyone find a torch or lantern, then we'll spread out and work our way to Town Road. All of you stay within hearing range and if you see something, speak up."

There was a flurry of activity as the men hurried to follow Luke's instructions. Soon a line of torch lights was moving slowly through the field and toward the road. Joshua stayed close behind Zekiel, nervously glancing behind and to the sides. He had refused to stay behind in the shack by himself, or run alone through the dark barnyard to the main house.

The line was about fifty feet from the road when they heard the sound of voices and hoof beats coming from the north, heading toward Grantsville. As they came closer, Luke could barely make out three figures on horseback but couldn't distinguish who they were. He called out to them and they reined in their horses and waited. He told his men to hold up and he went forward alone.

"Did you fellas hear any shots in the last half hour or so?" he asked, as he held the lantern near his face so they could see who he was.

"Yeah, that was us, Martin."

Luke recognized the deep raspy voice of Jerry Ellis. He assumed the other two must be his sons, but it was a little too dark to be sure.

Ellis continued in a mocking voice, "You sure you got all your nigras there? We thought we seen a black bear at the edge of the woods across from your place but it was too dark to really tell fer sure. Ain't seen no black bears round here before. Maybe it was a runaway, maybe it was a bear, but it sure was black."

The two men with Ellis chuckled quietly.

The only thing that held Luke back was his conversation with Henry the day before. *"Play it careful, Luke."* He could hear Henry's voice echo in his mind.

"Jerry, we'll get along just fine if you don't go shooting anywhere near my place. Too much chance for an accident. My son plays around here, and I graze my stock right here in this pasture."

"Well, I'll try to take your advice to heart, Martin. Too dark to tell, but I don't think we hit anything. Gotta be gettin on home, though. It's already darker than I like it to be when I travel." Then, as an afterthought he chuckled and added, "You sure you got all your negroes? Better count 'em again. Don't want no runaways in these parts, now do we?"

Luke understood the intention of his comment. There had been a growing problem with the Quakers to the north, and what some called, "the Underground Railroad." Ellis was making it clear that plantation owners in the area knew Luke's beliefs about slavery. It was a subtle warning against taking part in helping runaways find this so-called 'railway system'.

Luke's flesh was in a huge battle with his spirit as the sound of the three horses faded into the darkness. He wanted so much to shoot a horse out from under someone. He actually chambered a shell and started walking fast down the road toward town. He was imagining himself shooting into the darkness. Maybe he'd get lucky and hit Jerry's horse.

"I'm better than that, Luke!"

Luke stopped in frustration. He stared into the darkness for a moment and then removed the shell from the chamber. He took a deep breath, and his flesh surrendered.

The line of torches in the darkness had not moved forward.

"Is everything alright, Luke?" Pastor Davies called out.

"It is now, Matthew. Everyone keep moving forward and watch the ground. We're possibly looking for a dead animal or tracks and blood. When we get to the road, go on across Chester's field. We'll search clear up to the woods, just in case."

The line of torches began moving forward once again.

Chapter 15

Toby had gone to the barn and knocked loudly on the barn door but got no response. He repeated Luke's instructions three times before he opened the door and went in, calling Hope's name. He didn't hear anything, so he climbed the ladder to the loft. He held his lantern up and saw the empty bed in the straw. Now he was becoming worried and hurriedly dug around in the straw piles. Nothing!

Toby jumped down the ladder, looked around, and called out her name. "Hope? You in here?"

Still nothing!

Sally and Frank were sitting nervously at the kitchen table listening intently for any sounds from outside. Sally ordered Frank to stay away from the windows, just to be safe.

"Probably just coon hunters, but it doesn't hurt to be careful!" she had reminded him.

As they sat waiting, they thought they might have heard Toby calling to someone, but they heard nothing else. They waited. They looked at each other and listened. Suddenly there was a loud thump, thump, thump as Toby ran up the steps and across the porch. Bang! Bang! Bang!

In a fraction of a second, Frank was under the table and Sally had let out a squeal as she almost fell backward out of her chair.

"Miz Martin! Miz Martin!" Toby yelled, as he continued to pound loudly on the door.

Sally recognized Toby's voice and gathered herself together, sucked in and blew out two cheeks full of air, and then opened the kitchen door. Toby was beside himself as he envisioned Hope laying somewhere out in the darkness wounded, or worse.

Once all three had calmed down, and Sally had confirmed that Hope was not with them, it was agreed that Toby would check with Sadie and then search the perimeters of the farmstead. Sally would stay put with Frank.

Toby walked out onto the porch to the steps, then hesitated, turned, and returned to the kitchen.

"Miz Martin?"

"Yes, Toby?"

"In all my worryin', I believe I forgot sumthin' big. D' Lord will help us if we ask him."

Sally was humbled. "Thank you, Toby. I'd forgotten, too. Maybe that should be our next step. Would you lead us in prayer?"

Toby was caught off guard by her request. Had she forgotten that he was the slave? Slaves don't lead, they follow. "Uh, ma'am?" he stammered,

Sally realized his dilemma and reassured him, "The Lord knows you, Toby. He hears every word you say. This isn't about you or me. It's about Hope."

"Yes, ma'am. Well, uh," he fidgeted. "Okay, then. Uh, Lord? This's me. Toby. You probably see Miz Martin and Massuh Frank here, too. Well, we are real worried bout Mis' Hope, suh, 'n I, uh, we, is askin' for your help finding her. And we is askin' that she be alright. Oh, and Massuh Martin and d' others need your help, too. And … thanks for listnin', suh. And thank you for helpin'. This's Toby. Amen, suh."

All three heads raised, and Sally smiled at big ole Toby.

"That was a mighty fine prayer, Toby. I believe things will be okay, now. Thank you for reminding me of what I forgot."

Toby was still uncomfortable and anxious to get back out looking for Hope. "Yes'm. I'll go find her now." A quick nod and he was out the door.

He had expected a quick answer to his prayer and was disappointed to hear that Sadie had not seen Hope since supper. He looked to the east and saw the torches, still spread out in a line in the distance. That meant that they hadn't found anything yet.

Toby held his lantern up and tried to see into the darkness. "Lord, dis is Toby again. I hear you can see in the dark better'n a coon. I don' see nuthin', so you take the lead 'n I do my bes to keep up, if it okay with you, suh."

Toby began to walk toward the corral. After only a few steps he heard a faint, unnatural, scraping sound off to his right in the darkness. He stood perfectly still and listened for a long time. He finally continued in the direction of the corral, but now he felt alone and even a little afraid. "What changed?" he asked himself.

"You're not following me, Toby."

Only once before had he heard that inner feeling, or, voice, so clearly. Unsure how to respond, he stopped and whispered a barely audible, "Yessuh."

A strange, unfamiliar sensation came over Toby, and he felt as if God was heading off into the darkness toward the sound he had heard, and he needed to follow Him. He held his torch up again, but it failed to remove the darkness. Toby gulped, and then took slow, hesitant steps, following his Lord into the darkness.

He had gone only about twenty feet when he began to make out a tall dark object in the faint light of his lantern. He hesitated, and then slowly moved forward. A few more steps, and the dark form took the shape of an outhouse. Toby stopped again and listened. He heard nothing. He moved forward quietly as he approached the outhouse, listening for any sound at all inside. His foot snapped a twig just as he was about to ask if anyone was in there.

At the sound of the twig snapping, the door flew open and Hope exploded out of the outhouse running square into Toby and knocking them both to the ground. The lantern went flying from Toby's hand as they fell.

Hope was screaming, "No, no, no, no!" as she kicked and scratched at her perceived attacker. Toby almost punched her right in the face, but then recognized the girl's voice and wrestled her to her back, and held her down, pinning her shoulders to the ground.

"Dat you, Mis' Hope?" he asked, breathing heavily. He looked around for the lantern and noticed a small grass fire flickering to life about twenty feet away.

Hope continued to struggle, whimpering now, "Please don' hurt me. Please don'!"

"Tis you! Mis' Hope, this is Toby. I ain't gon' hurt you none. We been lookin for you. We thought maybe you was in trouble on count of d' shootin' an all. It's okay, Mis' Hope. You safe now."

As the flames began to rise, they lit Toby's face and Hope recognized him. She ceased her struggle and every muscle went limp as she began to weep.

Toby released her and rolled over to a sitting position on the ground beside her. His heart was pounding and he was exhausted from the adrenaline rush. He took a deep breath of air and let it out. He looked up suddenly and realized the outhouse was very well lit up!

Once they had reached the edge of the trees, Luke gathered everyone together. Nobody had seen anything out of the ordinary so he thanked his three visitors for their help, and then told the others to go on back and get some rest. As they turned to head back to Town Road, everyone noticed the far-off flames racing across the fallow field, toward the corn field.

If an outside observer had been looking on in the darkness, he might have thought a general had given the order to attack! The glow of torches moved swiftly down the slope and across the fields, to the accompaniment of shouting men in the small marauding army!

Sadie watched from her window and Sally and Frank came out onto the porch.

As Pastor Davies ran by the house, he pointed and yelled, "Fire in the field!"

Sally sprang into action when she looked to where the pastor was pointing. "Grab some buckets, Frank! I'll get Sadie!"

The yelling men attacked the water troughs. They filled buckets, grabbed their torches, and ran off to battle the weed fire. It was, indeed, a sight to behold.

Soon every man, woman, and child was on the fire line, giving everything they had to protect the corn crop. Fortunately, the breeze had kept the fire away from the outhouse and other buildings.

It took over two hours to put the fire completely out. Afterwards, there were barely ten feet of weeds between the corn field and the smoking black ground. All divisions of color, age, and position, were completely forgotten as the weary firefighters shouted hallelujahs, hugged, and patted each other on the back, relieved to have saved the crop of corn.

While everyone had been busy fighting the fire, a lone figure arrived, unnoticed, on the opposite side of the river.

Chapter 16

Tom Grant had been sitting on his porch smoking a cigar and enjoying the silence of the evening when he thought he heard rifle shots across the river. Shots echoing in the hills were a common sound. Tom himself enjoyed varmint hunting for a change of pace once in a while. He didn't think anything more of the sounds and took a few more puffs on his cigar. Then he heard two more shots. This time he smiled to himself, "Missed the first time, did ya, Martin?"

Standing up, Tom looked in the direction of the river and yawned. Then he walked to the porch railing and surveyed his kingdom. The main buildings of his plantation and a small forest of trees blocked his view of the river a mile away. A hundred yards to the south, near the hog pens, a stream ran between two rows of slave shacks which Tom called 'Shanty Town'. The shacks, eight in each row, had the look of a military encampment, except that the 'tents' were made of wood. Tom's grandfather had separated his slaves, two to a shack, believing that by sleeping separately, it wouldn't be so easy to consort amongst themselves and stir each other up to revolt. When they became in a family way, well, that was their problem. They just had to cozy up a little tighter. As the years went by, the shacks began to fill with children and adults, but no more buildings were built. Life was barely tolerable for them, and yet once in a while, when Tom got a hankering, he would purchase another slave and stuff him in with the others. How many did he have now? Forty? Fifty? He wasn't sure.

At the end of the rows nearest the house stood a newer, larger, building that the slaves used for cooking, eating, and some socializing.

A light was shining out of the windows and Tom could picture what was going on inside. Lizzy would be cooking up a big pot of beans and rice. Maybe she was even cooking the possum he'd seen her boy Jackson haul in this morning. The rest of the slaves would be sitting and eating quietly, too exhausted to say much. "That's the way it should be!" his father had told him. "Work and sleep! Work and sleep! Won't get no trouble from 'em that way. No sir!"

From the kitchen in his own house came the sounds of pots clanging together and his thoughts turned to Etta, his house servant. She had been with the family for over forty years and, though Tom hesitated to admit it, he had become quite fond of her. In his weaker moments, he would even say that she reminded him of his own grandmother.

But God had not given Tom a story-book life, and his bitterness would not allow him to dwell on such thoughts for long. He was the only child of an alcoholic father. He had not done well in school and often had been picked on by the ever-present school bullies. Tom had had dreams for his future on the large plantation, only to have those hopes dashed because his dad needed cash to pay off huge gambling debts. A large portion of prime land along the river had been sold off to Luke Martin.

Tom dreamed of having a beautiful wife, and children playing in the yard. And for four years he had that much, at least. But a few years ago, a hurricane had swept up the east coast, bringing heavy rain and high winds. Unknown to Tom, who had been sitting comfortably by the fireplace going over some financial papers, his wife Lillian had bundled up their daughter and taken some leftovers from the last few days' meals down to the slave family that had a new baby. On their way back to the house, a rotting oak tree (the only tree on the whole plantation to blow down) had landed on his wife and daughter. Tom was now all alone.

His life *had* been a hard one, and he was most comfortable looking at himself as a victim, because it allowed him to blame someone else. He blamed Luke for taking advantage of his father's "weakness." He blamed the negroes for the death of his wife and daughter. Most of all, he blamed God for not submitting to his dreams and desires, though he would not have worded it exactly that way. In his own mind, blaming others gave him some of his lost dignity back. Since he couldn't get back at God, he chose to take it out on the negroes. And that had worked well for him until about six months ago, when his wagon axle broke during a thunderstorm and he had to walk three miles home in the dark, soaking wet. All of the way home he yelled at God and ordered him to knock a tree down on him, since God thought it was such fun to kill people that way. But God didn't obey him, and that made him even angrier.

When Tom finally arrived home, he had stomped up the steps and stormed into his house. He burst into the kitchen, commanding Etta to fetch him some dry clothes immediately. No matter how fast she moved, it would not have been fast enough. He started pushing her to move faster, and before he knew it, he was beating the old slave woman with both fists.

When it was over, Etta was sitting on the floor, leaning against the wall with blood running out of her nose and both eyes swollen nearly shut. Tom was standing over her, looking down at the fruit of his anger and panting; his knuckles red with blood.

All of a sudden, as if in a vision, Etta's face became the face of his grandmother, the only woman he had ever loved other than his wife and daughter. For a moment, a light shined in his darkened soul and he saw what he had become. Tom was visibly shaken. His wife had loved the old woman, and he remembered his four-year-old daughter following Etta around the kitchen as she cooked, hanging onto her skirt and chatting happily. Suddenly, he began to feel physically ill. Leaving Etta to herself on the floor, he slowly turned and walked to his bedroom and sat down on the edge of his bed. He stared at the floor for quite some time. Eventually, he stood and walked to his dresser and removed a pistol from the top drawer. A photograph, set in a beautifully carved wooden frame, stood perfectly centered on a doily on the dresser top. His wife, Lillian, holding his young daughter, smiled at him from behind the glass. They were both so beautiful, and looked so happy. Tom's body began to shake and he began to whimper. Then he began to cry. Slowly he raised the gun to his head with his finger on the trigger.

"Yo' sweet lil girl 'n yo' missus would not fogive you fo' shootin' d' man dey loved, suh."

Tom was taken completely by surprise. He turned to see Etta walking slowly toward him. Her face was unrecognizable, swollen and bloodied. Her dress was torn and bloodstained. She stopped a few feet in front of him. He stared at her in a daze, and then lowered the gun to his side.

As she looked at him through the narrow slits that were her eyes, she said, "Dere's a better way, suh. Yo' women saw a better man in dere, somewhere."

Tom's shoulders drooped and he shook his head. "He's dead, Etta."

Etta turned, and as she shuffled to the door she said, "No, suh. Dey would say he ain't, suh." Then she slowly and painfully walked down the hall, back to the kitchen.

Tom stood looking at the empty doorway for a while, then lifted his pistol and studied it thoughtfully. Placing it back in the drawer, he walked down the hall and stopped in the doorway to the kitchen where he watched quietly as Etta, with great effort, knelt to clean up her own blood from the floor.

He remembered the image of his grandmother on her knees cleaning the mud he had carelessly tracked into her kitchen on a rainy day. She had scolded him, but she had also offered him cookies and milk. Etta kept scrubbing and didn't look up.

"Soon's I get dis mess cleaned up, I kin make sum hot coffee 'n some supper fo' you, suh," she said through her swollen mouth.

Tom was in a daze. The long walk in the rain, then taking his anger out on the old woman, and then his crying, had drained him of all energy. He wasn't totally sure that what he had just heard was real. Had she actually offered to cook him a meal, after what he had done to her?

"*Want some milk and cookies, Tommy?*" came a voice out of his past.

Not sure of what it was that was moving him forward, Tom went to Etta and helped her to her feet. "No, Etta, you go lay down. I'll send Danny to get Doc Jeffords."

That was as close to an apology as Etta would hear that night. But she recognized it and a trace of a smile crossed her cut lips.

"Yes, suh," she sighed deeply, "mebbe I lay down a bit."

Tom leaned on his porch rail and took another puff of his cigar. His eyes were still on the windows of the slaves' dining shack when he was brought back to the present by the sound of a pot or something hitting the kitchen floor. He could hear Etta scolding herself.

Etta had not been the same since that night in the kitchen. She moved slower and seemed a bit absent-minded at times, sometimes completely forgetting to make supper for him or to shine his boots. But Tom never spoke harshly to Etta again.

A middle-aged black woman came out of the dining house and closed the door behind her. Tom watched as she walked in his direction. He had purchased Belle to help Etta with the housework and the cooking. That was the same day he had shot the big slave.

"Such a shame," Tom thought to himself. "That big ole boy could have done a heap of work. He would have been trouble, though."

Tom wondered if Luke was getting any work out of the kid. He hoped not.

"Etta is in need of some help in the kitchen, Belle," he spoke, as she came up the steps. "And you can tell her I'll be eating out here on the porch tonight."

"Yessuh," Belle had stopped to listen as he spoke. She kept her eyes from meeting his.

"Get on in there. She might have my supper about ready. Help her bring it out."

"Yessuh." The slave woman continued on into the house as Tom thought about how well his purchase had turned out. Belle was hard working, and a quick learner. She was obviously of much better breeding than the field slaves. Field slaves were unpleasant. "*Not nearly as smart,*" he told himself.

Tom lit the lanterns around the porch walls as Belle brought out his platter of ham, baked potatoes and bread. Etta poured a glass of tea and set it on the table by the railing. She didn't smile, and Tom wondered if it was out of kindness to him, not wanting to remind him of her three missing teeth.

After all these years, he still had not gotten used to eating alone.

His way of dealing with it was to slide into his victim mode. As he buttered his bread, he watched some of the Negroes leaving the dining house. He noticed that most of their clothes were in tatters. Men and women alike had trouble being modest, because he had refused to give them any cloth or even old cotton sacks since his wife and daughter had died. After all, she would not have been outside on that fateful night if it hadn't been for the slaves. If it hadn't been for them, he would not be eating alone.

As Belle carried the empty dishes into the house, Tom stood and stretched, looking in the direction of the river. There seemed to be a strange flickering glow over the trees. He heard some voices coming from the slave quarters and saw three of the slaves standing in a doorway, pointing and watching the illuminated sky. He remembered the shots he had heard earlier in the evening. "*Well, well, well,*" he grinned, "*it seems it wasn't coon hunting after all. Looks as if Martin's got himself a little rebellion going on over there.*" Tom reached for his hat and a lantern. "*Tonight won't be as dull as I thought it would be, and Luke will be supplying the entertainment.*" He went to the screened door and yelled inside, "I'm going for a walk. Don't know when I'll be back." Without waiting for a response, Tom grabbed a lantern and headed down the steps and followed the trail through the woods to the river.

Tom was out of shape and panting hard as he came out of the trees and down the slight incline. About a hundred yards away, beyond the river, he could see men, women, and children running back and forth from the barnyard with buckets of water to throw at the field fire that was blazing its way toward the corn field just across the river from where he stood. Some were shouting instructions and encouragement to each other, and some were just moving silently from the water supply to the fire and back. After he lit a cigar, Tom blew out his lantern and sat down on the river bank to watch the action. As the fire moved along, the river became a source of water closer than the barnyard. Tom was disappointed that no buildings were burning and there didn't appear to be a rebellion in progress but still, it was better than nothing.

The flames shown on the face of the Baptist minister as he ran to the river with an empty bucket. Tom was surprised to see him, but pleased when he tripped over something in the dark and was sent sprawling on top of a black slave running to the fire with a full bucket. Tom almost laughed out loud at the sight, but then grunted his disapproval when the pastor picked up the Negro and dusted him off while apologizing profusely.

As the fire neared the corn field, Luke and his people began to get it under control. Everyone was puffing wearily and walking, instead of running, with their remaining buckets of water. In the light of two remaining hot spots, Tom witnessed a disturbing sight. Sally Martin walked over to the slave called Mabin and gave him a big bear hug. There were shouts of 'Hallelujah' and 'Praise the Lord', as they all began congratulating each other with hugs, handshakes, and pats on the back. "You, my friends, were wonderful!" Luke said loudly, and with unhidden emotion. "I am proud of every one of you!"

From where Tom now stood in the darkness, every word seemed to be miraculously clear over the sound of the gently flowing waters. He watched as Luke walked up to the older slave and hugged him saying, "You're the best friend a man could ever have, Mabin, my brother!" Then Luke turned and walked over to a male and female slave standing together, and shook the man's hand, "Thanks, Tal. You and Sadie gave one hundred and ten percent tonight."

"You're a good man, suh. It's an honor to work for you, suh."

A confusing wave of emotions washed over Tom as he listened to their foreign conversation. The feeling of loneliness brought on a feeling of anger which was replaced by confusion, and then sadness. He had never had people talk to *him* like that. As he watched the shadows moving toward the distant barnyard, Tom was swept with envy. As he stood listening to the sounds of the river that divided them, he began to understand how great a chasm lay between himself and the rest of the world.

As Tom walked back through the trees to his house, he decided to have a talk with his two slave drivers in the morning. He was not foolish enough to think they liked him any more than his field slaves did. What they liked was the power they had over the slaves and, of course, the money he paid them. *"Makes sense,"* he told himself with self-loathing. *"I like Etta, and look what I did to her."* He walked over the rise to his house, trying to think of what there was to like about Tom Grant.

Chapter 17

Luke set up a rotating fire watch for the rest of the night to put out any little flare-ups. The rest of the group gathered around the pump to drink and wash up. All were covered with a combination of soot and sweat, too exhausted to say much.

It was Sadie who noticed the blood running down Toby's face and arms as he washed up.

"What happened to you, Toby? You look like you took on a wildcat!"

To his embarrassment and Hope's dismay, all attention turned to Toby.

"I'm jus' fine, Miz Sadie. I took a tumble, dat's all; landed in some brambles or sumthin'."

Sadie shook her head, "Took more than brambles to do that! Miz Sally, do you have some ointment in your house, ma'am?"

Sally nodded as she stared at Toby, "Frank, run up to the cupboard and fetch that ointment and some clean rags please. You know where they are."

"Yes, ma'am," Frank and Joshua both ran off to the house together. As they ran, they passed Tal coming out of the shadows carrying a blackened lantern in his hand.

"I was curious what mighta caused the fire. Found this down by the outhouse."

Toby quickly intervened, "I s'pose I start d' fire when I fell. It was me dat dropped d' lantern." He looked over at Luke and Sally, "Din' mean to cause no trouble, suh."

"No, Massuh! Dat ain' true!"

In unison, all heads turned to Hope, who had been standing unnoticed near a torch mounted on the barn wall. Her already threadbare and tattered dress was now barely hanging on her. It was blackened by soot and smoke, mixed with some dirt and weeds.

"It's all my fault. Please don' beat him, Massuh!" she begged Luke, as her tears began to flow freely. "Please, Massuh, it's my fault! I hurt him! Made him drop d' lantern."

Hope was crying hard as she pleaded with Luke to have mercy on Toby. For a moment no one knew what to do or say. Then Luke walked slowly to Hope with a grim look on his face. He stepped in front of her as she closed her eyes and braced herself to be struck.

But Luke reached out and gathered Hope into his arms and hugged her. Tears built up in his eyes and in the eyes of half of the onlookers as Luke held her tight. It took a while before he was able to speak.

"It's like Sally told you when you first came, Hope," he said, looking past her into the darkness as he held her to his chest. "It really is different here."

"Amen to that," confirmed Pastor Davies as he walked up to the man and his slave. "It is sooo' different here. A whole lot of work, a whole lot of excitement, a lot of laughing - even crying. But nobody gets beaten around here, Miss Hope; mostly, a whole lot of Christian lovin'!"

Frank and Joshua suddenly came running into the somber group proudly holding up the clean rags and a jar of ointment.

"Here y'are, Mama. What happened to Toby? Did he get attacked by a mountain lion? Did he kill it? Do we have to go to bed tonight? What was the shootin' about? Is Teddy staying here all night? When do we........?"

"That's enough questions for a year, Frank," his mother interrupted. "Hush up now and give us time to figure everything out."

Sally's attention was diverted to Toby as she realized that he had left and quickly returned with a blanket. As he walked over and placed a blanket around Hope to cover the torn dress, Luke stepped back and Sally put her arm around Hope and walked her to the house. She paused a moment to instruct Tal and Sadie to take Toby to their place and get him cleaned up. Then she proceeded to take the young sobbing girl into her home.

Luke was exhausted. Even before the fire, it had been a hot, humid night. He looked around at the ragged group.

"Pastor, it's too late for you three to go home tonight. I hope you're all right with bedding down in the barn. I think Sally will be keeping Hope in the guest room tonight."

The three nodded their ascent.

"Fine with me," said Teddy. "I'm so tired I believe I could sleep on a bed of nails."

Luke looked over the rest of the group, "I don't expect to see anyone out of their beds before noon. Tomorrow I'm going to put all of the pieces together and figure out what happened tonight, and why. But for now, I'm going to bed. Goodnight, and thank you all so much for your help."

Luke turned and walked to the house, then without turning around, he said, "C'mon, Frank, you too."

"Aw, shucks," Frank came out from behind Mabin, kicked the dirt, and followed his father.

Chapter 18

Late morning on the following day, Luke and Matthew were having coffee. Sally had gone upstairs to check on Hope, saying they would both be down soon. She had just finished explaining to the men the things Hope had told her when she had brought her into the house to clean her up.

Luke was relieved to hear Hope's version of what had happened. When he had gone to bed the night before, he prayed that things were not as they appeared. Hope had badly scratched Toby, and Luke wondered if it had been in self defense. It didn't look good for Toby. And he was very bothered that it had all started near the outhouse.

But Hope cleared things up by explaining that after eating the evening meal with Tal and Sadie, she had stopped by the outhouse on her way back to the barn to get some rest. It was while she was inside that she heard the gunshots.

The last time Hope had heard gunshots was when her previous master had been killed by an old black house servant who had taken the master's gun off the wall and shot him dead. The old woman committed the crime to protect Hope after he had dragged her upstairs to his bedroom. The result was that Hope had been sold to Jeb and the old slave woman had been hung from a tree in front of the slave quarters by the master's son.

So when Hope heard the shots, she stayed hidden in the outhouse, not knowing what was going on but fearing the worst. She had blown out the candle and stayed as quiet as possible for nearly half an hour in the blackness of the outhouse.

Eventually a lantern light, shining through a couple of cracks in the boards, revealed that someone was slowly and silently approaching. She had no way of knowing he was as nervous as she was. The snap of a twig told her where her perceived attacker was standing. She chose the element of surprise, and in total terror, she struck first. Now Toby had what would probably be a permanent scar, and Hope was terribly ashamed. Sally tried to assure her that her response was understandable and that Toby would hold no hard feelings.

After only a couple hours of sleep, the deacon and his son had slipped out of the barn and gone home to help with the morning chores. They woke Matthew up and told him they would be back in the early afternoon.

Matthew had chosen to stick around and now, after hearing Hope's story, he was of the opinion that Toby deserved to have all doubts or suspicions cleared up. So Luke instructed Mabin to gather everyone together for a final debriefing of the night's events.

There was not the usual lighthearted chatter among the workers as they wearily leaned against the corral fence, or a wagon, or a tree. Mabin offered a tired greeting as Tal and Sadie dragged themselves up to a bale of cotton and plopped themselves down. The adrenaline rush that had gotten them through the night before had deserted them all. A couple of the men shook their heads in wonder as Joshua and Frank ran up to Mabin and began to talk nonstop about the fox they had chased away from near the chicken coop. Not one of the adults could remember when they ever had as much energy as those two boys.

Joshua was in mid-sentence when he suddenly stopped speaking and stared across the yard past Mabin. It didn't take more than a second for all eyes to focus on Hope. Walking beside, but slightly behind Miz Martin, she looked like an altogether different person. It was obvious that she had gotten all washed up and someone, possibly Miz Martin herself, had brushed and braided her hair. But the greatest change of the package was the wrapping. The new dress she had on was homemade, and nothing fancy, but with Hope wearing it - and compared to the rags they had last seen her wearing - the dress was beautiful.

When Hope realized that every eye was on her, she became

uncomfortable and embarrassed. She stepped further behind Sally as they walked up to the group. Sadie stood up and went to her and put her arm around her. Luke stepped away from the women, intending to take everyone's attention off of Hope, but it didn't work. Not until he spoke.

He began with the gunshots, and used the Ellis family as a reminder of how dangerous the world was for black people, and that they needed to be especially cautious whenever they were in town. He instructed them to all keep their eyes open because they still had no idea what the three Ellis men were shooting at.

"It could've been an animal, or possibly a person, or even a tree stump. We just don't know."

Then Luke proceeded to tell Hope's story of her past, and about the fire, and how Toby had done all the right things, adding, "Sometimes, doing the right things can be painful, but don't let that stop you from doing them." Luke assured the men that because of last night, his respect for all of them had grown even more.

With impeccable timing, Deacon Al rode into the barnyard. It was time for everyone to take advantage of the five remaining hours of daylight. At least it would be a shorter work day, after such a long night. Al begged off working on the roof saying his balance wasn't what it used to be, but Luke was welcome to use his tools. He also explained that the family milk cow was ready to drop her calf and so Teddy had remained at home in case he was needed. Luke chose Mabin, Toby, and Zekiel to help him put the roof on the new building. Pastor Davies asked the slaves for permission for Al and himself to join them in the fields. He said he wanted to turn all of his blisters into calluses. Not accustomed to a white man asking their permission for something, they shifted uncomfortably but agreed to the pastor's request. Tal finally spoke for the others as they were all climbing aboard the wagon.

"We wuz all talkin' this mornin bout how we can't go to the white man's church, but dis white man been bringin church to us."

Matthew laughed, "I promise not to take up an offering, but you fellas gotta speak up if I get too long-winded."

"No, suh. Makes the day go by faster."

"Well, that's mighty nice of you, Tal. Let's get going so that I can start speeding up the rest of your day," said Matthew.

Meanwhile, Luke noticed that Hope had started walking toward Mabin, Zekiel, and Toby.

"Zekiel, Mabin, would you come over here? I need to talk to you two for a minute!"

All three men started walking over to Luke, but Hope walked purposefully up to Toby and he stopped. Zekiel and Mabin continued on but both wore an, ever so slight, smile.

Sally spoke loud enough for Hope to hear, "Sadie, I'll help you at the gin house until Hope comes. She'll be along in a few minutes."

"Yes'm," smiled Sadie, as she walked away listening to Sally telling of her meal plans for the evening.

Hope had approached Toby with a purpose and she didn't hesitate.

"I want to say I'z sorry for d' trouble I caused you."

Toby noticed that she was not looking him in the eyes, but instead, she was staring at the deepest gash on the cheek under his left eye. Unconsciously, he raised his hand and touched the wound.

"You done jus' what you shoulda done, Miz Hope. I shoulda call out sooner. You had no way o' knowin'."

"I feel real bad bout what I done to your face."

Toby smiled a little, "You sure a fighter. Thought I had hol' of a bear for a minute. Glad it was only you."

Her gaze lifted from his cheek to his eyes. He began to feel self-conscious and uncomfortable. He put his hands in his pockets and they both turned their eyes to the ground as Hope nudged a rock with her toe. Both searched for something to say and finally Hope said, "Miz Martin giv me dis dress. She says her and Sadie made it jus' for me!"

Toby looked at the dress and then at her.

"You make it look real good, Miz Hope."

They both became uncomfortable again, so Toby said, "I best be gettin on over and helping Massuh Martin." He paused a moment, "I'm glad you okay." Reluctantly, he began to shuffle off in the direction of what would soon be Hope's new house.

As she watched him leave, Hope realized that she felt safe for the first time in her entire life. She didn't feel old, beaten, and weary anymore. She felt young! On a whim, and without thinking about who else would hear her, she called out, "And Toby! Thank you fo lookin' fo me las night!"

Toby didn't turn around, but he did raise a hand in acknowledgement.

Hope walked quickly and lightly to the gin house.

Toby felt a little lighter himself.

The four men worked well together. Zekiel and Toby were both in their twenty's and in prime physical condition. Of the three slaves, Zekiel had been at the farm the shortest time. Luke had actually bought *him* out of need, rather than in response to nudging from God. Until Zekiel came along, Toby had done all the heavy lifting. Tossing full baskets of stomped cotton on and off of wagons all day was something none of the others were built to do. Luke knew that Toby needed some help.

Two years ago, an Englishman, down on his luck, had come to town offering to sell his slave in exchange for fare to England. Luke was the first man he'd met in Grantsville. At first sight of the man's tall, muscular, young slave, Luke was quick to close the deal. Luke had even escorted the man down to the ferry dock and personally purchased the fare, and food for his trip. Luke had no doubt that Zekiel was the best bargain for a slave of his caliber that a man could possibly hope for.

Luke watched as the two strapping young men lifted boards and beams, climbed ladders, and swung hammers. He realized that they were both a piece of God's mysterious plan that had been going on around here for quite some time. It had *not* been a matter of chance that the Englishman had run into Luke before anyone else. And as he thought about that, he also remembered that when he gave his first bid for Hope, the bidding had stopped. Nobody had bid against him!

Many men attribute their good fortune to luck. But Luke knew that 'luck' was not God's name. He also knew that his three friends from church showing up to work for a few days was a personal message of love from this God whose name is *not* 'luck'. Then he remembered a very different message that had come from this God of his, through Henry. Henry's was a message of rebuke, warning, and caution. But now, as Luke thought about it, he felt it was a message with direction hidden in it. Could it be that he could be of more help to the black man if he kept his mouth shut a little more often?

Luke's mind wandered back to his trip to Baltimore in '56, two years ago. In a bookstore he had come across a narrative written by a former slave by the name of Frederick Douglas. The name was familiar to Luke. The man had traveled around New England telling his story at anti-slavery rallies. The mere mention of his name, south of the Mason-Dixon line, could easily result in a brawl. Douglas was apparently very successful at removing the fantasy of southern plantation culture, from the minds of the northerners. Out of curiosity, Luke bought the book and read it during his trip back to Grantsville. He had been deeply convicted by Douglas' opinion of 'plantation Christianity', but as he had told Mabin recently, he had been afraid to take the big step.

Near the end of his trip, Luke had been sitting in a small café in Savannah, reading the book for a second time, when a man walked boldly up to him and grabbed the book from his hands and tore it up. Frederick Douglas was clearly not welcome in Georgia.

Luke wondered if maybe, just maybe, God was about to let him in on the plan, or at least how he, Luke Martin, fit into the plan. As the tension between South and North, slavery and freedom, rose to fever pitch, Luke's was not a feeling of dread. Instead, what began growing inside of him was anticipation. Beyond head knowledge, it was a knowing in his soul. God had a plan to work, right in the center of strife and dissension. And, right in the middle of it all, God was going to use him! He was sure of it. Luke began to pray about Henry's warning, as he worked on the roof. He felt sure his assignment was near!

"Wood pile's getting low for the cookin' stoves, suh," Mabin's voice drifted into Luke's thoughts as he worked. "Tol' the boys I'd be makin' col' coffee for 'em soon if we din't start workin' on it. Thought maybe Zekiel and Toby'd go up on the hill with me after we finish dis roof."

"Good idea, Mabin," Luke agreed. "Deacon Willis and his son said they'd come tomorrow for one last day. That would give us enough...." Luke stopped and thought for a minute. "No, on second thought, let's you and me go up there. We haven't talked for a while. It would do me good to fill you in on a few things I've been thinking about and get your input on them."

Mabin held his chin in his hand and nodded thoughtfully, then said with a smile, "That'd be fine, Massuh. Even while talkin, we get mo' work done den dese two boys."

Toby shook his head, "No, suh! Can't do it, Mabin! Ain't no one gets mo' work done den dese two boys." He pointed at Zekiel and himself. "And dat's a fact!"

"Oh, really?" Luke challenged. "You think a couple of middle-aged men can't keep up? Well, Toby," Luke pointed to the forested rise to the north, "you look up there tomorrow night and there probably won't be a tree left on that hill for a bird to set on. What do you think of that?"

Toby smiled, "Dat won' be good fo' d' birds, suh!"

Luke noticed Sally coming from the house carrying cups and a pitcher.

"Well, we'll leave a few for the birds, if you wish. Let's take a break and have some lemonade. We deserve it!"

Sally lined up the cups on a stack of boards and poured the lemonade. "Toby, would you take some over to the girls at the gin house, please?"

Toby was quick to stand up from the rock he had just sat down on. "Yes'm. I sure could!"

Sally didn't miss the look of gratitude he gave her as he picked up the cups and pitcher from on the boards. "Thank you, Toby, it would be a help."

"Glad to help, ma'am."

"Bet you are," Zekiel laughed.

Mabin couldn't help but chime in, "Don' you go sittin' down for a chat now. We gots work to do. You come right back."

As Toby hurried off, the three men chuckled and Sally shook her head in disgust. "Honestly! Men can be so cruel! What's the matter with all of you?"

Luke put his arm around her, "Just telling him we like him, Sal."

"Gettin even with 'em fo' saying we can't works hard as 'em," Mabin added

While they rested and enjoyed their lemonade, Luke watched Zekiel sitting against the wall with his knees up, slowly sipping his drink and looking toward the corner of the barn where Toby had disappeared with the girls' drinks.

Chapter 19

Teddy Willis was twenty years old and his next younger brother, Nathan, had recently turned nineteen. Both boys showed up with Pastor Davies and their father Saturday morning and were anxious to join the others in the field.

"I figure if these boys hear the pastor's message twice, they *might* remember it," Deacon Willis told Luke as they climbed down off their wagon. He was a good natured man about eight years older than Luke. He was proud of his sons and they knew it. Al was always willing to take what he dished out, and Teddy was more than willing to dish it back.

"Pa wants us to remember it 'cause every Sunday at the dinner table he asks us what the sermon was about. I think it's because he was daydreaming and can't remember half of what the pastor said."

Al squinted his eyes and scrunched up his mouth, pretending to glare at Teddy. "You're not supposed to tell family secrets, boy! Just for that, you have to take two baths this month instead of one!"

"I thought you weren't supposed to tell our secrets!" Teddy smirked. "Now they know how many baths I take."

"I'd better quit while I'm behind," chuckled the deacon. "Let's go, boys. We got us a messy field to clean up.

The Willis men and the pastor went off to join Frank, Joshua, and the others already picking cotton in the field. The three ladies were in the house, trying to get as much housework done as possible before the first wagon of cotton arrived to be ginned. Mabin and Zekiel finished Hope's roof, while Toby and Luke worked on the loft.

By late afternoon, the addition was finished and Sally was hanging a curtain over the window. Hope's new home was almost a mirror image of Tal and Sadie's, except the bed was smaller and the view out the front door was of the woods to the north instead of the farmyard to the south. Luke had purchased another small woodstove from Wally, and had just put the finishing touches on the smokestack. Mabin walked in the door carrying one end of a ladder and Toby arrived soon afterward carrying the other end. They stood it up against the loft floor and Toby nailed it in place with spikes.

The four of them stepped back and admired their work.

"Do you s'pose we be buildin' more o' dese soon, Massuh?" asked Mabin, "We sure be getting' good at it."

Luke agreed. "It does look good, doesn't it?"

Toby took a deep breath and let it out. "Guess I'll go help Zekiel clean up outside."

"S'pose I will, too," agreed Mabin. "Den us three kin finish d' day hoein' d' salad patch. Dem weeds been sneakin' in while we wasn't lookin'."

"Good idea," Luke concurred. "It's too late to cut wood anyhow. You and I will go up on Monday. We do seem to be growing a healthy crop of weeds on this farm. Too bad there's not a good market for weeds."

When Mabin and Toby were gone, Luke and Sally sat on the edge of the bed and looked around the room. The quietness felt good. Luke took Sally's hand. She squeezed it, and for a while they just sat there.

"Sadie says that even though she knows she's a slave and we own her, she feels free. Tal told her that living with the Pennington's and now us, is like salvation. Jesus bought her so she's still owned, but she's free from the bad master. The good master owns her now, but the world is still dangerous. She says Tal's favorite line is, "We may be free cuz o' Jesus, but heaven don' come til later."

It took a while for Luke to think through the implications of what Sally had just said. She sat patiently, looking around the room while holding his hand.

"It's true, what Tal said." Luke looked up at the ceiling and quietly said, "Wow. That man understands some things better than I do." He paused, lost in thought. "I'll bet all of them could teach us a thing or two, if we would listen, and if they all knew how to read and write."

"What?" Sally was caught completely by surprise. "You want to teach the others to read? That's a pretty big step, don't you think?"

"Yeah, it is," he admitted. "Ever since Sid told us about Tal and Sadie, I've been thinking about it. Sometimes, I feel like a young kid looking at a 'Don't Touch the Wet Paint' sign, because it could get us even further onto the bad side of some people around here if they found out. Maybe even some jail time. But I think it's something to consider. I've been told that some of the large plantations south and west of here have schools for their slaves so they can read the Bible and get religion." He looked at her quizzically and asked, "What do *you* think about all that's been going on around here lately?"

Sally felt a rush of heat in her face as she turned slightly red. She stood up and began walking around the room. "Just think about it, Luke. Think about the weather," she said.

"The weather?"

"Yes, the weather," she said firmly. "There's been flooding from Alabama to Texas this year, but we've had our best growing season yet."

"Ah, yes. The weather."

"And two years ago, in the fall, a hurricane nearly sunk Florida but all we got was the rain we needed. And the drought up north last year! We had less rain than usual, but we had enough." Sally was wound up and walking round and round the room. "Luke, we've had three years of protection. Even when the weevil started spreading this way and everyone feared the worst, the worst went around us. I could go on and on, Luke. Like years ago when the hurricane did hit us. It came after our crops were in. The river rose nearly to our house but didn't hurt any of our buildings."

"It blew that tree down on Tom's wife and daughter," Luke added seriously, "and it flooded his shanty town."

Sally stopped walking, looked at Luke sadly and nodded. "I don't understand why certain things happen to some people and not others." She stuck her index finger in the air and shook it, then began walking again. "But I do know that we've been blessed and we've bought more land than we can work and we have more money in the bank than we have ever had!"

"When you put it together that way it doesn't seem accidental, does it?" Luke agreed. "So, what did you have in mind?"

"We need to buy more slaves!"

Luke cleared his throat and tried to act calm. "Excuse me. Did you just say...?

"I said we need to buy more slaves!" Sally interrupted. "Think about it, Luke!"

"The weather?"

Sally pretended frustration and rolled her eyes, "No! This house! It's big enough to put another bed down here and two more in the loft. And the men's bunkhouse has two empty bunks in it, right now. We could start shopping right away!"

"Shopping?"

"Yes, shopping!" She sat down on the chair at the table and faced Luke who was still sitting on the bed trying to think of what to say. Then she stood up again and commenced pacing back and forth while she talked. "Shopping and praying are the same thing in this situation. We ask the Lord to show us who the ones with the bad masters are, and how to buy them! It's as simple as that."

Sally sat back down in the chair. "So, what do you think?"

"I think things are starting to pick up speed around here. I surprised you and you surprised me. Both of our ideas are aimed at helping slaves. So, I say we give it a few days, and then see if we're still as sure. A little prayer and a little counsel never hurt. So, if you don't mind, I think I'll see what Mabin and Matthew think.

Sally nodded her approval, "I guess I was given a new way of thinking, when Sadie shared with me. I guess I sort of got wound up. Thank you, Luke, for listening."

She leaned over Luke to give him a big hug and kiss, and he fell back on the bed happily smothered by his wife.

Chapter 20

Just after dawn, two white tailed deer raised their heads and listened intently. The woods were silent, the air was still, but still they listened. There had been a sound. The gurgling voice of a raven drifted through the trees, but that was not what disturbed them. Nor was it the squirrel that chattered from its hiding place high up in the cottonwood tree. Eventually, the smaller of the two returned to nibbling a patch of wild grass. Another raven drifted across the sky calling out to the other. Soon they began circling in synchronized flight above a small stream that trickled down the hill to the Martin plantation. Eventually the doe lowered her head and joined the fawn in grazing. Suddenly both heads shot up again, and they listened. There it was again. They stared at the fallen log near the stream, ears pointed forward. One of the ravens swooped down and landed on the log and was soon joined by the other raven. Both deer jumped in unison and ran a few steps up the hill as a coyote appeared from the base of a rocky ledge downstream. They turned and watched as the coyote inched slowly toward the fallen log, sniffing the ground as he went.

The hill and foliage must have blocked the sounds, because the distracted animals didn't seem to hear the wagon until it suddenly appeared through the trees on the logging road.

Luke and Mabin enjoyed the scene as the two deer sprang away from them in the direction of the coyote. The surprised coyote landed in the middle of the stream as it jumped away from the men and deer.

In a matter of seconds, all three animals were out of sight and all was peaceful again.

Luke pulled back on the reins and the wagon came to a stop. "I guess we ruined their morning, didn't we?"

The squirrel scolded from the tree above them. Luke looked up at the squirrel, "You'll get over it."

Mabin laughed and scanned the slope, "Dat's a good stand o' trees up ahead. Easy to load, bein' right by d' road."

Luke urged the horses forward to where the work was to be done. The men unloaded axes and saws, then moved the wagon out of the way of the trees. Both men grabbed an axe and stood on opposite sides of the tree they had chosen.

Mabin took a deep breath and took a warm-up swing at the base of the tree. At the sound of steel meeting wood, the two ravens noisily departed their resting place on the fallen log. The unexpected flutter of wings caught the men's attention.

They looked at each other and Luke shrugged, "Guess we disturbed their breakfast."

Mabin looked back down the hill at the log. "If we din't, dat coyote probly woulda. Mus' be sumthin' dead down dere."

Luke spit on his hands and took hold of his axe handle, "Well, they can come back and have it for supper. Right now, we've work to do."

The two axes pounded at the base of the tree with a steady rhythm. It wasn't long before the tree came crashing to the ground. The two friends worked at piling the branches to the side and then cutting up the tree and loading it into the wagon. About mid-morning, they were ready for a rest. They sat side by side on the back of the wagon sharing water from the jar they had brought with them.

Mabin was listening to the tapping of a woodpecker echoing through the trees as he soaked in the scenic view of the forest and fields below. The red tinted soil of the fields contrasted beautifully with the green trees and blue sky. Even the cotton plants and the thousands of white spots of cotton looked nice from where he sat. As he listened to the gurgling of the small stream, Mabin's attention fell on the group of men and women working across the river. Sadness swept over him as he thought of the contrast between his life and theirs.

Luke followed Mabin's line of sight down to Tom Grant's farm, then looked back at Mabin. "Beautiful here, isn't it?"

Mabin let out a big sigh and looked around him. "You surely are blessed, Massuh Luke. I don' know why d' Lord would choose to bless me by lettin' me be here, too."

He raised his eyes to the sun shining through the trees. "Seems a mighty good place for God to come meet a man fo' a talk, don' it?"

Luke looked at the ground and smiled, "Mabin, I need your advice on something."

Mabin focused on Luke, "You do, suh?"

"Yes, I do." Luke hesitated and cleared his throat, "You see, Sal and I think God has been telling us to do something. Something big! At least it seems big to us. I'm hoping you're right, and God might meet with us here and speak through you, to let us know if what we think we're hearing is plain crazy, or from Him."

Mabin looked down below at the workers, stooped in the fields. "Don' rightly know what his voice sound like. Toby thinks he might have heard him sum. You might do best askin' Pastor Davies, or Toby or sumthin'."

Luke slid off the end of the wagon and stretched as he looked out over the flat countryside below. "I do intend to talk with Matthew about this, Mabin. But you are a very wise man and I've known you longer than anyone." He turned and looked directly at Mabin, "I will not move forward on this until I've heard your council."

The men looked silently at each other for a short time, as though trying to read each other's mind, and then Mabin slipped off of the wagon and did something no slave would dare do to his master. He stood square in front of Luke and reached out and grasped his shoulders. He closed his eyes and lifted his face toward heaven. Luke closed his eyes and bowed his head.

"We jus' men, Lord. Jus' men," Mabin spoke in a firm voice. Luke could hear the confidence and determination, and it pleased him. Mabin continued, "Seem like sumthin' might be hapnin' round here. If you're doin' sumthin', well, we'd like to be in on it, suh. But if we about to mess sumthin' up, you be sure 'n let us know. We here fo you to do d' talkin' and we do d' listnin', if dat's okay with you, suh. Amen."

Just that quickly, it was over. Luke opened his eyes to see Mabin smiling at him. Mabin gave Luke a pat on the shoulders and walked over to a large rock and sat down.

"All right, Massuh Luke, tell me what you think he might be tellin' you."

Luke was ready. Boy, was he ready! The words of his story spilled out like water over a dam. For over an hour, he talked. Once in a while Mabin asked a question but mostly, he listened.

The sun was past its zenith when Luke finally wound down, but neither of the men could have said where the time had gone.

"So what do you think, Mabin?" Luke asked as he plopped down on the ground beside the rock Mabin had been sitting on for so long.

"I think I've been sittin' too long," Mabin said as he stood up and rubbed his sore backside. "You hungry? I'm hungry. What say we feed d' horses and ourselves, and listen fo' a minute?"

Without waiting for an answer from Luke, he walked to the wagon and grabbed the feed bags they had brought along for the horses. Luke was surprised by Mabin's response. He watched as his friend hung the bags over the horse's heads. Something had changed in Mabin's countenance. Luke stood to his feet and joined Mabin as he rummaged through the basket of food Sally had made. This was highly unlike him to not wait for the master's lead. Luke recognized the confidence that he had heard in Mabin's voice when he had said the prayer. A curious anticipation began to build in Luke but he held his tongue and waited. Mabin stood lost in thought, looking out over the land as he chewed on a leg of fried chicken. Luke leaned against the wagon and watched Mabin. He wasn't the least bit hungry.

Mabin soon came back to the wagon to fetch another piece of chicken. "My Mama say God don' know d' difference 'tween black folk 'n white folk."

He took a bite and chewed on it while staring at the wood they had piled in the wagon, then added, "Sadie say God see inside a man, and dey's all d' same color in there."

Luke leaned quietly against the wagon, not wanting to interfere with Mabin's thoughts. It seemed as if maybe he did his best thinking while he was eating.

Buttering a biscuit, Mabin spoke again, "You bein' against ownin' slaves 'n all." He glanced over at Luke with a sly smile, "Could be d' Lord is tellin' you to buy more slaves. It sure don' sound like *you*, but it sound like sumthin' *he* might do, don' it? Sumthin' dat don' make sense to us."

"I need help, Mabin, help hearing him." Luke scuffed his foot along the ground as he scratched his head. "Sally and I believe God is telling us to bring you and Matthew, and maybe Tal and Sadie, into this project with us. All of us would have to stay in close communication as to what we're hearing the Lord say. After all, this has to be *his* plan, not our own. There would have to be a certain degree of secrecy among us because of the prejudice that seems to be running rampant around here."

The two ravens glided over their heads and landed on the fallen log.

"Kinda give life a bigger purpose don' it?" Mabin said as he watched one of the ravens jump to the ground behind the log. "Who would think God would put together a team o' black men 'n white men in Georgia, to bring some light to dis dark dark place."

"Does that mean you don't think we're crazy? Could we really be hearing from God on this?" Luke asked hopefully.

"I don' want to go speakin' fo' God, Massuh, but I do admit it has me mighty interested."

"That's all I needed to hear for now, Mabin. God could stop us at any time he chooses, but until I talk with Pastor Davies, we sit on it, and pray.

Both men heard a strange noise and looked down at the log as the two ravens flew away.

"Sounded like a growl, didn't it?" Luke looked at Mabin curiously.

"Maybe so, or a groan or sumthin'."

As if on cue, both men began to slowly walk down the hill to the log. As they approached they heard some sort of movement. Luke looked over the top of the log as Mabin walked around the end. Wedged against the lower curve of the log, half covered in twigs and leaves was the body of an old black woman. Mabin knelt down and rolled her over. It appeared as if she had been shot in the right thigh. Mabin checked for other injuries but could find none. "Wouldn't have been too serious, if she hadn't lost all that blood."

Luke scanned the immediate area. "The ground isn't stirred up. It was probably her that the Willis's were target practicing on. She got this far, then hid herself under this log. That would mean she's been here for days. If there's any life left in her, it isn't much."

"Lord, have mercy. We gots to get her outta here real careful-like," said Mabin, as he looked up to the wagon. "I'll toss a leather strap down here to tie around her leg, Massuh. Then I get to turnin' d' wagon around."

He stood to his feet and ran up the hill. Luke brushed the dirt and leaves from the old woman's face.

"If this is part of your plan, Lord, she's gonna have to live."

He wet his cheek and lowered it to her mouth. He thought he could feel a faint breath.

"Not much left of her, Lord. Maybe you let us find her so we could give her a proper burial."

The woman's eyelids flickered, and then she groaned.

"Not quite ready to be buried yet, huh? Well, you're gonna have to keep fighting, young lady, and we'll give it our best shot."

The leather strap flew through the air and landed on the log. Mabin was already running back to the wagon. Luke went to work applying the tourniquet to her leg.

"I guess that coyote won't get any breakfast *or* dinner today," Luke said to himself. He glanced up and saw that the wagon was turned around and Mabin was throwing firewood onto the ground to make room for the woman.

Luke patted her cheek lightly, "Are you still with us?"

Her eyes moved under the eyelids, but they remained closed. Then she made another barely-audible groan.

Soon the men were laying her gently into the wagon. They had been surprised at how little she weighed. Mabin climbed in beside her and cradled her head in his lap.

"Take it slow and easy, Massuh," he cautioned Luke with the

confidence of an equal, but it didn't bother Luke at all. "A few extra minutes won' hurt her so much as bein' all banged roun'."

Luke nodded and urged the horses slowly forward. Both men were sweating profusely as they began the slow, tedious journey down the logging road. They had no way of knowing it, but they both were lost in the same thoughts. They were both aware that they were a team. Both also knew they would have to be cautious, because the country was so filled with prejudice and hate. But neither Mabin nor Luke was afraid. In fact, they were surprisingly relieved - and yet filled with anticipation - because at last, after so long, a sense of purpose was beginning to form. They both believed it had been given to them by their Maker, and wondered if this old woman was part of the plan. If she was, they knew she would not die.

When the wagon rolled into the farmyard, all was quiet. Not a person was in sight. Luke drove the wagon up to the door of Hope's new home. Few words were spoken as they proceeded with their mission. Luke knocked on the door, then pushed it open. Both men gently carried their patient to Hope's bed and carefully laid her down.

Mabin straightened his back with a big sigh and gazed down at the aged face.

"You best go gets d' women, Massuh. If she wakes up 'n sees yo' white face, she may just give up d' ghost, if you know what I mean." Luke cracked a weary smile and agreed, "We sure don't want to scare her to death after all she's been through, now do we? I'll be right back."

Turning, he walked quickly to the door and then broke into a run to the gin house. Soon, Mabin could hear people running to help. Sadie burst through the door, followed by Hope. They both froze and stared at the grey-haired woman in the bloodied dress.

"Massuh Martin gone to the big house to fetch Miz Sally," Sadie said, as she approached the bed. "Is she dead, Mabin?"

"No, she ain't. But she as close as she can git without bein'."

Mabin stood up and backed away.

"I don't rightly know what to do 'cept pray."

"That'd do just fine, Mabin."

Sadie sat down on the edge of the bed and felt the woman's forehead. "She's cold and damp."

Without taking her eyes off of the frail, seemingly lifeless face, Sadie gave instructions. "Mabin, you run and tell Miz Sally to bring some scissors and a knife with her. It'd be best to cut these clothes off instead of movin' her around much. And Hope, start some water warming so we can clean her up."

"Yes'm," Mabin was out the door almost before he'd said it.

"Come here, Hope. Untie them rags from her feet and rub 'em some."

Hope quietly knelt at the foot of the bed and removed the makeshift shoes. Tears began to silently slide down her face as she gently massaged the old, tired feet. She couldn't take her eyes off of the gaps, where the middle toe of each foot had been cut off.

"Dear Lord," Sadie said softly, as she brushed the hair out of the woman's face. Hope glanced up and both women stared at the side of her head. It was clear that someone had taken a knife and cut off most of her left ear.

Hope looked down at the feet she was rubbing. More tears trickled down, "I seen it before. Dis woman din always do what her massuh say to do."

Sadie nodded gravely, but couldn't speak.

The old woman took a noticeable breath, and then another. No eye movement, but it was at least hopeful.

The sound of Luke and Sally on the porch announced their arrival. Luke followed his wife to the edge of the bed, carrying a sharp knife. Sally held the scissors and carried one of her night robes over her arm.

"How's she doing?" asked Sally as she placed her hand on Sadie's shoulder.

"Showed signs of breathin' for a minute. Not much else."

Sadie moved the tangled grey hair aside so they could see her ear. Then she directed their gaze to the missing toes. A sad silence filled the room. Hope continued to stare at the feet as she worked them with her thumbs.

"When a man thinks his Negro ain't workin' hard 'enuf, he hurts d' wife. When d' girl won't go do things wit d' man, he hurts d' girl.

Maybe cut a toe or finger. Sometimes the man don't need no reason at all. Jes want to keep 'em scared." Hope's tears were flowing freely now and she could hardly finish speaking.

With moist eyes, Luke stepped behind her, and put his hands on her shoulders.

"Jesus brought you here," he said, "because it's different here. He brought this woman here because it's different here."

Hope kept looking at the feet and rubbing. She sniffed and nodded her head up and down, but she couldn't speak.

Attention was brought back to the need of the moment as Mabin walked in with a large, steaming pot of water. Sally directed him to set the pot on the table. "You men have done all you can for now." She reached out, and Luke handed her the knife. "We'll get these wet clothes off, and get her cleaned up and under some warm blankets. We'll call you if we need anything."

"I think you may need a needle and some thread," said Luke. "The bullet entered cleanly enough, but the exit is a little ragged. I couldn't really tell if it hit the bone. It's pretty clear, though, that she was shot from behind."

"The needles and thread are in the parlor closet," Sally said, as she focused for the first time on the hole in the woman's dress, "Should we send for Doc Atwood, Luke?"

Luke thought about that for a minute and then addressed Mabin, "Doc's plenty willing to work on Negroes, but he's not at all favorable to abolition."

Mabin rubbed his forehead with his hand, "Wouldn't be good for word to get out, if she's a runaway."

"Better she be dead!" No one missed the firmness in Hope's voice.

"As close as she is to it anyway, I would have to agree," said Luke. "Mabin, you can take the wagon back up and pick up the wood. I'll get the needle and thread, and the whiskey from the medicine shelf."

Sally steeled herself for action, "OK, then. Let's get at it. Luke, please bring some towels and rags with you when you come, and the bottle of rubbing alcohol on our dresser. I guess it's time to practice my mending."

Chapter 21

Tom watched from the house as the two white men drove the wagon to the storage shack. He had sent his two slave drivers to Grantsville at sun-up to stock up on food supplies, but also to get enough whitewash to paint his house. Without giving them a reason, he also ordered them to buy four bundles of sackcloth from the general store, and also twenty heavy duty needles, and some thread.

Before the wagon had even come to a stop, George, the larger of the two drivers, called out to the two slaves that were scraping the paint from the siding on Tom's house.

"Get your black behinds down here and unload this thing. C'mon now. Run!" George yelled.

The two black men immediately broke into a run. George climbed down from his seat. As the slaves arrived at the wagon, he kicked the feet out from under the last to arrive. Both slave drivers laughed as he picked himself up, yet not daring to brush himself off.

"I said run! You call that running?" mocked George.

Both slaves remained silent and kept their eyes focused on the ground.

"Your master wants those bundles of cloth taken down to your eatin' house. The rest of this stuff goes in this storage shed." George put his face about four inches from the older slave's face. "Now get this thing unloaded, and you'd better run while you do it!" George yelled.

The two black men ran to the back of the wagon and each grabbed a bundle of sackcloth and then turned to run down to the eating house. Del, the second driver, stuck his foot out and tripped the older slave. The bundle went flying as the slave landed on his face in the dust.

The two white men howled with laughter as they slapped each other on the back and leaned against the wagon.

"George! Del! You two get up here right now!" Tom yelled.

George and Del looked at each other and frowned.

"The man's been an old grump for a few days now," said George, as they walked to the porch where Tom was standing.

"Musta been something he ate," chuckled Del.

George tripped on the second step and he and Del broke into laughter once again. Tom stood there waiting as they calmed down and pulled themselves together. "I see you brought the smell of stupid home with you," Tom said grimly.

The two men looked questioningly at each other.

"Stupid, is what I smell whenever I walk near the bar in Grantsville. Stupid, is the perfume that my daddy wore most of his life!" Tom looked at them with cold, steely eyes. "I hate that smell!"

The intense glare of his eyes bore into them and held them transfixed.

"A bottle of stupid is why my daddy sold all that nice land to Luke Martin. I suspect a few bottles of stupid are why I got three men slaves and two women slaves laid up in their beds unable to pick my cotton! Your job was to motivate, not disable them. Am I right, gentlemen?" Tom asked.

Del was beginning to feel a little dizzy while staring into Tom's eyes. Before he knew what was happening, he had landed on his back in a poof of red dust. Tom drew in a large breath of air, held it, and then slowly breathed out.

"You have one half hour to clear out," said Tom. "Stop by for your pay when you leave." He turned and walked inside, slamming the door behind him.

As Tom stepped inside, he was surprised to see Belle and Etta standing to his left, suspiciously near the open window. Belle's look reminded him of his daughter when she got caught with her hand in the cookie jar.

"What are you two looking at?" he asked gruffly, "Don't you have something to do?"

"Yessuh," said Belle, as she quickly scurried off to the kitchen.

Etta looked at him with eyes that no longer moved in perfect unison. "Yo' missus was right. She say dere's a better man in dere, Massuh."

Tom shook his head, somewhat irritated. "I told you he's dead, Etta," he said. "What you saw out there, that was selfishness. Now, get in there and help Belle."

Etta stood her ground. "Not dead, suh, jus' in prison. You done got him locked up."

"That's enough!" Tom said, raising his voice, "Now get out of here!"

"Yessuh," Etta said, as she shuffled off toward the kitchen.

Tom suddenly felt guilty as he remembered how he had treated her the last time he was angry. "Etta?" he said, "I'm sorry."

Etta did not stop or turn around. She merely said, "Dat's him, suh," as she disappeared into the kitchen.

Tom looked at the ceiling and let out a groan of frustration as he walked down the hall to his study. *It feels like Grandmother came back as a black woman,* he mumbled to himself. He stepped into the room and closed the door behind him, sealing himself off from the world. He needed time to think.

"Right now, she's still unconscious," Sally said. "Hope refuses to leave her bedside. She's managed to get a few drops of broth into her, but not much."

Sally and Luke were sitting together on a bench swing on the porch. Matthew was sitting in a chair nearby. Sunday morning, after the service, the Martins had invited him out to the farm for dinner and to stay the night. They told him they needed his advice on a very important business decision that had come up. Mabin was also present and leaning against the porch railing. Luke had asked him to join them after he finished his dinner.

Sally had not felt good about telling some of the details at the dinner table with Frank present, so she was filling them in while they sipped their cups of coffee or tea. "All I could do was reach inside the wound with my fingers and feel around for bone chips. I found three pieces. The bullet grazed the bone but didn't shatter it, so I think there's hope she'll be able to walk, if she lives. She might not be too happy with my sewing job though."

"She's going to live, Sally," Luke interrupted. "Mabin and I both talked about this, and I personally think that old woman was on our shopping list."

"I beg your pardon?" asked the pastor. "Shopping list?"

Luke scratched the back of his head. "Well, possible shopping list anyway. That's why we asked you to stay the night. Sally and I have a lot to run by you before we move forward with any of it. I've also brought Mabin into this because I trust both you and Mabin to tell us the truth, even if it might disappoint us. We think we're hearing from God, but our emotions might be misleading us."

"This sounds pretty important," Matthew said. "I'll try to help in any way I can. But don't be afraid of your emotions. They can be the very tool God gives you to push on through very difficult times. But you're wise not to use emotions in your decision making. Speaking for myself, I find tremendous strength when I embrace my emotions." Matthew leaned back in his chair and crossed his arms, "So fill me in. I'm a captive audience."

"I'll start with the main ideas and then fill in the details of how we arrived at them," said Luke. "As you know, I long for slavery to be abolished. I'm also smart enough to know that I can't bring that about. I've been reasonably sure God is urging me to buy more land than I can keep up with, and more slaves than I wanted to own. It's really frustrated me, not knowing what was going on."

Luke leaned forward holding his hands together, with his elbows on his knees, bringing himself closer to Matthew. "You might not believe this, but Sally now thinks God wants us to buy more slaves, and *I* think he wants us to teach them to read and write."

Pastor Davies eyebrows shot up and he tilted his head. "Now you're startin' to sound like Sid Pennington," he said.

Mabin stood up from the railing, suddenly looking a little nervous. "Uh, Massuh? Could I talk wit you fo a minute?"

"Sure, Mabin," said Luke. "Go ahead."

"Uh, not wantin' to be rude or nothin', suh, but could we step away for jes a minute, suh?"

Luke looked at Matthew and then Sally. She looked curious but nodded.

"Sure, Mabin," said Luke. Standing to his feet, he looked back at his pastor and smiled, "If you'll excuse us, we'll be right back."

"I got all night," said Matthew. "Take your time. Sally and I will enjoy our tea, and the crickets."

Luke and Mabin walked to a nearby pecan tree. "What's up, Mabin?" asked Luke.

"I was goin' to mention dis to you when we was on d' hill, but I guess you might say I got a little distracted by d' woman. When you spoke o' readin', I remembered what I needed to tell you, suh." Mabin gave a nervous glance to the porch and then looked around him as if worried he might be overheard. "I don' like to say what I ain't sure of, suh, but since you mentioned learnin' us to read 'n all.... Well, I suspect that maybe Tal and Sadie already knows sumthin' 'bout readin'. Don't want 'em in no trouble, so I kept quiet."

Luke put his hand on Mabin's shoulder and smiled reassuringly, "They not only can read, but they can write, and add and subtract. Sid taught em." Luke laughed, "What do ya think of that, huh?"

Mabin leaned back against the pecan tree in relief and amazement, "I'm glad you knew, suh." He paused in thought for a few seconds then looked over to the porch, "Dey know numbers? I don't rightly know what to think of that. Dat why you said dey might be part of this plan, maybe?"

Luke took a deep breath, "Let's go see what the good pastor thinks." They walked side by side back to the house.

Mabin was having trouble sleeping. He had never had that problem before. A life of slavery, even with a good master, meant hard, backbreaking work from sunup to sundown. When a body is weary to the bone, it grabs sleep as soon as it's offered, but not tonight. It was not the snoring of others that kept him awake, it was his thoughts. It was revelation and wonder. It was hope.

What had he just experienced today? Could it truly be that God doesn't see a man's color? Is the color of skin something that matters only to men desperately trying to find something to be proud of? Or to look down on?

"If this your doin', Lord, you either didn' notice dat I'm a black man, or you don' care dat I'm a black man." He whispered his prayers as he lay on his back in the dark, with his hands linked behind his head. "Thought I was too old to learn to read," he mused to himself. He rolled onto his side and could hear young Joshua mumbling something in his sleep. Mabin envisioned Frank and Joshua fishing and climbing oak trees together. As the boys got older, that would all change. Or ҇ maybe not. Maybe God was changing something else. He replayed in his mind what Luke had told Pastor Davies. "I not only consider Mabin my friend," Luke had said, "but a partner in this with Sally and me and, hopefully you, Matthew. Sal and I have decided we won't make any major decisions about this without input from the both of you. We can't do this alone. We need a team. At the very least, we need your prayer support."

"How kin this be?" Mabin wondered. "How did it come 'bout? What if we' all making a big mistake? How kin I know?"

"The Woman."

Mabin instantly raised his head and listened to the darkness. All he could hear was Zekiel snoring softly in the corner of the room. Eventually he laid his head back down on his arm. It wasn't long before he faded off into a peaceful sleep while thinking about what he had thought he heard.

The coyote was walking in a wide circle around the old woman in the bloodstained dress. She was standing beside a small stream and didn't appear to notice the hungry animal, or if she did, she seemed unafraid . The coyote continued to walk in an ever shrinking circle as he sniffed at the ground and the air. The woman slowly kneeled with great effort and cupped some stream water in her hands and took a drink. The coyote darted in for a test strike, then yelped as if something invisible had struck him and he jumped back to resume circling, but from a little farther off. The coyote stopped for a moment and surveyed the area around him then turned his head back to gaze at the old woman. She was now sitting in a rocking chair in a field of green grass and flowers. She was holding a baby in her arms, and a young boy was picking flowers at her feet. The coyote lowered its head and lunged again at the woman. Again, the animal let out a yelp at some unseen cause of pain. He watched longingly for a few moments more, then turned and walked away.

The earth began to shake beneath his feet and Mabin heard a young voice calling out his name.

"Mabin! Mabin, wake up! Massuh Martin says you should come. You gonna sleep all day? You done missed breakfast already!"

Mabin forced his eyes open, only to find Joshua standing over him and shaking his shoulder.

"What you talkin 'bout, boy?" mumbled Mabin as he sat up and looked around the empty room trying to get his bearings. "Where'd ever'one go?"

"They's loaded up and headin' out to pick," said Joshua. "Massuh Martin tol' me to fetch ya before I go with Frank to hoe the garden."

Mabin stood and stretched his arms to the ceiling. "Well, consider me fetched. Now go on, an don't make Massuh Frank do all d' work."

Joshua ran out the door yelling, "Hey, Frank! Wait up. I'm a comin'!"

Mabin groaned and splashed a handful of water from the tin wash basin onto his face. He slipped on his clothes and stepped out into the bright morning sun. He could see Luke and Matthew standing by the pastor's horse lost in deep conversation. As he walked, he rehashed the events of the night before, finally clearing away the fog of sleep that was stubbornly clinging to his head. Not wanting to interrupt, Mabin stood by quietly as Pastor Davies said something about writing Sid Pennington. Then both men turned to Mabin.

"Morning, Mabin," greeted Luke with a smile.

"Mornin', Massuh. Sorry about bein' late," Mabin apologized.

Luke shook his head, "Matthew and I would still be asleep if Sadie and Sally hadn't started banging pots and skillets around, down in the kitchen.

"Mabin," Matthew interrupted, "I have to be heading home, but I want you to know that I feel real good about being in on this plan. However, we all need to be totally honest with each other. If you feel hesitant in any way, please let us know. You could be saving us all from some possible disaster that the rest of us didn't foresee."

Mabin was encouraged by the realization that he didn't feel at all inhibited by the two white men who were staring curiously at him, hoping for a positive response. "No, suh. I ain't so good at hearin' God as ya'll. Feels right, but I ain't quite as sure about it as ya'll. Don't mean to disappoint ya none."

Pastor Davies was indeed disappointed. Both, Mabin and Luke, could see it on his face.

On the other hand, Luke felt a pride well up inside that surprised even him. He was sure he had not misplaced his trust, and it was comforting to be leaning on a man of integrity, who would not just 'go with the flow' to keep everyone happy.

"Do you think we missed it, Mabin?" asked Pastor Davies hesitantly. "Should we back away from this?"

"We don' back away yet, suh. We stays put. If this is God's plan, it will change everything. I need sumthin'. Sumthin' I can hang on to if things get bad. Don't rightly know what that is."

"That's fine, Mabin," said Luke, "We wait then. We'll wait for that something, whatever it is."

The pastor climbed up onto the saddle, sat there for a moment, then sighed and looked down at Luke. "Well, my friend, if Tal and Sadie are half as wise as this man, it will be an honor to be on the team." Turning to Mabin, he smiled and said, "Take your time. Get it right. I can't wait to hear from you." Then Matthew turned his horse and trotted down the road, waving at the two boys working in the garden as he rode by.

Luke put his hands in his pockets and watched the pastor ride away. "With all that extra help in the fields and the distraction of the old woman," Luke said, "we've gotten behind at the gin house. I guess you and I could spend the day helping catch up at the gin, then tomorrow, we'll take a load to Henry's. Sadie is cleaning up in the house. Sally and Hope are with our mystery woman. What do you say we check in on 'em before we get to work?"

"I guess I am kinda wonderin' 'bout her, Massuh," said Mabin.

"She must still be alive. No one has come to get us," said Luke. "Let's go see."

The door was half open so the men entered quietly. Hope was sitting in the chair beside the bed and Sally was standing at the table stirring something in a tin cup.

"Good news, Luke," Sally said in a low voice. "Hope has spent the night feeding her broth, one drop at a time. She says that sometime before dawn, she noticed the woman's breathing had grown heavier." She pointed to the woman's stomach, "See? You can see her stomach rise and fall now. So Hope decided to try a half spoonful of broth."

"I talked to Jesus then poured it in her mouth, suh," Hope interrupted, with a smile. "She coughed a little, then swallowed. She kept it in so I waited some, 'n then tried it again. She choked, but den she swallow again. Done it six times, now!"

"She hasn't opened her eyes, but she's still breathing smoothly," said Sally.

"She gonna live," said Mabin, not taking his eyes off the woman.

"Sally, you and Hope stay with her as long as you need," said Luke. "Mabin and I will gin the cotton today. Tomorrow we'll be heading to town with a load."

"Thank you, Luke," Sally put the spoon down and walked over and gave Luke a big hug. She looked up at him and said, "We'll call you if there is any change."

As they walked side by side to the gin house, Mabin said, "The woman! I had a dream. She was in it." His face seemed to light with excitement. "Dat's what it is!"

"That's what what is?" Luke asked.

"When I need sumthin' to hang on if things get hard, I remember d' woman. We were up dere trying to hear God, and d' woman showed up."

Neither man looked at each other. They just kept walking, each silently reviewing the events on the mountain.

"That works for me, Mabin," said Luke matter-of-factly, and without another word the two men went inside and set to work ginning the cotton.

Chapter 22

"You should have been happy with what you had, Rena! Your ma and pa will be very sad to see you go."

Wilton Hatch, a skinny Louisiana white man was circling her like a hungry vulture, never taking his eyes off of her eyes. His white suit was in stark contrast to the black audience that had been forced to observe the proceedings.

"Tie her hands together!" said the tobacco baron and failed politician. One of his slave drivers stepped forward with a leather strap and tied the girl's wrists together tightly.

"Now string her up by her hands from that branch so she's standing on her toes!"

The driver followed his instructions and then stepped back. The girl's eyes watered but she made no sound. Many in the group, including her mother and father could not stop their tears, but they also remained silent.

The plantation owner resumed his journey around and around the girl. The man had never been elected to public office, and yet he insisted that his slaves call him, "Governor". He had not gained his power by love or wisdom. He simply didn't have the resources to rule in that manner. No, this man ruled from the throne of money, and the evil desire to inflict pain. He actually enjoyed these times. His sarcastic smile taunted her. He thrilled at the sight of the growing fear in the girl's eyes. It was at times like these when he really felt like he was somebody to be reckoned with. Somebody important!

"Your hands won't be so good at stealing when I'm done with

you, Rena. You stole some of my chickens. Good thing I went for a walk last night. I woulda never known. I hope they tasted real good, Rena."

Hatch suddenly went into a frenzy with his whip, striking her hands time after time until they bled. When he finally stopped, he was sweating and breathing heavily as he looked around the group of slaves until he found Rena's father. "Come here, Hack, and make it quick!" The black man hurried up to his master, looking down submissively. The man in white handed Hack his whip. Hack raised his eyes to the master, puzzled. "A good father punishes his children when they steal, Hack. Now you be a good father. You whip her backside from her shoulders to her knees, 'til I say stop!"

"Please, Governor, she won't do it no more," Hack pleaded.

The planter suddenly grabbed Hack by the throat and yelled, "You bet she won't steal no more! 'Cause if you don't whip her, I'll see to it she don't walk away from this tree!" He shoved Hack to the ground and walked over to his white chair. With his back to the slave he yelled, "Now, get to it!" Then he turned and sat down and took a glass of lemonade from the servant standing beside him.

Hack slowly stood to his feet and, for what seemed an eternity, he beat his daughter. Tears streamed down his face and the faces of those forced to watch. When Hack had no energy left to raise the whip another time, the master ordered him to stop. Shoulders slumping, the grieving father dropped the whip and walked away without looking back. Rena was no longer standing on her toes. She felt as if her shoulders had been torn from their sockets as she hung limply by her wrists. What was left of the back of her dress was crimson red.

Still in his chair, Hatch gave orders to his drivers, "She was carrying my chickens in her right hand. It won't be so easy to steal with two less fingers. When you've taken care of the finger problem, go and get the wagon and bring it down here to the tree." He stood up, picked up his whip and waved it in the air. "This is what happens to thieves. It'll happen to you if you so much as steal a spoon, do you hear me?" Every one in the group nodded their heads. "Now, get back to the field and get to work! You've had enough school for one day!"

It was mid-afternoon when Rena's father and mother saw their daughter again. They were standing in the cotton field as the wagon rolled down the road away from the plantation. They could see her lying in the bed of the wagon, bound hand and foot, still wearing what was left of the dress that her father had bloodied. They watched until the wagon disappeared over a hill, then with tears flowing freely they bent down and continued to hoe the master's soil.

Luke and Mabin worked through the rest of the morning, ginning cotton and discussing the ramifications of the plan. It would mean planting more acres with cotton and planting a few unused acres with peanuts. No other planters in the area grew peanuts, but a year ago Luke had tried an acre of peanuts just for fun, and the results were surprisingly good. Another wagon and more horses would need to be purchased. Food storage space would have to be expanded. Construction of a central eating area for the slaves would be necessary. The list seemed endless, but they were not discouraged.

Their conversation was interrupted when Frank and Joshua showed up complaining of hunger pangs. Luke agreed it was time to break for lunch, thinking he would also check on the old woman. As they stepped out of the gin house into the sun, they met Sally, who said there was no significant change in the patient. Mabin and Joshua headed to the men's slave quarters to have a bite to eat. The Martins went home to find out what Sadie had cooked up. As they sat around the table enjoying bean and rice soup with fresh slices of buttered bread, Frank asked if Joshua could go to school with him after harvest was over. Sally reminded him that black people were not allowed in his school.

"But it's not fair," said Frank. After a moment of silence, he added, "Joshua don't seem to know nothing at all! I've been teachin' him the alphabet and some small words."

Luke noticed Sadie give a quick glance at Frank. He couldn't decide if her look was one of surprise, or concern. She turned her attention back to her work but her head was cocked as if she was very interested in how Luke would respond.

"You don't say," Luke said, taking a sip of his coffee. "Does he seem interested in learnin'?"

"Yes, sir, he does. I can't figure why he likes it so much," Frank said, with a puzzled expression.

Luke smiled at Frank and then said thoughtfully, "Maybe it's like a rich man wondering why the poor man is so happy when he finds a coin or a man with a full stomach wondering why the starving man licks up every crumb."

Sally watched as Frank sat quietly staring at the slices of bread on his plate. He appeared to be deep in thought as he pushed a few crumbs around with his finger. He looked over to Sadie and studied her for a while as she busied herself putting wood in the cook stove. He returned his attention to the bread and the crumbs.

Sally looked down at her bowl of soup, "Maybe we have so much that it doesn't seem special any more."

Frank glanced at his mother then looked back at the crumbs and nodded.

"Maybe school would be more special if your goal was to collect bits of knowledge to bring home to share with Joshua," Sally said.

Luke looked up and nodded, "That would be a good attitude for all of us. It could make our work and school more important to us if it gives us something to give."

Luke noticed that Frank was looking at Sadie again. Sadie caught the boy's eye and smiled at him as she wiped her hands on her apron. Luke watched Frank watch Sadie as she took up a basket and went outside to collect the laundry off of the clothesline.

"Mama," said Frank, still staring at the door. "Sadie's little shack is more special to her than our big house is to me." Frank turned and looked at his mother, "And Hope likes her new dress more than I like all my clothes. And Joshua has more fun with a few words than I do when I read a whole book."

Sally looked across the table at Frank. She was amazed at how perceptive her young son had become. Where did her little boy go? She finally spoke, "It's the same with me, Frank. I need to be more grateful, too."

"Me, too," Luke added. "It would do me good to look up to heaven about a hundred times a day and just say 'thank you'. But I get too busy. So now, while I'm thinkin' of it," he looked to the ceiling, "Thank you! Thank you for my son and my wife. Thank you for the work you've given us to do this afternoon. Help us to do it well."

Luke scooted his chair back from the table and stood up, "Time to get to work, Frank. Isn't it exciting to know that when you hoe the weeds in the garden, you're giving food to someone else?"

"Do you mean I have to appreciate work, the same as my house, my clothes, and my learnin?" protested Frank with raised eyebrows.

"It's up to you. It would help your day go better. But either way, it's time to get at it. Joshua's probably already out there waiting to learn a new word." Luke gave Sally a kiss and nudged Frank toward the door.

"I guess I could give it a try," Frank conceded. "I'll let you know how it goes." He walked out onto the porch and then broke into a run as he set off to find Joshua.

Luke stood at the door and turned to Sally, "Mabin's on board. He says the old woman is God's answer. He says he had a dream, or heard God say something, or maybe both, but now he's convinced. We've been talking about it all morning."

Sally shoved her chair back so fast that it tipped over as she stood up and ran to Luke and gave him a big hug. "I knew it! I knew it! I've been praying, and I just know the Lord has already set things in motion. But we have to pay attention and recognize them when he puts them in front of us."

She stepped back and looked up at Luke. It seemed to him as if her face was almost glowing with anticipation. It reminded him of the day he had proposed to her. The excitement on her young, beautiful face had been etched into his memory forever. He couldn't help but smile.

"One step at a time, girl," Luke said. "This could be hard, as well as exciting. But I agree. We might as well get started. Mabin and I have quite a list for town. We won't be able to get everything in one trip, but if you could make a list of the things you need, I'll get them tomorrow. I'll take Zekiel and Mabin with me in the morning. Addison, the blacksmith, has a wagon for sale. It looks to be in real good shape. We'll be needing another one if everything goes as planned. It looks like we'll also be keeping the sawmill in business for a while."

"I guess we might need to talk to Tal and Sadie this evening, huh?" Sally asked.

"Every step is an adventure, isn't it? I wonder what they'll think of this?" said Luke.

"Well, if they don't feel comfortable teaching, I guess we could ask Frank," Sally smiled and hugged Luke again, "but somehow, I've got this feeling…"

Chapter 23

When Luke arrived back at the gin after lunch, he found Mabin and Toby unloading baskets from the wagon. Toby reported that the northwest field should be completely picked by the end of the day. Luke helped them finish the unloading while he laid out his plan for the final pick of the southeast field down by the river.

"Mabin and Zekiel and I will be in town all day tomorrow, so maybe the boys can help Sally and Sadie at the gin. How long will it take you to finish the southeast field?"

Toby thought about it as he handed the last basket down to Mabin and Luke. "Should take three o' four days I s'pose, suh. Depends on how wet d' fields get," he said, nodding his head forward as he looked past Luke to the horizon. Luke hadn't even noticed the gathering clouds.

"Hmmm," Luke studied the sky for a moment. "It sure would be nice to have the northwest field totally finished before the rain falls. I'd like you to send Tal in early; I need to talk with him. Try to get all the baskets into the barn to keep 'em dry. I'll be taking only one wagon to town tomorrow so once you get a wagon unloaded, put it here in the gin house. We can load the bales first thing in the morning in here where it's dry, and if it's still raining we'll cover it all with canvas."

"Yessuh, we can do dat," Toby said, climbing onto the wagon. He sat down and picked up the reins. "Suh?" Toby looked down at Luke. "We been wonderin' how d' woman's doin'?"

"No change yet, Toby. But there will be."

Luke looked over at Mabin, who was just beginning to crank the gin. He lowered his voice. "Hope's bent on seeing her through, so she hasn't had much rest. I was thinking that maybe you could stop in for a few minutes before you went back to the field and give her some encouragement."

Toby held a serious look on his face. "Dat an order, suh?" he asked.

"It is," said Luke.

A trace of a smile came across Toby's face, "Be glad to, suh. Thank you, suh." Toby snapped the reins and guided the wagon toward Hope's shanty.

Throughout the afternoon, the dark gray line pushed its way closer to the Martin farm. The growing rumble of thunder demanded everyone's attention. The air cooled as the blue sky disappeared, which was a good thing, because everyone was working as hard and fast as they could to beat the storm. Frank and Joshua had been dispatched to the field with Toby and were now working alongside Gideon, helping to fill his bag. Necks were aching and backs throbbed, but neither man nor child eased up.

Tal's body worked as hard as the rest of them but his mind had gone in a different direction. He was trying to figure out why Massuh Martin would want to meet with him and Sadie. It's amazing what an imagination can do. All of the possible good and bad reasons bobbed in and out of his head like a storm fighting a sunny day. Had something gone wrong, or had something gone good? Maybe the massuh only needed help shoeing a horse. But if so, then why would he ask for Sadie also?

The wagons were moving slowly along the end of each row as Toby and Zekiel loaded the full baskets with great effort. Muscles ached severely as they pushed themselves beyond their normal limits. When they neared the end of the rows, others joined in, and as the last basket was lifted and pushed into its place on the wagon, five were pushing and grunting together as one.

"We done it!" said the slave they called Otis.

For a few seconds, the group stood staring at the finished field. All was quiet and calm. Joshua flopped down on the ground. Others stretched out sore backs and legs.

"Probably won' even rain 'tall," said Joshua, from his place on the ground.

Suddenly, a bright bolt of lightning lit up the hills a few miles away. Three seconds later the sound of the explosion reached them and the air began to stir.

"Oh, it gonna rain, boy," said Toby, jumping into action, "and we better have dis cotton all tucked away in d' barn 'fore it starts!"

The trees at the edge of the field began to sway and the wind arrived with a vengeance. Another flash of lightning and a loud clap of thunder worked as well as a crack of a whip. In no time at all the two wagons, loaded with cotton and topped off with people, were rumbling down the road to the barn. They hadn't quite reached shelter when the air crackled around them and the sky lit up again. Lightning struck a tree across the river with the ear-splitting noise announcing an imminent downpour.

The sky was now dark and ominous, and a slight breeze began to move the still air. Tom Grant stepped out of the stable and watched as Abel shouted instructions to the slaves walking behind a full wagon down the narrow dirt road from the upper fields. Abel was a large black slave to whom Tom had given the position of driver. There was a roughness about him that Tom hoped would command the respect of the rest of his slaves - if not respect, then at least obedience. Abel appeared to enjoy his promotion and the authority that came with it, having become comfortable with a bullwhip almost overnight. He seemed to love the sound of the crisp pop as he cracked the whip over the heads of the workers.

"I'll have to keep an eye on him," Tom thought to himself. "He might get to enjoying it a little too much."

Tom patted the butt of his pistol in his holster. It was always loaded, always ready. He was now the only white person on his plantation, but it was not supposed to have been that way. He had planned on a wife, a daughter, and sons, many sons. Once again, as he dwelt on his loss, bitterness began to stir deep inside. Almost on cue, a sound began to build somewhere in the distance. It was as if all of his sleeping demons were awakening. It began with a breeze, but in what seemed like only a moment, the storm front slammed the farm with a sudden mighty wind that shook trees, buildings, and people.

Tom grabbed his hat and held onto the doorpost of the stable as a lightning bolt struck the hill above the returning slaves. The roar was deafening. Almost instantly, rain poured down from the rumbling sky overhead, soaking everything and everyone that wasn't under a roof. Tom stepped back a couple of steps inside the stable, out of the rain, and watched as the procession of slaves continued down the road to the slaves' quarters. It seemed peculiar to him that they didn't run for shelter. They just continued walking. Their nearly worthless clothing clung to them like their own skin, the winds tearing at what threads remained, but they didn't seem to notice. They just slogged silently through the mud, as if they had no spirit left in them.

Without warning a great blast of wind swept across the valley and smashed against the slaves shacks. Four of the rickety buildings fell like dominos. Then, just as quickly, the wind died down and the torrents of rain slowly began to diminish until the only sound Tom could hear was that of a gentle rain peacefully watering the earth.

Tom stepped back into the doorway and watched as the slaves stood about, surveying the damage. A four-year-old girl and a ten-year-old boy held their mother's hands as their father, who Tom called 'Big Joe', walked up to the pile of wood that had once been their home. If Tom remembered right, this was the family his wife had brought food to, on the day of her death. A few of the others began digging through the rubble picking out blankets, tin cups, and other treasures. Big Joe just stood there, then turned to Abel who quickly threw up his hands as if to say "It's your problem, not mine," and pointed up the hill to the big house as he spoke something that Tom could not hear.

For some reason, Tom looked up to his house where Abel was

pointing. Etta and Belle were standing on the covered porch. Belle had been sharing a shack with an older slave couple who had no children. Hers was one of the four that had collapsed. She looked as if she was crying.

And then Tom noticed Etta. She was not watching the others. Instead, she was watching Tom. When their eyes locked, Etta smiled and then, to Tom's surprise and wonder, she nodded her head as if she was communicating something to him that he was supposed to understand. The old woman crossed her arms, tilted her head slightly, and watched him. Tom had the impression that she expected him to do something and she had no doubt in her mind that he would do it. He began to feel uncomfortable under her gaze and forced his attention back to the shanty town.

Abel had gone inside his quarters as had many of the others whose homes had been left undamaged. A few had remained outside and were helping the now homeless ones carry their belongings to the pecan grove seeking some form of shelter under the trees.

Tom cursed the weather. It was a storm like this that had destroyed his family. A storm had also preceded Etta's beating. And now it was another storm that had left some of his slaves standing in the rain, shivering and homeless. He cursed again.

For some reason, he turned back to Etta. As if cast in stone, she had not moved, nor had she taken her eyes off of him. He wanted to turn away but could not. Tom stood transfixed with the slave woman. Her face was not mocking; neither was she enjoying the catastrophic scene before her. Unbelievably, she looked as if she was proud of him. Proud of what he had done? Surely not! He had kept every building on the plantation in top notch shape, except the slave's homes. They had not been repaired since his grandfather had built them. Proud that he had almost killed her with his bare fists? Proud, that his slaves were too afraid to ask him for shelter? Why was she looking at him like that?

It slowly dawned on Tom that he had seen that look before. It seemed strange to him that Etta could so easily draw out memories of his grandmother. She too had looked at him like that. He remembered distinctly the time when, as a youngster, he had come home from school and told his father that some of the bigger boys had been teasing him because he was so skinny and couldn't read as well as the others.

His father had scowled at him and said he was a disappointment to the 'C.P. Grant' family name. He remembered the smell of alcohol on his dad's breath as he pushed Tom aside and staggered out of the house. Tom had been devastated. He just wanted to die. With tears in his eyes he turned to run from the room but was surprised to see his grandmother standing at the entrance to the hallway blocking his exit. She had that same look on her face that Etta had now.

"Do you know why your father is so angry with you, Tom?" his grandmother had asked.

Tom had said nothing.

She continued, "It's because you're so much better than the three C.P.'s . The comparison is too hard for your dad to face. It would be so much easier for him if you joined him down on his level. Don't do it, Tom. I know he's my son, but he's like those boys at your school. Chadwick may be disappointed in you, but I'm proud of you, Tom." Then his grandmother had kneeled down and hugged him long and hard, as he cried.

The tears became rain again as he was drawn back into the present moment.

Etta nodded again as if repeating her unspoken message. This time Tom nodded his head slowly up and down at Etta, "Alright, Grandma Etta, you win." Tom spoke the words as if she could hear him, then he turned and walked into the stable.

Belle was completely unaware of what had just transpired between Etta and the master and so was not expecting Tom to come out of the stable driving an empty cotton wagon. She could hardly believe her eyes as she watched him pull up in front of Abel's shack and call him and the others back out into the rain. When everyone had climbed on, the Massuh himself drove the wagon down to the pecan grove. Belle was so caught up watching the Massuh working side by side, soaking wet, along with the others, loading the women and children and all of their belongings into the wagon, that she didn't even notice as Etta leaned forward and placed her hands on the porch railing and said, "Dat's him, suh!"

Chapter 24

Lightning struck somewhere across the river and it took no time at all for the accompanying boom to arrive, causing Hope to jump out of her chair. She let out an involuntary squeal as she dropped the cup of broth onto the floor. Groaning in frustration, she grabbed a rag from the table and dropped to her hands and knees by the bed to begin cleaning up the mess. The sounds of the wind shaking the building and the rain beating on the roof engulfed the room.

"Praise you, Lord Jesus!" she prayed as she stood up and went to the door. She stepped out onto the porch to rinse the rag in the waterfall coming off the roof. As Hope wrung out the water from the rag, she shuddered as she looked up to the hill where the woman had been found. She imagined herself lying up there somewhere, alone in the rain and bleeding to death. As she slipped back inside, she looked long and hard at the old woman, and then once again knelt down to finish wiping up the floor. "Praise you, Lord Jesus!" she repeated, as she closed her eyes in prayer and sat back on her heels. She didn't move for a while. As Hope listened to the storm, a welcome peace swept over her. She opened her eyes and turned her head to the woman. Letting out a shriek, she lost her balance and fell sideways away from the bed. Quickly scrambling back to the side of the bed on her hands and knees, Hope looked into the face of the woman, who was now looking back at her. A two foot space separated their faces as Hope just stared with her mouth open. "It's you!" she finally said. "I mean, hello. My name's Hope."

The woman's eyes followed Hope's as Hope stood to her feet. Hope could hardly contain herself as an indescribable joy engulfed her. "You're alive!" she said in amazement.

There was no expression of acknowledgement but the woman blinked twice.

"I can't bleve it!" Hope wanted to jump up and down. "No. I do bleve it! I can see it! Thank you, Jesus! Do you want a drink of water or sumthin'?" She grabbed the cup she had set on the table, and ran out to the porch and filled the cup with rainwater then quickly returned to the bed. For the first time, Hope held the woman's head up and she drank from the cup. When she had finished, the woman closed her eyes and went back to sleep. Hope fell back into her chair with her arms hanging to her sides, one hand still holding the tin cup. Her attention was focused on the woman's eyes expecting they might open at any moment and she didn't want to miss it. A wave of exhaustion swept through her. She had been so caught up in taking care of her patient that she hadn't allowed herself a long, restful sleep in days. She watched and watched the woman's eyes. Her own eyelids became heavier and heavier until finally, the tin cup clattered to the floor as both the young and the old shared a peaceful sleep.

On the other side of the double wall that separated Hope from Tal and Sadie, Tal was eating some dried perch and pacing nervously.

Sadie was sitting on the edge of the bed rubbing a tired foot. "I'm telling you, Tal, they were all fine at lunch. Massuh Martin didn't seem at all upset when young Massuh Frank mentioned teaching Joshua to read."

Tal kept pacing. "Do you think it's a coincidence that they been talking so much to Mabin lately, and then Frank says he's teachin' Joshua, and now they want to come and talk to us?"

Sadie shook her head and switched to rubbing the other foot. "No, Tal, but I'm just saying they showed no sign of any problems." She lifted her eyes from her aching foot to Tal. "It was you who told me we were blessed to be here. I still believe you were right."

The knock on the door interrupted their conversation. Sadie quickly stood and straightened her dress as the confidence she had just voiced to Tal quickly disappeared. Tal walked slowly to the door and opened it.

The rumbling thunder in the darkened sky seemed out of place behind the smiles on Luke and Sally's faces as they stood in the doorway.

Southern protocol would have the slave come to the master. However, because of the need to finish the field before the storm, Tal had been unable to come back early, so Luke had told him to go ahead home and get cleaned up and he and Sally would come calling after they had a bite to eat.

"Good evening, Tal, may we come in?" asked Luke.

Tal was confused. Masters do not ask permission from a slave to do anything! *Do I actually have a choice?* he wondered.

Luke seemed to understand Tal's dilemma and added, "If we stay out here too long we'll probably both get soaked." As if to accentuate his point, there was a loud clap of thunder and it began to rain a little harder.

Tal backed into the room and stood beside Sadie. "Yessuh. You both come right in, suh."

The Martins stepped inside and Luke gently pushed the door closed as Sally stood beaming at the slave couple. Sadie began to relax and offered Sally a seat at the table. Sally quickly accepted and Luke opened the conversation by asking if there were any leaks in the roof and did they need anything to make them more comfortable. Tal assured him that they were more than happy with what they had. What slave would dare say otherwise, even to a kind master? But in this case, it was the truth. Eventually, Luke got to the point of their visit. "Tal, Sid told us that he taught both you and Sadie to read and write, and that he also taught you arithmetic."

Without thinking, Sadie stepped back and sat down heavily on the bed. Tal stared dumbly at Luke as if he'd been caught stealing.

Sally instantly understood what was happening and hurried over and sat on the bed beside Sadie and took hold of her hand. "This is wonderful, Sadie! We're thrilled about it!" She looked as excited as she sounded. "We think it fits right in with what we think is God's plan."

"That's right, Tal," interjected Luke. "We've decided to make some changes around here and we'd like your help to pull it off."

Tal felt as if he had stumbled into the middle of someone else's conversation. He had no way of guessing where Luke was going with this. "I'm sorry, suh. Sadie was pretty sure Massuh Pennington told you. I should have said something, but Massuh Pennington said most white folks don't much like the idea of black folks readin."

Luke nodded in agreement, "Not around here, they don't. Actually it's illegal. But Henry Blackstone, the man that owns the feed store, and Sid have both seen some larger plantations around New Orleans and one in Mississippi that actually have plantation schools where the slaves learn to read."

Sally squeezed Sadie's hand. "We want you to teach the others how to read and write!" she said, as she looked excitedly into Sadie's eyes.

Sadie's jaw dropped. "But missuz...."

"She's right, Tal," added Luke, looking directly at Tal. "I managed to dig up two old Bibles in my study that could be used as reading materials. And I can pick up some slate boards at Wally's store."

Tal stared blankly at Luke, totally speechless. *Can slaves say no? Is this some sort of test?* Myriad thoughts were flying through Tal's head as Luke talked on. *Could this really be true?*

"The abolitionists in the northern states have started printing newspapers," Luke continued. "Articles describing the true conditions of the black slaves living in the south are mixed among regular news articles. Anger is stirring up on both sides of this issue. Sally and I tend to agree with Sid that it's entirely possible that sometime in the near future slavery will be illegal. We want to help prepare everyone on this farm for whatever might happen." Luke pulled a small piece of paper from his jacket and handed it to Tal, "Henry Blackstone slipped this to me in church on Sunday. A cotton buyer from Philadelphia brought some of these with him at great risk to himself. It adds another dimension to some of the changes we have in mind."

Luke stopped talking as Tal read the writing on the small piece of paper. Tal read slowly and carefully. "It says a man named 'Hopper' is trying to form a secret escape route for slaves who want to live free in Canada. It says he's looking for safe stations along the route from the south to the north." Tal turned the sheet over and noticed some ink scratches in the lower corner of the paper that were so small they were almost unreadable. He took the paper over to the lamp and studied it closely. "Hackquakmithston." He looked up from the paper and repeated the word 'hackquakmithston' puzzling over the meaning.

"I can't figure it out either," Luke commented, "but we're sure there's a meaning to it. The paper isn't handed out to just anybody. They are being cautious. Henry was told that if he found a reliable person that was interested, he was to contact them and they would explain."

Tal began pacing back and forth, rereading the flyer. Luke and Sally politely waited while he thought through the implications of what he was reading. Eventually, Tal looked at Luke and then around to Sally. "You want us to teach the others to read so's they can go to Canada, suh?"

"Well, not exactly," said Luke. "Sally and I are finally convinced of God's purpose for us. We intend to turn this plantation into a special place. That might entail a variety of things, including intentionally purchasing more slaves, but according to their needs and not our own. We'll need God's help in being selective in our 'shopping', as Sally likes to call it. A boy without a father and a woman with a bullet hole in her leg seem to be examples of what God might have in mind."

Luke smiled and nodded toward them, "A man needing to stay with his wife might be another example."

"Another thing we would like to do is take up Sid's idea of educating, to prepare slaves for emancipation. That's why we are hoping you'll work with us and Pastor Davies, and Mabin."

"Mabin knows all of this?" Tal and Sadie both asked at the same time.

Sally nodded and answered, "He's suspected you could read since you came here but he's kept quiet, not being sure. He didn't want to cause any problems. It all came out when we told him that we believed the Lord wanted the six of us to work together on this."

"It's not like we're going to be announcing this to the town," Luke interjected, "but we won't be able to hide the fact that I'm planting more crops and buying more slaves, and adding more buildings. But we plan to stay as low-key as possible and let the Lord handle the rest."

"What about this paper here, suh?" asked Tal, holding up the flyer.

"Yeah, that could add another aspect to this whole project that we hadn't planned on. It would definitely add another layer of risk to my family if we got involved, but Sal and I haven't ruled it out. Maybe we should all get together and discuss it before you make your decision. Sally and I will head on back to the house now and let you two talk. I was going to take Mabin with me to town tomorrow, but I've changed my mind. The fields will be too wet to pick tomorrow, so I'll take Toby and Zekiel instead. I would like you to get together with Mabin and let him fill you in on what he's thinking about all of this. I'll get Pastor Davies' opinion about this flyer when I'm in town tomorrow and then the rest of us can talk again tomorrow night."

Luke hesitated, and then said, "I want you both to understand that you are free to decline our request. We're not talking right now as master and slave. It would have to be as six Christians working together on an assignment from the Lord, not as three blacks and three whites. We might all feel uncomfortable at times because we're used to another structure, but I want you to feel free to give your input at any time with no fear of reprisal."

The window lit up and thunder followed. "I hope you've been here long enough to see that I'm more uncomfortable treating you all as slaves than I am treating you as regular people who are the same as us. I would rather be an employer than a master."

Tal shuffled his feet and looked uneasily at Luke. "I don' know nothing but master and slave, suh. Don't know if I can do different. But I have been here long enough to see what you're sayin'. Sadie 'n me will talk."

"Thank you, Tal. We'll be going now," Luke held out his hand to Sally who stood and joined him at the door.

"At the very least, we could sure use your prayers," said Sally as they stepped out and closed the door behind them.

Tal walked over and sat down next to Sadie. They both sat there listening to the steady rain. Eventually Sadie sighed and said, "Well, I guess that would be a good place to start. We could pray for them."

Tal nodded and took his wife's hand, and they prayed.

Chapter 25

"I made one once, years ago," said Addison, "It had a metal bottom frame and the bed was half inch wire screen. The sides were screened, too. That allowed the air to come up from below." The blacksmith drew himself up with pride. "Didn't even have to unload the peanuts to dry em. Just stirred them once in a while, right there in the wagon."

"You do build a good wagon, Addison," said Luke. "I'm thinking of experimenting with more peanuts this coming season. If it proves successful, I may be asking you to make me a peanut wagon." Luke noticed that Zekiel and Toby had finished hooking up the mules to the new wagon. "Looks like it's ready to go. I'm going to give it a strength test right away. My next stop is the mill. Can she hold a whole load of lumber?" Luke asked, feigning concern.

"If she can't, I'll carry the whole load out to your place on my shoulders," laughed Addison.

"It's a deal," said Luke, as they shook hands.

Addison returned to his forge, and Luke turned to leave. He handed a sheet of paper to Toby. "Here's the list of board sizes and amounts that we'll need to get started. Give it to Harvey and he'll take it from there. You'll need to take both wagons with you."

Luke looked down the muddy road that led to the river and the mill. "Hmmm. You know, Toby," he thought aloud, "now that I think of it, tell Harvey to only load the top half of the list today. The roads were pretty sloppy coming into town. If we take it all, we'd be inviting problems. Distribute the weight between the two wagons, and we'll make a second trip tomorrow. Meet me down at the stables when you're finished."

After the wagons had departed, the first place Luke went was the parsonage, located next to the Baptist church. He informed the pastor of Mabin's decision and of the talk with Tal and Sadie. Then they discussed the flyer Henry had given him.

After his conversation with Matthew, Luke headed for Main Street. Mostly men occupied the boardwalks of Grantsville on this particular morning. The rain had stopped sometime in the night, but most of the ladies were unwilling to risk getting mud on their petticoats.

Grantsville had about four hundred yards of roadway that was paved with brick. But it wasn't on Main Street, in the business district. Business in Grantsville played second fiddle to the clean Sunday dresses worn on Sunday mornings. Church Street was the only road in the entire town that wasn't muddy today.

As Luke walked through town on his way to the bank, he noticed a group of men standing around a table that had been set up in front of the barber's shop. Al Willis and his son Ted were among the group. George, the barber, was sitting behind the table, dipping a quill into an ink jar and handing it to anyone willing to sign his petition.

Luke's curiosity motivated him to step out into the mud that was called Main Street and cross over to the barber's shop. Halfway across the street, Al noticed him. Pointing to Luke, he said in a loud voice, "Gentlemen, you are looking at the reason that we all need to sign George's petition!"

Luke felt as if every eye in town was on him as he paused, wondering how he had suddenly become the focus of everyone's attention.

"Look at him," Al continued, as a few of the men shook their heads and chuckled, "standing there with mud almost to the top of his boots. What a sorry sight! If he were to slip and land on his keester, his boots would be the least of his problems."

That drew a laugh from the group of men. As Luke resumed his journey to the boardwalk, he heard someone say, "The last thing this place needs is Luke Martin, sitting in the middle of the road covered with mud when a stagecoach filled with fine Louisiana women pulls into town!" Then the mocking voice of Jerry Ellis could be heard over the laughter, "Oh, I don't know, I think the sight of Martin layin' in that slop could help cheer this town up."

As Al reached out and pulled Luke up onto the boardwalk, Luke looked Jerry in the eye and smiled, saying, "God bless you, too, Jerry. Need some cheering up, do you?"

Jerry returned a stiff smile and responded, "I'm doing fine, Martin. Just fine."

"Hey, Luke!" called George. "We need you to sign this petition to get the mayor to pave Main Street. I've got over three hundred names in less than a week. The town council says they'll accept signatures from folks as far as ten miles out. The cost will be split, two thirds from town businesses, and one third from all non-business residents in the ten mile area." George raised his voice a little for the benefit of those walking by, "The good news is that Ben Statler, at the bank, has offered to donate two thousand dollars to the project, and The Boston Textile Company, which buys a good amount of our cotton, has offered five thousand dollars if we start the paving by spring."

"Count me in, George. Those donations should make this more affordable than Church Street was," said Luke. George handed him the quill and he signed his name, then stepped aside for another man and his wife who had stopped to sign. Luke looked around for Al and Ted and pulled them aside from the others.

"I'd like to hire Ted and Nathan for a couple of months to help build a dining house for my workers." Luke turned to Ted and said, "I need some strong backs and good attitudes, and you and your brother fill the bill."

"I'd like that, sir," answered Ted. "I'm hoping to hire on here, in the spring, if this paving project goes through. When I get enough money saved, I want to go to school in Philadelphia. Working for you will give me an early start to my savings."

"You wouldn't have to be hiring young Teddy here, if you had enough slaves, Martin!" grunted Jerry Ellis, interrupting the conversation. "I've got a couple of no goods with strong backs I'd sell ya. But wait a minute! You don't much care for slavery, do ya, Martin?"

"It's not polite to listen in on other people's conversations, Jerry,"

Luke said, with a condescending look, "but as a matter of fact, I *am* interested." Jerry, Al, and Ted all raised their eyebrows in surprise.

"I've had a change of heart." Luke smiled at him. "I plan on expanding my crops next year so I'll need some more help."

"Greed helped you see the light, did it?"

Luke ignored the comment. "Can I come out to your place and take a look at them sometime soon?"

"Any time you like, Mister 'Christian Slave Owner'," Jerry stressed his last three words.

"Why did you call them no goods?" asked Luke, once again ignoring Jerry's mocking words.

"Cause one of them's stupid as a rock and can't hear straight. And the other is a runaway I bought off a guy in Savannah seven months ago. Healthy enough, but I gotta keep him in leg irons or he tries to run off. I tried beating some sense into him, but it don't work with him." Ellis looked right at Luke with a deadly serious face. "Do you *still* want to come out and look at them? These nigras would fit right in at your place. They're lost causes, just like you." Jerry gave a wry smile and added, "But they wouldn't cost you much, and you wouldn't have to hire kids."

Luke noticed Ted's face drop. "I'll be out in a few days to look at them," he said, pretending to ignore Jerry's insult. "You could be right. They might be just what I need." Luke turned to Ted, "Can you and your brother start work in a couple of days?"

Ted cheered up, "I know I can, sir, but I'll have to check with Nathan."

Al nodded, "They'll be there the day after tomorrow, Luke."

The next stop was to be the bank, but as Luke passed the stables, he noticed that Jeb had eight male and female slaves roped to the fence. He was setting up his platform, preparing for his day's work.

Luke stopped, said a prayer, and then went 'shopping'. Slowly he walked along the fence row of slaves. He studied how they stood, the expression on their faces, how healthy and how strong they looked.

"You buy all eight and I'll give you the deal of a lifetime, and I can go back home to Savannah," Jeb said to Luke, as he and another man continued to assemble the platform.

"Tell me about them. Where are they from? What do you know about them, Jeb?" Luke stood back and studied them as a group.

"I got it all. Young, old, male, female, tall, short. No problems with any of them, 'cept that gal there's about to drop a foal. The man that bought her about eight months ago didn't know she wouldn't be worth much for awhile. I got her on my way up here to Grantsville. He dumped her on me for a song."

"The old guy over there has spent his whole life as a house servant. He's got some class. He could train the rest of your staff real nice."

Jeb stood up and walked over beside Luke - the proud salesman, selling his wares – and continued, "That one on the end spent the last ten years in a blacksmith shop. He's learned the trade real well. He's strong and healthy. The rest of them would be good as pickers and planters. Two don't speak English very well. None of 'em would be any trouble. Jeb stuck out his chest, "Yep, I got a real good bunch this time. What d'ya say, Mr. Martin?"

"I'll think it over, Jeb."

"Suit yourself. I'll be right over there, if you need me." Dukett left him and went back to work on the platform. As Jeb put the finishing touches on the platform, Luke moved to one of the benches under the largest oak tree and sat down to pray.

A couple of men Luke didn't know walked up to the slaves and began their inspections of each one. Luke had seen others do it all his life, but he himself had never poked and prodded a slave as part of his pre-purchase inspection. He felt the usual distaste for slavery welling up inside him again, as he watched. The old slave and the blacksmith both wore shoes. The other six stood barefoot in the mud, accepting the white men's inspections without emotion.

Looking around, Jeb saw only three possible customers. He cursed the mud, then quickly put on his practiced smile and walked over to the two men to begin his personal sales pitch.

Standing up, Luke walked over to the blacksmith and asked, "Have you done any carpentry?" The slave looked puzzled, but didn't speak. Luke tried again, "Built anything, like houses, sheds, or barns?"

"No, suh," the slave answered very quietly, keeping his eyes to the ground.

"Can you cook?"

"No, suh."

"How about animals, are you good with animals?" Luke asked.

"Real good, suh," answered the slave, showing no emotion or movement.

Luke walked down the row of slaves quietly asking each one about any special skills. The responses were the same, "No, suh." No movement. No eye contact. When he came to the pregnant woman, he didn't bother to ask anything. He returned to the bench, sat down again, and prayed.

The two men had stepped away and were discussing something between themselves, while Jeb turned his attention to a man who was walking toward the stables. Twenty minutes went by before Luke noticed that the others had left without making any purchases. Jeb was angrily yelling instructions to his helper, telling him to take the slaves to the barn, and that it had better be a sunny day tomorrow.

Luke walked over to the girl and asked, "Can you cook?"

She stared at the ground. "No, suh."

"Can you learn to cook?"

"Don't know, suh."

"You still here, Martin?" Jeb turned from his helper and was focused once again on Luke. "Why don't this fool town pave its streets? How's a man supposed to do any business when it rains? Everyone's afraid they'll get their lily-white boots muddy. I got a mind not to come back here. This place is a slop bucket!"

Luke nodded his head in agreement, "You're right, Jeb. We got a petition going around to pave Main Street. You oughta take some of that passion up to George's barber shop and help him convince people to sign it."

The man working for Jeb began to herd the slaves toward the barn.

"But before you go," Luke added, "I'm interested in buying the blacksmith."

"Hold on there a minute, Willy!"

Luke found it interesting how quickly a salesman could switch into his sales mode.

"Bring me the blacksmith, Willy." Jeb's smile was back, "He's all yours, Martin, for a mere thousand dollars. He's the best one of the bunch and you will not be disappointed. Shall I write up the papers?"

"That's more than I planned on spending. Sorry, Jeb, but I'll pass," Luke began to walk away as Jeb cursed the mud again. "Maybe I'll come back tomorrow and see if I get lucky at a lower price."

Then a thought entered Luke's mind that he knew wasn't his own. Turning back to Jeb, he said, "I'll tell you what. You said you got the woman for a song? Throw her into the deal and I'll give you $800."

Dukett was well aware that none of the other three men had given the woman more than a glance. "A thousand dollars for both," Jeb folded his arms and tried to look firm.

"Sorry, Jeb," Luke shook his head, "not today. $800 tops." Turning away, he said over his shoulder, "You never know around here. Tomorrow, we could have a downpour." As he left, he could hear Dukett calling Grantsville and the weather a variety of creative names.

"Get back here, Martin! I shouldna ever bought her in the first place." Next, Jeb yelled over his shoulder, "Willy! Bring the woman!"

As he had done with Hope, Luke left the two newly acquired slaves with Jeb while he went to the bank. While there, Luke gave Ben the short version of the direction he and Sally appeared to be heading. After taking a minute to digest what he had heard, Ben asked, "So the two you just bought, did God tell you to do it?"

Luke fidgeted and cleared his throat, "This time I'm not so sure, Ben. There were a couple of field slaves that I think would have been really helpful. They were young and strong, and could have done a lot of hoeing and picking. I tried to talk the Lord into choosing them, but came up blank. No voice, no feeling, nothing.

"All of them kept their eyes to the ground as they do, but just as I was praying about the blacksmith, he looked up at me. I tell you, Ben, there was something about that look. It was as if he knew I was asking the Lord about him. The others all looked so defeated and hopeless, but this man seemed to sense something."

"I know I can't go around buying up all the slaves in the state of

Georgia. I need to listen carefully and try to let God do the choosing. But I have to admit to you, Ben, I think I just bought a slave because he gave me a look of kindness."

Ben shrugged his shoulders, "I can think of worse reasons to buy a slave. What about the woman? You say she's pregnant?"

"Very! She looks to be around thirty years old. Apparently the baby's father got sold about eight months ago, and so did she, but to two different buyers. I can't tell you why, but I got this last-minute urge to see if Jeb would throw her into the deal. Maybe it was God, maybe not. I'm not real clear about it, but I hadn't made any conscious decision to buy her."

Ben laughed, "I guess you didn't *really* buy her. She was thrown into the deal for free!" Ben stood and walked around the desk as Luke rose from his chair.

"You lead a fascinating life, Luke. I like watching you to see what's going to happen next."

They walked to the door and shook hands. Ben made Luke promise to bring Sally with him the next time he came to town, so Ben's wife could take her shopping and they would all have lunch together.

Chapter 26

When Luke arrived back at the stables, his two loaded wagons were waiting. Toby and Zekiel were relaxing at the back of one of them, talking about something that appeared to be humorous. Luke joined them and asked how things had gone. Toby told him it was a good thing they'd only picked up half a load today, because another customer, who had lost some buildings in the storm, had taken a huge wagonload of lumber just before Toby and Zekiel had arrived.

"Mister Harvey say for you not to bother coming tomorrow. He'll be runnin' both saws from sunup to sundown, but the load he ordered from upstate don't come for three more days."

Luke studied the load of wood as he spoke to Toby, "Well, we can't pick tomorrow; the bolls are too wet. But since we have all the posts and beams, we can dig the holes and tar the posts, anyway. It won't hurt everyone to take it easy another day."

Luke glanced toward the barn where Jeb had taken the slaves. "I've made a couple of additions to the family, fellas. We'll be on our way after I get them from Jeb."

Turning, the two young men looked behind them at the barn, and then at each other.

"One is about thirty-five or forty. Still strong, though. Should be a big help in the fields. He says he's good with animals, and was a smithy for quite a while. The other one – well, she's younger, but I doubt she'll be much help for a while!" Luke smiled mischievously, leaving them to wonder what he meant.

It wasn't long before their questions were answered. The black woman waddled along beside Luke, trying to keep up with him and the other slave. When the mud got deep, they each took an arm and helped her along.

"This is Dinah," said Luke, as they arrived at the wagon, "and this here's Washington." Luke put his hand on the man next to him. "You three men ride on this wagon, and I'll have Dinah ride with me. We'd best get going. The mud could slow us down."

The clouds had begun separating into patches of blue sky and sunshine. Heat and humidity come fast in Georgia and a steamy mist was rising up from the roads, forests, and marshes. As they traveled along, sparrows were flitting from tree to tree, and Luke watched a robin having a tug-o-war with a worm which regretted having come up from the ground to see the view.

As the wagons rounded a bend, they came to the fork in the road leading to the bridge that crossed the river. The slippery road was banked the wrong way at the turn for a top-heavy wagon. Sure enough, a wagon was lying on its side at the fork. Luke pulled his wagon up near the tipped-over wagon. Two men slogging around nearby were picking lumber up and wiping off what mud they could before stacking it in the weeds out of the way. Covered in mud, they had obviously been thrown from the wagon when the load shifted and it rolled over. Whoever they were, it was clear that these men were miserable. And then the realization came to Luke.

"What are you smiling at, Martin?" asked Tom Grant from under an armload of wood.

Luke had wanted to howl with laughter, but he could almost feel God himself putting His mighty hand over Luke's big mouth. Luke removed the smile when he realized that Tom was more miserable than angry.

"So you're the guy that beat us to the lumber this morning!"

Tom grunted and answered, "Need every bit of it and more. If I would a known the mill was runnin' low on wood, I would a brought more wagons. Then you'd be going home empty-handed." He turned his back on Luke and went back to work stacking lumber as "Big Joe" cleaned each piece off in the weeds. Tom felt the gaze of the others bearing down on him like a weight on his back as he slopped over and picked up another board. He felt humiliated and anger began to rise within him.

"Let's give him a hand, fellas," Tom heard Luke's voice behind him. "Dinah, you stay put."

Tom glanced back to see the four men, almost in unison, jumping off the wagons and into the mud. "Don't need no help!" He pretended to ignore them as he continued working.

Luke held his tongue. The four of them stood together watching for a minute and then Luke forced himself to say, "You're a good man, Tom. You wouldn't hesitate to help us, if we needed it. We'd like to do the same."

Tom stopped and looked at Luke. "You don't want to get them nice clean clothes all dirty, now do ya?" He looked down at the front of his clothes and then back at Luke. "Can't tell which one of us is the nigra an which one's not. Now, get out of here and leave us alone!"

Luke was fighting a mammoth battle inside his head. He had done his Christian duty by offering to help and Tom had even given him permission to leave.

After standing there for a short moment, Luke knelt down in the mud, cupped his hands, scooped up a heaping portion of mud, and dumped it on his own head. As it oozed down his face and over his ears, he stood up and wiped his face with his muddy hands. He gave Tom a challenging look and said in a calm, serious voice, "It washes off, Tom. Please let us help."

Luke could see right through the mud on Tom's face and read the confusion. There was a struggle going on inside both Tom and Luke at the same time. They both disliked each other; always had. Neither one wanted to be there at this moment. It was as if the Father had grabbed the two kids by the collar and plopped them down in the mud facing each other and said, "Now you two boys figure out how you're going to get along, or you'll be sitting here all day and all night!"

With five slaves quietly, but curiously, watching to see how the scene would play out, Luke finally said, "It would do me good to do something for someone else."

Tom thought about it for a moment and then said, "Suit yourself. You're a mess already anyway."

With six men working, it took very little time to unload and clean the remaining boards. Then all six of them lined up side by side and, with one loud groan, they tipped the large wagon back on its wheels. Big Joe and Tom hooked the team of horses back to the wagon as Luke and the others began loading boards and beams. As the wagon began to get full, Luke suggested that they evenly disperse the rest of the wood in all three wagons. Tom seemed genuinely surprised at Luke's offer, and Luke was genuinely surprised when Tom accepted.

The line of wagons pulled up to the slave huts, and Luke and his slaves stared at the mess. Now he understood why Tom needed so much lumber. They watched as Abel directed the other slaves in the clean-up. A huge bonfire had been lit to burn the old splintered and rotten wood that used to be their homes.

Luke climbed down and stood beside Tom, shaking his head. "Anybody get hurt?" he asked.

"Nope," replied Tom, pointing to a shack that was still standing. "The two that had stayed home sick were in that one over there, but the rest hadn't quite gotten back from the fields. Etta, my house servant, calls it a miracle." Then he nodded his head in the direction of a shack at the end of the second row. It was leaning precariously, looking as if it could fall over any second. "That one could've hurt someone. Last night, it looked fine, but it must have been weakened in the storm. Four of my nigras were sleeping inside when it started creaking and tipping. When I woke up this morning, those fellas were all sleeping in the horse stable."

"Where are the others staying?" asked Luke.

"I got 'em all jam-packed in the cook house for now."

Luke nodded in understanding, and then called to his three men to start unloading Tom's wood. While they worked, Tom observed Toby walk over and quietly say something to Luke. Nodding, Luke smiled and turned to Tom, "Toby seems to think that your need might be greater than ours. He says maybe we should leave all three wagon loads off here and fetch ours from town next week."

Tom was stunned. He didn't know what to say. He glanced at Toby curiously and then at the wagon loads of lumber. The truth was, he suspected that if another storm came, more shacks would come down. And if it happened at night, he could have some dead slaves.

"I don't need charity, Martin," he said.

"I wasn't offering charity," Luke countered. "I've got the bill from the mill right here in my pocket. You can pay me full price. I think a good safe shelter for your people is a higher priority than our new cook house. We can wait a week longer and it won't hurt us."

Luke was right, and that made Tom angry, "You hymn singers are always going around trying to look all righteous and pure." Then he looked up and saw Etta standing on the porch, watching him. Distracted for a moment, he wondered, "Who *is* she, anyway?" He could swear that she was hearing every word that was said, even so far away.

Luke looked over his shoulder to see what Tom was looking at. Turning back, he said, "Just trying to do what's right, Tom." Then he grudgingly added, "Just like you are."

Tom frowned as he tore his eyes away from Etta's grasp. His pride wouldn't let him be gracious. "Paid good money for each of them nigras. Wouldn't do me any good to have a house fall on 'em now, would it? Okay then, Martin, I'll go up to the house and get your money." He called all of the slaves to himself and gave out orders. By the time Tom returned with the cash, only the supplies that Sally had requested were left on the wagons.

"You're a mess, Martin," said Tom. "Guess we'd all best go get cleaned up." And with that, Tom turned and went toward his house. On his way past Toby, he paused, and stepped out of character for a brief moment, "Sorry about the whippin'. Won't happen again."

Then Tom proceeded on to his house, going up the steps and inside without looking back at any of them, not even Etta.

Chapter 27

Sometime during the night, Hope had moved from the chair to the floor. When she opened her eyes at dawn, the old woman was sitting on the edge of the bed looking down at her. For the second time, she scrambled to her feet in excitement. Breathing heavily, her eyes were wide open as she resisted the urge to run out the door and shout her news to the world.

The old woman spoke first, "I in you' bed?"

"No, ma'am. I mean, yes, ma'am. I mean, you jus' stay dere, ma'am." Hope looked around the room flustered, then saw the pot of broth and brought herself back under control. "You don' have much strength. If you kin stay sat up fo' a time, I give you some broth; then you kin lie down 'n rest while I go get Massuh Martin and Miz Sally 'n tell them you not dead!"

The woman turned her gaze to the floor thoughtfully, "Guess I *ain't* dead yet, am I?"

Hope moved quickly to the table, poured a cup of broth, and brought it to her.

"No, ma'am, you very much 'live. Jus' like Mabin say you would be. Here now, drink it slow. You hardly had anythin' to eat fo' some time now."

The woman was too weak and shaky to hold the cup herself, but she drank the entire serving as Hope held the cup to her mouth. When she finished, Hope fluffed the pillow and eased her back down on the bed.

"You get some rest. I'll go tell d' others, but I be right back."

A serious look came over the woman's face as she reached weakly for Hope's hand. "This place, 's it good, o' bad?"

Hope leaned down and asked, "Do you hav' a name?"

"Mahta," the woman responded weakly.

Hope stroked the side of her head that was missing the ear. "This a good place, Mahta. You'll like it here."

Mahta didn't smile, but looked deep into Hope's eyes, searching for the truth in her words. Hope gave a slight smile and nodded her head. Mahta finally gave a faint nod of her own and closed her eyes. Hope tiptoed to the door and slipped outside. She walked softly across the porch and down the step. But as soon as she hit the ground, she broke into a run; she could hold in the good news no longer.

Rounding the corner of the feed shed, Hope could see Toby, Zekiel, and Massuh Martin far down the road on their way to Grantsville. Momentary disappointment filled her; she had wanted Toby to be the first one to hear the news. Hope ran to the house and knocked on the kitchen door, but the house was empty. She whirled around and down the porch steps, jumping over the bottom three and landing in the slippery mud. Suddenly, she was sliding along in the mud on one foot with the other leg and both arms flailing in the air as she tried to maintain her balance. The young slave, Otis, was half-way across the yard carrying a bag of potatoes to the house. He watched wide-eyed, expecting her to land flat on her back in the mud, but she regained her balance and continued her charge to the gin house, yelling, "She's awake, Otis!" as she flew by him. Otis watched her disappear around the barn, then cranked his head back around forward and shifted his load of potatoes to the other shoulder. He proceeded on his way, speaking aloud to himself, "Dat's good, Mis Hope. You done reeeeal good."

Frank and Joshua were helping Sadie and Sally in the gin house. They all looked up at once as Hope came running into the building squealing with delight. "Her name's Mahta 'n she woke up 'n she tol' me her name 'n she ate some broth 'n now she's asleep again 'n I jus' had to come 'n tell you!" Hope bent over with her hands on her knees trying to catch her breath.

"Lord Jesus!" exclaimed Sadie as she straightened up.

Sally quickly instructed the boys to go tell the rest of the men.

They obeyed instantly, and at a full run. Next, Sally hugged Hope and told her how proud she was of her. "And now, if you will take us to her, we'd like to meet our new friend."

As the three women walked across the barnyard to meet Mahta, Hope was telling the whole story as fast as she could get the words out. Then she asked if she could sleep on the floor and give Mahta her bed, to which Sally responded, "Absolutely not! Some of the men will build a second bed, this very day. With the cotton being wet and all, they are probably looking for something to do, anyhow."

Hope reminded the women that Mahta's dress had been cut off, and that the old gown they had dressed her in would not do when she became strong enough to leave the house.

Sally appreciated Hope's concern. "Actually, it would be good if you all had a new set of clothes. Some of them are getting quite worn and everyone needs to keep a second set for when the other is being washed."

By the time the women approached the building they were planning a huge sewing project. It was decided that they would begin by making two new cotton dresses for Mahta, even though Sadie had offered to give her one of the three dresses she had brought with her to the farm.

Sally held a finger to her lips signaling them to be quiet as they approached the door. Hope carefully opened the door and the women silently entered the room. The old woman still slept. The three of them stood and gazed at the miracle. Sally noticed right away that the look of death on the old wrinkled face had been replaced by new life and a restful peace. She almost wept when she heard Hope whisper softly, "Ain't she beautiful?"

Chapter 28

The time spent helping Tom Grant had added an extra couple of hours to Luke's trip to town, but they would still be home by sunset. Now that the wagons were not full, Luke had Washington ride with him in the wagon, along with Dinah. He spent the ride home trying to put them at ease about the new experiences that they were being forced into. He told them about the farm, the family, the other slaves, and even the old woman.

Eventually, Luke asked them about themselves. When he asked if Dinah had a husband and where she came from, she told him the marriage of slaves was not allowed on the plantation where she came from. The baby's father had been sold a few weeks before her. She had been a field slave until she could not keep up with the rest of the workers and was sick too often. One morning before sunup, she was taken out of her shack, put onto a wagon, and sold.

Her new master hadn't known Dinah was pregnant and worked her hard. When the field driver complained to the master about her lack of energy and speed, she told him she was expecting. He had her whipped a few lashes for good measure. For a few months, all she did was carry water and do errands then, once again, Dinah was hauled off before sunup and sold to Jeb.

As for Washington, Luke was pleased to learn that he was a Christian man who saw his role in life as ministry. He showed no fear, and yet no animosity or anger, and he carried himself with confidence mixed with humility. The blacksmith shop he had worked at was near the home of the town's only minister. Washington's white master was not a Christian man but did not object when the pastor began visiting with his slave, "just as long as the nigra keeps working," he had reminded the pastor.

In a couple of weeks, Washington had gotten "saved" and for the next few years, the pastor had taught him from the Bible while he forged horseshoes and repaired iron wagon wheels. During that time, Washington had led two other slaves to Jesus and eventually started "lightly" witnessing to his white master. But after a few times of that, Washington was informed that he should "back off and keep his religion to himself." Washington had respectfully obeyed.

Apparently his witnessing had already had some effect. About a month later, the master had come to the shop with two other men. They all had been drinking. The three men stripped off Washington's shirt and strapped him tightly to a pole; then his master had heated up a horseshoe-shaped branding iron. He held the iron against Washington's back long enough to burn a permanent brand into his flesh, though not long enough to badly injure the muscles. Then, tossing the iron into the fire, he'd said, "Jesus is not your master, Washington. I am! And that is my brand of ownership!" It was as quick as that. Without another word, the three men walked back downtown to the bar, leaving Washington strapped to the pole for over four hours as people passed by and stared.

"It wan't long after, that I 's sold to dis man, Massuh Dukett, 'n now I'z in dis here wagon with you, 'n you say you bleve in Jesus too!"

Luke switched his attention to Dinah, and asked her how she was feeling.

"I'z fine, suh."

"When is the baby due?"

Dinah absent-mindedly rubbed her stomach, "Don't know, suh." Then she added, "Soon, I s'pose."

"Sorry about the long ride. I'm sure the detour to unload wood didn't help," said Luke. "When we get you home, we'll let you rest up for a couple of days. I'll have the doc come out and check on you to make sure everything's okay."

As Dinah stared at the horses ahead, her brow creased as she considered if this man was for real. She was not accustomed to such casual conversation with a white man; the master's wife maybe, but not the master.

"There it is - the Martin plantation." Luke looked proudly up the tree-lined road to the white house at the far end. A few white chickens meandered across the road as the two nearly-empty wagons squeaked and rattled along under the great oaks. The clouds in the western sky were outlined with the golden light of sunse, as the last rays of sun shone sideways through the trees. The effect was magical, and it was not lost on Washington.

"It's as if God 's givin' us a welcome," said Washington respectfully.

Luke nodded in agreement, "It is, isn't it? I don't remember seeing it like this very often."

As they pulled up to the end of the drive, Luke called ahead, instructing Toby to take his wagon on to the gin house and brush down the mules. While he was speaking, he noticed off to his right that Otis and Gideon were carrying what looked like a wooden bed frame. Following close behind them in parade fashion walked Frank and Joshua with a straw filled sleeping mat on their heads.

Luke climbed down and walked around the end of the wagon to the other side. "Washington, come around here and let's help Dinah climb down."

Dinah began to protest but Luke held up his hand and stopped her, "We wouldn't be gentlemen if we didn't help a lady in your condition get down off of a wagon." The two men each took a hand and Dinah stepped gingerly to the ground. She was surprised to discover that this man's hand felt the same as a black man's hand. She had never touched one before. She had expected it to be smooth and soft, but there was no sign of a leisurely life in that hand. It was as calloused as any working black man's hand. Dinah was embarrassed because her belly stuck out so far that it strained the worn cotton dress. She was sure the whole world could see when the baby moved inside of her.

It took a moment for her to realize that the world around her was beginning to spin. Washington noticed that she had begun to swoon and she was holding her hands out as if to keep her balance. "Massuh, sumthin's wrong!" he said, as he took hold of her arm and shoulder.

Luke took her other arm to steady her. He looked around and said, "Let's take her to a bed." Luke jerked his head in the direction of Tal and Sadie's place and they began the slow journey across the barnyard. When they got Dinah to the porch, Luke knocked with his foot and Tal opened the door. Luke could see Sadie and Mabin inside and realized he had interrupted them.

"Sorry to interrupt you, Tal. We need a place for this lady to rest, and yours was the closest."

As men are sometimes inclined to do in situations like this, Tal and Mabin reacted slowly. Sadie, however, was at Dinah's side in the blink of an eye, and Washington stepped politely aside.

"We'll take her right 'round to Hope's side and put her in bed. Miz Sally just had the men put in a second bed." Not wanting to make the woman feel bad, she didn't say that it was to be Hope's new bed.

"I'z better now; not so dizzy," Dinah said weakly, somewhat uncomfortable with all the attention.

Sadie nodded, but held firm, "That's good, honey, but by the looks o' you, your child's knockin' at the door 'n you'll need to be rested 'n ready."

Luke and Sadie guided Dinah around the building to Hope's side. The three black men followed wordlessly.

As they approached the door, Sadie told Luke, "The old woman's sittin up in bed, suh".

"Say her name's Mahta," Mabin added. Luke heard the confidence of victory in Mabin's voice.

"God's been busy today!" said Luke.

Hearing Sally's voice through Hope's open door, Luke walked right in. Sally was giving instructions to Otis and Gideon as they set up the new bed against the wall. Two young faces were peeking down over the edge of the loft, watching the action. Hope perched on the edge of the other bed, holding a small plate of cornbread and fish. Leaning against a stack of blankets and pillow, Mahta was facing the door and so was the first person to see Luke enter. She stopped chewing, and swallowed. Hope turned to see what caught Mahta's attention. Spotting Luke, she jumped up and spun around. She couldn't keep the grin off of her face.

"She's up 'n eatin', Massuh Martin!" Her excitement rose afresh and she lifted up and down on her toes a few times as she said, "Her name's Mahta 'n she's come through. Ain't it wonderful?" As she held her position on her tip toes, she clasped her hands together to her chest waiting for his response.

Luke momentarily forgot about Mahta and everyone else in the room. The look of pure joy mixed with anticipation on this young girl's face stirred something deep inside of him. It was a feeling similar to what a father would feel, watching his daughter walk down the aisle on her wedding day. Luke smiled at her in wonder. "My, how far you've come in just a few weeks. Yes, Hope, it absolutely *is* wonderful!" He pried his attention away from Hope and introduced himself. "Ma'am, my name is Luke Martin." He tipped his head toward his wife, "I'm with Sally. It sure is good to see you awake and sitting up." Luke leaned over and extended his hand. Mahta looked uncertainly at Hope who smiled and nodded that it was okay to shake this master's hand. Slowly she raised a feeble hand and said, "I'z called Mahta, suh. Don' mean t' put yo' all out like I done." She kept her eyes lowered.

Luke chuckled and shook his head. "You don't get to take any credit for that, Mahta. You didn't choose this. We are all of the opinion that the good Lord placed you right here, as a message directly from Him to us. This is His doing, and it is a good thing. No apologies are necessary."

Sally moved in and put a hand on Luke's arm, "Maybe Hope can finish helping Mahta with her supper while you tell us who it is that's peeking in the door."

"Oh!" Luke exclaimed. "I completely forgot! Washington. Dinah. Come on in here and meet everyone."

The man and woman entered politely and Luke introduced them. He swung his hand in the direction of the man, "This here is Washington," and then to the woman, "and this is Dinah. Washington is a blacksmith and he has experience working with animals. As you can see, he's in good shape to help us with the crops. Dinah here has been a field worker, but as you can also see, she will be taking a break for a while."

In her youthful excitement, Hope jumped right in. "This is

wonderful, suh! Miz Sally jus' had Miz Dinah's bed brung in. Now all's we need is more blankets."

Sally and Luke loved her even more because of her selflessness. Most of them knew that the bed had been made for Hope, and yet here she was, bouncing around at the opportunity to give it away, calling it Miz Dinah's bed.

"Otis," Sally calmly spoke her instructions as if it had all been planned days before, "you and Gideon can return to the shop and start building the two beds for the loft."

"Yes, ma'am, we get right to it," they replied, as they went out the door.

Sally looked at Luke and shrugged, "Well? We've gone from one to three so fast, we might as well be prepared."

"Makes sense to me," agreed Luke. "Mabin and Tal, would you show Washington his quarters while we get things settled here? Then Washington can help Otis and Gideon, while you two, and Sadie, finish your visit. I'm sorry we interrupted you."

As the three men left, Sally asked Dinah when she had last eaten.

"Yesterday evenin', ma'am. Ha' some fish 'n carrots 'n a turnip d' massuh give us." Dinah looked weary. Traveling from Savannah and then enduring the humility of the auction, before a long wagon ride to new surroundings and people, had taken its toll on her.

"Sadie?" asked Sally. "Would you go up to the house and get that half-loaf of bread on the table, along with some cheese and water? After you bring them here, then you can take the rest of the day off."

"Yes, ma'am," she said cheerfully. Sadie looked around at Dinah, Mahta, and Hope. "It sure is nice having more women around the place," she said as she hurried off.

Sally guided Dinah over to the empty bed. "You sit down here and relax, Dinah," she said, and then looked up to the loft. "You boys run and fetch a pillow and a couple blankets from the storage shed, and then you can each have a cookie." The boys only hit two rungs of the ladder before they were on the ground and out the door.

Luke moved behind Sally and put his hands on her shoulders. "I've got some things to do, but Sal will stay awhile so the four of you can iron out the details of what you'll need. You'll be living together. This is your home. I hope we all become good friends. My wife and my son and I are a Christian family, but if you are not a believer, it makes no difference. I only require that everyone be treated well."

Luke turned to leave, and then paused, "Oh, yeah." He looked at Mahta and Dinah, "The first job for you two is to rest and get your strength back. We will see to it that you eat regularly and are comfortable."

"Sadie and Hope can help prepare for the new arrival," added Sally. "Diapers will need to be made, and I think I know where there is a basket that will hold a baby."

As Luke said goodbye and stepped out onto the porch, he overheard Mahta say, "I don't want to be no trouble, ma'am. I don't need nothin'."

He smiled at his wife's response.

"I will not have all of you drinking out of the same cup and sharing the same fork," she said.

Luke knew things were going to be okay when he heard Mahta chuckle and say, "You're right, missus. I guess I do need a few things."

Chapter 29

We ben digging for three days now, an we gots a hole big nough to put a bear in," said Joshua, as he plopped down on the cool soil at the bottom of the hole. He held his hands against the ground, "This hole's deeper dan d' last one we dug. How come d' ground's gettin' cooler 'stedda warmer?"

"Don't make sense, does it?" Frank replied thoughtfully. "Must be like bein' on top of a mountain."

Joshua looked confused, "We in a hole, Frank."

"Pa says the higher the mountain, the colder it is on the top. It doesn't make any difference that it's closer to the sun. Must be the same with lava. The closer you get to it, the cooler the ground gets."

Joshua still looked confused. "D' closer you get to d' sun d' colder it gets? You sure he say dat?"

"Maybe the sun's not as hot as it looks," said Frank, as he sat down beside Joshua and looked around. "Boy, this hole looks even bigger from down here!"

"Big enuf to hol' two bears?" Joshua asked.

"Probably big enough for two elephants when we get done," said Frank confidently.

"Wha's bigger, a bear or elephant?" asked Joshua.

"Elephant."

"How high's 'n elephant?" asked Joshua thoughtfully.

"Pa says he couldn't reach the top of it when he tried." said Frank.

"Your pa's seen an elephant?"

"In Boston, at the circus. I guess I was a baby then. I don't remember it. Mama says its ears were as big as American flags, and its nose was as long as a giant snake."

Joshua absorbed this information. "It sounds scary lookin'," he said.

"Sure does," Frank agreed.

"Anybody down dere?" Toby's voice brought the boys quickly to their feet as they grabbed their shovels and began shoveling. Ground level was now neck high to the boys and the hole had been marked off at twelve feet by thirty feet. They had been working hard for three days. Toby's assignment was digging the holes for the posts of the new dining hall, but he also put in a couple of hours each day helping the boys on the hole for the root cellar.

"I brung another wheel cart. You boys climb on out of dere 'n haul dis dirt over to d' new garden 'n spread it aroun'. I'll fill d' second cart whiles you empty dat one," he said, pointing to the full cart. Toby jumped into the hole, "I finish tarrin' dem posts 'n now Mr. Ted 'n Mr. Nathan 'n me will finish diggin' dis cellar. We'll keep you sweatin' wit' dose wheel carts. Mabin say dis here hole's gotta be twice dis deep, maybe more."

Frank and Joshua ran up the slope that had been left at the far end of the hole. Tossing their shovels on top of the filled cart, the two of them together pushed the cart to the new garden site.

"Twice as deep would make a good swimming hole," said Frank, as he began tossing dirt out of the cart.

"Do you spose dere's wild elephants in Georgia?" asked Joshua, deep in thought.

"My teacher says they come from the other side of the world. A country called India," said Frank.

"Den dere's wild elephants in Georgia!" said Joshua, excitedly.

"How do you know that?" asked Frank.

"Cause I hear'd dey's Indians in Georgia!"

Frank thought about that as they shoveled more dirt out of the cart. "Maybe they escaped from a circus like the one my pa and mama saw. Probably not too many, though - maybe twenty."

"Twenty elephants," Joshua said as he worked. "Could be four or five wandered from Boston down to Georgia."

"Nah. At most, maybe one or two," said Frank, "but it never hurts to keep our eyes open."

Luke and the deacon's two boys stood by the lumber filled wagons, talking out the plan for the afternoon while they watched Frank and Joshua.

"The posts and beams should be nearly all cut, tarred, and ready for both buildings. We'll need to start with the root cellar and get the storage shed built over it as quickly as possible, or we might have a swimming pool if a storm comes," said Luke.

Luke was only telling part of why he wanted to cover it so quickly. The root cellar was to be located near the dining hall for convenient access from the kitchen. But only half of the underground section was to be used as a root cellar. He and Sally, and his new team of advisors, had decided to make it larger after Luke had returned from visiting Henry Blackstone four days earlier.

After his visit with Henry, Luke had invited Pastor Davies to come for dinner and spend the night. After the meal, the group had gathered in the Martins' kitchen. It was the very first time Tal had ever sat at a master's table, and the first time all six of them had met together since Tal and Sadie had come on board. They sat around the table drinking coffee and tea and enjoying a bowl of hot pudding that Sadie had put together for the gathering.

"Henry says that the guy's name is Bob Hackett," explained Luke. "He's part of that Quaker group up in North Smithston, hence, 'Hackquakmithston'. Hackett is working with some fellow named 'Hopper' up north, helping slaves escape to Boston or Cleveland. They're trying to establish a more direct route, or at least an alternative, in case some of the others get shut down."

"Heard about it," said Mabin. "Mr. Higgins's slave tol' me 'n Toby. He say he knew of a connection if we knew any slaves dat was in trouble. We tol' him we didn' know of any right den."

Everyone sat quietly as they pondered the implications. Luke looked around the group and settled on Tal. "What do you think, Tal?" asked Luke, "Any gut feeling about this?"

Tal could feel all eyes on him as he fidgeted.

"I'm still havin' trouble thinkin' different from slave and massuh," he finally admitted.

"Fair enough," said Luke. Then he looked around at the others. "I'm not telling you what you should believe, or how you should think, but I will tell you what Matthew here has taught me, and what has become my belief. The Bible says, in I Peter Chapter 2, that God has created a whole new people. White men are not my people. Black men are not your people. Color is out, belief is in!"

"Amen to that!" injected Pastor Davies. "It's man, not God, who has messed this whole thing up."

Tal looked at Sadie and thought for a minute, and then cleared his throat and spoke. "Well then, suh, I think we should be ready for whatever might happen, so long as we don' push to make it happen. But it don' make sense t' have someone show up needin' help 'n then have t' wait for us to call a meetin' to decide just what to do."

Everyone was in agreement with Tal, to stick the toe into the water but not dive in the river quite yet.

"Where would we hide them?" asked Sally.

"In the root cellar, maybe?" suggested Sadie.

"That's the first place slave catchers look," said Matthew.

A light went on in Luke's mind. "Yes! The root cellar! With more people living and working here, we need to store more food. We're digging a second root cellar, down by the new dining hall."

"First place they'll check," Matthew insisted.

"We can dig it twice as long and put in a false wall. Once the supply shed is built over it, no one can tell how long the cellar is," Luke was getting excited.

"It might work," Tal said.

Matthew offered, "I could ask Henry to contact Bob Hackett for more information as to how the system works, but to tell him we're not ready to make any commitments, yet."

Mabin nodded thoughtfully, "Yes suh. Dat would be a good way to do it, suh."

The others agreed.

Luke scooted his chair up to the head of the table and poured himself a glass of water as he spoke.

"Let me fill you in on my latest slave purchases." He looked uncomfortably at Tal, Sadie, and Mabin. "I will continue to use those terms because of the social environment we have all been born into. But you are all aware that in my mind, you are all friends and employees, NOT 'purchases'."

"It has to be dat way, suh, for now. We understand," assured Mabin. "Maybe things change soon."

"Thank you, Mabin. I hope so. I appreciate you saying that." Luke took a sip of water, then looked at Matthew and continued. "I bought a pregnant woman named Dinah. I had the doctor come out, and he says that she's in good health and could deliver any day now."

Sally picked up the story. "Hope says Dinah is not a Christian. She is very bitter at the white man who took her man away. She says that if there is a God, he's not a very nice one."

"On the other hand," Sally continued, "Hope tells me that Mahta is a believer, and says that Mahta keeps telling Dinah that the Lord's watching her, and he'll show her that he's alive and he's good. Dinah always changes the subject right away."

"Speaking of the Lord being good," interrupted Sadie, "Mahta stood up today and limped around the room a couple of times."

"That in itself is a miracle," said Pastor Davies. "It sounds like Dinah is in good hands."

Everyone agreed.

"Washington is the man I bought the same day as Dinah," continued Luke. "He also is a believer, and he seems to be totally at peace with his life and his slavery. He says it's his calling, his ministry. He's suffered some for it too."

"We have an unusual percentage of Christians here, Pastor," said Sally. "Only two of our field workers aren't interested, and now Dinah. That's only three out of twelve."

"Twelve," Luke shook his head in amazement. "In only a few months, I've doubled the number of slaves."

"It's not whether you own zero or twelve, and it's not whether you're slave or free. It's the heart, not the situation or the color," Matthew explained. "Do you love Jesus, and have you repented for what he had to go through for you? *That* is what God is concerned about."

"Well, twelve may just be the beginning," said Luke, "You'll never guess where I'm going on Friday."

Everyone looked at Luke, waiting for him to continue.

"I'm going to visit Jerry Ellis."

Matthew sat back in his chair and crossed his arms, "Isn't he the one we believe shot Mahta?"

Luke nodded his affirmation, "He said he wanted to unload a couple of lost causes that would fit right in, because I am also a lost cause. I think I surprised him when I said I'd drop by." Luke paused and smiled, "However, I don't think he believes I'll show up. I'd like everyone here to pray about my little 'shopping' trip."

The clatter of two shovels being tossed into an empty wheelbarrow brought Luke's mind back to the present. "Ted and Nathan, I want you to unload this lumber on the flat area between the dining hall and the root cellar. Once you've finished, grab some shovels from the tool shed and help Toby and the boys get that hole dug. After lunch, I'll be hauling a load of cotton back to town and will bring back another load of boards."

Luke turned from watching Frank and Joshua to see Gideon coming from the field with a wagon filled with baskets of fresh cotton. "I'd better go help Gideon get those baskets off and get the clean cotton loaded. I'll send him over here to fetch one of these empty wagons to take back out to the field." He turned his attention to Ted and Nathan. "As you can see, we've got a lot going on. I sure am glad to have both of you here."

The boys set off to unload the wagons as Luke headed quickly to the gin house. Luke stopped short just inside the door, totally surprised at what he saw. Hope was stooped over the cotton gin turning on the crank handle. Sadie, with much effort, was dragging a full basket over to the gin as Sally fed cotton into the hopper. All three women were in a deep sweat, working hard. Sitting in two chairs near them, were Dinah and Mahta. Dinah was sewing a dress that lay across her expanded belly, with Mahta carefully watching Dinah's hands and giving instructions.

No one had seen him enter, and all five women instantly turned to look at him.

"What a wonderful sight," said Luke, "five beautiful ladies, all working together in one place. It sure is good to see everyone up and around," said Luke, looking at Mahta and Dinah.

Sally, Hope, and Sadie all smiled. Standing up from the basket, Sadie brushed off her dress and said, "Don't know about five, Massuh, but four beautiful ladies will still be here after I leave to fix lunch for you all."

As she headed off to the kitchen, Gideon arrived and began unloading the wagon.

Sally finished filling the hopper and walked over to give Luke a big hug. "A few months ago, I was surrounded by men." She looked up at Luke, "Not that there's anything wrong with men, of course. But I'm so happy having these girls around." She gave Luke another tight hug. "I just can't explain it, but it's great!"

"You don't have to explain it," smiled Luke, as he gazed fondly at his wife. "I can't imagine being the only guy on a farm full of women."

"Well!" Sally pushed him away in a pretend huff. Luke quickly held up both hands, as if fending her off. "I'm just saying it's good to have a little of both. Now calm down, girl, 'cause I don't want to have to sleep in the barn tonight." He heard Mahta give a quiet chuckle.

Sally held the pout on her face, "Well, okay then, but you watch what you say about women 'cause if you don't, you'll be sleeping in the outhouse - not the barn!" Spinning around with her chin in the air and a proud smile on her face, she returned to the gin and resumed filling the hopper.

Gideon had climbed up onto the back of the wagon, listening to the bantering. He gave a quiet, shy laugh, "Best leave it there, Massuh, lessn you can sleep standin' up."

"You're right at that, Gideon, "agreed Luke. "Beautiful women always get the best of a man. We'd better get to work or I'll stop getting fed, too."

"Yessuh," Gideon handed a basket down to Luke. "Don't want that, now, do we?"

"No, we sure don't!" chuckled Luke.

As Luke sat at the table with Frank and Sally eating lunch, his mind was on Gideon. Luke wondered what that healthy young man really thought of what he heard in the gin house.

"Luke?" He looked up as Sally spoke his name. "This might sound silly, but would it be wrong to shop for a couple more girls? Not so I'd have more women around me. I'm thinking of young girls."

"Girls? Zekiel and Gideon's age?" interrupted Frank.

Sally and Luke both stared at him.

"Are you sure you're only twelve?" Luke finally asked. "You're starting to worry me."

"No, sir, I'm gonna be thirteen next week!"

"Amazing," Luke said as they both continued to stare at Frank.

"I saw Toby and Hope walking down by the river and they was holding hands," said Frank.

"They *were* holding hands," Sally corrected.

"Yeah, they were. You saw 'em too, huh?" answered Frank.

"They were?" interrupted Luke.

"No. I mean, no, I didn't see them," said Sally.

"I did," smiled Frank, proudly. "And it was my idea."

"What was?" asked Luke, looking a little confused.

"Buying Hope, Pa," said Frank with some frustration in his voice. "Don't you remember?"

"I remember." Luke looked thoughtfully at his plate for a while as he pushed the beans around with his fork. "I was thinking the same thing," he said.

"About buying Hope?" asked his surprised, almost thirteen-year-old, son.

"No, Frank. I was speaking of your mother's idea about girls, and Gideon, and some of the others."

"I was the one that said that about Gideon and Zekiel." corrected Frank, not wanting to miss out on the credit. "I even thought about 'em last night, while Toby and Hope was sittin on a rock throwin' stones in the river."

"They *were* sittin' on a rock," corrected Luke.

"You saw 'em, too?"

"No, Frank!" said his mother. "We are talking about using 'was' instead of 'were'."

"Oh. Right," said Frank. "Sorry."

"Well, it appears that the entire Martin family is on the same track with this one, so I'll keep my eyes open and see if the Lord agrees." Luke scooted his chair away from the table and stood up. "It's time for me to get to Grantsville. There's a lot to do if I'm going to squeeze in a visit with Jerry Ellis."

Chapter 30

"Well, what do you know? Look who's coming," Jerry stood on his porch and pointed to Luke, coming through the gate.

Del took a large gulp of whiskey from the bottle he was holding. "My ex-neighbor has come a-callin'," said Del. "Did you invite him to supper?"

Jerry shook his head, "I told him I'd sell him Ambrose and the idiot. Martin's not stupid. He knew I was pushing him. I was just havin' some fun. I didn't think he'd show up, though."

"Maybe he's stupider than you thought," Del replied, "or maybe he's playing with you and calling your bluff, leading you on a little."

Jerry gave a sly smile, as he watched Luke pull his wagon up to the house. "I'd be the winner of this game if I could unload them two problem children onto Martin's back and get 'em off mine."

Sauntering down the steps, Jerry inspected the load of lumber in Luke's wagon. "Looks like you're gonna try to build somethin'. A home, maybe? For those two slaves you're buying from me?"

Luke remained seated on the wagon. "Didn't say I was buying. I just said I'd have a look, and here I am."

Jerry nodded and gave him a mocking smile. "Well, here you are, at that. A man of your word." He turned to Del, still sitting in the shade of the porch. "Del, go fetch Ambrose from the field and tell Glenn to find the idiot. He's probably back of the barn, talkin to the hogs."

Del stood and reluctantly walked down the steps, glaring

menacingly at Luke. Luke noticed the bottle in his hand. He gave Del a polite smile, "I haven't seen you across the river lately."

"Got a better job," Del said without any emotion, as he walked away.

Luke climbed down from the wagon, then removed a handkerchief from his back pocket to wipe the sweat and dust from his face.

Jerry couldn't resist throwing jabs at people he disliked. "You must not have anything better to do with your day than to waste your time looking at losers. I told you they weren't any good." He was trying to embarrass Luke into buying the slaves. "If you had any common sense, you would have stayed home."

Luke ignored the comments. "Why do you call the one an idiot?"

"Cuz he is!" said Ellis. "He can't even get the right food to the right animals. And he swears that the animals talk to him. I tell him to take water out to the nigras in the field and I find him giving the water to the pigs 'n goats instead." Jerry folded his arms and smirked, "Whippin' him don't do no good at all. He just gets dumber afterwards. Yesterday afternoon, I found him sleepin' with the cows under the shade tree. He said he was talkin with his family when he dozed off."

Luke chuckled and said, "Sounds like you got yourself some pretty steady entertainment."

"You wasted your time, Martin. You can't say I didn't warn you." Jerry was pleased with himself, for having lured in a sucker.

"It wouldn't be the first time, Jerry. And it won't be the last. I mess up every once in a while, just like everyone else." Luke wiped his face with his handkerchief again. "Hot and muggy today," he said. "Maybe you're right. I should've stayed home and gone swimming."

"You'll find out, soon enough. Here they come," said Jerry.

Del and Glenn were pushing two black men ahead of them. The larger of the two slaves was drenched in sweat and was wearing ankle chains. The other was not sweating at all, and as they approached the wagon, he looked up to the sky and waved at a couple of crows as they flew overhead. He had the look of a man lost in his own world, who wasn't even aware of the other people around him.

"I need a few minutes alone with them," said Luke.

"What for?" asked Jerry.

"I'd like to talk to them, and ask a few questions, and then maybe pray about it."

Del, who had been taking a swig from the bottle, suddenly sprayed the whiskey from his mouth as he burst out in laughter. Glenn and Jerry joined in the revelry.

"So when it's all said and done," Jerry laughed, "you can blame God?"

Luke just relaxed and leaned against his wagon, looking at them as if they were a bunch of goofy children. When they finally calmed down, Jerry looked at Luke and said, "Sure, go ahead, Martin. Do your thing. We'll be up on the porch in the shade." They turned and left him standing with the two slaves.

The smaller slave bent down and tried to get an ant to climb onto his finger.

"What's your name?" asked Luke. "I know it's not 'Idiot'."

"Don' make no differnce, now do it?" replied the man, as he intently watched the ant. "Dey don' call me it, nohow."

Luke squatted down beside him and looked into his eyes, "Do you get a lot of rest, sleeping with the cows?"

Luke detected a twinkle in the slave's eyes as he focused on Luke for a second.

"Might say so. Sun gits hot. Cows fine shade 'n sof' grass to lie on. Ain' bad place t' be." He stood up and watched the ant scurry up his arm.

Luke stayed squatted for a moment and looked at the other slave's bleeding ankles. It was clear that he wore the chains day and night. It took Luke a moment to bring his anger under control, and then he stood up.

"Why the chains, Ambrose?" he asked.

Ambrose stared straight ahead and showed no emotion as he responded. "They say I needs 'em, suh."

"What would you do if the chains were gone?"

"I go, suh."

Luke nodded, "At least you're honest." He leaned against the wagon and said a prayer asking for direction, and then he asked

Ambrose, "Where would you go? And why would I want to pay a lot of money for you if you were just gonna run off?"

"No reason to pay money, suh. I can't stay."

"Even if I treated you well? No chains, no beatings, good food, clothes, and shelter?" asked Luke.

"No, suh. Gotta find my Dinah, suh," Ambrose answered.

Luke froze. His jaw dropped and he stared at Ambrose. Suddenly he had butterflies in his stomach and he could almost feel the goose bumps go up his back.

"My Lord and my God!" Luke mumbled to himself.

The two slaves looked each other, puzzled by his reaction.

Luke spun around and walked determinedly around the wagon and up the steps to the porch.

"How much?" he asked, looking down at Jerry as he sat in his chair.

Jerry laughed, but remained seated, "I knew those two would fit right in at your place."

"I only want Ambrose," replied Luke with firmness in his voice that caught Jerry's attention.

Jerry stared at him as if trying to read into his mind and find out why Luke was suddenly so intense. "He'll run on ya."

"Maybe. Maybe not."

"You're dumber than the idiot over there. You must like throwing money away. Of course, I don't mind helping you out in that," said Jerry. Then his expression changed as he realized, "Oh, I get it! You think you'll get him saved and he'll turn into a little angel slave. That's it, ain't it?" Jerry stood up. "This'll be a fun one to watch, Martin. He won't be around long enough for you to say 'In the beginning' if you take those chains off."

Del's and Glenn's laughter suddenly seemed to irritate Ellis. He turned and said, "You two get on back out to the field. Them negroes is probably all sound asleep by now!"

Del and Glenn quickly got up out of their chairs and left. Jerry grabbed the whiskey bottle out of Del's hand as he went by. "Take the idiot with you. I guess I'm stuck with him!"

When they had gone and the paperwork was done, Luke drove the wagon out through the gate, loaded with wood and what Luke was pretty sure was a miracle. Ambrose was high atop the stack of lumber where he couldn't see the huge smile on Luke's face.

It was almost too dark to see the road in front of him when Luke pulled off Town Road and started up the drive to his house. He couldn't remember when he had been more excited, and so he was a little disappointed to be arriving so late. He could only see a couple of oil lamps glowing from the kitchen windows. The rest of the house was dark. The yard lanterns were burning and he saw a lone figure, about the size of Otis, walking to the men's bunkhouse. By the time he pulled into the barnyard, there was no one in sight. There was light coming from the window of the bunkhouse, and from Tal and Sadie's place. He hopped off the wagon and tied the horses to a post. A horse neighed from the corral and one of his team horses responded. The door of the bunkhouse opened and Toby stepped outside.

"Dat you, Massuh?" he called.

"Yeah, Toby, I'm back," answered Luke. "Could a couple of you fellas come out here and give me a hand please?"

Toby disappeared inside and then reappeared with Mabin and Otis. When they arrived at the wagon, Luke pointed up to the man sitting on top of the stack of lumber. "Could you help Ambrose get down from there? He's got ankle chains on, and it was hard enough getting him up there. I don't want him breaking a leg getting down."

The three sprung into action and in a matter of seconds he was on the ground.

"Welcome to the Martin farm, Ambrose," said Luke. "Otis, would you unhitch the horses and feed and brush them? Mabin, would you go to the house and ask Sally and Frank to come out here? And Toby, I need you to get Hope, and ask her to bring along her newest roommate, please."

When they were gone, Luke turned to Ambrose. "Ellis tells me you are from Savannah. Is that true?"

"Yessuh, it is," said Ambrose.

Luke was beginning to feel like a little kid at Christmas time. He smiled at Ambrose as he took a key out of his pocket. "Then I think you won't be needing these chains any longer." He knelt down and unlocked the chains and they fell to the ground.

As he stood back up, Ambrose spoke apologetically, "I tol' you I won' be stayin', suh."

Luke held up his hands with palms out. "You owe me something for taking the chains off. Give me a few minutes before you decide to leave or stay, okay?" he asked excitedly. "I've got a real good hunch that you'll want to stay."

Ambrose thought for a minute, somewhat perplexed at the tone of the request.

"Yessuh," he answered.

The sound of women's voices could be heard in the darkness.

"One more favor. Take these chains into the barn and stay there until I call for you." The voices were getting louder. "Hurry!" Luke urged anxiously.

Ambrose vanished into the blackness as the group arrived. Luke tried to act calm as he leaned against the corral fence. Mabin and Toby were glancing around, wondering where Ambrose had gone. Toby almost asked, but Luke caught his eye and shook his head.

"Is something wrong, Luke?" Sally asked, as she walked up to her husband.

Luke acted surprised. "Wrong? No, nothing's wrong. As a matter of fact, I think something's real good." He paused and smiled, "I want to show you all what I brought home from my trip to town this afternoon." Heads turned and stared at the wagonload of lumber.

"It's just wood, Pa. What's so great about wood?" Frank asked.

"Not the wood, Frank. It's what was *on* the wood that I want to show you."

All eyes glanced to the top of the stack of wood and then quickly back to Luke.

Dinah felt a contraction coming on but was afraid to let on. Sally finally realized that Luke was playing with them and decided to give him a push.

"Well, I am completely and thoroughly blessed to see all that wood, and my husband home safely, but I am now going back to my sewing. I've got clothes to make." She turned to the house, pretending that she was going to leave.

"No, no, Sal. This is better than wood, or even me for that matter, if you can believe that." Luke turned and called to the barn, "You can come out, now."

Sally stopped and turned around, just in time to see a lone figure step slowly out of the shadows. Dinah's contraction was fading now as she also watched the man step into the torchlight. She became confused. The man resembled her own man Ambrose, but in the low light she couldn't be sure. She took a couple of steps forward to see more clearly, and as she did, she also stepped into the light of the lantern that Mabin was holding.

Luke noticed that Ambrose was looking humbly at the ground, as he had been trained to do. "Look up here, Ambrose. I want you to see something," he urged.

"Ambrose?" said Dinah, in an almost whisper.

Ambrose heard his name and looked past Luke to the woman standing in the lantern light. Recognition exploded in his head and his eyes grew as round as saucers. Without thinking, he took a couple of steps forward, then the years of harsh training took over and he remembered his place. He stopped and looked back at Luke.

"I think they know each other, Sally," Luke said, as he watched the tears well up in Dinah's eyes.

Sally was in a state of shock. She nodded silently while searching for words that didn't come.

Hope suddenly took over and gleefully clapped her hands and gently began pushing Dinah forward. "God gives a gift, you grab it! Dere's your gift, Dinah." She gave a little squeal and jumped on Toby's back and hugged him. "Oh, Toby, I can't bleve it!" she exclaimed.

Ambrose looked pleadingly at Luke.

Luke smiled at him. "I thought I might have a pretty good reason for you not to run away." He nodded towards Dinah. "Go ahead, Ambrose. I think your search has ended."

Ambrose and Dinah approached each other with slow, hesitant steps. Tears were now flowing freely down Dinah's cheeks.

Sally finally found her voice and spoke to the group. "It's time for the rest of us to get on home, now."

"Yes, ma'am, I bleve tis," Mabin agreed. "Cmon, fellas, let's go finish our supper."

Staying in the mood of things, Toby said, "I'll walk Hope home, Mabin. Then Ibe back to eat, so save me some." He took Hope's hand and they walked into the darkness, both looking over their shoulders at the new couple.

Mabin got Ambrose's attention and pointed to the bunkhouse. "We gots an empty bed down there wid us when you gets ready to turn in."

"Thank you, suh," Ambrose responded politely.

Mabin and Zekiel headed to the bunkhouse, talking and giggling about Toby and Hope.

Luke, Sally, and Frank were halfway to the house when they all three couldn't resist taking another peek. As if on cue, they all looked back over their shoulders and saw Ambrose and Dinah looking down at her stomach. Dinah had her hands on top of his, holding them against her belly. Then Ambrose leaned over the large protrusion and kissed his girl in the lantern light.

"Ahem!" Sally pretended to clear her throat. "This is shameful! Here we are, all being nosy. Turn around and leave them to themselves." They all quickly faced the house. "I've got some cake inside to celebrate with," she added.

"This is kinda like a miracle farm, ain't it, Pa? This stuff just keeps happening," said Frank happily.

"A year ago you were telling me this place was boring, Frank," Luke smiled down at his son as they went up the steps.

"Well, it ain't boring no more!"

"Isn't boring," corrected his mother.

"No, ma'am, it sure isn't."

As Luke reached out to open the screened door, they heard someone yell. They all walked back to the porch railing.

Ambrose yelled again, "Someone, come quick!"

Chapter 31

Ambrose, with Dinah leaning heavily against him, was looking desperately to his new masters for help. In a matter of seconds, the couple was surrounded by the Martins, along with Toby, Hope, and Mabin. "Don' know what happen! She say she were gettin all dizzy and den she groan 'n hold her stomach." Ambrose was clearly frightened.

Dinah gave out a low groan. She continued to lean on him with her eyes closed. Sally noticed the moisture on her dress and told Frank to run and get some blankets from Tal and Sadie.

"Is she gonna die, Mama?" asked Frank.

Ambrose stiffened and looked at Sally through watery eyes.

Sally looked directly back at Ambrose as she spoke to Frank. "Nobody's dying tonight, Frank. Dinah has had these dizzy spells before, but tonight something's very different." Then Sally broke into a smile, "Dinah was waiting for her man. Now it's time for her to deliver his baby."

"Wow!" whooped Frank. "You gotta be kiddin me! Tal! Sadie!" he yelled into the night as he ran to get them, "Mama needs some blankets, quick! You gotta see this!" His voice faded with him.

Sally was still smiling at Ambrose.

"You mean it, ma'am?" he finally looked hopeful. "She gonna be okay?"

Sally nodded and felt Dinah's belly as she groaned again. "She's having another contraction. Her water broke."

The fear returned to Ambrose's face. "Sumthin's broke? Dat can't be good!"

Sally smiled and put her hand on his shoulder. "This time it is good. It means God opened the door and someone's coming out to meet papa and mama."

Ambrose let out a big breath in relief.

"Ambrose?" Dinah spoke his name as she opened her eyes and looked up at him.

"I'm here, girl. I ain't leavin!" The emotions of the moment had become too great and he broke down and cried. "I swear I ain't leavin."

With Sally leading the way, Ambrose and Luke helped Dinah to her bed. Sadie and Hope both set about boiling water on their woodstoves. Toby brought a fresh bucket of water to each of the houses.

Mahta was sitting at the table casually sipping some tea and watching Dinah. The room seemed particularly crowded this night as it filled with anxious, curious onlookers. Though it was beginning to cool down outside, the stove and the extra bodies made it quite stuffy.

Dinah groaned more intensely than before. She was sweating profusely as she spoke to Ambrose. "You go on, now. I'll be jus' fine."

Ambrose shook his head with determination. "I ain't goin' nowhere, girl! I jus' found you again!"

"I'll be right here, Ambrose. You jus' have to go out for awhile." Her words faded right into another groan as the contractions closed in on her.

Sally faced the men. "Gentlemen, it's time for you all to step outside."

"Aw, Mama! Do we have to?" Frank whined.

"No room for arguing on this one," Sally planted her feet firmly and folded her arms. "Well?" There was a playful, yet menacing tone to her voice.

Mabin put his arm on Ambrose' shoulder. "C'mon, my friend. You don' want to argue with her. Nothin' good *ever* comes from *dat*."

"That's for sure!" chuckled Luke.

"I heard that, you two!" Sally grinned, "Remember the outhouse!"

"Outhouse?" asked Mabin as they all stepped outside.

"The outhouse is my doghouse, since we haven't got a dog," Luke answered.

"Oh, I see," nodded Mabin, as if he understood. Then he gave a confused glance Luke's way as the door closed behind them.

As Frank and the five men stepped off of the porch, Frank asked, "Where's Ambrose gonna sleep, Pa?"

Luke put his hand to his chin and gave the question some thought as they all walked to the barnyard.

Tal broke off from the group and headed to bed. Mabin decided to help Luke out with the decision. "He be sleepin' in d' bunkhouse with us tonight. We gots a couple empty beds."

"That'd be jus' fine, suh," said Ambrose.

"Pa, look at his ankles!" Frank exclaimed, as he stopped and stared.

Because of the distractions of the moment, Luke had failed to notice that when the ankle chains had fallen off, raw, infected skin and muscle had also been ripped off. As the men looked down, it was clear to all of them that Ambrose had not had the chains off for months. There was no skin left, and his feet were soaked in blood.

A fresh wave of anger swept over Luke as he thought of Jerry Ellis.

"Toby!" he said, sharply.

"Yessuh."

"The chains are in the barn. Take them to the river. I don't ever want to see them again!"

"Yessuh," Toby immediately changed directions and headed to the barn.

"I'll jus' wash up, suh," said Ambrose.

Luke shook his head. "If we don't deal with the infection, you could lose your feet. For your family's sake and your own, we need to soak them in whiskey and wrap them up until we get the doctor to look at them."

Luke and Frank went up to the house and Mabin took Ambrose to the bunkhouse to clean his wounds. Luke sent Frank back to the bunkhouse with bandages and the whiskey bottle from the medicine shelf. It had been decided that when Ambrose was bandaged and taken care of, they would all meet on Hope's porch and hang around until the ladies could tell them the results. Luke brought biscuits, jerky, and coffee.

Toby went on to bed, but young Frank and the other three men settled in, side by side on the edge of the porch, staring at a lantern that Mabin had set on the ground three feet in front of them. They listened to the women's voices and Dinah's occasional groaning inside the shack as they nibbled the food and sipped their coffee.

At one point, Ambrose shook his head in wonder and asked, "How'd you know, suh?"

Luke understood the question. "I asked my family and friends here to pray. And I said a short prayer when I was there. It's not just a coincidence that real soon after that, you said you had to find your girl, Dinah, and that you were from Savannah."

Ambrose did not respond. He just took another bite of biscuit and stared at the lamplight.

After a period of silence, Luke said, "This has been quite an extraordinary year here on the farm, Ambrose. God has been leading me in ways I would never have imagined." He let out a long slow breath. "But I've gotta say, I was not a bit prepared for what he did for you and Dinah. I still feel kind of stunned, setting here with you right now."

Ambrose studied Luke's face for a moment and then turned back to the lantern.

"If things go well tonight, suh," the slave paused, then continued, "well den, I has some things I needs to think about."

Dinah gave out a louder groan and the men sat silently, listening. They could hear voices but couldn't understand what the women were saying. They heard a strange, but faint, squeaking sound, but couldn't quite place what it was. Three of the men sat and listened intently. The fourth, and smallest one, had leaned his head against a post and was snoring softly.

The women were speaking more quietly now and could hardly be heard at all from out on the porch. Tension began to build in Ambrose. He shifted and turned an ear to the door and listened carefully. Possibly a faint squeak, but other than that, nothing. They waited. There was the sound of a metal pail bumping into a chair or something, and then Luke thought he heard Sally say something.

"Maybe I'll check and see how things are going in there," Luke said, as he stood up.

Ambrose and Mabin looked relieved. They had been wishing he would do so a long time ago.

Luke raised his hand to knock on the door, but it opened before he connected. Sally stood in the doorway, a little surprised to see him.

"I was just coming to find you. Where is Ambrose?"

At the mention of his name, Ambrose stood and came to the door. Sally looked across the porch and saw Frank, asleep against the post, and Mabin, still seated but waiting anxiously for whatever news she had to offer.

Sally returned her attention to Ambrose and saw the worried look. She gave him a comforting smile and said, "It went well." Then she curtsied and added, "Your son awaits you, sir," as she stepped to the side.

Ambrose was flooded with relief, but was hesitant to enter the room. Luke gave him a nudge from behind and said, "Go on, Papa. Your family's waiting."

Ambrose slowly entered the building, and Sally stepped out onto the porch to invite the others inside. Mabin nudged Frank awake. "C'mon, young suh. You got sumthin' to see." It took only a moment for the fog to lift, then Frank jumped to his feet, gave another whoop, and ran for the door, only to be blocked by his mother.

"Oh no, you don't!" she spoke firmly. "You will go in there quietly and in a gentlemanly fashion, or you won't go in at all!"

Frank gave a low groan, then drew himself up to his full height and entered quietly and politely. Luke and Mabin followed close behind, each removing their hats as they approached the bed.

Sally was the last to enter and made sure the men understood that they could only stay for a few minutes. She stood beside Mahta, who still sat in the chair enjoying her cup of tea. Sally noticed that the room had filled with the comforting aroma of her men. A mixture of hay, cotton, barnyard dirt, and sweat. Strangely enough, it made her feel good.

Mahta chuckled at the sight of the three and a half men, standing in a line beside the bed, clutching their hats to their chests looking down with as much reverence as they would have if they were in church.

"Wow!" Frank finally whispered.

Ambrose, starting with a whimper, began to cry. No one in the room could know what he had gone through to get to this moment. The fear, the despair, the beatings, the anger, the pain, the determination, and finally, the grudging desperate prayer he had offered up to the God that he was so furious with. And now, here he was, looking at the son that he had had no idea God was preparing for him.

Sally and Hope were both wiping their eyes, trying not to make a scene.

Dinah opened her eyes at the sound of his crying. Ambrose tried to pull himself together but only accomplished a weak smile through more tears.

Dinah didn't say a word. She just returned the smile and lifted her son to his father.

As he drew the baby to his chest, Ambrose heard Luke say, "He looks jus' like you, Ambrose - only much, *much* smaller."

Ambrose immediately became concerned. He turned to Luke all flustered and began to ramble, "Oh, suh! I forgots my place! I surely didn' mean to be like this. I guess I forgot *you* was here. I mean, I forgot where *I* was!"

Luke smiled and was about to speak when Hope interrupted and said, "Missuh Ambrose, suh? It's okay. Massuh Martin, he don' mind." As Ambrose and the others turned to her, she smiled and added, "It's different here!"

"That it is," Sally quickly agreed. "Now, I think it's time to take *my* men home and put them to bed. Mabin, you must be getting kinda sleepy yourself," she hinted, making eye contact and giving him an instructional smile, along with a nod of her head.

"Oh, yes'm. I mus' be. I guess I be gettin' on home 'n take a lil nap. I be needin' to get up soon and start cookin' breakfast." With his eyes on Sally, he nodded his head toward Ambrose, who was now looking down in amazement at his son.

"Ambrose will be along soon. Leave a lantern lit in the yard," Sally responded. Then she added, "Frank. Luke. We need to be going."

Frank yawned and then stood on his toes to reach up and rub the baby's head. "Can I see him in the morning, Mama?"

"Everyone will be wanting to see him, but we musn't overwhelm Dinah. You'll see him when they're both well rested." She guided them toward the door, "C'mon now, you guys. Let's be going."

As the group filed out of the room they overheard Ambrose saying, in amazement, "He don' weigh nothin' at all, Dinah. He don' weigh nothin' at all!"

Hope closed the door and walked over to the woodstove. She poured herself a cup of tea and refilled Mahta's cup. "Would either of you like sumthin' to drink?" she asked, as she placed the pot back on the stove.

Dinah thought some cool water would be nice, but Ambrose scarcely heard her.

As Hope poured from the water pitcher and handed Dinah her tin of water, no one spoke a word. Peace had enveloped the room, and nobody wanted to disturb it. Hope sat down in the chair across from Mahta and silently watched Dinah watching Ambrose watch the baby. It wasn't long however, before the baby began to squirm and squeak and then give out a cry of discomfort. Ambrose tried a few different ways of holding him but nothing seemed to quiet the boy down.

"I'll take him now, Ambrose." Dinah reached up and received the baby, as her man willingly handed him to her. She took the baby to her chest, and Ambrose sat down on the bed beside her and took her hand. With teary eyes, he sat watching the most beautiful sight he had ever seen, and for a fleeting moment, he wondered if this had anything to do with the prayer he had prayed. Peace had once again entered the room.

But the quiet was soon interrupted when Mahta snickered, and commented in a low voice to Hope, "I guess dere's a few things a papa jus' can't do."

Probably because they were so tired, the old woman and the young girl got the giggles. They covered their mouths with their hands, but they just couldn't stop.

The family across the room didn't even seem to notice.

Chapter 32

"I'm beginning to feel a little overwhelmed, Sally."

The worn-out couple lay in bed listening to the rooster as he proudly pointed out to all the late risers that he was fully awake and on duty. They could smell the coffee and hear Sadie clanging pots in the kitchen as she prepared breakfast. Luke would normally have been up an hour ago, but this morning, he couldn't bring himself to get out of bed.

Sally lay on her back, staring at the ceiling. "Feels kind of like riding a runaway horse, hanging on for dear life."

Luke agreed. "The cotton is piled high in the barn *and* in the gin house waiting for us. Ted and Nathan should be getting here any time to finish the root cellar. The posts are set, and the lumber is stacked and waiting for someone to get the time to build the eating house. And now, with this latest, unexpected twist, we need to come up with housing for a small family."

Luke groaned, and then threw his legs over the edge of the bed and sat up. "I didn't give Mabin any instructions for Ambrose, but all of the other men, and the boys, have been in the fields since before sunup. And like a lazy taskmaster, here I sit."

Sally rolled over on the bed to sit behind Luke and rub his neck. Luke let his head drop. "And here I shall stay," he said with another groan. "But I'm going to feel sooo… guilty."

Sally smiled, "Sadie's going to all of that work, making us breakfast. I suppose we should go down and eat it. Don't you think so?"

Luke raised his head and arched his back, as Sally dug her thumbs into his back. "Eventually, I suppose."

Sally leaned forward and spoke into his ear, "It'll get cold."

Luke nodded in agreement and said, "Ain't nothing worse than cold oatmeal."

He got up from the bed and stretched. "Dear Lord, give us strength!"

Sally rolled back over to her side of the bed and hopped up. "Looks like it'll be a while longer before we have bacon for breakfast. No time to slaughter pigs yet."

As Luke buttoned his shirt, he suddenly remembered that he hadn't told Sally about Ambrose's ankles. He filled her in as they finished dressing. "I should leave right after breakfast and fetch the doctor. He can check on Ambrose's family at the same time."

"You don't suppose the Lord would do us a favor and make the sun stand still until we get caught up, do you?" Sally asked, as they went down the stairs.

"I'll settle for the moon standing still tonight, so we can catch up on our sleep."

"Goood morning, Sadie," greeted Luke with a yawn as they stepped into the kitchen.

"Hi, Sadie," said Sal, and then added, "Sorry we're so late."

"Mornin', suh. Mornin', ma'am. Got some coffee, biscuits and fresh eggs this mornin'." Sadie set two cups on the table and filled them with coffee. "I bin noticing Mr. Ambrose pacin' back 'n forth down by the men's place. He looks to be limpin' some, suh."

Sally hurried to the window and looked out. "The poor man. I suppose he's anxious to see his family."

Sadie placed a plate with three biscuits and four eggs on the table in front of Luke. "Thank you, Sadie," he said, as he broke open a biscuit and spread a thick layer of butter on both halves. "You'll have to let the dust settle here in the house, today. I really need you and Sal to do what you can, down at the gin house. I'll go fetch the doctor and Sal will take Ambrose down to visit Dinah at Hope's place." Luke looked up from his plate. "And Sal, if everybody's okay down there, we need to have Hope help you two girls work the cotton. Ambrose can fetch you if the others need anything."

Sally salted her eggs. "Just don't go bringing anyone back with you - with the exception of the doctor, of course. It seems like nearly every time you leave, someone follows you home. Would you slide that butter plate over here, please?"

Luke pushed the butter to his wife. "Today, I intend to shop for seed potatoes, peanuts, a doctor, and that's all. Oh, yes, and more lumber, and that's all. Oh yeah, and that dress cloth you asked for, and that's all."

Sadie chuckled and added, "And whatever *else* the Lord sends home with you, suh." Then she added, "An thas' all."

"Humph!" Luke slid an egg off of his fork onto a biscuit and stuffed a large bite into his mouth. He sat quietly chewing because his cheeks were too full to respond to Sally's witty comment of agreement with Sadie. As they giggled to themselves, he swallowed and pushed away from the table, stood and took one last gulp of coffee to wash everything down. He placed his empty cup down on the table and said, as he walked to the door, "I'm going to go hitch up the wagon. The horses don't give me nearly so much guff as I get around here."

Abel was enjoying standing in the shade and supervising his fellow slaves as they dug in the rain-softened ground and placed posts for the new, and slightly larger, slaves' quarters. He had decided that, as field boss, he should have nicer quarters, so he planned to move Big Joe and his family into a small shack, and he would take over one of the larger, new buildings. Of course, the old shack would be too small for Joe's family *and* the new young slave girl who had been living with them, so Abel had decided to help solve the problem by, conveniently, letting her stay with him in his new home. She had been rather standoffish around the male slaves, but he told himself that she just needed to get to know him better.

Abel leaned comfortably against the large Magnolia tree and watched the scene before him. Every man, woman, and child, (except Abel, of course) worked at clearing away the old and rebuilding the new. He smiled as he thought of their resemblance to a colony of black ants repairing a damaged ant hill.

Abel noticed with some irritation that the massuh was coming from the eating house carrying a bucket of drinking water in each hand. Belle was walking along behind carrying a basket of bread, and one of fruit.

The massuh was making Abel look bad. Didn't he understand that bosses were 'sposed to supervise the work, not actually *do* the work? He grunted in frustration and stepped into the sun and walked to Tom. When they met, Tom set the buckets on the ground and said, "Time to give 'em a break." Then he turned and walked back to the house.

Abel guessed that the massuh might be expecting him to pick up the buckets and take them on down to the nearest workers, but that was not a precedent he wanted to set. Instead, he instructed Belle to set the baskets down, and then he turned and cracked his whip in the air, calling the slaves to come to *him*.

When they had all arrived and had each received their portion, Abel gave the instructions for the afternoon.

"D' cotton won' dry fo' nother day or two, so I wants you to work on finishin' d' house nearest de eatin' house. Dat will be mine; sooner I gets out of my ol' shack, d' sooner Joe 'n his family kin move in it."

In response to the scattering of puzzled looks, he added, "I knows it'll be too crowded fo' Rena to stay wit Joe's family, so she be staying wid me in d' new house." He patted the palm of his hand with the handle of the bullwhip. "Any questions?" he asked.

Rena's eyes clouded over as a mental numbness swept over her. "So dis is it," she thought to herself. "Dis is what's in store for me. And ain't nothin' I can do about it."

"No, Missuh Abel. We kin fit her in wid us, even if tis a little crowded." Big Joe spoke in a voice that Abel detected as a little unsure, even though Joe was the larger, and stronger, of the two men. Abel understood that this was a defining moment, and it was critical that he establish his authority swiftly, leaving no doubt in anyone's mind as to who was in charge.

There was a fleeting moment of silence. Suddenly, Abel raised his hand and swung the whip behind him and then sent it forward, aiming to give a warning snap by Big Joe's left ear. With an instinctive twist of his head, Joe turned to his left to protect his face. But he wasn't quite fast enough, and the whip struck his right eye with a loud crack. In an instant he was on the ground writhing in pain, holding his face in his hands.

Joe's four-year-old daughter stood frozen in place and started to cry. His wife and son fell to their knees beside him screaming, wanting desperately to help him but not knowing what to do. As blood began to seep between Big Joe's fingers, his son flew into a rage and jumped to his feet and ran to Abel and began beating him in the chest with his fists. Abel was in a state of shock, himself. He hadn't intended to actually strike Big Joe. He wasn't sure what he should do about this unintended consequence of his attempt to establish the pecking order. In fear and confusion, he pushed the young boy to the ground and backed away. He raised his whip as if to strike the boy in self defense. One of the slaves yelled his name, and he looked up to see some of the men running at him. Abel immediately dropped his whip and turned to run. He took about three steps before he was tackled by the angry mob, and they began to beat him.

It wasn't long before a loud explosion brought an end to the melee. Everyone rolled off of Abel and scrambled backwards away from the noise in fear. When they got their wits about themselves, they all looked up to see Tom Grant standing over the scene, holding his now empty black powder rifle, still aimed at the sky.

As the smoke drifted away, the men remained frozen in place. They understood that the silence was like the calm in the eye of a hurricane. A bird flew out of the barn, as Tom glared down at the disheveled group of men. A child's whimper caused him to look over to the group huddled over Big Joe.

When Tom took his eyes off of him, Abel suddenly moved, intending to jump to his feet and run. Without hesitating, Tom dropped his empty rifle, and with a quickness that surprised even him, he drew his pistol from its holster and aimed it directly at the big man's chest.

"Don't nobody move a lick!" he shouted.

And nobody did, not even Tom. The tension in the air was palpable. Every nerve in Tom's body was on high alert. He watched and listened for any sign of movement as he gave himself time to think. He had no idea what had just happened but it appeared to him as if the slaves were in revolt.

He could hear Big Joe moaning and his family weeping over him. He chanced a glance in their direction and then quickly returned his attention to the others. Another glance, then quickly back again to the men.

"Belle, tell me what this is all about!" Tom was yelling but didn't know it. He was so high strung right now, if anyone would have moved even slightly, he would have pulled the trigger. He was keenly aware that if they chose to, this group of black men could over power him with very little effort.

"What's going on here, Belle?" he asked, but not quite as loud as before.

"Missuh Abel dun whip Joseph for no reason, suh." Belle had taken a big risk by speaking so boldly. If her master didn't believe her, she would be punished severely by Abel.

Tom thought about what she said. It was plausible. Abel did seem to love his job way too much. Tom noticed a small group of the young children huddled fearfully under a tree with some of the women. He had an idea.

"Belle, bring the children over here and don't let the women say anything to them before I talk to them. Bring them to me. Everybody else, stay put!" He raised his voice to emphasize how serious he was. His eyes bore through Abel as he watched Belle with his peripheral vision as she urged the children toward him. "Why don't all you fellas lie down and relax. Look for shapes in the clouds or somethin'," he added sarcastically. "I don't want anybody sittin' or standin' while I'm talking to the younguns'."

When the slaves all complied, Tom began to relax a bit. He lowered his gun and returned it to the holster. He recognized the boy standing in front of the smaller children. "William? Is that your little sister standin' there behind you?"

"Yessuh."

"How old is she?"

"She five, suh."

"What's her name?"

"Name Misha, suh."

"Well, Mister William, if I let you stand right there with her so she'll feel safer, do you think Misha will answer me a couple questions?"

William glanced uncertainly behind him to his mother; she nodded, concern in her eyes. Tom watched the boy's eyes as he turned back to his master, and nodded apprehensively. The boy appeared anxious to have a turn at telling the story himself.

"Misha?" Tom spoke gently. "It's okay, Misha. Come out and stand by William for a minute."

Misha peeked around her brother's leg and shook her braided head 'no'.

Tom looked to the men lying on the ground and reminded them to keep watching the clouds. He then knelt down to be closer to Misha's size, hoping to be less intimidating. But he was careful to have immediate access to his gun.

"Misha. Now that's a real pretty name for a real pretty girl." Tom forced a smile and concentrated on sounding calm and friendly, "Misha, can you tell me what happened so I can help everybody?" He raised his brow inquisitively and waited.

Soon, the little girl wrapped one arm around her brother's leg and, while still standing behind him, reached around front of William and pointed to Abel.

"Dat man, hurt dat man!" She spoke in a shy little voice as she then pointed to Big Joe. "Den dat boy, hurt dat man," Misha said, pointing back to Abel. "Den, dose mans hurts dat man too." Then she quickly disappeared behind her big brother.

"Thank you, Misha. That was real helpful." Tom slowly rose to his feet. "Okay, William, can you tell me why you think all of those men began hurting each other?"

"Yessuh, I can!" William answered hesitantly. Then, almost as if he were relating an exciting adventure he had read, he forgot his caution and the words tumbled out. "Missuh Abel, he done say he was takin' Miss Rena to live with him in his big new shack. But Missuh Joe, he say is okay fo' Miss Rena stay with them in Missuh Abel's old, little shack. Den Missuh Abel done took d' whip to Missuh Joe's face."

"Hold on a minute, boy. You got to tell me the truth!" interrupted

Tom, "Abel don't *have* no big new shack! And if I'm not mistaken, the girl Rena already *was* living with Big Joe's family!"

"Yessuh," William responded, a little shaken. "Missuh Abel say dat's all gonna change, suh."

"He did, did he?"

"Yessuh." William, suddenly remembering his place and who he was talking to, dropped his eyes and tried to evaporate into the group stepped back.

Tom paused and took a deep breath to relax. Then he looked to the rest of the children and asked, "Do you children all agree with William here?" They all nodded in affirmation and with no hesitation.

"Belle, you got anything to add?"

"No, suh, 'cept Missuh Abel say we was to finish the building on the end nearest the eatin house first so's he could move in."

"That so?"

Belle nodded. "Yessuh."

"Okay, Belle, you can take these children back to their mamas. Then bring Rena to me. She can tell me, herself, who she would like to stay with."

Tom turned and walked over to where Abel was laying. He stood over him with his hand on his pistol. He looked down and asked, "You got anything to add to or change about that story?"

"Din't mean to actually hit him, suh. Jus' mean to put d' scare to him."

It seemed to Tom as if a dark cloud had suddenly covered the sun. He slowly pulled the gun from the holster.

"I heard those very words spoken when I was a kid in school," Tom was speaking stiffly, and in a low voice. "Only difference is, the bullies that picked on me were white. The teacher caught 'em once, and they said those very words."

Tom aimed the gun to Abel's head. "The teacher let them go, Abel," he said bitterly.

He pulled the hammer back with a click. Abel sobbed and closed his eyes and waited for the thunder. It seemed like eternity before he heard another click as Tom released the hammer and replaced the gun to his side. With his eyes still closed Abel heard the master mumble under his breath something he didn't understand. "That was real close, Etta," Tom whispered, and then, after a long pause, "I wanted to, real bad. But I didn't do it! You proud of me?"

Still frightened, and now a little puzzled, Abel slowly opened his eyes to see Tom still standing over him, but looking off toward his house.

Tom let out a big sigh, told the rest of the men to get up, and then instructed some to tie Abel to the nearest tree. Next, he turned decisively and strode quickly to Big Joe, who was sitting up and leaning against his wife. His children had been taken away so they wouldn't see the damage that had been done to their father.

"Sorry to leave you sitting here for so long, Joseph. I was just sitting down to eat when I heard the ruckus. Got here as fast as I could but I couldn't take any chances. Had to sort things out."

Joe was holding both of his bloody hands over his right eye and groaning quietly. His wife held him in her arms, whispering the words, "sweet Jesus, sweet Jesus," over and over as she wept. Tom knelt down, reached out, and gently pulled Joe's hands away from his face. Tom's mouth fell open, and he stared in shock. The eye was totally missing; ripped out by the whip. An uncontrollable shudder swept through him and he returned Joe's hands to his face. As he stood up and took a step back, he continued to look down at the two slaves, his 'livestock', as he had jokingly called his slaves in the past. They hadn't responded or acknowledged him in any way. It was as if they didn't even know he was there. As if they hadn't heard a single word he had said.

Tom was in unfamiliar territory now. A strange, almost spooky feeling had come over him and it was as if he had stepped outside of the scene. It was more like he was entering a dream. Revelation began to sweep through his entire being. Was he hearing, or feeling, a thought that didn't feel like his? He wasn't sure.

"A husband, and his wife!"

Tom stood looking down at his two black slaves. He couldn't move.

"A husband!"

His eyes were held firmly on the man in agony.

"His wife!"

Tom was suddenly drawn to the weeping woman. He could tell that she had once been beautiful, but her face was now marred with the lines of time, pain, and weariness.

As Tom watched, he slowly began to understand.

A wife, weeping for her husband. Not livestock!

A familiar feeling from the past began to engulf Tom and he fought to regain control. It wasn't working. Despair was defeating him. Slowly, reality began to mix with this surreal scene that he was swimming in. A faint, female voice was whispering, "Sweet Jesus, oh, sweet Jesus." The voice grew closer and closer until it matched the movement of the lips of the woman sitting in front of him.

Tom had no idea how long he had been standing there. Maybe seconds, maybe minutes. It didn't matter. What did matter was that guilt had arrived to reinforce despair. Tom realized that he didn't even know the woman's name. He *had* known it, but over time, he had forgotten.

"Sweet Jesus," she whispered again, as she stared straight ahead, at the level of his knees.

Tom had an idea that she wasn't really seeing anything at all.

"He hears you, ma'am," he assured her in a low, unsure, whispering voice. It actually surprised Tom to hear himself say those words, but the guilt told him the words were true.

"Sweet Jesus," she whispered again, staring blankly.

Tom stepped forward and knelt down. Taking her face in his hands he aimed her face directly at his, "Jesus hears you."

Guilt and despair teamed up and struck him again with full force. His eyes began to well up with tears. One escaped, and rolled down his cheek.

"I can't even remember your name," he confessed, with guilty disgust, "but he does. He's listening. Somehow, he knows you and he's listening."

Even as he spoke, a look of recognition crossed Joe's wife's face, as she returned to the present.

"Please, help him, Massuh." She pleaded so quietly he had barely heard. But it was enough.

Tom jumped to his feet! "Yes! What on earth is the matter with me?" he reprimanded himself. "I have to get him to a doctor!" He looked down at Big Joe and remembered what it looked like behind those blood drenched hands. Was Joe going to die from loss of blood? The couple appeared to be going into a state of shock.

If what he had just told Joe's wife was true, God was watching! And if God *was* watching, he was probably real mad! Tom glanced up, as if expecting lightning to strike. He spun around to call for help and was surprised to see most of the adult slaves standing a few feet away. "How long had they been there?" he wondered, but only for a split second before he quickly began to give out instructions.

"Jackson, bring the buckboard down here as fast as you can! William, you run up to the house and have Etta get you some whiskey and some rags. Lots of em! Move fast, William! Run! Belle, have the gals round up some blankets and get them down here!"

The plantation became a flurry of activity. Men ran to help Jackson hook up the horses to the buckboard. A mother sent her boy upstream where he would find cleaner water to fill a bucket. William had reached the house and gave the message to Etta.

As the blankets arrived, the women wrapped them around Joe and his wife. The devastated couple didn't respond. Belle took the whiskey bottle from William and knelt beside Big Joe. She poured some whiskey on a clean rag and reached up to remove Joe's hands.

"No, Belle!"

Belle turned to Tom. She looked confused.

"He needs to be cleaned up, suh."

"No, Belle."

"Suh?"

"It's real bad, Belle. You don't need to see it."

Tom reached down, took her arm and pulled her to her feet.

"I'll do it," he said, as he took the rags and the bottle from her. "Have the boy bring that bucket of water over here and then send him away."

He looked over his men and chose the two biggest. "You two will need to hold him so I can clean him up." He turned back to Belle. "Maybe you and ..." Tom nodded in the direction of a big woman standing nearby. "What's her name?"

"Her name's Anna, suh."

"Yes, that's it, Anna. I want you and Anna to help Joe's wife not to have to see this."

"Yes, suh."

As everyone took their positions, Tom knelt down and nodded to the slaves. They lowered Joe's arms and held them tight. Joe seemed to be in a trance, and did not resist. Tom shuddered at the sight, then took a deep breath and proceeded to clean out the wound as best he could with water. Next, he took a clean rag and poured some whiskey over it.

"Okay, boys. Hold on tight. Big Joe ain't gonna like this, I'm bettin'."

As Tom touched the whiskey'd rag to the empty eye socket, the pain exploded in Joe's head with a fury! The two slaves needed every ounce of strength to keep Joe down as Tom held the rag firmly against Joe's face while the battle raged.

Across the river, heads turned to the distant sound of a man's scream.

"Help him, Lord," Toby muttered, as they all stopped work for a moment and looked in the direction of the Grant plantation. He had no idea who he was praying for, but it really didn't matter.

"Thas' fo' sure," Gideon agreed. Then he shook his head and returned to his picking.

The two young boys moved closer to Zekiel. The sound had unsettled them, and various scenes played out in their minds as to why the man had screamed. As Zekiel and the others resumed their work, the boys continued to stay close. It wasn't long before they were all singing a song about "a better place" in harmony, as they continued down the rows.

When Big Joe screamed, his wife covered her ears and cried out to Jesus. Belle couldn't help herself and looked over her shoulder at the struggling men. She had a momentary glimpse of the eye socket as Joe fought against the pain. The blood began to flow afresh as Tom continued his struggle to clean out the wound. Belle couldn't fight back her tears.

In only a matter of a half a minute or so, it was over. Joe lay limp on the ground as Tom finished cleaning and bandaging the eye.

"He dead?" asked his wife, as she stared straight ahead, afraid to turn around and look.

"No, ma'am. He only passed out. But it's better this way; he doesn't feel the pain right now."

When the buckboard arrived, the group of black men worked as a unit to get the unconscious man and his wife settled in the back.

As Tom climbed aboard and sat down on the seat, Belle stepped up to the side of the wagon, still wiping tears from her cheeks. "We can't find Rena, suh. Seems no one's seen her since the whipping. But I'll look around more, suh."

Tom swore under his breath. "Probably a runaway," he said, half to himself.

"Have everyone keep looking. She might be hiding in the barns or something. You never know. All this ruckus probably scared her."

Tom looked over to the tree where Abel was tied. His fellow slaves had tied him in a standing position, facing the tree. His hands were at his sides, and the rope was wrapped round and round the tree holding him tightly.

"When it rains, it pours." Tom said, as he shook his head and cracked the horsewhip over the horses. He drew the buckboard up to the tree and spoke to the three men guarding Abel.

"We very much need to get these houses finished while the weather is good. Get everyone back on it." He motioned toward Abel with his head. "You got him tied real good. He ain't goin' nowhere. No sense wasting a man just to stand here."

Tom looked at Abel and shook his head in frustration. "You really messed everything up, Abel." He stared at the man but couldn't think of anything else to say. He watched as a lone tear ran down the cheek that wasn't pinned to the bark, then swore again and sent the horses trotting towards Grantsville.

Chapter 33

As Tom came to the end of his road and turned toward Grantsville, he caught sight of Luke Martin heading home in his wagon. He had a passenger sitting alongside, but Tom couldn't place who it was as they disappeared around a bend and into some trees. He had other things on his mind as he urged his horses to pick up the pace. He knew time was of the essence. He glanced at the couple behind him. The woman was trying to make Joe comfortable even though he appeared to still be unconscious. "What *was* her name, anyway?" he wondered as he rode along. "Why haven't I paid more attention to these people?" He thought about how ragged and immodest he had let their clothes become, and the rotting condition of their homes. He remembered the weariness on their faces.

As he rode along he had a flashback of pulling the trigger and putting an end to what he now understood to be a young boy's father. When he closed his eyes, Etta's bloody face looked back at him.

"Why did I let Etta talk me out of it?" he despaired. *"If I had pulled the trigger, I could have put an end to this mess."*

Guilt and self-loathing, led him to what he thought was the only right answer. *"I have to put an end to the C.C Grant bloodline. But now is not the time. The need of the moment is to find a doctor for Big Joe."*

He pictured in his mind what the doctor's response would be to Joe's condition. After all, this was not a common injury. For some reason that he couldn't explain, his thoughts went back to Luke and his passenger. The man that was riding with Luke was wearing a hat and coat like the one Doc Jeffords wore when he came to help Etta. The memory of having to explain to the doctor what had happened to Etta brought another wave of shame and guilt.

"I'm some piece of work," he grumbled out loud to himself in disgust.

Tom remembered, with embarrassment, that as the doctor put on his coat and hat to leave, he had reminded Tom that Etta was too old to take another beating like that. He'd suggested that the next time he felt the need to vent his anger, he might consider splitting a cord of wood or something. As Tom had watched the doctor ride away in his buckboard, he'd wondered to himself how fast the word would spread around town that 'Tom Grant beats old women'. But the doctor had kept it to himself. He had not spoken of it again, not even to Tom.

Suddenly, Tom pulled back hard on the reigns. That man! The man riding with Martin! It was Doc Jeffords!

Tom turned around in his seat and spoke to the slave woman, "Hold on to him. I'm gonna turn this coach around. I just realized that the doctor is going to the Martin place."

Joe's wife said nothing as he maneuvered the horses back and forth with great difficulty until he was facing back in the direction from which he'd come. He cursed the swamp on one side of the road and the trees on the other, but eventually he was successful and on his way back. He glanced behind him and noticed that, with all of the jostling, blood had begun to soak through the thick bandages. Facing forward again, he urged his horses to move a little faster.

Tom looked up at the blue sky through the scattered clouds. "If you're really up there, you're probably real mad at me," Tom said out loud. "But it ain't me that needs the help right now. Those folks in back need you something fierce. So don't let me be wrong about the doc, okay? You can take up the matters about me, later!" He looked down the road, thought for a moment, and then added, "If it's okay with you, that is. I don't mean to be bossin' you around or nothin'. You probably wouldn't like that."

As he traveled, Tom thought back on what he had said. Had he gone mad? Who was he talking to, anyway? Then it crossed his mind that he was glad that the Ellis boys and Sheriff Roily hadn't been there to hear him. He'd never live it down.

The oak tree was dropping children like a plum tree drops ripe plums. Ted and Nathan had brought a younger brother and sister along when they came to work that morning. When Frank and Joshua delivered a load of cotton to the gin house at lunch time, they were given permission to play with their guests for a couple of hours after lunch. One at a time, the two younger children dropped to the ground, followed by Joshua and Frank. The four of them lined up beside the road and stared as Tom passed by them and proceeded to the main house. When Frank saw the passengers riding in the back, he suggested they all go find his dad. They broke into a run, making a beeline to what was now called the Women's Quarters.

Tom pulled his wagon in near the one that Luke - and hopefully the doctor – had been riding in. He barely noticed the children, who disappeared around a building far off to his left. Turning to the house, he yelled out, "Luke! Mrs. Martin?"

Two young white men working on the roof of a new building a hundred yards away apparently heard him calling. Tom saw them stop hammering and look his direction. He called out to the house again, but still there was no response.

He turned and spoke to the woman in the wagon. "Must be they're busy elsewhere. Guess I'll go ask those fellas where Martin is."

Tom climbed down and scanned the barnyard. He saw Martin's boy run out from behind the building where he'd last seen the children, then stop and point at him while saying something to someone Tom couldn't see. The other children joined the boy, staring at Tom. Tom was about to call out to them when Luke came around the building. He paused slightly and then quickly approached Tom, with the children following close behind.

"Afternoon, Tom," Luke greeted him with a curious look. His neighbor had not set foot on his farm for many years so he guessed it had to be something important to bring him here. He looked past Tom to the black woman sitting in the back of the wagon.

"I'm in real need of a doctor, Martin," said Tom, not wasting his time with greetings. "I got a man in bad shape back here," he added as he moved to the back of the buckboard. "Lost a lot of blood."

Luke stepped forward and looked over the sideboard, while the children ran around behind for a better view. The little girl gasped and turned her face against her brother. The three boys stood gawking at the blood soaked bandages.

Luke turned angrily and faced Tom, "What on earth have you gone and done now, Tom?"

Once again, Tom didn't waste time. But he could feel the heat rising in his face as he stared at Luke and said, "The children should not be seeing this." Then he added forcefully, "My man needs a doctor, and if the doctor is not here, you tell me right now, so's I can get him on to town!"

Luke looked at the children and realized the truth of Tom's words. "Frank, take the others and go fetch Doc Jeffords."

When they hesitated, he added, "Go right now! And when you get there, send your mother with the doctor. You all stay there with Hope. Now get going!"

After they had gone, Luke joined Tom at the back of the wagon. "By the looks of those bandages and their clothes, it must be *real* bad," Luke spoke under his breath with his head slightly turned in Tom's direction.

"It's worse than that," replied Tom, staring at Joe.

Luke considered Tom's response, then nodded his head decisively. "Okay then, let's get him into the house and put him in our guest room. A long ride to town could really mess him up, I'm guessin."

"It could," Tom agreed.

As Luke climbed up to help lift the big black man out of the wagon, he realized that the woman did not seem to be responding to anything going on around her.

"Are you okay, ma'am?" he asked.

She looked up at him with a blank look but said nothing.

"I'm not so sure she is," Tom answered for her. "This here's her husband and all of this seems to have sent her over the edge."

Luke felt his temperature rising and he held his mouth tight shut and glared at Tom. He finally snapped, "It does happen to people, Tom! There's only so much a person can take!"

Tom leaned forward resting his hands on the wagon as he gave Luke a steady, even slightly defeated look. "Yes, it does happen. And if it makes you feel any better, after some of the things that have happened today, I think you're probably right. There is a God. And it was him that got this man to a doctor. I was taking him in the wrong direction. And this will really cheer you up, Martin. All these people that have had the misfortune of being bought by me? Well, their lives are really screwed up, right now. So, if there is a God, and I'm beginning to think there is, then I've probably bought myself a train ticket straight to hell!"

Tom stood up straight and finally took a breath, "Now, let's get this man inside before God strikes me with lightning and you have to carry him in by yourself!"

Luke was dumbfounded. He had nothing to say. He numbly nodded his head and lifted Big Joe by the arms as Tom grabbed his legs and eased him to the back of the wagon. They draped Joe's arms around their necks and worked their way up the steps to the front door. Both men worked silently, each lost in their own thoughts.

As the two men got Big Joe settled into the bed, they could hear hurried footsteps coming down the hall. Joe was beginning to moan as the doctor entered the room and walked over to the bed. Sally stopped at the doorway when Luke held up his hand and shook his head.

"Care to tell me what happened, Tom?" asked the doctor, as he set his bag down on the end of the bed.

Tom could feel every eye trained on him, but he just stood there looking down at Big Joe. He knew they had already convicted him in their minds. His history justified their disgust. He didn't blame them. He was pretty disgusted with himself right now too.

"A bull whip took his eye out."

Luke took in a big swig of air and slowly let it out. He folded his arms in front of him and slowly shook his head, frowning.

"I see," said Doc Jeffords, squinting his eyes at Tom, expecting to hear more of the story.

"A bull whip?" Sally questioned in a whisper.

Tom didn't have to look at her to know that she was struggling to comprehend how a human being could possibly have fallen so low.

"You all do what you have to do to help him. His wife's out at the wagon. I'll go out and try to talk to her." With that, Tom turned and left the room.

"How could he, Luke?" Sally looked pleadingly at her husband.

Shaking his head, Luke walked to his wife and held her close. "I don't know, Sally. I don't understand it, either."

Doc Jeffords adjusted his eyeglasses. "Well, I'd best get to work here. We can't undo what's been done," he said as he sat down on the edge of the bed.

Joe gave out a low moan as the doctor began removing the bandages.

"He din' do it," the slave said quietly.

The doctor leaned closer. "What's that you said?"

"The massuh didn' whip me." He gave another moan then, with great effort, he said, "Nother man done it."

The man groaned again; but he was too weak to say more. Doc sat up straight and glanced back at Luke and Sally, asking with his eyes if they had heard what Joe said.

Luke closed his eyes, put his hand to his forehead, and rubbed it as if he had a headache. "I reckon I'm feeling as bad as I was just wishing Tom felt."

Sally looked out the bedroom door. "We need to go talk to him, Luke."

"Not now, ma'am," the doctor said, shaking his head as he removed the bandages and analyzed the job ahead of him. "I'll be needing both of you right here. This is going to take some work. Tom will have to wait."

She heard the boots coming down the steps, but didn't turn to look, even as they approached, crunching on the gravel. When they stopped right behind her, she didn't move, but she was aware of his presence. The woman sat in the back of the buckboard with her arms holding her knees to her chest. Her head rested on her knees as she stared at nothing.

Tom stood for a moment, searching for what to say. As he walked around to the back of the buckboard, he noticed the two young men on the roof had stopped working again to watch. He looked directly at them and put his hands on his hips as a challenge. Embarrassed, they quickly returned to their work. Tom turned his attention back to his slave woman and cleared his throat uncomfortably.

"Ashamed to say, I forgot your name," he finally said bluntly.

"He dead, ain't he," she stated, without any emotion or movement.

The words caught Tom off guard. It was glaringly clear how little he understood about the emotional needs of others. In the tension of the moment, he had left her outside, all alone, not knowing the fate of her husband. She had been bracing herself for the very worst news, and here he stood telling her that he couldn't remember her name.

"Oh no, ma'am!"

Tom usually responded to embarrassment with a display of anger. His pride would lead him to somehow throw the focus and blame onto the other person, believing that by doing so, he was exonerating himself. But not this time.

"No, Joe's not dead. He's a fighter. The doctor is working on him now. It's good we found the doc so quick."

She gave a barely detectable nod and closed her eyes as if in prayer.

Tom became uncomfortable, not knowing what to do. But again there was none of the usual anger rising from his frustration. He merely took off his hat, dusted it off and looked at the ground, and waited. The second time he glanced up, her eyes were open again. He took a chance, and spoke.

"I don't think they'd mind if you were to come in and sit with Joe. Why don't you at least get down and stretch your legs a bit while I go check."

Joe's wife gave it a thought, and then slowly scooted to the edge of the wagon. It didn't cross Tom's mind to offer a hand of assistance. That wasn't something he'd ever done for a slave before. She lowered herself to the ground and looked to the house.

"It Maybeth, suh," she said as she half-heartedly brushed some of the road dust off of her bloodstained dress."

Tom lit up as she spoke. His memory came flooding back when he heard the familiar name.

"Yes, that's it! Maybeth! I feel bad for forgetting," he said, as he tried to think of what to do next. His eye caught sight of four young faces peering from around the corner of the building, and that caused him to look over to the two young men on the roof of the other building. They were also watching again. For some reason, this flustered Tom and he quickly turned and climbed the stairs to the house, speaking as he went, "C'mon, Maybeth, let's get on in there and check on your Joe."

He let the screened door slam behind him, leaving Maybeth with not much choice but to follow the 'massuh' inside.

Chapter 34

Luke held Joe's head up off the pillow as Doc Jeffords finished wrapping the fresh bandages around his eye and head. Sally was busying herself by gathering up the bloody bandages when Tom knocked lightly on the door. He stepped into the room as Sally opened it and asked if his slave woman could see her husband for a few minutes.

"Absolutely!" Sally said without hesitation. She grabbed up the used bandages and the bowl of red-stained water. "I'll get some clean water and show her in."

As she stepped into the hall, Tom thanked her and moved to the end of the bed where he silently watched the doctor.

Sally walked into the kitchen where she came upon the black woman standing helplessly just inside the door, gazing down at some drops of blood on the floor. Sally paused slightly before continuing to the counter to set down the water and bandages, then quickly returned to her guest.

"I'm glad you came in," she said with an understanding smile. "My name is Sally, what's yours?" she asked.

"Maybeth, missus," the slave woman answered respectfully and quietly.

"It's nice to meet you, Maybeth. I'm so sorry about the circumstances. If you'll follow me down the hall, I can take you to your husband. Seeing you would be good medicine for him."

"He awake, ma'am? He can see?" Maybeth asked, surprised yet hopeful.

"He's got about as much energy as a spent fire, but there's still enough spark there to rekindle a flame. I have a feeling you'll be the kindling." Sally paused, then continued, "Yes, he can see, but he only has one eye. The doctor says he'll be wearing a patch from now on, but there are no other visible marks on his face. He's right down this hall. Come with me."

"You can do what you want, Tom. After all, he's your property."

The doctor's words suddenly made Tom uncomfortable. Livestock, animals, property. Yep, that's how he had related to his nigras. That's what they had been to him. But that all had slowly begun to change since the night he almost killed Etta, and himself. And today, the dream, or voice, or revelation; whatever it was, it had destroyed his old way of thinking and left him with nothing to replace it. He understood that he was pretty poor at relating to white people and now he had to add the nigras into the mix. Maybe he should go off into the woods and be a hermit. It would be a whole lot easier. A wave of the old anger tried to stick its foot in the door but Tom fought it off.

"I was telling Tom that the nigra shouldn't be moved for a few days." The doctor explained, as the two women entered the room. "We want all of those little veins to seal off. He's also going to need to rebuild his blood supply, and that requires rest and a good diet. The dressings will also need to be changed, often at first."

"Since I'll be coming out to check on your nigra's ankles, Luke, maybe you could put this fellow out in the barn or something. Then I wouldn't have to go hopping from place to place.

"Absolutely not! We wouldn't even think of it, would we, Luke!" declared Sally.

"That's okay, Mrs. Martin," Tom answered quickly. "I'll take him on home with me."

"But all the bouncing around in the wagon could start up the bleeding, Tom!" Sally sounded exasperated, and her pleading eyes totally confused Tom.

"But, I thought…" Tom began, but Luke cut him off.

"What she meant was that we wouldn't think of putting him in the barn. If the doctor doesn't think he should be moved, then he should stay right here in this bed."

Tom was flabbergasted.

"Maybeth?" said Joe quietly, taking advantage of the gap in the conversation.

Everyone except Tom looked down at the man on the bed. Tom stared at Luke as he tried to register what Luke had just said.

"Yea, Joseph," Maybeth moved to the bed at Sally's nudge.

Big Joe cracked a smile meant to encourage his wife. "Dey say I be fine," he said weakly. "You jus' hafta get use' to livin' with a pirate, thas all."

Too much had happened in too short of a time. Maybeth couldn't think of what to say. As she stood by the bed, all she could offer was a slight nod, a weak smile, and a few tears of relief.

"You'd do that? You'd keep a nigra in this room where your guests stay?" Tom asked.

As they turned to respond to Tom's inquiry, Luke and Sally both noticed that Doc Jeffords appeared to be as surprised as Tom was. Luke managed to smile at them both.

"This *is* a guest room, Tom. Joe and Maybeth would be our guests," he replied, trying not to sound like he was teaching a simple fact to a child, though he was sorely tempted.

Tom was beginning to realize that change was not going to be easy for him. "All of the 'C. P. Grants' would be rolling over in their graves at an idea like this," Tom thought to himself, smiling. Yet Martin was talking as if this idea was as natural as buttering a biscuit.

"Well, now that you mention it, he *is* already lyin' in the bed, now isn't he?" Tom looked at Big Joe, "Didn't mean nothin' by it, Joe. It's just that I got a lifetime of different thinkin' in my head."

Joe nodded his head weakly but didn't speak.

Tom turned, looked at Luke in the eye, and frowned. "I know you two are thinking I'm lower 'n a skunk, and you're right about that. I don't hold a real high opinion of you, neither. But this ain't about us, now is it? If the doc thinks Big Joe should stay, well then, I guess I could come back for him in a couple of days."

He turned from Luke to Sally, "I hate to put you out like this, ma'am. I was raised to take care of my own problems. When Maybeth and I come back for him, I'll be glad to reimburse you for all the trouble I've caused."

Sally flushed with embarrassment, "We made some wrong assumptions, Tom."

Luke cleared his throat. "Joe told us that you didn't do this to him. He says all you've done is help him."

Tom's gaze returned to Joe, who nodded in affirmation.

"I owe you an apology," Luke added.

"The Bible says that pride leads to a fall," Sally added. "I'd say we fell flat on our faces. Please accept our apologies, Tom."

Now it was Tom's turn to feel uncomfortable. He felt like they were putting him on the spot. He didn't like having everyone staring at him, waiting to hear him let them off the hook, as if he owed it to them or something. His pride began to flare up. "I guess you are beginning to see that all that hymn singing and Bible-thumping don't make you perfect after all."

"There," thought Tom to himself, "that ought to put them in their place."

"It's the hymn singing and Bible (reading) that keep reminding us that we're *not* any better than anyone else," said Luke.

Tom wasn't ready for Luke to be so agreeable.

"Yeah, well, I ain't got time for a sermon right now. I have some things to deal with at home."

"Would it be alright with you if Maybeth stayed here with her husband?" asked Sally. "It wouldn't be any trouble for us at all."

By now, Tom was feeling a real need to get away before the Martins tried to get him saved right there in front of his slaves and the doctor. He was not about to let them beat him to the punch with words like 'it's the Christian thing to do' or something.

"Sure, I suppose that would be fine. I'll pay you for their food when I come back for them." He caught the doctor's eye and thanked him, saying he'd pay up when he was in town the next week. Then he nodded at the Martins, and walked quickly down the hall and out of the house.

Rena had stayed hidden in the bushes near the river until nightfall. When she crossed the river it was so dark she could see absolutely nothing but the lights of the Martin plantation. During the crossing she had slipped and fallen twice and was now sitting, soaking wet, in a small shed, huddling behind a pile of burlap bags filled with what she guessed was potatoes or onions or turnips or something.

She was silently berating herself for being so impulsive. On impulse, she had stolen the master's chickens and paid dearly for it. On impulse, she had run away when Abel had struck Joseph with the whip. Rena wanted to go back, but she knew Abel would take his anger out on her for shaming him by running away.

Rena had no plan. She kept her fears at bay by scolding herself for her stupidity, but that tactic could only last so long. The darkness lasted longer. She began to shiver, partly because she was wet and cold, but mostly because she was a young, frightened girl. It was nearly dawn when she finally cried herself to sleep.

Chapter 35

Luke and Sally stood together at the rail of the front porch, their arms around each other's waist, collecting their thoughts. The doctor had just left for town after his second visit since Big Joe had arrived. He was pleased that the bleeding had stopped and there seemed to be no sign of infection. On his way home, he would stop in and tell Tom that he could pick up his slaves the next day. The doctor also gave a good report on Diana and the baby. Ambrose's ankles were a different story, however. The infection seemed to be worsening, with increased redness and swelling up to his knees.

"You may have to put him down," the doctor said matter-of-factly, as he climbed into his buckboard. "It'd be for his own good, and he wouldn't be of much use to you, anyhow, if he lost his feet." As the doctor settled onto the seat, he added, "We'll give it a little more time. But it doesn't look real hopeful."

With a nod and a tip of his hat, he rode away down the driveway.

As the couple stood quietly watching the scene around them, Sally shuddered.

Luke looked down at her and gave her a squeeze, "No matter what happens, we'll take care of him, Sal. We aren't going to 'put him down', as the good doctor says."

"It's the way he said it, Luke. He was so cold, so unattached, as if he has no feelings."

Luke nodded and sighed, "Yeah."

They were quiet as they watched Gideon and Zekiel finish hauling the bags of peanuts into the potato shed. Nearby, the Willis boys were putting the finishing touches on the new pantry. All that was left for them to do was hang the doors and the building would be ready for use.

"Nobody would know by looking at it that there was slave storage underneath that building," said Sally. "The boys have done a good job."

"Mabin and I will build the false wall and shelves after they're gone. No use having any more people than necessary knowing about it," Luke responded, as he watched Zekiel and Gideon come out of the shed. They looked around, and then at each other. Then Zekiel said something and they both climbed onto the empty wagon and headed to the field where the last of the cotton was being picked.

"When the picking's done we'll put Washington, Otis, Tal, Frank, and Joshua, to cleaning up the fields," said Luke. "I'm thinking to put the rest of the guys on building the cookhouse. The sooner we get it built, the sooner we'll have the rooms on the top floor ready for Ambrose and his family."

"How will Ambrose get up and down the steps, Luke?"

Luke gave Sally's question some thought. "I'm praying we won't have to face that problem. I'm praying he gets healed."

"So am I," Sally agreed. "I don't know when I've ever seen a more faithful husband. He's put himself through a lot to get back together with Dinah." Sally suddenly realized how that might have sounded to Luke. "I mean, except you, of course," she added.

"I've never been put to that kind of test," said Luke with a half smile. "I wonder how I'd do."

Sally turned to her husband. "I have no doubt that you, sir, would pass with flying colors!"

At the sound of the screen door, Luke and Sally turned to see Big Joe and Maybeth step out onto the porch. Leather strings held a leather patch over some fresh bandages where Joe's eye had once been.

Luke smiled and gave a quick nod of greeting. "It's good to see you up and around, Joe." Then he added, "The Doc says you might be leaving us tomorrow."

"Yessuh, Massuh. You been real good to us." Joe spoke quietly, avoiding eye contact.

Sally took a step toward them and said, "You have been wonderful guests. It's been no trouble at all to have you here. You've been such a help with the mending and candle-making. I only wish we had time to get to know you better."

Without thinking, Maybeth glanced up and met Sally's eyes with a curious look. During the three days they had stayed in the Martin's house, they had been treated as if they were white. Miz Martin had even brought food to their room. At times, Maybeth had listened from the bedroom doorway as Miz Martin and a female slave had worked together in the kitchen preparing food while telling each other stories and laughing as if they were best friends.

"We was wonderin', suh, if you had some work for me to do to repay," Joe said. "I could stack bales, shoe a horse, or help wit dat building I see over there. I could ...."

"Not a chance Joe!" Luke interrupted. "Doc says you shouldn't put any extra pressure on those blood vessels. You need to let 'em seal good and strong."

Sally noticed Joe's look of disappointment.

"I've got a lot of cooking to do tomorrow, Maybeth. Sadie and I could sure use some help with that while Joe is resting," offered Sally.

"Yes, ma'am. I make a real good coon stew. Sometimes I have to use possum, though."

Sally glanced up at Luke, then back at Maybeth. She cleared her throat uncomfortably. "Uh, we happen to be out of those right now, but it would be fun to have you help Sadie and me with some sausage and potatoes, and green beans, I have planned for dinner. Then, if there's time, you can help us make some pies."

"Yes'm, she could do dat," Joseph quickly agreed. Maybeth nodded.

"Okay, then," said Luke. "In the meantime, you two might want to go for a short walk, or maybe sit on the porch and get some fresh air. Take it easy, and in a couple of hours, Sally and Sadie will be back here to get dinner." He turned and walked to the porch steps and looked out at the pickers in the field. "It looks like they might even finish up today," he said, half to himself and half to the three standing behind him. "If you need anything, Sal will be over there in the gin house." Luke pointed in its direction, and as he did, he noticed a wagon coming up the road toward the house. Two men on horseback were leading the way. One of the men was Sheriff Roily.

"It looks like we have company." Luke turned and gave Sally a quick kiss on her forehead, "I'll see you all at dinner."

Luke moved quickly to intercept the procession at the barnyard entrance. A quick glance revealed three male slaves chained together and sitting in the back of the wagon. Luke did not recognize the two men who accompanied the Sheriff.

"Afternoon, Sheriff," Luke greeted politely as they all came to a stop.

"Afternoon, Martin."

"Can I help you with anything?" asked Luke, as he eyed the cargo in the wagon.

The sheriff took his time in answering, puffing on a cigar as he surveyed the area around him. "Rounding up a few strays. Been gone a couple-o-days, but before I left, Tom Grant said a young gal had run off on him." He paused and took another puff, then slowly blew smoke into the air. "Seen anything?" The sheriff stacked his hands on the saddle horn and the leather creaked as he shifted his weight and turned to study the workers picking the field.

"As a matter of fact, I've got two of Tom's people here, right now. Tom will be picking them up tomorrow. But there's no one here that isn't supposed to be." Luke stood with his thumbs stuck in his belt watching as Sheriff Roily took another puff on his cigar and slowly studied the farm and buildings as if trying to memorize the layout for future reference.

"Musta done good this year," the sheriff finally commented. "You're adding some buildings." Then he began to scan the woods at the edges of the fields.

Luke guessed he was imagining a runaway slave behind every tree.

"It hasn't been too bad," Luke said. "I plan to work more fields next season, so I'm adding more people, and buildings to handle them," said Luke.

"Adding more nigras," corrected the sheriff, without taking his eyes off the woods.

Luke stiffened and put his hands on his hips. "I got better things I could be doing right now, Sheriff. Is there anything else I can do for you?"

Without looking at Luke, the sheriff asked, "Been in your woods lately?"

Luke looked perturbed. "No, I haven't, but we will be cutting more wood in the near future." He gave a fake smile, "I'll be sure and let you know if I see anything."

"Good idea," said the sheriff and, without acknowledging Luke, he turned his horse and rode away with the others following.

As the sheriff and his entourage rode past the cotton field, Zekiel spoke to Gideon in a low voice.

"Jus' keep workin' like you don' even know dey' dere. Don' look at 'em."

After the wagon and horses turned onto Town Road, Gideon stood up and stretched. "Dey was lookin' for her," he said.

Zekiel stayed bent over and continued to pick. "Good thing we din' tell Massuh."

Gideon agreed, "Dis way, Massuh don' have to lie or get caught lookin' guilty or sumthin'."

"We do have to tell him, Gideon," insisted Zekiel. "She been in dere fer days. Massuh Martin would help her."

Gideon began dragging his full sack to the basket at the end of the row. Zekiel looked around at the others. Not wanting to be overheard, he also dragged his sack to the basket.

"Things are good here," said Zekiel. "We don' wan mess dat up. Massuh Martin, he trust us."

Gideon was frustrated. "You heard her, Zekiel. She ask us not to tell. Last time she git caught, she lost some fingers. Can you imagine what she look like afta dat big guy wit d' bullwhip finish wit her?"

"The Martins know Jesus," Zekiel insisted. "If dey know d' whole story, dey won' send her back fer no whippin'. D' Lord would show dem what to do."

For a short time, the two friends packed the baskets tight with cotton.

Gideon finally surrendered and gave a big sigh, "Okay, den. But we wait til after her massuh come 'n gets dem other two o' his."

The two slaves carried their empty sacks back to the rows where they had left off. They worked for a while without saying anything, though each knew what the other was thinking about.

"She's a nice girl," Zekiel said, without looking up from his picking.

"Mmhmm," agreed Gideon.

"Sure is scared."

"Mmhmm."

The men worked silently for another few minutes.

"Rena's a nice name."

Gideon looked over at Zekiel and then back to the cotton.

"Nice name," he said.

The sacks were half filled by the time either spoke again. It was Gideon who broke the silence. Still bent over, and nearing the end of a row, he said, "It been a long day. My back is tired and I need extra rest tonight. Be okay wif you if I don' go wif you to bring her food t'night?"

"You sure?"

"I'z feelin' real tired, even now."

Zekiel pretended to give it some serious consideration. "I'm feelin' pretty good today."

Even without looking, Gideon could sense the smile on his friend's face.

Chapter 36

Another two hours and the sun would be tucking itself in for the night. The last wagonload of the season had been unloaded at the gin house. There was a joint sense of satisfaction and accomplishment shared by all - men, women, and children. Despite the distractions and unusual turns of events, the crop was in.

The next day, following a tradition Sally had started years ago, tables were set up on the front lawn. Everyone would share a feast of potatoes and gravy, roast beef, perch, a variety of garden vegetables and, of course, a pile of biscuits with butter and jam. It had worked out especially well to have Maybeth and Sadie helping her in the kitchen all of the previous day. The boys had willingly spent the morning peeling potatoes and running errands as they anticipated what was now spread before them. Never before had there been a table completely dedicated to pies. The pecan pies had been donated by Liz Willis. Deacon Willis's entire family was invited to share in the meal, as was Pastor Davies, and Ben and Wilma Statler. The dessert table was encircled by children, each claiming they would be able to eat twice as many slices as anyone else.

As everyone gathered round, the Reverend offered up a very lengthy prayer of thanksgiving, encouraged by an occasional 'amen' from the adults. The children were not quite so appreciative, however, and when Matthew finally deemed the prayer sufficient, the adults opened their eyes to discover the two youngest children were missing.

It wasn't long before the tablecloth was lifted to reveal two stolen biscuits being devoured by the two culprits.

"Wisht I thought of dat," murmured Joshua, nudging Frank with an elbow.

It wasn't long until plates were full and everyone had found a spot to eat. The children were clustered on the front steps of the house, listening as the older boys told tall tales of their greatest hunting escapades. Ambrose sat on the ground, leaning against a pecan tree with his bandaged legs stretched out in front of him. Dinah had filled his plate and hers before joining him on the ground. Tal and Sadie soon made it a foursome.

Luke sat next to Ben, Al, and Matthew as they ate and watched Sally and the other women sitting in a half circle of chairs with the baby on a blanket at their feet. Ambrose had named the baby Eli. To Luke's left, and not far away, Mabin sat on the grass with the rest of the slaves. He stabbed a chunk of roast beef with his fork and dragged it through the potatoes and gravy. Holding the bite up, he studied it for a moment before stuffing it into his mouth. He closed his eyes and chewed slowly.

"Seein' yourself at the Lord's banquet table, Mabin?" asked Toby with a chuckle.

A smile crossed Mabin's face, but he didn't open his eyes. He savored the flavor for a moment longer and then swallowed. "Easy to do at times like this," he finally answered before repeating the motions with his next bite.

The men didn't feel the need for much conversation as they concentrated on the work at hand, but there was a comment or two about how the women were able to multitask as they ate, and talked, and passed the baby around from person to person. By the time most everyone had finished a second plate of food and started working on the pies, the shadows had grown long.

Toby loaded his plate with a slice each of cherry and pecan pie, and then walked over to stand beside Hope as she cuddled the infant in her arms.

Luke swallowed his mouthful, then gave Matthew a mischievous look. "I think we'll be needing your services one of these days, Pastor," he said.

"I was thinking the same thing. Maybe you should concentrate on family housing from now on," chuckled Matthew."

"If I add another sixteen feet onto the cookhouse, I'd have three large rooms on the top floor and one living area behind the kitchen on the bottom floor." Luke had been thinking about this expansion for a few days now, but seeing all of his friends and fellow workers gathered in one place made it clear how large a group he was now housing and feeding.

"Have you ever performed a double wedding, Pastor?" Luke asked suddenly.

The question got the attention of the rest of the slaves that were close by. Until now, they had thought the master was talking only about Ambrose and Dinah.

"Well, no, I don't guess I have," said Matthew, after giving it some thought.

"Wouldn't hurt to make things right. I don't think Ambrose and Dinah would be against it, do you?" asked Luke.

""To them, that would be the frosting on the cake!" smiled the pastor.

Otis, Zekiel, and Gideon looked totally confused until Mabin smiled and pointed across the yard to where Hope was handing little Eli over to Toby. Eyes grew wide and then big white smiles formed, as realization swept through the group, followed by some good-natured joking.

Eventually Mabin brought them all back to earth, as he began passing out assignments. First, he instructed Washington to light the torches and lanterns around the house and barnyard. Otis was sent to make sure all of the animals were bedded down. Next, Mabin called Toby over and set him, Gideon, and Zekiel to cleaning up the area of food, tables, and chairs. Soon others joined in the work, spicing it up with comments about being too stuffed to breathe or how perfect the roast had been.

Mahta had dragged her chair over to the pecan tree and visited with Dinah as the baby nursed and Ambrose rested his head on Dinah's shoulder. Sally watched from a distance, silently thanking her Lord for all of these souls He was gathering together on their farm. The emotions welling up in her heart brought her to tears as she looked around at all of the happy people. She was glad it had gotten dark. She didn't want to make a scene. She needed a short time alone to express her gratitude and to allow what was happening to solidify her faith. She could almost feel her Maker's arms around her as she prayed for each person.

As Sally began to pray for Ambrose, a strange thing happened. From two opposite directions, Pastor Davies and Washington walked over and began to talk to the couple on the ground. She could not hear what was being said, but they had Sally's full attention as each placed a hand on the slave couple's heads and prayed. While they were praying, Mahta struggled slowly to her feet and placed her hands on their heads also. Soon, Toby and Hope joined them. When the Statlers and the entire Willis family joined the prayer group, Ambrose began to weep, hugging his wife and sleeping child. Mabin and the others soon gathered around, and Sally could no longer see the three on the ground, but mostly because of her own tears. Luke's arms suddenly slipped around her waist; she could tell by his silence that he was as moved as she by what was going on before them.

"Oh, Luke, I've never seen anything like this before!"

Luke did not respond.

Soon a song of praise began to rise into the night and the couple moved out of the shadows to join the choir.

The faint sound of singing put the finishing touches on a weak, frightened, and very lonely girl. She lay crumpled on the storage room floor in total blackness. Her body shook as she cried and sobbed and surrendered herself to whatever fate lay before her. She longed to be surrounded by that kind of singing for the rest of eternity, and death was what she prayed for.

The song eventually ended and she lay sniffling in the silent darkness until she made her decision. She would return to Massuh Grant and he could give her to Abel to do with as he pleased. She hoped Abel would put a quick end to her life so it would finally be over. She tried hard not to think of some of the other things he might do to her. The image of Big Joe's bleeding face was clearly before her. She touched her hand where her two fingers had once been. She drew herself up to a kneeling position. She felt so weak. She fought off a sudden desire to lie back down and go to sleep. She must go now, before she lost her resolve. With great effort, Rena rose to her feet and opened the door of the shed. Outside, it was just as dark as inside and she could not see where to go, but it didn't matter. She could hear the distant sound of the river and turned in that direction and walked into the black nothingness, not really thinking about anything.

The sound of approaching voices helped Rena shake the fog out of her head. She broke into a full run, but she had traveled only about twenty or thirty paces before the blackness got blacker, and she was once again hearing what sounded like angels singing.

"Did you hear dat?" asked Gideon.

"I hear sumthin'," Zekiel answered as they rounded the corner of the shed. He held the lantern up as they approached the door. "Uh-oh, door's open. Dis ain' good."

"Rena?" called Zekiel, as he followed his lantern inside. "Rena, it's okay. We needs t' talk t' you. You in here?"

"She's not here, Zekiel."

"Rena," Zekiel continued. "Massuh Martin's coming. We tol' him you was here. He help us work dis all out."

"She's not here," repeated Gideon. "We shoulda tol' him sooner."

They both stepped out of the shed and Zekiel handed Gideon the lantern. "You go git Massuh Martin 'n Mabin, 'n some more lanterns. Don' tell nobody else, though. I'll go t' d' river 'n call around."

Gideon agreed and left to find Luke. He had barely gotten past the shed when he heard Zekiel grunt and then mumble something.

"You okay, Zekiel?" he called behind him.

"Jus' hit my head 'n tripped over a log or sumthin'. I'z fine."

Gideon turned around. "I'm bringing you d' lantern. Clumsy as you is, you need it more den I do," he joked.

"Whaa...? Wait a minute," Zekiel sounded confused. "This ain' no log! Gideon, come quick!"

Gideon moved in the direction of Zekiel's voice as he held the lantern out in front of him. He soon came upon the shadowy figure of his friend, kneeling over what appeared to be a body. Gideon lowered the lantern and stopped paying attention to his surroundings as he hurried to get to Zekiel. With no warning, his face slammed into a thick tree branch and he dropped to his hands and knees. Zekiel instantly grabbed the lantern as Gideon came up holding his nose.

"Guess I shoulda' warn you, Gid. I hit it too, but not so hard."

"Ooh, dat hurts. I wasn't thinkin' where I was. It's my favorite tree, too." Gideon shook the cobwebs from his head, "Dat d' log you tripped over?"

Zekiel nodded and held the lantern up to reveal Rena's face. A knot was forming on her forehead at the hairline. She had a slight cut, but it was barely bleeding.

"Guess she hit it too."

They both watched her stomach rise and fall to make sure she was breathing. Zekiel raised one of her eyelids. "Out cold," he mumbled as he looked up to see Luke coming toward their lantern light.

"Look out for d' tree, suh," said Gideon as Luke approached. "It ain't bein' too friendly tonight."

Luke ducked under the branch and stood over the men and the girl. "This her?"

"Yessuh, is Rena," Zekiel confirmed. "Don' rightly knows why she out here. We come to d' shed 'n she was gone."

Luke held up his lantern as he looked back toward the shed and then up at the branch.

"It looks as if she was running away from something or someone in the dark."

He squatted down and felt her neck for a pulse, then checked her eyes and her breathing. "Can't say for sure, but she seems okay," Luke said as he stood up. He noticed Zekiel brushing the hair from her face with a finger. It helped him make the next decision.

"Zekiel, you carry her up to the house. Gideon will stay with you and carry the lantern. I'll go on ahead and move the pastor from the guest room out to the barn."

"Yessuh," both slaves responded together, as Luke turned and hurried away.

With very little effort, Zekiel placed Rena's arm around his neck and picked her up. Gideon held up the lantern to shine it on Zekiel.

"You two look good t'gether, Zekiel," he said with a grin.

Zekiel frowned and kicked some dirt at Gideon. "You hush now! Dis ain' no time to be makin' fun! Now, get goin'!"

"All right, all right, I'z a'goin'. No need to get all stirred up." Gideon turned and led the way.

About halfway to the master's house, Rena stirred with a groan. The two men stopped and Gideon turned around with the lantern. Rena opened her eyes for a moment and looked up at Zekiel, and then she closed them again. "We in heaven?" she asked quietly, barely moving her mouth.

"Not yet, girl, not yet," answered Zekiel as they continued on. He couldn't tell if she was still conscious or not. They walked in silence for a while, with Gideon leading the way. As they approached the barnyard, Rena asked, "You hear d' singing?"

Zekiel looked down at the seemingly unconscious girl as he continued walking. Then, after giving it some thought, he replied, "Yeah, I hear it."

Gideon glanced back curiously as he walked. The girl's eyes were still closed and Zekiel was staring straight ahead as he walked. Gideon looked back forward again as he wondered what they were talking about. As far as he could tell, there was no singing.

It was nearing midnight and not a candle, or lamplight, was shining anywhere in a ten mile radius of the Martin plantation except for the one in Luke's drawing room. In that same radius, most of the human population was asleep in their beds, regaining energy for the work of the following day. The three exceptions included Luke, who was wearing out the rug as he paced back and forth in the drawing room, and Sally, who sat at a small writing table with a lamp, a closed Bible, and a cup of hot tea. The presence of the third was unknown to Luke and Sally. His dark skin blended in with the night as he knelt outside, beneath the open window.

"She was hiding here for five days while Tom was coming and going and trusting us with two of his slaves." Luke threw up his hands and spun around to resume his journey across the room. "What were they thinking?"

"They were thinking of what it would mean to send a young girl back to a big angry driver with a bullwhip." Sally picked up her teacup and took a sip as she watched Luke pace.

"I guess blacks can mess things up as much as whites," murmured Luke.

"They didn't know what to do, Luke."

"I was talking about Tom's driver."

The room fell silent for awhile as Sally sipped her tea and Luke paced.

Luke finally spoke, "Maybe it's time for that Quaker-Smithston project. It's either that, or send a runaway slave back to her angry master. Not much of a choice, is it?"

Sally's mind began to pick up speed as she searched her memory for a thought that seemed just out of reach. "Isn't there something.....?" Her voice trailed off as she tried to remember, "Something in the Bible somewhere........?" She reached for the book on the table and began thumbing through the pages. She couldn't quite place it but she knew it was in there. "Something about a runaway slave......?"

Suddenly it came to both of them at once. "Philemon!" they spoke in unison.

"Yes, that's the one," Sally continued with growing enthusiasm. "Paul sent one of his friend's runaway slaves back to him with a letter."

"This isn't quite the same thing," Luke interrupted. "This particular slave owner doesn't like me. And to make matters worse, I don't like him either, and he knows it. "

"That's true. We'll have to work on that part."

"What?" Her comment had brought him up short. "He's not a good man, Sal."

"Something about him was different this time, Luke."

"Now you're talking like Henry did a few weeks ago." Luke thought back for a minute. He did an instant review of Tom's words when they had helped Big Joe into the house. He had to agree, something had changed with Tom.

"He even agreed to take the pie that I offered him when he came to get Joseph and Maybeth," Sally added.

"Yeah, but he took it grudgingly," Luke agreed, just as grudgingly. "He probably didn't even share one slice with Big Joe, or even with Maybeth, who helped make it."

"Luke, God can change Tom, and God can change us," Sally exhorted. "Unless, of course, we've gotten too comfortable with the way things are."

"Ouch," said Luke, as he walked over to the open window. He stood looking out into the dark as he gave Sally's last words some serious consideration. "Are you saying that maybe I don't want him to change because, if he does, that puts pressure on me to change?"

"I'm beginning to think you and I should assume that Tom shared the pie, until we find out differently," suggested Sally.

Luke turned around, sat down on the window sill, and smiled at his wife. "Now, *that* will take some imagination, but you're right. It won't be easy, but I'll give it a try."

"What shall we do about the girl, Rena?" asked Sally, drawing the conversation back to the problem at hand.

Luke perched on the sill with his hands on his knees, staring at the floor as he considered the options before him. "I suppose that if Tom has softened and is actually sharing a few slices of the pie, then that big slave she called Abel would be the main problem. I'm not so sure a letter would work in this situation. I guess I'll have to go over to his place tomorrow and try to have a rational talk with the stubborn old goat."

"Luke!"

"Sorry. I forgot for a minute that he shared the pie." He smiled at his wife and added, "I said it wouldn't be easy, didn't I?"

Luke walked over to Sally, took her by the hand, and raised her to her feet. "Let's get some sleep. My imagination works better when it's rested." He picked up the lamp and together they left the room.

The last thing Zekiel heard was Sally giving a big sigh and saying "Lord, please give this stubborn old goat that I married some more faith."

When all was quiet and he was sure it was safe, Zekiel slipped away from the window. As he walked back to the bunkhouse, he said a little prayer of his own, "Lord, I sure would like it if I could see Rena again. Anyways, help dat man across the river t' not hurt her. Seem to me he done 'nuf bad stuff to people."

Chapter 37

Luke's stomach began to churn as he neared the junction in the road that led to Tom's farm. "This couldn't be worse timing!" Luke thought to himself, as he watched Sheriff Roily approach the junction. He was apparently coming from Tom's place. Luke pulled his horse to a stop as the sheriff came alongside.

"'Lo, Sheriff," greeted Luke, without enthusiasm.

"Heading to town, are you?" asked the sheriff, without returning a greeting.

"Nope, just out for a ride. Thought I'd drop in on Tom for a neighborly visit."

The sheriff smirked, "You and Tom ain't never been neighborly, Martin."

"Maybe we've called a truce."

Roily stared at Luke for a minute wondering if that was even possible. When he reached his conclusion, he gave another smirk and said, "Ain't no way that's ever gonna happen." Then he kicked his horse and rode off toward town.

Luke leaned on the saddle horn as he watched him ride away, then turned to look down the road that led to Tom's place. He took in a deep breath of fresh air and breathed out, then urged his horse forward at a steady walk.

"Seems like being a Christian should be easier than this, Lord."

Luke stared at the back of his horse's head as he moved along. "I'm pretty sure you like Tom. But me? I'm pretty sure I don't. I mean, it's not like he's likeable or anything."

Luke rode along in silence for a while. He felt like his attitude toward Tom was reasonable, but try as he might, he couldn't seem to reconcile his own opinion with what he knew was the Lord's opinion of Tom Grant. *"While we were yet sinners Christ died for us"*. Luke thought of another Bible verse. *"For God so loved the world, He gave his only son...."*

The frustration built until he raised his head and looked searchingly at the blue sky. "What on earth do you see in that guy?" He held his gaze. It was almost as if he was expecting to see someone appear.

"I guess," Luke finally conceded, "what I'm saying is, I'd appreciate it if you would let me in on the secret."

"He needs me, Luke."

Before it even sank in that it was the Lord who was speaking from deep inside his soul, Luke shot back with a quick, "Boy, does he ever!"

But then the strangest thing began to happen. Luke could actually feel an ache begin to grow deep in his heart. It felt almost like a sad yearning. Desire, smothered in sorrow, began to overwhelm him.

Without knowing why, Luke swung his horse around and rode back in the direction from which he'd come. When he arrived at the river, he dismounted and tied the reins to a bush, then walked under the bridge to sit down in the shade. "What's going on?" he wondered, as his eyes began to tear up. "Why do I feel this way? What's happening to me?"

Luke was so focused on his situation that he was surprised when the Lord interrupted his thoughts. *"I want him but he won't come."*

"Who?" Luke spoke out loud, "Who won't come?"

"Tom is in great pain."

"What!" exclaimed Luke. "It's Tom who's causing everyone else pain!"

"He doesn't know who his enemy is."

Luke sat quietly, once again engulfed in the strange sadness. He lay back on the ground and closed his eyes.

In his mind, he began to see a terrified little boy, somewhere around five or six years old, lost and alone in a dark forest. Something out there was trying to destroy him but he couldn't discern who, or what, it was. The boy was carrying a long stick and whenever he sensed something near him, he began swinging wildly at the darkness. With tears streaming down his face, the boy was crying out for help.

"He thinks his enemy is you, Luke. He thinks it's the slaves. He thinks it's his family."

There was a long pause.

"He thinks it's me."

Luke rolled over onto his side and rested his head on his arm. As he replayed the conversation and the vision in his mind, he began to wonder if he had made the whole thing up. When he was young, he had often had conversations with frogs and birds, even horses. Was he doing it again?

He rolled back over on his back and stared at the bottom of the bridge as he listened to the river move along on its journey.

But what about the emotions? He could never have made that up. Not in a million years! What was that all about? Was that how the father of the prodigal son felt when his child walked away? Was that the grief of the father whose son had rejected his teachings in the book of Proverbs?

Was that how God, the Father, feels when His child thinks He is the enemy?

"He needs me."   *"Tom is in great pain."*
　"I want him."　　　　　　*"He won't come."*
"He doesn't know who the enemy is."　　*"He thinks it's me!"*

Luke reviewed the words over and over again in his mind.

"No," Luke decided. "I would never have made those words up, especially about Tom! He murdered Joshua's father! He beat Toby with a whip!"

He sat up and plucked a long blade of grass, stuck it between his teeth, then locked his arms around his knees. As he watched the water, he reminded himself that, if the Spirit of God was in him, then it wasn't so odd that the Spirit's voice came from within him.

Things suddenly became very clear. Tom had been deceived into thinking God was the enemy, and Luke himself had also been deceived, believing Tom Grant was the enemy. Luke's pride had led him to trust his own understanding of what he saw in the visible world. Now, he realized he had been suckered into blaming all of the destruction on everyone except the devil himself. And while he and Tom were blaming each other and throwing punches, the destroyer was laying back, munching on a snack, and enjoying the fight.

Luke was embarrassed and ashamed. "Tom needs you, Lord. You want him, and I've been a stumbling block." Luke nodded his head. He knew what he had to do.

Slowly, he stood to his feet and stepped down to the rivers edge, "I'm so sorry. I repent of thinking I was better than Tom. Please forgive me, Lord. I need your help to lower my opinion of myself, and raise my opinion of Tom."

Luke stood watching the river, lost in thought. It crossed his mind that the water in front of him was not the water that had been there when he had arrived at the bridge. That water was long gone, and this water was new. He smiled and closed his eyes. When he opened them again, he knew he was not looking at the water that had been there when he had closed his eyes. He considered that for a minute, then lifted his face to heaven and said, "I don't want the dead sea. I want the river of life!"

Luke felt the ache begin to fade. Eventually, he resumed watching the river again. "I've still got a lot of dirt needin' washed off. Keep the water coming, Lord. Keep it coming."

A leaf caught Luke's attention as it floated down from upstream. With his eyes glued to the leaf as it drifted by, he said, "I place my low opinion of Tom on that leaf."

He watched as the leaf got smaller and smaller, fading into the past. "And I never want to see it again," he mumbled under his breath as the leaf disappeared around the bend in the river.

Chapter 38

Luke rode slowly up to what was known as 'The Grant Mansion'. He was a little surprised to see weeded flower beds and well-manicured hedges. The house and fencing were freshly painted. The barn and carriage house looked to be well-kept, as did the gin house and the storage buildings, even without a fresh coat of paint. He realized that he hadn't paid any attention to his surroundings when he helped deliver Tom's lumber.

In stark contrast to the rest of the plantation, past the carriage house and what he now knew to be the eating house, his eyes fell on the dilapidated, unpainted slave shacks that still remained standing since the storm. They stood as a testimony to life as a servant of Tom Grant.

Luke reminded himself of the picture of the leaf disappearing around the river bend. As he did so, it seemed his eyes were opened to notice two newly-completed houses nearest the eating house, noticeably larger than the rest and ready to be painted. There was also enough lumber stacked nearby to build at least two more houses, maybe more.

"Wow," he spoke to himself. "They've gotten a lot done in a short time."

He dismounted, went to the door and knocked. Etta informed Luke that Tom was out in one of the fields, though she wasn't sure which one. Luke thanked her and returned to his horse as she closed the door. He glanced around and, seeing no one else to ask, walked his horse down the road to the slaves' housing, jumped across the small stream, and approached one of the new buildings. He rapped his knuckles on the door and called, "Anybody home?" After a short time with no response, he glanced around again and, with a little bit of guilt and a whole lot of curiosity, opened the door and peeked in.

The first thing he noticed was a dividing wall, separating off a large bed on the floor made of straw and blankets from an area with three smaller beds also made of straw and blankets. To his surprise, there was a dresser, in fair condition, standing against the dividing wall in the section with the large bed. In the corner across from the larger 'bedroom', he saw a small old woodstove and a table and chair. Shelves built onto the wall which held metal bowls, cups and spoons, and a small knife. A window on the wall, right next to the kitchen table, caught his attention. The view was of the building next to it and there was no curtain, but the light coming through it made the kitchen area seem kind of homey.

"Kin I help you, suh?" asked someone with a deep voice.

Luke nearly jumped right out of his skin. He slammed the door closed and swung around in about the same time it takes for a man to blink. He stood facing a black man who was two or three inches taller and about fifty pounds heavier than himself. Luke figured it was either his response to the man's voice, or the look on his face, or both, that brought the discernable but fleeting smile across the big fellow's face. Then, at the very same moment, both men recognized each other.

"Oh, uh, hello," Luke stumbled for words as he tried to regain his composure. "Abel, is it? I'm Luke Martin. I brought a load of lumber here a couple of weeks ago."

"I 'member, suh."

"I guess I was getting a little nosy. I was curious to see how these turned out." Luke nodded his head toward the new building, "Is this your house?"

Abel's non-response made Luke uncomfortable, so he continued, "I came to talk to Mr. Grant. Do you know where he is?"

"The field, suh," Abel answered.

"But I thought *you* were the driver."

Abel's face suddenly became downcast and Luke regretted his words. "I'm sorry, that is none of my business. I apologize."

"I pulls weeds, trims hedges, and paints buildin's, suh."

Only then did Luke notice the paint pail in one hand and a brush in the other. He guessed that Abel must have been painting on the backside of the building that he had been peeking into. Apparently things have changed, he thought to himself.

"I didn't mean to interrupt you, Abel."

In the shade of a pecan tree at the far end of the row of shacks, Luke noticed two young children playing near a woman sitting on a wooden box. She was concentrating on her sewing, but glanced a couple of times in his direction, obviously curious as to his business. He wondered why he had not noticed her earlier.

"Where did you say I can find Mr. Grant?" Luke asked, turning his attention back to Abel.

"They's all over there," Abel said, "past dat line o' trees." He pointed northwest to a field away from the river.

"Thanks. I'll head over there and see if I can find him," Luke smiled.

"Yes, suh," responded Abel apathetically. He turned and walked away, back around the house to where he had apparently come from.

It crossed Luke's mind to peek into the other new house to see if it was the same, but he quickly came to his senses and walked back to his horse, all the while berating himself for having ever peeked into the first house.

As Luke climbed onto his horse, he turned and looked back at the pecan trees. The woman was still sewing, and the children were kneeling on the ground, looking at something in the grass. He shook his head. "I gotta be about the stupidest guy you've ever saved, Lord. I wonder how many others were watching from the barn or a cracked-open door, wondering why this white man was peeking into their house."

Some pots clanged together in the kitchen of Tom's house. Luke scanned the house and windows, but saw no one. "Maybe I should quit while I'm behind, and get myself home." Luke listened intently, hoping the Lord would agree with him. But he got nothing.

With a deep sigh, he turned his horse and rode off in search of Tom.

"You said you need to talk. So, talk." Tom looked up at Luke, who was still sitting on his horse, and continued dragging the full basket to the back of the wagon. An adult male slave took the basket and lifted it onto the wagon as Tom turned and walked down a nearby row to where a boy was struggling to dump a bag of cotton into another basket. With his back to Luke, he took the bag and emptied it, then handed the empty bag back to the boy without a word. As the boy moved down the row to refill the bag, Tom stomped down the cotton in the basket before dragging it back to the wagon where two other men had also brought baskets to be unloaded.

Sweat was pouring down Tom's face as he stood and arched his back to relieve the pain.

"So, talk. What do you have to say?" he asked, as he grabbed a canteen of water that had been hanging in the shade underneath the wagon.

"Is there somewhere we could go and talk?" Luke asked.

The question irritated Tom. As he lowered the canteen from his mouth, he was working hard to control his temper. Being caught doing manual labor alongside his slaves didn't do anything to improve his mood. Turning to face Luke, Tom put his hands on his hips, cocked his head, and scowled at Luke.

"Look at you, sittin' there all comfortable in your saddle and askin' if we could go sit in the shade and have some tea and crumpets while we have a little private chat. Well, in case you forgot, I have buildings to build, but I can't finish building them because I am way behind on the pickin' - because I've been building buildings!"

Tom swept a hand in a half circle at the field he and his slaves were picking.

"There's already patches showing signs of being past prime picking! I got a whole other field to do," he paused and shook his head, "and you think I got time to sit around and shoot the breeze."

Tom looked out over the field to see where he might be needed.

Luke watched Tom closely and spoke as casually as he could, "We found Rena."

Suddenly, Luke had Tom's full attention. Luke also noticed that others who were within hearing distance stopped picking and listened, without looking his direction.

Tom turned and looked up at Luke. He pointed at some trees lining the field. "Let's go talk," he said as he strode quickly toward the trees.

Sally sat down at the table and scooted her chair in close.

"So, tell me why you're here, Rena. What happened?"

Sally took a bite of buttered cornbread and waited calmly for the girl sitting across the table to respond.

Rena stared at the teacup she was cradling in her hands and said nothing.

Sally lifted her own cup to her mouth and sipped thoughtfully as she studied the sad young face in front of her. "I see you're missing some fingers," Sally added softly, but matter-of-factly.

Rena nodded slightly as she continued watching her teacup.

Sally pursed her lips, set the cup down and slid it aside. She leaned forward with her elbows on the table and her chin resting on her hands. "When Sadie and I got you out of your muddy clothes to wash them, we couldn't help noticing the terrible scars on your backside, Rena."

The girl slowly raised her eyes to meet Sally's and then returned them to the teacup. "Yes'm."

"Did ...?" Sally paused a moment, then continued uneasily, yet gently. "Did Master Grant put those scars there?"

Rena slowly shook her head. She kept her eyes on the cup and said, "No, ma'am." A tear rolled down her cheek as she added, almost in a whisper, "My daddy done it."

Although Sally was relieved that Tom wasn't the culprit, she was totally confused as to why Rena's father would do such a thing. Not wanting to pressure Rena, she simply said, "I see," as she took another sip of tea and waited for the rest of the story.

Eventually, Rena raised her eyes again and spoke. "Massuh made him do it. Daddy cried while he was whippin' me. Massuh say he would kill me if Daddy didn't whip me till massuh say stop. Then massuh cut off my fingers and sold me away."

Rena's tears were flowing freely now. Sally quickly moved around the table and sat down in the chair beside her, drawing Rena to her chest and holding her tight, as the sobbing girl melted in her arms. Sally's own tears were dropping onto the head of the young slave girl as she spoke her prayer for help to the only One who could.

Chapter 39

"So, how long have you had her, and why didn't you bring her with you?"

Tom had no intention of making this easy for Luke. He'd always enjoyed having the upper hand with people, especially Martin.

Luke sat down on a large branch that had long ago fallen from the tree above him. Tom stood with his back to Luke, watching his workers out in the field.

"Found out about her last night," answered Luke. "Two of my guys found her in a shed, sleeping behind some bags of potatoes."

"When did they find her?" Tom asked, as he continued to survey the field.

"I'm not sure. But that really doesn't matter."

"Why didn't you bring her with you?"

Luke straightened his legs in front of him and looked up at the back of Tom's head.

"Tom, did you share the cherry pie, or did you eat it all yourself?"

Luke's question surprised even himself, so he was not surprised when Tom wheeled around and looked at him as if he was crazy.

"What? What cherry pie?" Tom was incredulous. He had his hands on his hips and was leaning forward slightly, looking down on Luke. "Can't you stay focused for even a little while? Long enough to tell me why you didn't bring that runaway with you? I've got her on the sheriff's list and even put a price on her head. But don't you go thinking for one minute that I'll be givin' you a reward for hiding my property! Now you git right back home and fetch her before I turn you in to the sheriff for slave-stealing!"

Luke could tell this wasn't going to be a walk in the park. He pulled his feet back in and leaned forward with his hands on his knees. He stared at the grass at Tom's feet as he spoke.

"I'll have her here by dark. I was hoping you'd hear me out first. I have some things I'd like to discuss with you."

Tom threw his hands up and then dropped them to his sides.

"You're here, aren't you? We're standing here under this tree not gettin' anything done, aren't we? Who cares if a little more cotton rots?" In a mocking fashion, Tom leaned over to pick a daisy, then lowered himself to the ground and lay on his back with one arm behind his head. With his free hand, he held the daisy to the sky and pretended to study it.

"Got any lemonade?" he mocked, as he continued to study the flower.

"Tom...."

"Go ahead, Martin," Tom interrupted, "I got all day. I can't think of anything else I'd rather be doing." He lowered the daisy to his chest and closed his eyes, pretending to be napping.

Luke raised his eyes to heaven. Against the dark blue sky, he could almost see the leaf. He mentally placed his low opinion of Tom back onto the leaf where it belonged and imagined it floating down the river and disappearing around the bend, again.

"You should have been a preacher. So far your sermon is putting me to sleep."

"I'm not here to preach at you." Luke paused and then sighed, "I'm here to ask your forgiveness."

Tom opened his eyes, rolled his head to the side, and studied Luke for a moment. Then he lifted the daisy and spun it between his fingers.

"Your sermon is starting to get interesting, preacher."

Luke rolled his eyes upward and mentally asked for patience.

"About your train ticket to hell, Tom."

"That's it!" Tom quickly struggled to his feet. "Cherry pie, forgiveness, and my train ticket to hell! You have gone completely loony and I got no time for this nonsense!" He threw the daisy to the ground, strode to his horse, and put his boot in the stirrup. As he reached up and grabbed the saddle horn, he looked back at Luke and warned, "And that girl better be here by dark!" And then he pulled himself up into the saddle.

Luke raised his voice to make sure Tom heard, "I'll have ten people here first thing in the morning to help you pick for a week, but only if you shut your mouth for ten minutes and let me talk."

Acting as if he hadn't heard, Tom wheeled his horse and rode away. The horse had gone maybe fifty yards when Tom reined him in and wheeled back around. Luke remained sitting as Tom pulled up in front of him.

"You gotta' be one of the ten. I would enjoy nothing more than to see you sweat over my cotton."

Luke didn't hesitate. "Deal. Now get down off that horse and listen to me. But if you interrupt me one more time, the deal's off."

Tom smiled and dismounted. He reached into his pocket and pulled out a gold watch on a chain. He opened it, glanced at it, and then snapped it shut. "Time starts now," he said, as he slid the watch back into his pocket.

Luke stood up and took a couple of steps toward Tom.

"The day you brought Big Joe over to my place, you said that I was probably right, that God is real and not just a figment of my imagination."

"Now, don't you go an ......"

"Ah, ah, ah," Luke held up his hand. "No interruptions or the deal's off."

Tom groaned as he walked over and settled down on the log.

"Now you owe me another minute," said Luke. Then he continued, "You couldn't be more right than deciding that God is real." Luke began to walk around. "But, you couldn't be more wrong than thinking God wants to zap you with lightning. Now, I don't know if you've already bought that train ticket to hell or not, but if you have," Luke purposefully stopped pacing and looked directly at Tom, "well, it's not too late to return the ticket and get your money back."

"You idiot," Tom interrupted again. "You ain't got no idea what all I done. Who do you think you are, anyhow, pretending to know what God wants to do to me?"

Luke held up his hand again. "Ah, ah, ah. Now you owe me another five minutes, or the deal's off."

"Oh, for ..." Tom stopped, folded his arms, and stared grumpily straight ahead.

When Tom shut up and didn't get up and leave, Luke realized how much Tom needed the help with his cotton harvest. But he was too proud to admit it.

"I've got this pride problem," Luke continued. "I want people to think good of me and respect me. But since you already think I'm a bit crazy, I'm going to risk telling you something about me."

Luke looked at the ground and slowly took a few steps. He was keenly aware that, off to his side, Tom was now eying him.

"There have been a few times when ..." Luke looked up and paused as he tried to think of how to say it. He looked back down and took a step forward. "When ..."

As he paused again, he felt an urging from down deep inside to 'just say it like it is'.

Luke turned and looked directly at Tom. There was no feeling of pride or authority. Actually, Luke was surprised by a sudden feeling of confidence. Tom could 'take it or leave it'.

"Tom, there have been a few times in my life when I think I have actually heard God's voice." He continued quickly, so as not to allow time for Tom to say anything. "I guess I would say it's *almost* a voice, but not quite. I know this sounds nuts but it's like I'm actually *feeling* words and sentences in my mind." Luke shook his head, "No. It's deeper than that. It comes from deep in my soul, but it feels as if my ears are involved, too."

Tom was now looking off toward the slaves working in the field. Luke wondered if he had completely tuned him out.

"It's not my imagination. If it were, I could keep those conversations going all day. But I have no control over it. Sometimes it's only a couple of words, other times it's a few sentences, but when He's said what He had to say, it's over. Silence. No 'goodbye', no "see ya later," or anything. No matter how hard I try, I can't drum it up. It never fails, though - He always leaves me with lots to think about."

It appeared to Luke as if Tom was in another world, seeing something far off, way past his cotton fields.

"I'm probably making it sound like it happens all of the time. Actually, it's only been maybe four or five times in my whole life, until a few months ago. Lately, things seem to have picked up a bit."

Luke decided to find out if Tom had even heard a word he'd said.

"Has anything like that ever happened to you, Tom, or am I just plain crazy?"

Tom kept staring into space.

Luke waited.

"Maybe," Tom finally said, then added, "Maybe not."

"Maybe I'm crazy?" asked Luke.

Tom slowly turned his head. "That too, I suppose," Tom paused, deep in thought, "but maybe I've heard him." Then he added, "Once."

Luke was flabbergasted. He would never have expected to hear *that* from Tom Grant. There was an awkward silence, before Luke remembered he was losing minutes.

"Uh, Tom?" Luke spoke cautiously, not wanting to set him off and ruin his chance of the moment. "I've never been more serious than when I said I've come to ask your forgiveness. Well, I admit that's not what I originally came for, but on my way here, that voice (or whatever - and I happen to believe it's the Spirit of God), well ....,"

Luke made eye contact with Tom, who actually appeared to be interested in what he was hearing. "He sat me down and straightened me out on a couple of things, one of them bein' ... you."

Tom stiffened a little, but allowed Luke to continue.

"The other bein' me. I guess I've been a little thick-headed and ....,"

"A lot thick-headed," Tom calmly interrupted.

Luke dropped his shoulders in defeat. "All right, a lot thick-headed. Actually, I am ashamed of myself," he conceded.

Tom raised his eyebrows, but kept a straight face.

"By the way," Luke added, "you interrupted me again, so now I'm going to take all the time I need, to say what I gotta say."

"Will you get on with it, Martin? I ain't got all day, and you just got to the good part! Now talk, for pity's sake!"

"A deal's a deal," Luke stated flatly.

"Talk!" shouted Tom, as he threw up his hands and turned his back on Luke and watched his people work. The next moment, he spoke as if he wasn't the least bit angry or excited. "You've got my attention. Don't lose it," he said calmly.

Luke tried to remember where he had left off. When he remembered, he continued, "The Lord said that I don't see things as they really are, and that I've really been screwing things up."

Before, Luke would never have admitted that to Tom - even a few hours earlier. He would have felt like he was giving ammunition, aid, and comfort to the enemy.

"Go on," said Tom, without turning around.

"He doesn't like the way I've treated you over the years. He gave me the impression that He really likes you and wants you to like Him, but I'm part of the reason you don't. Of course, I found every bit of that a little hard to believe, at least at first.

Tom smirked, "You found it hard to believe He likes me?"

Luke looked slightly uncomfortable, but continued while he still had the nerve.

"Well, mostly I found it hard to believe that I had anything to do with *you* not liking *Him*. But ... Well, yeah ... I did find it a little hard to believe that God liked you."

"Hmmph. I thought so," returned Tom.

"Yeah, well ..., I was wrong, Tom. In fact, He says that I should be even more amazed that He likes *me*!"

An uncomfortable silence hung in the air for half a minute as Tom watched his slaves and Luke watched Tom.

Finally, Luke spoke again.

"I don't get the idea that God is so much interested in watching us sizzle at the end of a lightning bolt as he is in helping us change. It appears that we're seeing the junk on the outside of each other, but He seems to be looking past that and seeing something better on the inside of us."

"We're beyond fixing, Martin," said Tom firmly.

"Nope," said Luke, even more firmly than Tom. "If God speaks to us," he paused and then stressed, "*even once*," he paused again, "then that's proof we're not beyond fixing! God doesn't waste his time."

Luke's words seemed to make Tom uncomfortable. He pulled

out his gold watch and checked the time. "Yeah, well, it looks like I gave you more than your share of time. Have the girl here by dark." Tom snapped the watch shut. "And I expect ten of you here by nine tomorrow!"

"A deal's a deal," said Luke.

Tom walked to his horse and took hold of the reigns.

"Do you believe in angels, Martin?" Tom asked as an afterthought.

"I actually do, Tom," Luke answered.

"Well then, this ought to interest you." Tom looked gravely at Luke, "I think I beat one up." He paused as if he was seeing it happen. "In fact, I almost killed her."

Tom had a way of leaving Luke speechless. He watched silently as Tom put his left foot in the stirrup and hauled himself up into the saddle. Luke was still trying to get his mind around what Tom had just said.

"You ... what?" he murmured.

Tom either didn't hear him or was ignoring him. He placed his hands on the saddle horn and looked down at Luke.

"What I do with gifts I receive is none of your business. Where I come from, and I come from here, that's called being nosy. But since you probably won't be able to sleep tonight without knowing, I'll tell you. I gave most of the pie to Big Joe and his family. I did take out one large slice and gave it to the angel. I, myself, didn't have any, but tell your wife I'm sure it was good."

And with that, Tom rode off to the field and back to work. Luke was left standing alone, shaking his head and wondering if things had gone as the Lord intended. Personally, he wasn't sure. But he was amazed at how often people who don't like you tell you things you need to know about yourself, because they're not afraid of hurting your feelings.

Luke could feel himself blushing as he remembered peeking into the new slaves' quarters. *Nosy.* He hung his head in embarrassment and rubbed his forehead. What had gotten into him? *"Hey, Tom? What did you do with the pie we gave you?"* Nosy. Luke groaned, "What kind of jerk would ask a question like that?"

As Luke rode home, he thought about the devil's most powerful weapon. Pride. "All I have to do is blink," he said to himself with frustration, "and it slips right in the back door and hides in a corner. The more I know, the more control I have, so the nosier I get. And every time I get nosy, I'm back in Eden, choosing the Tree of Knowledge so that I'll be more like God, more in control. So I won't need to depend on God so much."

He thought about his Creator opposing him, and he shuddered. "God opposes the proud," Luke whispered the verse out loud. It soon crossed his mind that that was a good thing.

He remembered back to his boyhood when he and his dad were visiting a neighbor. The man's son had challenged Luke to climb into a corral that held their breeding bull, and to hit it with a rock. The boy claimed that he had done it, and that the bull's hide was so tough he didn't even feel it. When Luke hesitated, the older boy teased him, and then Luke's pride and reputation took over and became the idol he served. He went to the fence and began to climb. His father, Evan, saw what was happening and shouted for Luke to stop but Luke had placed himself in service to his idol, called "pride." He climbed to the top and over the other side. The neighbor's boy reached through the fence and handed him a large rock. Luke was surprised when he turned around and the bull was moving toward him at a fast trot. He quickly raised his arm to throw the stone. Suddenly huge hands grabbed both of his arms and, with all of the adrenalin and strength his father could muster, he opposed his proud son and lifted him back over the fence just as the bull arrived on the scene.

"Help me, Lord. I don't want to put you in the position that you to have to oppose me," Luke spoke to the sky as he rode home.

Chapter 40

Sally stepped out onto the porch to greet Luke as he arrived. As she started down the steps, her hair shown golden brown in the afternoon sun and, for the first time today, Luke was distracted from the seriousness of his mission. Sally looked different. Younger, maybe? Though she seemed to have lost a bit of her youthful figure lately, her face still had the same radiance of excitement that he remembered when he was courting her. Luke was suddenly entranced by the smile that so easily lifted the burdens of a hard day.

"How did it go with Tom?" she asked with a tone of anticipation, as if she was sure the answer would be wonderful. "Everything's good with Rena, right?"

Luke hit the ground at the same time she did and he took her in his arms and gave her a long, tight hug.

"You're beautiful, you know," he said, as he took a long whiff of her hair. He couldn't see her smile, but he knew she was smiling.

"Must be it went well?" she asked, as she snuggled tightly to his chest.

"I'm not sure, but I think so."

Luke held her back from him so he could look into her curious blue eyes.

"I'll fill you in on the details when I get back but, I must say, this has been one of the more unusual mornings I've ever experienced. Now that I think about it, I guess I forgot to talk to Tom much about Rena coming back, except that I'd have her there by sundown today."

Sally made a quick change from curious to indignant.

"What? Luke, how could you possibly forget about Rena's safety? I can't believe this! We can't take her back there to be beaten and abused by that big monster with the bull whip!" Sally began to plead with her husband. "She has had enough traumas to last a lifetime, Luke. Let's hide her in the new root cellar and send her to this Quaker fellow in Smithston. He can get her up north to Canada where she'll be safer."

She looked desperately up at her husband. "Please, Luke. Her missing fingers aren't the only thing that's happened to her. The devil himself made her own father beat her till there was no skin left on her backside. She told me she was on her way back to Tom's farm last night, hoping they would kill her and end the pain of this life. Please, Luke!" Sally was crying now, and hugging Luke tight.

Luke was silent. He was now questioning his whole experience at the river. Could God really have said he liked Tom? Luke wanted to run down the river until he could grab that leaf and stomp it to pieces. Mentally he had done just that, and the low opinion of Tom that he had retrieved from the leaf was now consuming him.

"I knew he was bad, but I have a hard time picturing him forcing her own dad to beat her like that." he said, trying to stay steady and not lose his temper.

"Who?" asked Sally.

Luke was deep in thought and hadn't heard the question. "I had no idea her father was even on the same plantation," he mumbled, more to himself than to Sally. He felt foolish and betrayed. What made him think Tom would, or even could change?

"You know the man?" Sally asked, backing away so she could see her husband's face.

"He murdered a boy's father. He whipped Toby. He treats his slaves like animals. Sally, he even said he beat up an angel!" Luke's anger was building steadily into a full-fledged tropical storm.

"I thought it was Tom that whipped Toby," said Sally, in complete confusion.

"And to think, I was going to go and help him finish his harvest! I oughta burn his fields instead of picking them!" Luke was so wound up he stomped halfway up the steps and then swung around and stomped back down. "Sally, if I wasn't a Christian, that's *exactly* what I would do! And then I'd bust him in the chops and feel real good about it, even while I was sitting in jail!" Luke said angrily.

"Bust who in the chops, the guy that beat up the angel?" Sally asked desperately.

"Yes! And by the way, he said the angel was a she, like Rena! He's a woman beater, Sally. He's a no-good woman beater!"

"So…, where and when did you meet this man, Luke? And, why didn't you tell me about him before now?"

"Are you kidding me, Sally?" Luke was mystified. "You know Tom. He lives next door! We let him in our house! We even gave the devil a cherry pie!"

First, it was bewilderment, and then, slowly, came the realization.

"Oh, Luke, no," said Sally, as her eyes grew large. She shook her head, "It wasn't Tom who made her father beat her. It was her previous owner, before Tom bought her."

Luke stared at his wife. He was, once again, stunned.

Sally continued, "Rena was running away from Abel, not Tom. She told me her whole story while you were away. She expects Abel will use his bullwhip on her when she goes back. Apparently, he announced to everyone that he was going to take her to live with him in one of the new houses. When Joseph opposed him, Abel took his eye out with his whip. That's when she fled."

Luke dropped his shoulders and went to the steps and sat down. He felt defeated. He could almost hear the devil laughing at him. Luke imagined him mockingly quoting scripture to Luke. ("*I guess you've been thinking a little bit more highly of yourself than you ought. Eh, ol' boy? Pride goeth before the fall and boy, did you fall! You're way too easy, Martin.*")

"Is something wrong, honey?"

"I keep getting reminded how weak I am," Luke sighed and looked up at his wife. "I had decided that I would get rid of my bad feelings about Tom. Kind of like setting them on a leaf in the river and letting them float away, never to be seen again. But it seems I can't just *decide* something into existence."

Sally sat down next to Luke and stared thoughtfully at the ground.

"Jesus said we can't do anything at all, without him," she said as she reached over and took his hand.

"Hmmph. What *I* tried to do didn't even last a few hours."

Sally nodded, "It happens to me, too. Way too often."

Luke gently squeezed her hand. "Well, I guess Jesus was right again - as always," he said. "So, when we take back something we've given over to him, we need to accept the resulting failure and then hand it all back to him and start again."

"And again, and again, and again," Sally chuckled.

"Okay, then." Luke closed his eyes, "Lord, I tried it on my own. I couldn't do it. I want to feel about Tom the same way you do. But I can't - at least, not without your help. I give myself to you. Help me to trust you enough so I won't take my 'self' back again."

"And please use us to help Tom come to you," Sally added, "whether or not he shared the pie."

Luke opened his eyes and looked at his wife. She was staring at the top of a tree or - past it.

"He didn't share it. He gave the whole thing away. He said to tell you that it looked real good, though."

Sally raised her eyebrows and turned to Luke with her patented, questioning look.

Luke nodded. "He gave a big slice to the angel and the rest to Big Joe and Maybeth."

"Did he tell you that?

"Yup."

"The angel he beat up?"

"That's what he says," Luke answered.

"Who *is* this angel?"

"I haven't got the slightest idea. But he was serious when he said it."

Sally thought about it for a minute and then said hopefully, "I hope someday he'll trust us enough to tell us about her."

"Yeah," Luke nodded in agreement and stood to his feet. "I hope I won't be the hindrance that I *have* been, up to this point."

Sally stood behind him and wrapped her arms around him, locking her fingers together in front.

"Well, now you know something you didn't know before," she said. "You know you need a lot of help doing this, and, you know that Tom didn't eat the pie. He gave it away. That's something good about him that you can hang on to."

"That's true. He's also building better housing for his slaves," Luke told his wife. Then he added, "But it took the Lord blowing them all down to get the old coot to do it."

"Luke Martin!"

Luke turned around, smiled, and put his hands on Sally's shoulders, "I was only kidding."

Sally's brow wrinkled in a pout.

Luke kissed the pout away and said, "I do admit that it's going to take both you *and* the Lord to keep me in line, though. By the way, where's Rena?"

"She's with Zekiel. He took her for a walk. He's trying to reassure her that you'll take care of everything and she'll be alright."

"With Zekiel, huh?" Luke thought about that for a minute. "She is kind of cute. Too bad she'll be so close, and yet so far away."

"Zekiel's not bad looking either. And he's so nice." Sally thought for a minute and said, "You don't suppose you could …"

"No, I could not," Luke interrupted. Then, "Well, at least not yet. First, I'm hoping he'll take her back without dishing out heavy consequences for running away."

"This is going to require immediate action!" said Sally.

Luke was instantly nervous.

"Like, what do you have in mind?" he asked.

"Prayer, that's what," she answered smartly. "I'm going to talk to all of the girls. We'll pray all afternoon while we're working."

Luke relaxed. "Wonderful idea! Keep the devil busy fighting an army of prayin women."

The screen door slammed and Frank appeared at the top of the steps. With his hands on his hips, he announced, "The meatloaf is getting cold, the salad is wilting, and *I'm* wilting from starvation."

Chapter 41

Every bone in him ached. It took quite an effort to appear energetic and unaffected by the day's labor as Tom climbed what seemed a mountain of stairs to his porch. As he eased himself down into his cushioned deck chair, Tom called for Etta.

"Yessuh, Massuh. I'm a'commin," she answered from inside the house.

"Can you bring me a large glass of lemonade? I've never needed it more, I don't believe."

"Yessuh, Massuh," Etta called out. "I b'lieve a big piece o' cake might go well wif it, suh."

Tom leaned his head back and closed his eyes. "That sounds reeeal good, Etta, real good." And with that, Tom fell fast asleep.

A few moments later, Etta stepped out onto the porch with a pitcher of lemonade and a small plate of chocolate cake on a tray. When she saw that her master was asleep, she walked quietly past him and gently set the tray down on the table next to his chair. As she straightened up to leave, she paused and looked down at the white man who had nearly killed her, sleeping peacefully. His hands were folded in his lap and his head was leaning back and slightly to the right. She watched his chest rise and fall. His breathing was steady and peaceful.

Finally she gave a sigh and shook her head. "*Lord, dis boy need mercy. He need somebody, somebody good.*" Etta spoke her prayer quietly, then headed for the screen door. As she pulled the door open, she glanced to her right and noticed a carriage approaching.

"Oh, dear Lord," she mumbled to herself, "Now, who this be?"

Etta quickly shuffled back to the table and picked up the tray and began to talk loudly. "Here your cake and lemonade, suh." She set the tray noisily down on the table as she pretended to accidentally bump his foot.

Tom's eyes opened slowly as he raised his head and looked up at Etta. Once she saw that she had his attention (however foggy that might be), she turned and looked down the driveway.

"Oh!" she exclaimed, acting surprised. "I do b'lieve summun's commin' up d' road, suh."

Tom's head quickly cleared and he sat up straight. He peered down the road, trying to make out who it was.

"Looks like Martin," he said. "He's supposed to bring Rena back." Tom noticed the surprised look on Etta's face. "Apparently they found her hiding at their place," he added.

"Poor thing," Etta clucked. "I hear she thought she was gonna be teamed up wif Abel."

"Yeah. Well, Abel and I have come to an understanding about that. Because of the trouble he caused, he can't have her. I made it perfectly clear that if he pesters her in any way, he'll regret it forever. Shoulda sold him right then and there, but I got too much work needing done. He ain't the field boss anymore, though. Proved he can't handle it," Tom said as he walked to the porch rail.

"There was a time when I'd have given the girl fifty lashes for running and then I'd have gotten rid of her." He hesitated, "Now, I don't quite know what to do. She did have good reason to be scared, I suppose."

The vivid image played out again in Tom's mind. "You should be glad you didn't see Joe's eye, Etta. But after what I done to you, I can't think ole Abel's any worse than I am."

"No, suh, he ain't no worse den you," Etta responded.

Tom took his eyes off of Luke and turned to Etta with a frown. Luke drew the carriage to a stop at the porch steps.

"But you is right to punish him, suh," she continued. "You d' massuh on dis here farm, 'n he done wrong. God give *you* dis farm, an' d' thority dat goes with it."

Luke and Rena sat quietly and listened.

"Just what do you mean, 'Abel ain't no worse than me'?" Tom was still frowning at her.

"I means you need d' Lord as much as he does!"

Etta showed no fear, nor was there any animosity. She was only saying what she thought he needed to hear.

Tom's face was beginning to turn crimson, and he might have raised his voice a little in his response, if he had not suddenly remembered that he had an audience.

He turned to Luke, then back to Etta, and then back to Luke. He cleared his throat and spoke. "Etta, bring another glass and another piece of cake. Mr. Martin will be joining me here on the porch."

"An' for the girl?" Etta asked properly.

Tom slowly turned and gave Etta his full attention. He spoke slowly, speaking each word stiffly. "The girl will not be joining us." Turning back, he looked past Luke to Rena and added, "She will probably want to be getting some rest, because she will be working *very* hard, and I mean *very* hard, to make up for the time she has been away."

"Yes, Massuh," replied Etta, as she hurried off to the kitchen.

"Rena," said Tom.

"Yessuh," Rena replied hesitantly.

"Joe and Maybeth are expecting you. You're staying with them in the new building next to the eating house. Now, get going." Tom had spoken firmly, but Luke saw no indication that Rena was in danger of serious retribution.

As an afterthought, Tom added, "And Abel won't be bothering you."

A wave of relief swept over Rena. She had expected to be sent directly to Abel. Even though Tom made it clear that he was not happy with her, Rena felt as if he had hugged her. She had taken beatings before, and she was not afraid of hard work, but she had imagined the worst with Abel. So, to be told she would be living with Big Joe and his family... Well, that was so much better than she had dared to hope.

Rena immediately hopped down out of the carriage. She smiled shyly and said, "Yes, suh. Thank you, suh," then turned and walked quickly away. Suddenly she stopped, turned around, and slowly returned to Massuh Grant.

"I'm sorry I run away, suh. You be right to beat me, suh. I shouldna' run. Won' run no more, suh." She looked at the ground, waiting for Tom's response.

Tom could feel Luke's eyes on him and he resented being put on the spot. His body began to ache throughout from his long day of work in the field. Tom grew angry and flustered.

"You *should* be sorry! I ain't gonna beat you this time, but don't try me again! Now, I said 'get going', so, git!"

The smile returned to Rena's face.

"Yes, suh. Thank you, suh."

"I said, 'git'!" Tom repeated with a raised voice.

Rena turned and, this time, ran happily to find Maybeth, Joe, and the children.

Tom turned his attention to Luke.

"You git, too, Martin!" he said gruffly. "I've decided that I'm tired, and I'm not up to havin' a tea party right now. It's been a hard day. Just be sure you git yourself here first thing in the morning. I expect promptness!"

"I understand."

Etta had come out onto the porch with a tray of cake and glass of lemonade for Tom's guest.

"And Tom," Luke added, "thanks for giving Rena a break."

Tom scowled. "I can't wait to have you working and sweating in my fields for a week," he said. "It'll be kinda like you taking her punishment for her. If you do a good job and work hard, maybe - just maybe - I'll let up on her a little."

"It's a deal," said Luke.

"I said, maybe," Tom reminded Luke, as he turned and walked away.

Etta watched Tom disappear into the house, and the screen door shut behind him. Turning to Luke, she held out the tray, offering him the cake and lemonade. Luke thanked her for fixing it, but declined, saying that he needed to be going on home.

As Luke turned the carriage around and drove away, Etta sat down in Master Grant's chair and helped herself to some cake and lemonade as she watched Luke disappear around the bend.

Chapter 42

"Here's the deal, fellas," said Luke. "You thought we were finished, but we have some more cotton to pick."

Luke watched the faces of his slaves as the gears turned in their heads. He knew they were searching their memories trying to remember which field had not yet been picked. They had all gathered in the large hay barn that evening, expecting to be given instructions about hoeing and weeding the fields in preparation for the next plantings of peanuts, cotton, and oats.

Luke continued, "Our neighbor, Mr. Tom Grant, has encountered numerous setbacks during this year's harvest and is in need of our assistance to save what remains of his crop."

The looks of surprise and confusion were expected so Luke quickly added, "The main reason Mr. Grant is behind on his work is because he is building better quality housing for his slaves. I have seen the new houses and I assure you he is improving the lives of his workers."

Luke paused and looked around the group. "I have offered our assistance, partly in exchange for Mr. Grant's humane treatment of the girl Rena, the runaway who was with us for a short time. Some of you had the opportunity to meet her."

Luke focused in on Zekiel. "Mr. Grant has made it clear that the man named Abel will not be having any dealings with Rena."

"I think he intends to work her extra hard for a while," Luke went on, looking at Gideon and the rest of the group, "but if we go over there and give our one hundred-percent effort, I am convinced he won't hurt her."

Luke's eyes honed in on the boy leaning against the barn wall with crossed arms. He had an angry, stubborn look chiseled on his face and stared hard at the ground.

Luke continued, "The man has done some terrible things, but I think the Lord is changing him. It's kind of like breaking a wild horse. The horse is fighting back, but he's getting tired, and the Lord has no intention of getting off his back."

"Joshua." When Luke spoke his name, all heads turned, and Joshua slowly raised his head to his master. The angry look did not change. "Joshua, I will not make you go with us."

Everyone noticed the boy's face soften and his body relax a lilttle.

Luke went on with his assignments, "You and Ambrose will remain here and tend to the animals and chores. My wife will be here along with Mahta, Dinah, and the baby."

He switched his attention to the others. "I intend to pay each of you for your work at Mr. Grant's. But the main reasons we are going to work hard are for Rena's safety and a man's soul. Is everyone with me on this? Do you understand where I'm coming from?"

Heads nodded and a few 'Yes, suh's' were spoken.

"Good. Let's all turn in and be ready to pull out at first light."

As the men were leaving, Luke came alongside of Joshua and put a hand on his shoulder. "Can I talk with you for a minute?"

"Yes, suh," said the boy as he looked up at Luke with curiosity in his eyes.

"Have a seat," offered Luke as he sat down on a bale of cotton and patted the space at his side.

For a long minute, they both sat silently and stared straight ahead. Soon everyone was gone and the yard was quiet.

Luke finally spoke, "I don't like him either."

Joshua didn't respond.

"I've spent most of my life not liking him," said Luke. "He's not a friendly man."

There was still no response from Joshua. The two sat together quietly as Luke tried to find the words to help Joshua understand.

"I feel like I need to explain to you why I'm doing this for Mr. Grant." Luke closed his eyes as he continued. "Your situation is so much harder than mine, and I understand that. But I think God showed me why Mr. Grant has acted so badly."

Luke opened his eyes and looked down at Joshua. "He's mad at God for killing his wife and his daughter, kinda like you're mad at Mr. Grant for killing your father."

Joshua looked up at Luke. "God kilt em?"

"That's what he believes. He also had a bad family life when he was young, and now he's turned into a very bitter man. He's running away from the only safe place there is."

"Where dat?"

"The arms of God," Luke answered. "Bad things happen on this earth because mankind turned from God and went out where it wasn't safe. But the Lord still loves us and wants us to come back."

Joshua looked thoughtfully at Luke, expecting him to continue.

"Did you love your father?" Luke asked.

Joshua nodded a yes and sniffed.

"Any brothers or sisters?"

"Yes, suh."

"Were they always nice to you?"

"No, suh. Sometime dey wern' nice."

"Did your father love them?"

"Yes, suh."

"How do you know?"

Joshua didn't answer immediately. Then he turned and looked up at Luke through tear-soaked eyes and said, "He cried when dey git sol'. He cry a bunch!"

Joshua turned away and tried to restrain a whimper.

Both sat for a moment and then Joshua added, "I lay in bed at night listenin' to him cryin' 'n prayin' dat d' Lord be wit' dem, wherever dey was."

"Did he ever punish them when they did wrong?" Luke eventually asked.

"Yes, suh. He punished all o' us."

Luke feigned mild surprise. "Even though he loved all of you?"

"Yes, suh, he did, but he hug us, too."

Luke nodded and looked down at the young boy sitting beside him.

"Joshua, I'm pretty sure God loves Mr. Grant. But Mr. Grant has been acting like a rebellious child who needed a whippin'. I remember a time when I was a child that I got whipped real good. Afterwards, I was pretty sure my dad didn't love me. When my dad was finished, he said all the right things about loving me and that it hurt him more than me, but I refused to believe him. Kinda like Mr. Grant feels about God.

"I stewed and stewed, and kept comforting myself by telling myself that I had been unfairly treated. I decided I would be better off without this man who had, in my eyes, just proved he did not love me!

"The following morning, I announced that I would be leaving because I was old enough to take care of myself, and I was no longer going to hang around an unfair father. I was around twelve or thirteen at the time. I'm not exactly sure."

"Bout same age as me 'n Frank," Joshua commented dully.

"Yep, 'bout the same age," Luke agreed, and then continued his story.

"My mom's eyes were watering when she handed me a bag of food as I walked out the door because I wouldn't even let them hug or kiss me. As I walked away, I heard my dad say, 'I love you, Luke.' But I just grunted and kept walking."

"I followed Town Road northwest, intending to get to the mountains and live the rest of my life as a man of the wilderness. No problem. I was going to hunt and trap for food and skins, the same way my dad had done. And I did fine until nightfall.

"During the day a few travelers on horseback or in a wagon passed by, but when it got dark, there was no one for miles around. I had not remembered to bring along any means of starting a fire. The clouds in the sky blocked out the stars, so I was in absolute darkness. I packed myself tight into a bunch of bushes and sat perfectly still trying to breathe as quietly as possible. I was scared. I prayed in my mind, but didn't dare say anything out loud that someone, or something, might hear. For hours I sat, wide awake, listening for the slightest sound. Eventually I was rewarded by the sound of a breaking twig. I was no longer scared. I was terrified! I began shaking, and I remember trying hard to relax and make the shaking go away, but I shook till I was totally drained of energy. The last thing I remember was praying that my father would come.

"The next thing I knew, the sun was shining brightly in my eyes. As I shielded my eyes with my hand, I saw a huge man on a huge horse that was stopped in the road, calmly smoking a cigar and studying me. His long beard was stained with tobacco juice and coffee and I'd guess he hadn't had a bath in his whole life. He made me awful nervous."

Joshua was now listening intently and watching his master's eyes. They were sparkling as they looked off into the distant past and saw it all happening as if it were today.

"The man had a deep, gruff voice, and when he asked, 'Ya lost, boy?' all I could do was shake my head. The gravelly voice was enough to scare a kid all by itself, but when added to his rough look and his immense size, I was pretty much speechless. The man sat and stared at me a moment longer, and then climbed off his horse. By the time his foot touched the ground, I was running through the thick brush, away from the road. I heard him yell behind me, but I didn't stop. As I ran, I kept looking over my shoulder to see if he was gaining on me, so I wasn't prepared to run hard, right into another man. That man held onto my shoulders as I tried to beat my way free of him, screaming and crying and pounding. But my enemy was persistent, and much stronger.

"He kept saying, 'Luke, it's okay. It's okay, Luke." I didn't stop to wonder how the guy knew my name, just kept struggling. I was nearly out of my mind.

He kept speaking. "I'm here, Luke. I'm here. Calm down now, it's okay.'

"Slowly, the voice became the voice of my father. I looked up in amazement and stopped pounding and screaming. Sure enough, out in the middle of nowhere, I found myself in the arms of my father.

"At that moment, the big man came crashing through the bushes behind me and stopped in his tracks. He was every bit as surprised to see my dad as I was. My father gently pushed me aside and picked up his rifle.

"Can I help you, mister?" he asked, as calm as if he was sitting at home drinking tea by the fire.

"It took a few seconds for the guy to respond. 'That there's my boy! We had a little argument, that's all,' he said. 'I was just coming to get him n' take him home.'

"What's the boy's name?" my father asked him.

"Now, that's none of your business! Give me my boy and we'll be going!" he said angrily, but he kept his distance.

"My dad pulled the hammer back, lifted the rifle a ways, and asked, 'Who's your father, Luke, him or me?'"

"Joshua, you should have seen that big guy's face when I answered my dad's question. He started slowly backing up while saying something about how much I resembled his son, and apologizing for the mistake. When my father raised the gun to his face and looked down the sight, the fella turned and ran through the thickets faster'n a frightened bear.

"My dad held his position until we heard the sound of a horse running full speed down the road. Then he lowered his gun and relaxed, and asked me if I still wanted to head north, or maybe come back to him and my mother. After I assured him that I was more than ready to come home, I asked him how he had gotten there.

"'Luke,' he said, 'I let you run away, but I never let you out of my sight.'"

Luke looked down at Joshua, who had not taken his eyes off him through the whole story, and said, "Me and Mister Grant are kinda like you and your brothers when you squabbled. Your father still loved all of you even though you weren't getting along with each other. Can you see what I'm trying to say?"

Joshua turned away and looked at the ground. "No, suh!" he said bluntly.

"My father was like God, in that instance," Luke continued. "God loves Mr. Grant and He loves me, even though we've been fighting. And even though Mr. Grant is mad at God and sins against him by running from him, God has never let Mr. Grant out of his sight. He's letting the man suffer some, but he is still close by."

Luke paused and asked, "Are you following me in this?"

"I suppose," Joshua mumbled grudgingly. "My pa loved us too." But then he added, with force, "But his kids din' kill each other!"

Luke's shoulders slumped in frustration. "Yeah, it's not quite the same thing as a squabble, is it."

"No, suh! It ain't!" Joshua responded firmly.

"Well, the truth is, Joshua, God's kids killed his son, Jesus. It grew to be much more than a squabble." Luke paused and cleared his throat. He took a deep breath, and continued, "God's been telling me that my hatred grieves *Him,* and He wants me to knock it off. Because everybody's sins are the reason His son, Jesus, was killed. So, even though I don't much care for the guy, God wants to forgive Mr. Grant and invite him into his family. And he wants to use me to do it."

"He don't deserve it!" Joshua said boldly.

"No, he don't," agreed Luke. "But, I don't either. I guess that's why forgiveness is called 'giving a gift' instead of 'paying a debt'."

Luke stopped a moment, wondering how he could help Joshua understand.

"By leaving them the way I did, I was telling my parents that I didn't need them any longer. And yet ....," Luke paused thoughtfully. "And yet, my father was willing to spend a cold night in the dark, and risk his life, to make sure I was safe. I didn't deserve it, Joshua," Luke added. "It was his gift of love to me."

Luke continued, "I don't want you to think that I've sided against you, or that I don't think Mr. Grant did a very bad thing when he killed your father. God was probably crying, too, when Mr. Grant did that. But I do want you to understand that I'm one of the people that killed Jesus, and I am grateful that God forgave me. I love Him and I want to please Him. So, even though it won't be easy, I am trying to obey Him in this, because I love God - even more than I dislike Tom Grant."

"Guess you do, Massuh," said Joshua, more sad than angry. "Don't know's I kin do it."

Luke turned and put his arm around the boy's shoulders and drew him close.

"Yeah. I have to admit I'm not all of the way there yet either. And it's gotta be so much harder for you. But we have to keep trying. We can't stop trying."

Luke stood to his feet. "What do ya say we get some sleep, huh?"

"Yes, suh," Joshua answered as he slowly rose to his feet.

Luke put out the torches and lanterns in the barn as they left.

"Good night, Joshua," Luke said softly, as Joshua walked thoughtfully to the bunkhouse. He waited until the boy had gone inside before putting out the two torches in the yard.

Standing in the darkness, he spoke, "I really *don't* know if I can do it, Joshua, but talking with you sure helped."

He stood for a minute, staring into the darkness after Joshua, thinking about the truth of what he'd been saying. Talking things through, trying to help Joshua understand, had actually helped Luke understand - even though all Joshua had done was listen.

"Thank you, Lord," he whispered. "I think this was more for me than him."

He turned and headed for bed, feeling much more ready for tomorrow than he had expected to be.

Chapter 43

Tom Grant's plantation had never been so busy. Day after day, full wagons headed to the barns and returned to the field empty, only to soon be heading back to the barns, filled again. For four days now, forty-five workers had accomplished twice as much each day as thirty-five had in previous days. By the third day, Tom had given up all pretense of being grumpy. He even admitted to himself that, for the first time since his daughter had been born, he was actually feeling a sense of elation, though he tried hard not to show it. On the outside, he remained serious and spent the days giving instructions and riding back and forth between the field and the barns and gin house.

There is a difference however, between grumpy and serious, and not one person on the plantation failed to notice the difference in Tom. Over the four days, Tom had gradually changed from being a ruling dictator to a supervisor, and he hadn't even been aware of it. The sun had cooperated and the fields were dry. Tom understood it was of no small credit to Luke that he was not going to lose his crop, but he did have to admit to taking a little pleasure in seeing the beads of sweat that ornamented his neighbor's face.

He also had to admit that Luke was a man of his word, and he was giving it everything he had in him. On the surface, Tom told himself that Luke was merely paying off his debt to Tom for his giving up valuable time to listen to Luke talk about religion and God; it was a trade, and nothing more. But the night before at dinner, Etta had insisted there was more to it than that. As she was pouring his coffee and filling his soup bowl, she once again was insisting the young boy that his mama and grandmother had known could still be given the freedom to show himself.

"Massuh Martin ain't here to pay no debt," Etta had argued. "He here 'cause d' Lord done drag him over here to show ya dere ain't nothin' God can't do!"

"Stop it, Etta." Tom tried to cut her off, but she would have none of it.

"Dem demons you listen to want you to shut me up, suh, cuz dey don' want you to know da Lord loves you."

"I said, stop it, Etta!" Tom pounded his fist on the table and stood up glaring at his house servant.

Etta continued slicing some bread as she proceeded, undaunted. "Dem demons you listnin' to tried to kill me once already 'n dey like t' try again." She sighed, "Dat be jus' fine. I'z tired, and I'z ready."

Tom had stood there, staring at the old woman. As he watched her spread butter on the slices of bread, a fleeting impression of Etta standing in the doorway of his bedroom, her face bloodied by his own hand, flashed in his mind. Tom's face had softened as he slowly sat back down in his chair. Etta slid the bread next to Tom's bowl of soup and walked over to the counter and returned with a jar of honey. She was completely unshaken and going about her duties as if everything was 'life as usual'. But her master was not eating. He sat staring down at his soup without seeing it. Etta had felt no need to either interrupt his thoughts or urge him to eat.

Tom was mulling over his conversation with Etta as he waited for the next wagon load, but his thoughts were interrupted and brought back to the present when Luke walked up to him. His shirt was soaked in sweat and he looked to be completely worn out from the day's labor.

"It looks as if we'll be done with the field a day ahead of time. Maybe a day and a half," Luke said, breathing heavily. "We could help get that lumber put up and some painting done for the rest of our time here. What do ya think?"

Tom was taken completely off guard. What he had expected to hear was a request to be let out of his time commitment early.

"Or," Luke added, "We could keep ginning and loading wagons for town, if you want your people to do the construction work. It's your call."

This was probably the first time in his life that Tom couldn't think of a smart reply to keep Luke in his place and, at the same time, maintain his own supposed dignity. His mind was racing to come up with something, but he had been disarmed. He could almost hear Etta's voice telling him to give up and 'let him out jus' this once. He's in there, suh'.

Tom surrendered.

"No, Martin, you kept your word. When the field's done, you go ahead and take your nigras home."

"The way I remember it, I offered you ten people for a week."

"To pick cotton."

"Then show me where the next field is and we'll pick it."

"It's all picked! There ain't any more!"

"Then I only kept half my bargain. What about the other half, the part about ten people for a week? Are you going to keep me from being a man of my word?"

"What exactly are you trying to say?" Tom was beginning to tense up.

Before Luke could respond, the sound of laughter drifted their way. They both turned toward the sound and saw Big Joe, Maybeth, Rena, and Zekiel working on adjoining rows. Apparently one of them had said something pretty funny, because all four were laughing and talking as they picked.

"I ain't heard that sound around here for years," Tom said, half to himself. "By the way, have you noticed that boy has been pickin' in the row next to Rena every day this week?"

"He's the one that found her hiding at my place," said Luke, as they both continued to watch.

"Looks like a strong one, a hard worker."

"The best."

"I don't suppose you'd be interested in selling him, would you?" asked Tom as he watched Zekiel.

"Nope." Then Luke asked, "I don't suppose you'd be interested in selling the girl, would you?"

"Nope."

The two men stood side by side scanning the field of men and women all bent at the waist.

"I'd pay top dollar for her," Luke finally commented.

"Nope." Tom glanced at Luke as he spoke, "But I might have mercy on you and let your people help me use up the rest of my lumber, and gin some cotton till Saturday night, but that's as far as I go."

Luke stared thoughtfully at the workers. "Throw the girl into the mix and it's a deal," he said, with a sly smile.

Tom exploded. "You have got to be kidding me!!" He threw up his hands. "Are you nuts? You just stood right here and told me that finishing the week was already a part of the deal, and now you're talkin like you'll do me a favor, if I throw in a little extra!!"

"Yes, I was and, maybe I am. Now calm down, will ya? I'm sorry. All right?" said Luke, with a hint of a smile.

"Yes, you was *what*?"

"I was kidding."

"Maybe you are *what*?"

"Maybe I am a little nuts."

Tom began to relax again. "Humph. No maybe's about that part."

"I said I was sorry."

Tom pretended to ignore the apology. "Looks like I'm one man short out there. What was that deal again?"

"All right, all right." Luke shook his head and pointed to an empty row next to Gideon. "I think I see the tenth guy over there. I'll go out there and make him get to work."

"It's about time," Tom said, loud enough for Luke to hear as he headed out to resume picking Tom's cotton.

The talking and laughing continued in Tom's cotton field as he watched Luke walk away.

Chapter 44

"Word around town has it that Sheriff Roily thinks you're hiding runaways out at your place, Luke. I've been waiting for you to come in for your order, to tell you."

Henry heaved the bag of grain onto the back of the wagon as he talked. Luke dragged the bag to the front of the wagon as he listened.

"That 'Lenny' fella was in here yesterday, bragging on how the sheriff asked him and a few others to accompany him on a surprise visit out to your plantation tomorrow night. It was supposed to be a surprise but I thought maybe you don't like surprises so much."

Henry leaned on the back of the wagon and looked up at Luke. "Ellis told Roily that him and his sons saw a slave slinking around in your woods a few months ago; even took a few shots at him, but think they missed him cause it was so dark out."

Luke jumped down from the wagon and the two men walked together into the feed room to get more bags.

"Also, Roily is a little bit furious with you 'cause you stole his reward. He's saying you hid one of Tom's slave girls til Tom put up a reward; then you suddenly showed up with the girl to collect the reward for yourself."

They arrived at the stack of bagged grain, and a black man lifted a bag onto Luke's shoulder. Luke stepped back and the man did the same for Henry.

"Both stories are basically true," Luke explained, as they approached the wagon, "except that I didn't hide her and I got no reward. It was she who was hiding from all of us, in one of my sheds. I took her back as soon as I found out."

They both dropped the bags onto the wagon at once. Luke turned to Henry and smiled as he raised his left eyebrow. "My reward, if you could call it that, was a week's labor picking cotton in Tom's field and building a slave shack. Now, why would Sheriff Roily be angry with that?"

Henry stepped back a step in amazement. "There's no way you did that! You're pulling my leg!"

Luke hung his head and admitted, "It's true, Henry. Eight of my workers, Frank, and I all got to share the reward."

Henry started laughing, "How on earth did Tom talk you into doing that?"

Luke grew serious. "Actually, it was my idea, not Tom's."

"I don't understand."

"Well, it was my intent that Tom might not be so rough on the girl, Rena, for running away. I think it did help, but our real reward in all of this was that, after a week of helping Tom out of a bind, there seems to be a whole lot less animosity between us."

"Well, hallelujah and praise the Lord!" Henry cheered, loud enough to turn some heads across the street.

"Now, don't go getting the idea that we're bosom buddies, but I do think the Holy Spirit might be grieving a bit less."

Some noise up the street caught the two men's attention. Frank, Joshua and two of Al Willis's boys were racing straight toward them. Joshua was in the lead, with Frank close behind, but the two Willis boys were gaining on them fast. As Luke appeared to be the finish line, he braced himself, preparing for the worst. If all four crashed into him at once, he would be in desperate need of a doctor. Even though it was probably too late, Luke held his hands out in front of him and yelled, "NO! STOP!!"

At the very last possible moment, the small mob split and ran by him, two on each side.

"I won!" shouted Joshua.

"It was a tie!" Frank insisted.

"I won," claimed the smallest Willis boy.

"You were last!" the other three insisted in unison.

"Was not! When you all 'bout hit Mr. Martin, you closed your eyes and I shot right past the whole bunch of you and won. You just didn't see it."

Frank turned to his father. "Who won, Pa?"

Luke shrugged his shoulders and said, "I was so scared, I closed my eyes and prepared to die. I didn't see anything."

Joshua went next to Henry, "You saw it, Mr. Henry, didn't you? You saw me win?"

Henry chuckled as he gave it some thought. "You fellas were all very fast!" he mused diplomatically. "That's the closest thing I've ever seen to a four-way tie, but I'd have to say I saw Joshua win by a nose."

Joshua gave a satisfied look of triumph to his friends as Frank admitted, "Yeah, okay, but only by a nose."

Henry rubbed his chin with his hand and nodded his head up and down. "That's right, only by a nose," he agreed, "but a nose is a nose, and Joshua won by it."

Luke reached into his pocket and pulled out ten cents.

"Congratulations, all of you," he said. "Head on over to Wally's and each of you get a stick of licorice. And Joshua," Luke handed Joshua the coins, "winning by a nose deserves an extra stick."

A few excited 'thank you's and then they were gone, leaving a cloud of red-tinted dust in their wake.

Henry chuckled as he watched them leave, but quickly grew serious.

"Luke, I've got a bad feeling about how Lenny 'just happened' to drop in and spill the beans about the sheriff's plans for tomorrow night. It might be a good idea to head on home real soon and take care of whatever might need to be taken care of, in case he got his nights mixed up and shows up tonight - or maybe at first light, tomorrow."

"Yeah, if he wants to see papers on all of them, I have one loose end to tie up," said Luke. "Do you remember I told you about an old woman we found in the woods? She said she was dropped off in the swamps south of here and left to die because her master thought she was too old and useless to keep feeding."

Luke became more animated. "And get this, Henry. The guy

apologized and even told her that he hoped everything would turn out okay for her. Can you believe that?"

Henry shook his head, "Helps take some of the guilt away, I suppose."

"Yeah, maybe," said Luke, halfheartedly.

"But that's a loose end you might need to take care of," agreed Henry.

"Thanks for the tip, Henry. I think I'll go find Al. He goes by my place on his way home. He might be willing to stop off and pick up a boarder on the way."

Henry shook his head. "Young kids have a way of blurting out things to the wrong people and Al's got a passel o' young kids."

"Well then, I guess it's time to test plan B. Kinda like a 'test run' for the railroad."

Henry grew very interested. "Do you have the place finished?"

"Almost as good as a hotel room," Luke replied with pretend pride. "It has hidden fresh air ventilation, two chairs, a small table, and even an oversized wooden platform for sleeping on. When someone's in there we can supply lots of blankets, food, and fresh water."

"Wonderful! Then I'd suggest you go right home and put the woman in there, as soon as possible."

Henry got even more serious. He looked around before he spoke. "The railroad can not afford to relax or take chances. This will be a good drill for you in case you decide to join. Always assume the worst. Assume the sheriff's little band will visit you tonight."

"That reminds me, Henry," Luke said, "Matthew's in on this with us, and we have all agreed to let this Quaker guy 'Hackett' know we're getting prepared, but that we don't think we're up for regular traffic, as yet." Luke smiled, "We're ready to get our feet wet, but not sure we know how to swim. But if there are any real serious emergencies, then we'd be willing to take them."

A look of relief swept over Henry and he closed his eyes for a moment and smiled. Luke guessed he was silently thanking the Lord. But the next moment Henry was once again 'all business'.

"That's real good to hear, Luke. I'll contact Hackett and let him know that you're on board in a limited way. But for now, you get on outta here. God bless you, Luke."

Chapter 45

"No need to apologize, ma'am," said Mahta, with a wave of her hand. "Even dis here is better than d' las place I live."

Butter and a loaf of bread had been placed on the table alongside two jars of peaches, a bowl of broth, and a pan of cornbread. On the floor near the back wall was a bucket of fresh water with a ladle. There were also two empty buckets and a few newspapers in case it was not safe for the travelers to go out to the outhouse.

Mabin and Luke had tested candles and lanterns in the dark and found that the glow of a candle could not be seen from the vent at the top of the storehouse, but that the faint glow of a lantern could be detected at night if someone was looking really carefully. Therefore, a lantern would be allowed during the day but at night, only a candle.

"I know that it's only for a couple of nights, Mahta," Sally said, as she handed the woman a jar of jam, "but you don't deserve this."

"Life be dangerous. Firs' time I feel safe is here wit' you folk, even down here, ma'am." Mahta motioned toward the dividing wall. "Even dat wall can't keep out da Lord. Here I am thankin' Him, and here you is, apologizin'."

Sadie laid a stack of blankets on the wooden platform and gave Mahta a hug.

"Dinah's going to miss Eli's nurse."

"Dat gal's full recovered," Mahta answered with a smile. "It's okay for an old woman to have some fun afore she dies."

"Right," laughed Sally, "Like this is going to be a party."

"Humph," Mahta grunted. "Dark babies ain't no dif'rent den

white babies. Dat sweet baby done makes noise in d' night jus' like babies 'sposta. I'm sayin' I'm gonna have some fun *sleepin*'."

Luke heard the laughter and stuck his head in the small opening of the wall.

"I don't know what's so funny, but Tal and I are out here ready to close her in and stack onion sacks to the ceiling. Henry was pretty serious about the possible danger tonight."

Mahta shuffled over to the sleeping platform and began arranging blankets.

"Sweet dreams, Mahta," smiled Sally.

Mahta put Sadie and Sally at ease with a great yawn and pretending to look longingly at the bed. When they were gone, she sat on the blankets in the candlelight and listened to the sound of onion bags being tossed against the wall. After the sounds stopped, she stretched her arms behind her and lay down to go to sleep.

As the four climbed the steps up from the root cellar, Gideon came running up to them. The worried look on his face spoke volumes.

"Massuh, d' sheriff and lots of white folk is up at your house askin' fo ya. Mabin is tryin' to slow 'em down by knockin' at your door and waitin' fo you to answer. Tol' 'em you must be nappin 'r sumthin'."

"I gotta start paying more attention to Henry," said Luke. "He said to expect the worst, and he was right."

The doorway from the storage building was on the corner closest to the half-built meetinghouse, out of sight of the main house. The group slipped through the meetinghouse and then ran in the opposite direction of the main house, carefully keeping the buildings between them and the sheriff's line of sight. As they neared the last of the outbuildings, Washington popped out from behind it and motioned for them to follow him, and then he ducked back behind the building.

When they arrived, the four panting adults were surprised to see Washington standing there with tools in his hands. They were even more surprised to find Hope holding out a picnic basket. As the runners fought to regain their composure and steady breathing, Washington explained the plan.

"Me 'n Tal will walk back and go to work on the cookhouse. Hope and Sadie will mosey on back to Hope's place as if they were out for a stroll."

"You folks will be havin' a picnic down by d' river," Hope interrupted, handing the basket to Sally. "We din't have time to put nothin' in it but some cornbread 'n butter dat Washington grab from d' men's house."

"Good plan!" agreed Luke. "The trail from here to the river is out of their sight if we hurry."

Luke took in a deep breath of air and said, "Lord, help us!" Then he took Sally's hand and they hurried on to their picnic.

Luke and Sally sat together at the edge of the river and waited. Luke occasionally threw a rock into the water as he told Sally the story of his placing his low opinion of Tom on a leaf and letting it drift away, hopefully forever.

When the faint sound of horses reached their ears, Luke said, "Well, we might as well give them their money's worth." He leaned over and took Sally in his arms and they kissed passionately until the hoof beats came to a stop behind them.

The couple feigned surprise as they quickly stood to their feet and Sally brushed off her skirt.

Luke acted irritated, "Don't you ever knock, sheriff?"

"I did, but you didn't answer the door."

"Well, maybe it's because I wasn't wanting to have visitors this afternoon."

"You got em' anyway! I need to see the papers on all your nigras. Word has it that you been hiding runaways and selling them back for reward and profit. Word also has it that you been hiding a batch of em' up in your woods. Right this minute, my men are rounding up every nigra on this place and putting them in that corral up by your house. I got six men combing your woods, and every nigra we find, you had better have papers for." Sheriff Roily gave a big smile and said, "What say we get this done so you can get back to your woman?"

Luke looked threateningly at Roily and answered, "If you've set one foot in my home when I was not present, I will have you in court before you even have time to kiss that bedroom mirror that you kiss every morning!

One of the men behind the sheriff chuckled. The sheriff's face flushed and he leaned forward in his saddle. "I got a man at each door so no one can escape, mister, and if you don't get right up there, I'll take my chances with you in court."

Luke squeezed Sally's hand to reassure her as they walked back to the house.

Both Luke's and Sally's blood began to boil when they saw every one of their slaves standing inside the horse corral along with the horses. Neither was surprised to see Billy Glenn standing guard at the gate.

Luke let go of Sally's hand. He walked over to Billy and began to talk to him as he would to a child that had difficulty understanding what was being said.

"Open the gate, Billy, and let my slaves out."

Billy stood with his feet spread, staring at Luke challengingly. Luke could smell the whiskey on his breath.

"One more time," said Luke. "Open the gate, Billy."

Billy stood still, in defiance. The sheriff sat quietly on his horse, clearly enjoying the entertainment while the others began to move in closer, hoping for some action.

Luke put his hands in his pockets and stared at Billy Glenn a moment, then slowly searched the area around the barnyard. When he spied a three foot length of medium chain hanging from a nail near the barn door, he walked over and removed it from the nail. As he walked back to Billy, Luke wrapped the chain around his wrist once and grabbed hold of the end, leaving about two and a half feet dangling and ready for use. Approaching Billy, Luke turned sideways, keeping the chain out of the other man's reach.

Sally held both hands to her mouth, closed her eyes, and prayed.

"Your time's up, Billy. Do it!"

Billy Glenn backed up until he bumped into the gate, but he made no move to open it.

Luke took a stepped toward him as he raised the chain as if to strike. Suddenly, Billy let out a growl and charged Luke. At the last second, Luke jumped back. His attacker flew by and stumbled and fell to his hands and knees.

"Drinking to build up your courage also slows down your reflexes, fellas," said Luke, as he looked around the group. His hand was still up and the chain was swinging threateningly in his tense grip.

Billy Glenn stood up and brushed off, but he didn't turn around.

"Go ahead, Leroy. Go on over and open the gate and let 'em out," said the sheriff, to a man at his left. "The fun's over. It's time to get down to business."

As Leroy opened the gate and the slaves began to file out, Luke walked toward his wife, his hand still gripping the chain. The men backed away and let him through. The sheriff climbed down from his horse and motioned Luke to the house. Luke was in no hurry.

"Mabin, Toby, Zekiel, all you guys; sit in a group with the women in the middle. If it comes to it," Luke paused for effect, "do what you have to do."

No one missed the insinuation. One of Jerry Ellis's boys cursed Luke.

Luke held up his empty hand.

"I'm not sayin'......" Luke paused again. "I'm just being careful, that's all. We protect our women."

Sally suddenly took hold of Luke's arm.

"Luke, where's Frank?"

Luke glanced down at his wife and then quickly scanned the area. Not seeing Frank anywhere, he turned and stared menacingly at Sheriff Roily.

"Where's my son, Roily?"

"I have no idea, Martin."

"I'm right here, Pa."

All heads turned to an open window, next to the front door. The sheriff's body gave a little jerk as he sighted the rifle aimed square at his chest.

"Frank!" exclaimed his mother. "What are you doing?"

"When they blocked both doors, Mama, I decided this wasn't a friendly visit."

Luke stepped between the rifle and the sheriff.

"You're right about that, Frank. The sheriff wasn't being too friendly. But you can put the gun down now. I'll take it from here."

Frank and the rifle withdrew into the house and the window closed behind him. Luke motioned for Sally to lead the way into the house and Luke followed right behind. When he reached the door, he turned back to the sheriff and said, "You are not welcome inside my house, but if you insist on entering, you will not leave my sight as you look around."

Roily glanced over at the window and then back at Luke. He raised his eyebrows and nodded his head.

"I insist on searching your house, but sticking with you might be a good idea," he agreed.

It took some time as the sheriff looked in every corner and every closet. He checked every inch of the attic and even in the kitchen cupboards. When the search was concluded and he was satisfied, he walked over to the kitchen table and pulled out a chair, all the while keeping his eye on the boy standing in the corner.

"Mr. Roily, we can do our business outside on the porch," Luke said as he picked up a stack of papers on the counter and tucked them under his arm.

The sheriff pushed the chair back under the table.

Luke held the door open and waited.

A disturbance outside caught the sheriff's attention and he quickly walked outside. Luke stepped out and closed the door behind him as Jerry Ellis and five other men rode up to the house in a cloud of dust. Roily stood at the head of the steps looking down at Jerry as he dismounted and came to the foot of the steps.

"Well? What did you find?"

"No tracks, no nothin'," Jerry replied.

"Well, that *is* disappointing," said Roily, "but let's see what we got in this bunch." He indicated the group of slaves sitting on the ground, as he descended the steps. "Martin, bring the papers."

It didn't take long to finish roll call, and all were present and accounted for. Roily scanned the farm with keen eyes.

"Did someone fork the bales and haystacks?"

"Will and I did," Leroy answered.

"How about the wagons?"

"I checked em'," said a man that Luke didn't know.

The sheriff's eyes fell on the newly completed building.

"What's in that one, Martin?"

"Root cellar below and supply storage on top."

"What's that you're building now?"

"Cook house," Luke replied bluntly.

"Anybody check them?"

"Yessir," someone said. "Me 'n Roy did."

Roily looked over at the slaves again, deep in thought. Eventually he came to some sort of conclusion in his mind and turned to Luke and said, "Looks like you're clean. Guess we'll be goin'."

He turned to leave but then remembered something he had been intending to ask. "Tell me something, Martin. How much did you make off of Tom for that Rena girl?"

"Not a thing, and by the way sheriff, where *is* Tom? I noticed he's not with your little gang today."

"Said he was busy."

Without another word to Luke, the sheriff walked to his horse and gave the order to mount up and head back to town. Luke thought he had sounded a little irritated.

Chapter 46

After the sheriff left, Luke thanked everyone for their help and pointed out various ways that the Lord had intervened for them all. He complimented Washington and Hope for their quick thinking and also mentioned the fact that God had gotten him into town to talk to Henry just in the nick of time.

Because of all that had happened and had just been said, Ambrose asked if he could speak. He was moved to point out that his infected ankles had clearly begun to heal on the day of the harvest picnic. "When ya'all prayed," he said, "me 'n Dinah, we been made to do some new thinkin' on there bein' a God, 'n if he is good'?"

Washington laughed and said, "There isn't anything good that happens 'cause *we're* good. No, suh! If any good happens, it's cuz da Lord's good. Yessuh!"

"Yessuh, He is! Thas right, Washington. I do believe that," agreed Sadie, as she took Tal's hand and pulled him to her. "Might as well tell everybody the good thing the Lord doin for us," she said as she looked up at her husband.

Tal looked at her and smiled. That's all it took.

Hope squealed and began jumping up and down. "I don't believe it!" she squeaked. "Yes, I do believe it. This is so wonderful, I can hardly believe it!"

Tal and Sadie just smiled.

Sally and Frank were sitting on the porch steps, listening. As they watched Hope's reaction, a look of absolute shock came over Sally. "This is unbelievable!" she said as she slowly stood to her feet.

"Believe what?" asked Frank, in confusion. "What's unbelievable?"

Without taking his eyes off of his wife, Tal announced, "Sadie and Mahta seem to think the Lord's been making us a child."

"I don't believe it!" Frank shouted excitedly. He leaped off the steps and ran over to Tal and Sadie. "How do you know? How do you know He's making a baby, Sadie?"

"Yeah, Miz Sadie, how *do* ya know?" Joshua's curiosity had led him to come and stand next to Frank.

"You don' look like somebody's in there," Joshua pointed to her stomach. "Now Miz Dinah, she sure did!"

The two boys stood side by side, looking up at the couple, waiting for an answer. The celebrating group of adults grew quiet. Tal looked blankly at the boys for a moment and then looked back at Sadie. Everyone was waiting to hear her answer. Tal gave her a look that said, "I'm turning *this* conversation over to *you*, so don't expect any help from me."

"Well, alright then." Sadie looked down at the boys and thought back. "Weeks ago, I started feeling funny inside."

"Funny?" both boys echoed.

"Not funny, funny. It was more like a strange funny," she smiled. "Sometimes it was a dizzy funny, sometimes a sick funny. Most the time it wan't funny at all. When I tol' Tal about all my aches 'n pains and sudden lack of energy even though I was eatin' so much more than I usually eat, we actually began to be afraid I was going to die. We spent lots of time in prayer and then one day I shared my fears with Mahta. She asked me a few questions and decided I was not going to die, but instead, was going to have a baby!"

"Wow," said Joshua with wonder in his eyes, "so havin' a baby feels like dyin'."

"Well, I don't know what dyin' *feels* like, so my mind was jus' guessin'," Sadie explained. A smile crossed her face and she looked at Tal as she spoke.

"When I told Tal, in bed that night, that he was gonna be a papa, he smiled real big 'n lay there a while, then he sighs 'n says, "You are so amazin', woman! It ain't yo time to die, after all. Heaven do come someday, but while we here, the Lord, he sends us a sneak peek o' heaven."

"So, does it hurt real bad?" asked Frank, still trying to sort out all this new information.

"It's not hurting at all, right now, but when it gets uncomfortable, it reminds me that someone's in there. Now I get excited, instead of scared."

Sally seemed stunned, as she stepped up and gave Sadie a hug.

Luke shook Tal's hand and said, "I'd sure like to see Sid and Maggie's faces when they get *this* news. They were very determined not to let you two get split up. If you want to write them a letter, I could get it sent for you."

Suddenly Tal's whole demeanor changed; he tensed and his eyes grew large, as he stared at the massuh.

The smile froze on Luke's face as he realized what he had just done.

All conversation had stopped and all eyes were on Luke as he mentally tried to figure out how to get his big foot out of his big mouth. Then he quickly dropped the frozen smile and tried to look as if this had actually been the plan all along.

"Well, uh, now that I have everyone's attention, I suppose this is as good a time as any."

Luke put his fist to his mouth and pretended to clear his throat. He grew serious and started in. "Ambrose says he's been thinking about whether God is good or not. Well …, most of the time, for the slave, it's very hard to see that this 'God' the white man taught you about is good. Mabin told me about a time, when he was young, when he was made to watch as his so-called 'Christian' master stripped a young black man and his wife and gave them each fifty lashes, because the master's wife was angry with the slave for not having the carriage ready in time for her to be early for church. After the beatings, his master put on his best Sunday hat and jacket and rode off in the carriage with his wife to church, leaving his two servants lying on the ground, naked and bleeding. It did not seem to bother the lady that taking the time to beat her slaves had made her even later."

"Think for a moment about some of the hard things *you've* experienced, when it was hard to think that God was good."

Luke looked around the gathering as some appeared to mentally relive a personal horror that they themselves had gone through, sometime in their past. One solitary tear rolled down Hope's cheek.

Ambrose just stared at the ground, and Joshua took in extra air as he let out a small whimper. Luke had no doubt as to what the boy was reviewing in his mind at that moment. Dinah's face was expressionless as she sat on the grass, looking at Eli as she held him in her arms.

Luke clapped his hands and rubbed them together, and allowed the smile to return to his face.

"And now, for the good part." He reached into his back pocket and pulled out a small black book. He took a moment to thumb through the pages until he found what he was looking for; then he surprised everyone by handing the book to Tal and pointing to a specific place on the page.

"Tal, would you read this out loud to us, please?"

Now, all eyes were bouncing back and forth between Luke and Tal.

"*What's happening?*" they were asking themselves. "*Can Tal do that? Why would the master ask him to do that?*"

Tal was looking up at Luke, his eyes asking, "Are you sure this is a good idea, right now?"

"Go ahead, Tal," Luke nodded.

Tal pulled the book closer to his face and began to read.

"'For my thoughts are not your thoughts, neither are your ways my ways,' declares the Lord."

Tal paused and looked up at his master who appeared to be anxiously waiting to hear more. The world had gone dead silent. The air was still. Not even a blade of grass dared move. Tal looked back down at the book and continued to read.

"For as the heavens are higher than the earth, so are my ways higher than your ways and my thoughts than your thoughts."

"Thank you, Tal," said Luke as he took the book and replaced it in his pocket.

All eyes were on Tal, and three or four mouths hung open in amazement.

Mabin smiled as he looked around at his friends. Finally, it was no longer a secret! Relief swept through him like a flood. "*It's one thing to know something good is coming,*" he thought to himself, "*but it's something entirely different, on the day it arrives.*" Even though he had never experienced any of these, he imagined it was like the day of a baby's birth, or a wedding day, or even, the day when the Lord will show up to fetch his people.

"Kin you believe dat? What Tal jus' did?" asked Mabin excitedly.

Luke's eyes were gleaming.

"Sadie can read too. And they can both write!"

Every eye had now traveled from Tal, to Luke, and now, to Sadie.

Hope asked the question everyone else wanted to ask. "You can read, you can write, *aaand* you havin' a baby?"

Sadie was suddenly feeling a little bit shy, having so much attention focused on her.

"Massuh Pennington ...," Sadie paused, and then added, "he taught us."

Luke walked over and stood beside Tal and put his hand on his shoulder as he looked at the others.

"We have a problem, and Tal and Sadie have agreed to help us fix it," said Luke. "The problem is that many people that call themselves Christians totally misrepresent the God whom they've told you about. Even I have done that, at times. And you have no way of knowing what is true or what is false about God, except what you have been told, or what you have experienced. I personally have found that it is very easy to be wrong in how I interpret my own experiences."

Luke moved on to Ambrose and looked him in the eye. "It would be very natural for you to think that God wanted you to have your wife taken from you, and that he wanted Mr. Ellis to put those scars on your back and ankles. It would be natural for you to be angry with God for wanting that. But, Ambrose....."

Luke reached out and put his hands on the slave's shoulders. "God sent you a personal letter!"

Ambrose looked confused, but before he could speak Luke continued.

"Tal has read you a portion of that letter. It's the same letter God sent to me, and the same letter he sent to Hope, and Joshua, and Sally, and everyone here. God dictated the letter through a few men and then delivered it to all men. But the thing is, when I sit down to read it, I read it as starting with 'Dear Luke'. And when Sally reads the letter, she knows it's a personal letter to her."

"So when God says to mankind in the letter, 'My thoughts are not your thoughts, neither are my ways your ways,' declares the Lord. 'For as the heavens are higher than the earth, so are my ways higher than your ways and my thoughts higher than your thoughts', you should hear it as, 'Dear Ambrose, what those men did to you was a display of *man's* condition, not mine. That wasn't me! My ways are higher than that.'"

Luke turned to Joshua and continued, "'Dear Joshua,' God is saying, "what happened to your father is proof of *man's* sinfulness, not mine. But it's not only proof of Mr. Grant's condition, Joshua; it's also proof of everyone else's condition - even yours."

Luke pulled out the book again and tapped it with his fingers.

"I want you all to be able to read this book. It says that we are so messed up there is no hope that we could ever save ourselves. We are so messed up, it would take someone greater than all of creation; someone perfect in fact, to be able to save us. In the part that Tal just read, God is telling us that our situation is not hopeless because that person does exist, and that person is God himself; the one who created us in the first place."

"Many of you already know this, and believe it to be true," Sally interjected. She was getting excited. "But there's something about reading, with your own eyes, the actual words that the creator of the universe, is speaking to us through this book."

Dinah looked doubtful. "But we don' know how, missus. We *can't* read," she said.

Mabin couldn't help but chuckle. "Gonna be a day when you'll teach dat baby in your arms how to read dem words," he said, with a confidence that puzzled almost everyone.

Tal looked to Luke for permission to explain. Luke nodded.

"Mabin said that, because he knows that Sadie 'n me have agreed to teach any of you who want to learn how to read and write."

There were gasps throughout the group.

Hope stood wide-eyed with her hands cupped over her nose and mouth. Her tears had come instantly and were flowing freely. Toby was standing behind her with his hand on her shoulder and his mouth hanging open, as he looked at Luke for confirmation of what he had just heard.

"Is that right, Massuh?" Ambrose asked. "We gonna learn how to read?"

Luke immediately became serious. "The problem is that the slave codes make it against the law to teach a slave to read. Our family has come to the decision that it's better to obey God, than men. I could realistically face months in jail, if the Lord wills. The same is true for Tal and Sadie, but they've come to the same decision."

Luke grinned at Ambrose and nodded his head. "A written letter is meant to be read. God wrote the letter to all of us, and all of us should read it."

As her husband continued speaking, Sally noticed Hope absentmindedly rubbing her belly. She couldn't believe what she was thinking. In a fog of wonder, she slipped over to Hope. Sally tapped Toby's shoulder and he stepped back from Hope. Sally whispered something in Hope's ear and the two women walked away from the group and over to the pecan tree near the horse barn.

"When the cookhouse is finished," Luke was saying, "the top floor, and a third of the bottom floor, will provide expanded housing for some of you and whoever else the Lord brings our way. But the cooking and eating area will also double as an unofficial learning place."

"I have acquired four more of these," Luke continued, as he held up the Bible from his pocket. "They will be your beginning readers. Tal and Sadie will meet with those who choose to, three days a week after the evening meal for a couple of hours. However, officially we will call it visiting. After the cookhouse is finished, I will be leaving for two weeks to visit my mother. It will be more discreet for me to purchase boxes of parchment and ink while I am away than to do it in Grantsville. In the meantime, Pastor Matthew Davies will bring enough supplies to get us started."

There was murmuring and nodding of heads. He gave them some time to process all that they had heard. He noticed the two women under the pecan tree but didn't give it much thought.

"Oh, and one more thing," he continued, "Pastor Davies has agreed to come out here to the farm twice a month to help you understand what God is saying through these words that you will be learning."

Joshua interrupted the discussion that followed Luke's last statement. "Massuh Martin?"

Everyone quieted down.

"Yes, Joshua?"

"Frank goes back to school next week," said Joshua. "Will he be learnin' what we be learnin'?

Luke nodded. "Well, he's had quite a head start on you. You'll have to start with the ABC's just like he did, but I wouldn't be a bit surprised if you eventually pass him right up."

"I can see the Lord's hand in having the sheriff get everyone together for this chat," said Luke, "but now, we all need to get back to work. Oh, and by the way, the longer we can keep this to ourselves, the smoother it will go."

As each person returned to their work, some were in deep thought while others talked excitedly with each other about this unexpected new chapter in their lives and what it would mean for their future. Hope had returned from her conference with Sally and was hugging Sadie. Dinah had joined them, and soon the three of them were talking about babies and comparing notes as they walked to the house to cook, clean, and fold laundry.

Luke felt a tap on his shoulder. He turned to his wife, who had come up silently behind him.

"Hi, I was...."

"We need to talk," interrupted Sally, looking serious.

"Okay. Let's talk after......."

"Let's talk now," she jumped in with a stressed, forced smile that almost said, "If we don't, I'm going to explode."

"All right," said Luke, giving her a look of curious concern. "I was going to ride a ways toward town to see if I spot anyone the sheriff might have left behind to keep an eye on us. I don't think we should bring Mahta out yet. Henry said I don't do 'careful' very well. But after what the sheriff pulled, I think I'm learning a little about 'careful'. We'll take the carriage instead of my horse, so you can ride along with me and talk."

Chapter 47

As the couple rode away from the house, there were about sixty seconds of silence before Sally started talking.

"We haven't had a baby around this place for twelve years. I remember how good it was to hear the noise of children running and yelling again, when Joshua arrived. Those boys became best friends in a matter of weeks. Now, the Lord has brought Ambrose and Dinah, and their baby, to us. It's so wonderful. Even hearing a baby crying is kind of nice."

Luke let his wife talk, nodding his head once in a while to let her know he was listening.

"And now, Tal and Sadie!" Sally's hands flew up, and back down to her lap. "Can you believe it, Luke? Two babies around the place? It's got to be God, doesn't it?"

Luke looked down at her. She seemed to be feeling him out about the whole situation. He smiled and nodded his head reassuringly.

"Sure seems to be," he agreed. "It feels good to have a baby around. And now, in seven or eight months, there'll be another one. It takes away any doubt I might have had about building the cookhouse and all the extra living space. We've talked before about how it's no accident that Mahta showed up when she did. And, that where she had come from, it was her job to take care of babies."

Sally seemed suddenly relieved. "Well, my dear husband, have I got some news for you!"

"I was guessing *that* back at the house," smiled Luke.

"Mahta will be busier than you think."

Luke tried to put the pieces together in his mind. Sally remained silent as she let him dwell on what she had just said.

Suddenly the memory of Sally talking to Hope under the tree came to him. Then he remembered Toby standing behind Hope with his hand on her shoulder.

"No way!"

"She thinks maybe so. She's noticed a few changes, but hasn't noticed the lack of energy that Sadie spoke of."

"No way! I can't believe this!"

"Hope hasn't told Toby because she wasn't sure, at least not until she heard Sadie today. But now that I've answered a few more of her questions, she's pretty sure."

"Well, that settles it!" Luke exclaimed. "I've been procrastinating long enough. A few weeks ago at the picnic, I told Matthew we might need to have a double wedding soon. So much has happened since then that I haven't given it another thought. How are we going to fit it all in? We have to get the cookhouse finished. I'll be gone for two weeks visiting my mother. Frank has to catch up with *his* schoolwork. Everyone needs to get moved into their permanent housing, which will include Toby and Hope now, won't it? And we must fit in a double wedding before they move in together - though I suppose they have already gotten ahead of themselves in *that* respect. And all of that should be done before Christmas!"

Luke and Sally rode along in silence for a while. There was so much to take in. It was close to being overwhelming.

Finally, Sally commented thoughtfully, "You might need to think of getting more help by spring. We girls won't be in shape to be very helpful."

Luke nodded. "Ted Willis might not be available as much; he'll be working on paving Main Street next summer. But his younger brother might be interested. And the Hutchen boy is back from college, so he might need some work, too."

"Maybe we could talk to Tom about renting Rena for six or eight months to do the housework or the cooking," smiled Sally. "The rest of us will be sitting around knitting baby booties on our big bellies."

Luke nodded. "That ought to be a sight. All you gals sitting around .....knitting booties ....on your big......."

"Wait a minute!!" Luke suddenly exclaimed. He pulled the horse to a stop and turned his whole body to face his wife. "But ..., I thought you were always so tired because ......"

He glanced down at her waist with a confused look. "I did notice you were gaining a little ...., but I thought ...., well, I just thought it was because that's what a lot of older women do."

"Lucas J. Martin! Exactly what do you mean by that?"

Luke immediately started backpedaling. "Well, I didn't mean ...."

"Humph! It sure sounded like you meant it to me!" Sally said, deciding to have some fun with her flustered husband.

"What I meant was ....., well ...., my mom ...., well, she..."

"Your MOM!!!? She exclaimed, in a pretend huff. "Are you saying I'm getting as big as your mom - or as old as your mom? Which is it?"

Luke sputtered for a few seconds before he held his hands out from his sides and said, "But we haven't had a baby for twelve years! That's a long time!" Luke was exasperated.

Sally brought her nose down out of the upper atmosphere and crossed her arms and smiled at him.

"I am your beautiful, young, thirty-five-year-old wife who just happens to be - though only temporarily, I might add - a little distorted."

"So what do you think of that, my dear young husband?" Sally asked, and kissed him on the nose.

Luke answered, in a daze, "I think ...., I think that I am beyond thinking. I think you caught me totally off-guard. I don't know what to say."

He was looking at Sally's stomach and noticing that she was bigger than he had realized. How could he have missed it? He thought about how easy it could be to hide it by always wearing loose dresses and loose nightgowns. And then, his thoughts switched to *who* God was forming at that very moment, right there before him.

"I think," he paused, thinking, "that I am staggered by the hand of God," he said quietly.

Sally nodded but said nothing. She realized that the mood had changed. Pure joy had blended into pure worship.

"Who am I, that I should be so blessed?" Luke was almost whispering to himself. His eyes were transfixed on Sally's belly, but he was no longer seeing her, as he thought back to six months ago. Five male slaves, one male child, and a wife. And then.......?

Luke's mind simply couldn't take it all in. It was as if the owner of the vineyard had returned suddenly, six months ago, and called his servants to action. In no time at all, the amount of land had doubled, the number of slaves more than doubled, and there was continuous construction with no end in sight. The vision took only seconds, and it ended with a sight that made Luke start chuckling.

"What's so funny?" Sally finally asked.

Luke continued to chuckle as he explained.

"I was picturing five women lined up on our porch sitting in rockers. On one end was Mahta, then next to her was Dinah holding her baby, and next to Dinah were two black women and one white one. The three on the end had huge bellies and they were all .....," Luke tried to hold back his laughter. "All five of you were knitting baby booties!" Luke broke out in loud laughter.

Sally frowned. "What's so funny about that?"

Luke took a deep breath and wiped a tear from his eye.

"Just picture it, Sal. Five women, all ....." He broke out laughing again. "All lined up on the porch in rocking chairs. Three of them….. side by side…" He made the form of a huge ball in front of him with his arms and that seemed to set him off again. He made a final effort. "knitting ... baby ....." And then he lost it completely.

Sally watched Luke as he tipped out of the carriage, landed on the ground, and rolled around in uncontrollable howling and laughter. A smile came to her face. She shook her head and began to chuckle too, but for a different reason. In her opinion, her husband was a whole lot funnier than what *he* was laughing at!

Chapter 48

Luke didn't wait until the cookhouse was finished before leaving to visit his mother in the city. Instead, he hired Ted and Nathan Willis on full time to help his men finish the project, and he left within a few days of finding out that his wife was with child. As Mabin guided the horse and wagon onto Town Road, Luke was already wishing the trip was over, yet at the same time, he was anxious to tell his mom all the news. They exchanged letters every couple of months, but this was special news and he wanted to deliver it personally. His mother loved city life and Luke knew that, but every time he visited her, he tried to talk her into coming home with him so he could take care of her as she grew older. He was hoping that news of another grandchild might be enough to convince her.

Luke brought Mabin along for two reasons. Luke would need help with loading the items he intended to purchase while in Savannah, the main item being a brand new cooking stove for the cookhouse. The other reason was that he enjoyed Mabin's company. On trips like this, they could drop the master/slave persona and just be friends for a few days. It was the third visit to his mother's home on which he had brought Mabin along. She had always been fond of Mabin and had almost taken him with her when she moved away.

After traveling a mile or so, both men stopped thinking about the trip ahead and their minds drifted back to the happenings on the farm.

"D' old woman say d' cellar's not too bad, for what it is," Mabin said, thinking of Mahta.

"She's something else, isn't she?" commented Luke

"She didn' mind a bit, havin' to stay in dere overnight jus' to be safe, even though d' sheriff already done left," Mabin said. "Had a dream 'bout her once," he added.

"Oh, yeah? Tell me about it."

"She was drinkin' fresh water from d' stream up where we found her. Den she was sitting in a rockin' chair, holdin' babies. All d' while, a coyote was circlin, tryin' to get her, but sumthin' was keepin' it away."

Luke gave it some thought and then said, "It sounds like the coyote might have been the devil."

Mabin nodded. "Dat's what I bin thinkin' too."

They rode along together in silence for a while. They watched a white heron glide over the road in front of them and land in the marsh near the road. It appeared to be totally unconcerned about the two men in the wagon as they passed by. The heron was in total contrast to the two mallards that exploded into the air quacking in alarm and beating their wings furiously to escape the supposed danger as the wagon rolled by.

"Dat heron knows sumthin' dat d' ducks don't," Mabin remarked. "Wit d' coyote circlin d' ole woman, she jus' keep rockin' dem babies. Mebbe she knew what was keepin' d' coyote away."

Luke chuckled, "How many babies did you see in that dream?"

"Two, suh, but one was older 'n playin' on d' groun'. I figure dat'n was miz Dinah's, 'n d' little one was miz Sadie's."

"What happened next?"

"Don' know. Young Joshua done woke me up afore I could tell."

"Well, I wouldn't be surprised if the next part of your dream would have had five women sitting on my porch, with three of them pregnant and all five knitting baby booties."

"Suh?" Mabin clearly did not understand.

"Was the baby in Mahta's arms black or white?"

"Couldn't rightly tell, suh," Mabin was totally perplexed. "Was all wrapped up in a blanket."

"I'm bettin' it was white!" said Luke proudly.

"You don' mean ....!" Mabin's eyes grew large.

"I sure do, Mabin," laughed Luke. "The expected birth order goes like this: Sally first, Sadie second, and Hope third."

This was way too much information for Mabin.

"But Massuh, dat means ….!" He didn't finish his sentence; instead, he just stared, wide eyed, at Luke.

Luke helped him out. "That means we will be stopping to talk with Pastor Davies on our way through town. We need to give him the heads-up about a double wedding that will be happening as soon as we get back. While we're gone, Sally will be talking to Toby and Hope, and Ambrose and Dinah about what the Bible says about getting married."

Mabin turned his attention to the road in front of him. He shook his head in wonder, and chuckled to himself, but said nothing. Luke knew what was going on in Mabin's head because, eventually, he chuckled again, and then again.

Mabin finally asked, "Five women lined up on your porch?"

"In rocking chairs."

Mabin laughed, "And three of dem ….?"

"Big as they can be," Luke interrupted.

Luke made a great effort not to laugh and so did Mabin, but they were doomed to failure when Mabin said, "And all five of them …."

They both spoke in unison, "Knittin baby booties!"

The uncontrollable laughter and howling could probably be heard for a half mile in all directions. More ducks flew off in alarm, but the heron seemed to understand, and probably would have smiled - if a heron could smile.

Chapter 49

Over the two-week period of time that Luke and Mabin were traveling, early winter weather had slipped into Georgia. It was not a freezing cold, but at night, it was an uncomfortable chill. It was great timing for the new cooking stove to arrive and with great fervor the men surrounded the stove and carried it to the center of the large gathering room. In this room, they would all soon be eating together, and learning together. The mood was festive, and as the men hooked up the stove pipe, the women drifted around the room in a group, discussing how they would decorate for the wedding. By the time Luke and Mabin returned, everyone had been filled in on all three babies, and moods had improved noticeably. The sheriff's little raiding party seemed a long-past memory, and the stove's arrival became the symbol of God's blessings. Luke had purchased enough colorful fabric to hang curtains over all twelve glass windows in the new building. Six of those windows were in the meeting hall.

Once the stove was in place, the men proceeded to move Mahta's bed and her few possessions into the living quarters abutting the cooking and eating area. Her room was large enough to accommodate two or three people, but for now, she would have the space to herself. All had agreed that this would be the perfect location for her, because it was difficult for her to walk long distances on her bad leg. It was also the ideal spot for her to help with the babies, and some of the cooking. Mahta was obviously pleased with the arrangement. Her heat source, her food source, and the hot water for her tea were all right at her fingertips.

Washington joined Frank and Joshua at a table as they enjoyed scribbling on three of the twenty, brand new handheld chalk boards. Frank was showing each of them what their names looked like, all spelled out. It didn't take long before the others gathered around to see what their names actually looked like. Frank was enjoying the spotlight and took great pleasure in the response when he wrote out the names, 'Toby and Hope', together on the same board.

He sounded out each letter and then had everyone copy him. He then said the words together. The whole group then repeated him in unison, "Toby and Hope", after which, they all broke out in laughter. The unofficial learning had begun.

On the day of the weddings, Pastor Davies arrived early in the morning, hoping for a warm cup of coffee, hot biscuits, butter and jam, and a bit of good ol' conversation around the Martin kitchen table. The air was cold and brisk, but he could not see his breath. Pulling back on the reins, he stopped the carriage and watched the smoke rising from the chimney of the cookhouse. The excitement he felt was not surprising. After all, a double wedding? And on the plantation of his favorite people. There was no doubt in Matthew's mind that God was indeed doing great things here. He felt privileged to be involved.

Zekiel and Otis carried a long bench from the barn to the cookhouse. Matthew watched as Dinah opened the door for them and then quickly shut it behind them. A few seconds later, he saw Frank run out of the cookhouse and up to the main house, obviously on an urgent errand. It amused him to see Dinah eventually come to the door and shut it again while shaking her head and saying something to herself or someone inside.

A gust of wind chilled the pastor into action and he urged the horse to move on up to the house. As he climbed down, he collected his Bible and two small gift boxes from the seat. He was halfway up the steps when Frank passed him, running the other direction.

"They seen ya comin'!" Frank yelled, as he flew down the steps. "Go on in!"

Sally was already pouring his coffee as he entered the kitchen.

"Good morning," she said as she handed him his cup. "What brings you out on such a chilly day?"

"I hear love is in the air on the Martin plantation."

"It's been in the air for a while now," Luke said, from behind the paper he was reading. "Today, we play 'Bible catch-up'." He chuckled and put his paper aside. "I can't wait for the teaching to begin, and for you to start filling in some of these younger ones on God's preferred timing for things like this." He stuffed a half of a biscuit in his mouth.

Matthew sat down at the table and scooted his chair in. Without even asking, he chose a biscuit from the platter and broke it open. Watching the steam pour out of the biscuit, he asked, "Why can't you do it? There's no law that says it's the preacher's job, is there?"

"Genesis," Luke mumbled through a mouth full of biscuit, "or maybe Romans." He gulped his bite down and added, "Maybe Revelations. I'm sure I read it somewhere."

Luke wiped his face with a napkin and sipped on his coffee as he watched Matthew pretending to think real hard.

"I think it's coming to me," the preacher finally said. "Yes, I believe you're right, Luke. I think I read it the other day in 1st Martin 3:8."

"There! You see?" Luke exclaimed, with the sound of victory in his voice. "I knew it was in there, somewhere. From now on, Matthew, I expect to see the weddings before the babies!"

Matthew feigned a look of disgust. "Sally, I'm putting you up for 'Wife of the Century" award. I have no idea how you've survived him."

"One day at a time, Matthew," she smiled. "One day at a time."

Henry, the Willis family, and the Statlers, all arrived within fifteen minutes of each other and the plantation became a flurry of activity. In a couple of hours preparations were complete and the meeting room was filled with people and food. The cook stove and warm bodies were more than adequate to heat the room, even with the ten-foot-high ceiling. The doors and windows were now open wide, and the sound of talking and laughter, combined with the smell of good food drifted out over the plantation. It was time to begin the ceremonies, and then celebrate with a feast.

Pastor Matthew called everyone to silence and asked them all to have a seat on the benches. He directed Ambrose and Toby to stand with him, one on each side. He opened with a prayer, thanking God that, even though many white men would not recognize marriage among slaves, he, the Lord, was not only going to sanction these marriages, he was going to bless these two couples and hold them accountable to their vows.

The baby soon began to squeak and shift around in Mahta's arms; then he put all his energy into one loud wail of protest against long prayers before dropping off to sleep. Pastor Davies got the message loud and clear. He quickly asked the Lord's blessing on the two babies that these couples had already been blessed with. Everybody joined in the "amen."

The brides entered from Mahta's room at the back. The girls each wore a clean, new work dress and a wreath with flowers in it on their heads. Although there was no music or singing as they split off and walked up the outside aisles that had been left open for them, there were lots of hoots and hollers and shouts of hallelujah. When the two couples came together and joined hands at the front of the room, all became quiet again.

"God is smiling," Matthew grinned, "and the angels are celebrating. There's a bigger crowd in here than you can see."

Oblivious to what the pastor was saying, Joshua was watching tears roll down the two couples' cheeks. He was becoming concerned. Turning to look back over the gathering, he noticed that Mrs. Martin was wiping tears from her eyes also.

Joshua nudged Frank. "I think sumthin's wrong dat we don' know bout," he whispered.

"No, there's not," Frank whispered back to his friend. "This is a wedding. Weddings are happy."

"Never seen no man cry when he was happy; and look at dem ladies. Sumthin's wrong, I tell you."

"Well, you have now," Frank said as he nudged Joshua and smiled.

"Shush, you boys. I want to hear this," whispered Zekiel, looking at them sternly.

Frank and Joshua immediately sat up and looked straight ahead. Joshua could have sworn Zekiel's eyes were also teared up when he had looked at them. "What was going on?" he wondered to himself. He looked around the room again. Most were smiling, but some weren't.

He nudged Frank again. "I don' think everone got tol' dat weddings were happy," he whispered.

"I been to two weddings at our church before," whispered Frank. "Trust me. Crying is part of a happy wedding."

"Shush, you two!"

When the pastor told the two men that they could now kiss their brides, Joshua watched in amazement. He had never actually seen two people do that before. The room broke out in cheers and praise. Joshua noticed that there was no one crying now, except Miz Martin.

"Ladies and gentlemen," Pastor Davies announced above the din, "I now present to you, Mr. and Mrs. Ambrose and Dinah, and Mr. and Mrs. Toby and Hope."

A loud cheer went up and out through all of the doors and windows and drifted across the river, faintly heard by Rena and those working with her. As she hoed the field closest to the river the cool weather actually made her hard work more comfortable. Rena began to think about Zekiel and his promise to meet her here at the river after dark, to tell her all about the wedding. It would be their third meeting since they had worked together picking cotton. She had not gone to Zekiel. He had come to her each time. His pants were always wet because of the river crossing. Tonight would be the coldest yet. She worried that he might get caught on one of his visits. As she chopped at the clods in frustration, Rena heard the distant sound of singing. She imagined Zekiel standing with his friends, and she prayed. She prayed that there would come a day when his visits would not be accompanied by fear.

Praise, worship, and spirituals rose to the heavens as the feast was set out on the tables. There were no tears now. Joshua watched as people hugged and congratulated the four newlyweds. The pastor had given each couple a Bible they could not yet read. Others brought forth hand-made items and baby clothes. Otis presented two chairs he had made for them in the barn in the evenings, and Gideon had made two cradles. Smiles were everywhere and Joshua finally came to the conclusion that whatever the problem had been, it must have been worked out.

While everyone was distracted by giving gifts, Frank slipped a flat board onto the table where each of the two newlyweds would be sitting. When it was time to eat, Toby came to his place at the table with Hope at his side. He saw the board and picked it up slowly and gently. They stared at it and smiled. Ambrose and Dinah did the same. The others watched them and wondered what it was that was holding them in rapt attention.

Finally, Frank couldn't stand it any longer and spoke loud enough for everyone to hear.

"I made 'em to put over your doors."

"What are dey?" someone asked.

"Hold 'em up, Ambrose and Toby," said Frank. "Show 'em what I made for you."

"We kin read it!" said Hope, as the men lifted the boards. "It say 'Toby and Hope'. It's beautiful, young suh."

Frank had carved out the names of the two couples in the boards and then painted the letters with left-over green paint from the house shutters.

Ambrose held his sign over his head so all could see.

"And dis say 'Ambrose and Dinah'," he said proudly. He looked at Frank. "We knows it do, cause you tol' us it do."

"Thank you, Massuh Frank," added Dinah as she smiled at the boy. "We shall hang it proudly over our door."

Frank was busting his buttons from all of the attention he was getting, and was slightly disappointed when Joshua changed the subject.

"When we gonna eat all dis food?"

There was laughter and Matthew announced, "brides and grooms dish up first."

"What for?" Joshua asked, disappointed.

"They done that at the weddings I've been at, Joshua," said Frank. "You'll just have to get used to it."

There was more laughter and bantering, and the feast began.

Joshua made sure he was first in line, after the brides and grooms.

Frank stood right behind him.

Chapter 50

During the weeks leading up to Christmas, the Martin plantation settled into a more relaxed lifestyle brought on by the cooler weather. Except for caring for the animals, the slaves were often left to themselves until after the day had warmed up a bit, when the men might be called to cut firewood, repair buildings, and do minor fieldwork. The women, because of old age, a baby, and pregnancies, helped with the cooking and cleaning in the Martin home and shared in the lunch and dinner preparation in the cookhouse. While Frank was at school each day, Joshua was milking the three cows, grooming horses, collecting eggs, and being the errand boy for whoever needed something.

About an hour before the sun set each evening, the slaves would gather in the eating room and share a light meal of vegetables, bread, and milk. After the meal, no one left. Every man woman, and child, was anxious to learn. The slate boards, chalk, and Bibles were passed out, and Tal and Sadie shared the gift of learning they had received from Sid and Maggie. First, they taught the alphabet, then how to sound out and write each personal name. No teacher ever had more eager and appreciative students. During the day, while working, they would drill each other on what had been taught the night before. They began to read small words like 'an', 'and', 'the', and 'if'. The challenge was thrilling to them. It would be nearly impossible for a young white student to understand how knowing just those few words raised the self esteem of a slave. Though the Martins had treated their workers as kindly as anyone in the South, and their slaves felt loved and respected, the ball and chain of ignorance had held their black friends back from feeling fully human. This discovery surprised both the Martins *and* their slaves.

One morning as they worked together, Mabin shared with Luke that even though he had always believed he was not an animal, and Luke had never treated him as one, for some reason he could not explain, he felt more complete now that he was learning to read and write.

"Tell me why, suh," asked Mabin, "why it is dat I bleved in God and dat he made me, but now, when I reads my name, I bleve he sees me and *knows* me?"

A wave of shame swept over Luke.

"Do you remember a few years ago when we were in town and saw the man who had lost both legs in the war?" he asked Mabin.

"Yes, suh, I do."

"You said it made you realize how you had taken for granted the gift of legs and feet and being able to walk."

"Yes, suh," Mabin nodded. "It was den I decide to stop feeling sorry for my position and start livin' grateful like."

"That's right," Luke agreed, "You always had arms and legs so they weren't special to you. I've always *had* reading and writing so that wasn't special. I see now that without any one of those things, a person is crippled."

Luke looked at Mabin and his eyes began to water.

"I've kept you all crippled, Mabin."

"No, suh," Mabin spoke firmly. "We was cripple, yes. If d' Lord say teach 'em to read 'n you don' do it, only den would you ben *keepin'* us cripple."

Luke gave Mabin's response some thought. "Thank you, Mabin. I appreciate that."

Luke handed him a stick.

"Here. Write your name in the dirt. I want to see it."

Mabin smiled, took the stick, and without hesitation carved the letters into the ground.

"Wow," said Luke, as he stared at the ground. "That must feel good to do that."

Mabin didn't say anything. He began writing in front of his name. Luke watched, nearly in tears, as the words 'God loves' took form in front of the name 'Mabin'.

"It feel good to do *dat!*" Mabin said.

Three days before Christmas, the morning brought with it a couple of unusual events. It doesn't often snow in Georgia, but on this particular day, large white flakes were cascading down from the sky in a beautiful, silent, tribute to the season. A thin, white, cottony blanket lay over the plantation giving a hushed message of peace and tranquility. As the sun rose to peek through the thin crack on the horizon between earth and clouds, it created a dazzling display of glittering wonder, though Dinah was the only one of the Martin plantation awake to see it. Sitting by the window, in the chair that Otis had made her, she was nursing baby Eli and thinking about all that had happened since she had been purchased and brought to the Martin farm. In a few short weeks, she had traveled from bitterness to blessings. As she watched the falling snow, all seemed right and good, and she thanked God.

Ambrose shifted positions and began mumbling something in his sleep. Dinah looked over at her husband and smiled. Her man was happier now than she had ever seen him. She repented again for her attitude toward God as he was leading them to this moment. As she looked again out the window, a distant movement caught her attention. Through the heavily falling snow, she could make out the image of a man riding in a wagon loaded with lumber. He appeared to have been traveling for some time. A layer of snow covered his coat and hat and he was hunched over in an apparent effort to keep warm.

Because there was no sign of anyone else being awake and aware of the visitor, Dinah placed the baby on the bed and shook Ambrose's shoulder.

"Ambrose, wake up."

"Huh? Whatsa matter? You okay?" Ambrose rolled over on his back and attempted to clear the cobwebs from his head.

"Summun's commin', 'n everyone's asleep 'cept us."

Ambrose opened his eyes and looked questioningly at Dinah.

"Who be coming at dis time o' mornin'?" he asked, as he glanced at the window.

"A man in a wagon dat looks to be loaded with lumber," she said, moving back to the window to watch. "He pull up to d' massuh's house 'n jus' sittin' dere. Looks like he talkin', but dere's no one dere but him."

Ambrose scrambled into his pants and went to the window.

"He sure enuf is. Maybe he a crazy man," Ambrose said quietly, as he stood next to his wife, watching. "S'pose I should go see if I can do sumthin'."

Ambrose sat on the edge of the bed to pull on his shoes as Dinah brought his shirt and jacket. Baby Eli began to fuss so Dinah picked him up, bouncing him up and down to quiet him as she returned to the window to watch.

"What he doin'?" Ambrose asked her, walking to the door.

"He climbing down from d' wagon, but he still talkin'."

"Hmmm. Keep watchin' 'n if anythin' happens, go next door 'n wake up Toby."

"I will."

Ambrose went out and closed the door.

Dinah watched as the man climbed the steps and then paused to look around as if wary of being watched or followed. She instinctively pulled back from the window, not wanting to be seen. Eventually, the man went to the front door and knocked. He waited a moment and then knocked again. Dinah watched as Ambrose appeared below her window walking toward the house. The stranger was attempting to see in a window and did not notice him coming. Dinah decided the snow must have muffled the sound of her husband's footsteps, because the man returned to the door and knocked again without looking in his direction. Apparently, Ambrose said something as he arrived at the foot of the steps, because the man suddenly spun around with a startled look on his face. As he spun around, his hand reached into his coat pocket and it looked to Dinah as if he was pointing a hidden gun at her husband.

"Dear Lord!" she said nervously as she turned and placed the baby on the bed, ready to run and fetch Toby. But when she took one more look out the window, she saw that the man had relaxed noticeably as Ambrose was speaking. Then the front door opened and her master stepped out onto the porch looking very curious, and half asleep. Dinah saw the curtains part in the room above the door and Mrs. Martin looked down at the wagon.

There was a look of recognition and the two white men shook hands. Dinah noticed words were spoken and the men looked down the plantation road at the lone set of wagon tracks in the snow. After a short pause, Luke motioned for Ambrose to follow, and all three went into the house and closed the door.

The longer Dinah watched the closed door, the less she could stand it. Finally, she picked up the baby and went next door and knocked.

"Hope! Toby! Wake up!"

She rapped on the door again. "Hope! It's Dinah. Wake up in dere."

She heard some mumbling and a thump, and then more mumbling.

Dinah knocked again.

"I'm commin', girl. Hol' on," said Hope as she opened the door. "Brrr, dis floor is cold!"

She had a blanket wrapped around her to keep warm, but she was hopping back and forth on bare feet.

"Well, put your shoes on 'n bring Toby 'n come to our window. We kin see d' house from dere. Sumthin's hapnin'."

Dinah turned and hurried back to her room, not wanting to miss anything. It wasn't long before Toby and Hope joined her, staring at the wagon and the closed door as she filled them in on what had happened.

It seemed like forever before the door opened and Ambrose exited the house alone. He appeared to be totally unconcerned as he ambled across the barnyard, just enjoying the peace and quiet that comes with newly fallen snow. This wasn't exactly what Toby and

Hope had expected after hearing Dinah's story. They both looked at her suspiciously and she could feel their eyes on her as she watched Ambrose coming toward the cookhouse.

"Hmmm. Dat strange," she said, before they could. "I wonder what's goin' on."

They all heard the door close below them, and then it sounded as if Ambrose was running up the stairs as fast as he could. They all turned to the door, expecting him to burst in at any second. Instead, they heard him pounding on Toby's door.

"Toby! Hope! You need to get up! We got things to do!"

He pounded on the door again. "Come on, now! Get up, in dere!"

He then turned toward his own room, only to find three curious people standing in the hallway watching him.

"Hackett brought them in after dark last night; a pregnant woman and her two mulattos. Says her master is the father of her children."

Henry had retold the story to Sally as she moved around the kitchen making coffee and fixing up something for them to eat.

"It seems that, somehow, the wife found out for sure that this third baby is her husband's. She had long suspected the same of the other two, but this was the straw that broke the camel's back, and she ordered them all to be locked up and beaten to death the following morning, as an example to all of the other female slaves, as well as to her husband."

"So, the wife rules the roost," Sally commented, as she tossed some wood into the stove.

Henry chuckled. "And I think she might be thinking of killing the rooster," he said. "Seems he's kind of fond of this slave girl. He had one of his slaves sneak her and the children over to Hackett's place during the night. The next morning the wife went out early and set fire to the shack she thought they were locked up in, then she and her husband happily ate breakfast while they watched it burn."

"Are you making this up, Henry?"

"Honest, Sally, this is exactly how it was told to *me*." He took the plate of eggs Sally handed to him.

"When the wife discovered there were no bodies, she took her derringer and shot at her husband as he ran off into the bushes. Guess she missed him, though. All of this started a week ago, and by now she's got pretty much the whole state of Georgia looking under every rock."

Henry got up from the table and went to the window and looked out. "The Lord's pretty much got the tracks covered up. That's good." He returned to the table and sat down.

"Sounds like the type of thing Roily likes about his job. Suppose he'll be giving us another visit sometime soon?" asked Luke.

"That's why I came out in the dark. The snow's an additional bonus. All tracks leaving town should've been well-covered by sunup."

"Haven't had snow in about five years," said Sally, "It looks to me like God's seal of approval on what were doing here."

There was a knock on the door. The men stood up as Sally opened the door and invited Toby into the kitchen.

"Ready?" Luke asked.

Toby nodded, "Yessuh. Food, candles, blankets, n fresh water's all set, suh."

"Did Ambrose tell you we'll be unloading the wood next to the storage building?" asked Luke.

Toby nodded again. "So dere's a reason for all d' tracks. Dere's mix wit ours."

Luke walked to the window and looked out at the wagon. "I'm sure they're getting chilly out there, but we don't want to unload unusually early. Don't want to arouse suspicion. Stay casual. No running. Like I told Ambrose, walk at a normal pace as if you don't have a care in the world."

"Yes, suh," said Toby as he reached for the door handle.

"Is the cook stove fired up?" asked Luke.

"Yes, suh. Ambrose, he doin' dat while d' women are getting' some food ready."

Luke nodded his approval. "Good. Maybe we'll sneak them in there for a hot breakfast before we put them in the cellar."

Toby opened the door to leave.

"Oh, and Toby, stop by the wagon on your way out, pretend to inspect the wood, and tell them we'll be out soon to get them out of there."

"Yes, suh. I will," said Toby as he closed the door behind him.

Henry was gone by nine, and the snow had melted away before noon. The three guests were warm, well-fed, and tucked away in their new quarters by the time the sheriff and three men rode into the barnyard in the early afternoon. Sally and Joshua were collecting eggs when the men arrived. They backed out of the chicken house as they fought back the chickens that were trying to escape to freedom. Joshua used his foot to push a hen back in as Sally shut the door. Sally held the egg basket and Joshua carried the empty feed bucket as they turned to the house. Sally gasped in surprise when suddenly confronted by four men on horseback.

"Afternoon, ma'am."

The sheriff was wearing a self-satisfied smile because he took great pleasure in keeping others on edge.

Sally quickly pulled herself together. "I apologize, Sheriff. I guess I didn't hear you ride up."

"Well now, that's okay, ma'am. I kind of like it that way." He smiled again.

"Is this a friendly visit, Sheriff," Sally asked, "or should we be rounding everyone up again?"

The sheriff detected a slight nervousness in her voice, so he took a long draw on his cigarette and rudely looked her over. He didn't notice Luke walking up behind the horses.

Sally self-consciously put her hand over her stomach.

Roily gave a smart-aleck look and said, "Looks like you've been eatin' real good, ma'am."

One of the men laughed. Luke slapped the sheriff's horse on the side of the rump as hard as he could and the horse jerked sideways, bumping into the horse next to him. The sheriff nearly fell out of his saddle, but he desperately held onto the horn with both hands and managed to pull himself upright. He cursed at Luke as the four men calmed their horses down.

"A sheriff's job is to protect the citizens and make them feel safe, Roily!" Luke spoke threateningly as he walked up to the sheriff's side.

"My wife doesn't feel too safe with you around! You're supposed to protect us *from* the bad guys, not *be* the bad guy!" He looked down and stomped on the cigarette that the sheriff had dropped.

"Now, why is it that you can't seem to leave us alone?"

Sheriff Roily reached to pull another cigarette out of his shirt pocket but found that Luke had stomped out his last one. He gazed down at the flat cigarette and his face turned red as he lifted his eyes to meet Luke's.

"Runaways."

The sheriff stared hard at Luke, hoping to see even the faintest hint of a reaction in his eyes. He got nothing.

"Seen Blackstone lately?" he asked, still watching closely.

"Every so often, yeah," Luke answered.

"I mean, recently."

"Yup. He was here for breakfast. Dropped off some boards."

The sheriff looked around and his eyes settled on the small stack of lumber.

"Not much there," he said. "Whatcha building?"

Luke thought fast and didn't flinch.

"A covered walkway from the cellar to the cooking house to keep the rain off the ladies."

"Ladies," the sheriff smirked. "You make the nigras sound classy."

"They are," Luke said firmly.

Roily changed the subject.

"Has Blackstone mentioned three high-stake runaways and a big reward?"

"Ya know what? You oughta give up on this sheriff stuff and just go out and be a full-time bounty hunter. You don't give a hoot about right and wrong, but you give a real big hoot about cash!"

"Do you know about the runaways?" the sheriff repeated without flinching.

"Henry says the whole state of Georgia knows about them! Of course, I know about the runaways." Luke was not even trying to hide his irritation.

"And I'll tell you what, Roily," he continued, "there's lots of us who intend to help any runaway that comes through these parts. God's law of 'do unto others' trumps any slave law you might try to bring down on my head."

"Not to a judge," the sheriff said, in a matter-of-fact tone.

Luke took a deep breath and tried to calm down.

"Well, it does to *the* judge, the one that's gonna judge me 'n you."

"That so? Well, when that judge shows up, you may find that you're no better'n me, Martin."

Not wanting the conversation to go from bad to worse, Sally interrupted their exchange.

"There's still time, Mr. Roily. I hope when he does show up, we'll all walk into heaven side by side." She smiled at him.

Roily looked frustrated and rolled his eyes. "That's not what I meant, ma'am."

"I know that. But you could change." She smiled again.

"Let's get outta here, Sheriff," said the man next to him. "I ain't got time to be preached at."

The man turned his horse to leave and the other two followed his lead.

For a moment, the sheriff seemed undecided. He locked on to Luke's eyes and said, "Don't do anything stupid! You see something, you tell me. Ya hear me?"

"I hear."

The sheriff reined his horse around and followed the others.

Chapter 51

Christmas morning arrived warm and dry. The snow, three days earlier, seemed like an unlikely dream from somewhere in the past. There would be no work today except to care for the animals. It was in everyone's prayers that the day would be without incident. The previous day, a group of six bounty hunters had stopped by to ask if they could search the woods for the three runaways. The reward had been raised to two thousand dollars, and the men were determined to get it. In order to not raise suspicion, Luke granted them permission, as long as he rode along with them. Finding nothing, the men wished the Martins a Merry Christmas and rode north to the mountains.

Every morning, at the first sign of dawn, it was Tal's and Sadie's job to slip the three fugitives into the cookhouse to clean up and, after a visit to the outhouse, feed them a small breakfast and allow the children to run around in the eating room for awhile. After an hour, the three would be back in hiding and remain there until after dark, when the ritual would be repeated.

Today, however, was Christmas, and Luke and Sally had given permission for them to stay in the cookhouse for the morning and join the others for the midday Christmas meal. Two, large, smoked hams would be the highlight of the feast along with fresh-baked bread, yams, and rice. The Martins supplied the food, but preparing the meal had been left up to the slaves.

The master and his family would be spending this morning as they did every Christmas morning, reading from the Bible, opening gifts, and singing carols. Pastor Davies had arrived the previous evening with packages and was to be their guest for a couple of days. His daughter Missy, and her husband David, were spending Christmas at David's parents' home in Edgartown. It was Frank's idea to give Sadie the morning off, and he and his mother were cooking breakfast for the two men. As Frank cut slices off of the block of bacon and placed them in the iron skillet, he asked his mother why his father and the pastor had spent so much time in the study with the doors closed, last night.

Sally thought for a minute, trying to figure how she should answer.

"Frank, today everyone's lives are going to change. It's good that you know ahead of time, but you have to keep it a secret for a few more hours. Not a peep to anyone, not even Joshua. Can you do that?"

Frank stopped slicing bacon and stared at his mother. He had rarely seen her so serious, and he became concerned that something bad was going to happen.

"I don't know, mama. I think so. Is something wrong? Is the baby okay?" he asked.

Sally smiled, "Everything's fine. It's just that we are about to enter some unfamiliar territory that could bring a few problems along the way."

"Oh, is Grandma coming to live with us?" Frank asked excitedly. "That would be great!"

Sally laughed as she dumped a pile of sliced potatoes and onions into a large skillet.

"No. She's been invited, but she's a very independent woman, and she likes living in the city. Now, finish slicing that bacon while I fill you in."

Frank renewed his attack on the bacon while his mother talked. When he finished the bacon, he sliced a loaf of bread and was then sent to retrieve a jar of strawberry jam and a jar of peaches from the pantry. As he returned to the kitchen, deep in thought, he found his father leaning over the pan of frying bacon and breathing in the fragrant aroma. The sizzling grease in the skillet popped and Luke let out a yell and jumped back, rubbing his face.

"I guess the hog gets the last word after all," laughed Matthew, as he walked into the kitchen. "Merry Christmas, Sally. Merry Christmas, Frank."

"Merry Christmas," they responded together.

"No, he doesn't," said Luke, as he took another whiff from a safer distance. "I'll get the last word with every bite."

"All right, you guys, have a seat," Sally cut in. "This is a big day. Let's get it started off right."

She pulled a large pan of cornbread out of the oven and set it on a mat on the table. Everyone seated themselves at the table and Frank watched the adults as they joked and ate their breakfast, but he wondered what they were really thinking. Were their minds really on breakfast, or actually on what would happen this afternoon?

"Hey, Frank, are you in there?"

"Huh? What?" Frank realized his father was looking at him.

"I asked you to pass the butter."

"I told him the plan, Luke," Sally interceded for him, "I imagine he's a little distracted,"

"You did? That's good."

Luke looked at Frank. "While I was in Savannah, I met with your grandma's lawyer and he drew up all of the legal papers so no one could contest their emancipation. I had enough copies made to cover any future need, too. When I got back home, I met with Ben's lawyer and he assures me that state law recognizes a man's right to set his slaves free, but he warned me that there are those that have ignored the law and kidnapped and resold freed slaves."

"That's not fair, Papa! Wouldn't the judge make 'em go to jail?" asked Frank.

"A black man's testimony means nothing in court, Frank. That's why we have asked every white friend we have to come here tomorrow and witness the signing of the papers. Judge Wilkins has agreed to be present also."

"There will be risk," his mother added, "but each slave will have the choice of whether to take that risk, or remain as is."

"But then they could choose to leave!" protested Frank.

"Yes, they could," Luke agreed, "and some might. It would be very hard on us to have them leave. We've come to love them all so much."

"Do you mean that by tomorrow, we could be all alone here?" Frank was close to tears.

"Technically, yes, but that's not likely," Luke answered. "Today we tell them of our intentions. Tomorrow, they will all be set free. As of tomorrow, we will no longer own any slaves except Joshua. We have decided he will be safer as our slave until he turns sixteen, and then, he will also be set free. We are now employers. They can choose to stay and work for room and board and a small wage, or they can freely leave and try something else at any time. It's my hope that no one will choose to leave right away. They are safer here, and they are loved. But, sometime down the road they may feel the need to move on, and tomorrow, they will be given that right and that freedom."

Frank looked at his mother through watery eyes. "That wouldn't be fair to *us*, mama. We've treated them so well, and they are our friends. Why can't we keep them?"

"For the same reason we can't keep *you*, Frank," answered his mother. "There will come a time when you will choose your vocation, who you will marry, and where you will live."

"And what you believe," added Matthew.

"That's right, Frank," Luke agreed. "We might hope you would choose to stay on with us as a planter, but if you were to choose otherwise, you would be free to do so. True, your choices might break our hearts, and we'd probably cry, but they must be your choices, and that's how it should be with Mabin, or Toby, or any of the others."

A knock at the front door ended the conversation. "I'll make this as quick as I can."

"Frank, help your mother clean up the table, please. Then you three can move on into the parlor. I'll join you for our Christmas Bible reading and songs as soon as I see who's at the door."

Luke left the room to the sound of scooting chairs, tinkling silverware, and the stacking of plates and cups. He walked down the hall to the main entrance and opened the large door.

"Hello, Martin," Tom Grant greeted smartly. "You been missin' a slave, by any chance?"

Luke could see Zekiel standing slightly behind Tom, looking like a little boy caught with his hand in the cookie jar.

"Uh, if I was, I didn't know it," Luke said haltingly.

"Well, you was, and now you know it. He's the one that was working by Rena and Big Joe when you was over in my field." Tom put his hands on his hips. "Can you guess who I found him with?"

"Uh, I'm guessing it wasn't with Big Joe or Maybeth, was it?"

"No, it was not!" Tom turned halfway around and stared at Zekiel giving him a look of irritation until the big slave began to fidget, and then he turned back to Luke. "So what are we going to do about this problem of ours?"

"Problem? Of ours?"

"Yes, ours!" Tom spoke loud enough that he attracted the attention of the other three persons in the house. "Can't you see that we've got us a full-fledged romance goin' on!"

"*We* have a romance going on?" Luke was aware that there were now three people standing behind him.

"Don't be ridiculous, of course *we* don't. *They* do!" Tom pointed with his thumb over his shoulder at Zekiel. "They was at least honest enough to admit he's been over there six or seven times now."

Luke raised his eyebrows and looked curiously at Zekiel. Zekiel slowly looked up and nodded his head slightly, and then resumed his study of the front porch decking.

"Hmmm. This does present a challenge," agreed Luke. He looked at Tom and raised only his left eyebrow. "Does this remind you of when you were young? It sure does me."

"Luke!" said Sally, indignantly.

"What are you insinuating, Martin? Are you saying that I .....?"

"I'm just saying that my parents had this same problem with me and the beautiful lady standing behind me, that's all."

"Luke!"

"What do you think, Tom? Shall we set up some sort of courting rules or something?" Luke pressed on. "Maybe ..., hmmm, Friday nights, for dinner at your place?"

Zekiel raised his head and studied Luke, trying to determine if he was serious or joking.

"Very funny, Martin. You know you have to keep him away," said Tom.

"Why? Did he keep her from her work?"

"No, but...."

"Did he steal anything?"

"No, but...."

"Did he cause any sort of trouble?"

"Well, no, but he can't just come sneaking around in the middle of the night!" said Tom, with a great deal of frustration.

"I agree."

"You do?" Tom asked in surprise.

"Certainly. It's a good way to get shot!"

Luke looked over Tom's shoulder. "Zekiel, it would be better if you went to visit Rena in the daytime or the early evening. And you need to set it up ahead of time, so Mr. Grant knows when to expect you."

"Wha ...? Wait a minute here .... I didn't....." Tom was clearly flustered.

"That's very kind of you, Tom," Sally jumped in. "I'll send a hot pie along with him the next time he comes over. I hear you didn't get to taste the last one."

"But ma'am, that's not what I meant," he said, begging her to understand.

Luke turned serious. "Zekiel, you may go help the others prepare for the Christmas meal. We'll talk later."

"Yes, suh," he said quietly as he turned and walked away.

"Would you please come in, Tom?" Luke motioned him in. "There's something you should know."

Tom hesitated, but finally agreed to stay for a short time.

When everyone had taken a seat in the parlor, Luke began to explain the coming events on the Martin plantation.

"You are very well aware, Tom, of my distaste for slavery."

"Very," Tom agreed with a look of disgust.

"Well, as of tomorrow, we will be conducting an experiment here on our farm. We want to see if it is possible to run a profit-making plantation using only employees instead of slaves."

"You're a fool, an idealist!" sputtered Tom, "You'll die a slow death and eventually you will have to sell this place back to *me*."

Tom paused and thought about what he had just said. He smiled. "When ya sell your nigras, I'll give you a good price on that Zekiel fella. That could well solve our problem with Rena, don't you think?"

"Well, Tom, *none* of them will be sold. I'm setting them all free."

All eyes were on Tom Grant as he sat in stunned silence, staring at Luke.

Luke finally continued. "We are hoping that all, or most, of them will choose to stay on and work for room and board and a small wage. But they will be free to choose, the same as any other human being."

"*Any other human being*," Tom repeated inaudibly to himself as his eyes fell to the floor.

"God showed you, the same way he showed me," said Luke. "You told me he showed you."

Tom finally came back around and looked up again at Luke.

"Those papers don't mean much to Roily, and some others around here, Luke."

"Was that the second, or the third, time he had ever heard Tom call him by his first name?" Sally and Luke both wondered.

"Today we are planning to inform everyone of our decision," said Luke. "Tomorrow, Judge Wilkins, Ben Statler and his lawyer, the Willis family, and Henry Blackstone will all be here to witness the signing of the papers by Sally and myself, and the judge, and the pastor. Oh, yes," Luke suddenly remembered, "the sheriff will also be attending, shall we say 'grudgingly', at the insistence of the judge. Mr. Wilkins wanted no confusion as to the validity of the papers."

Tom looked at the Christmas tree and thought about everything he had just heard. He looked at the gifts under the tree waiting to be opened. His eyes settled on Frank and he said, "I hope your Pa don't lose it all for you, young man. But who knows, maybe he's right and the rest of us are wrong." He slapped his knees and stood to his feet. "Looks like you've covered your people as best you can, Martin. I guess this means you can't, or won't, keep this Zekiel fellow away from Rena?"

"I could talk to him, I suppose. What would you do, if he went back over to your place some night?" Luke asked.

"There was a day when I'd a done what you suggested earlier."

"You'd shoot him?" asked Frank incredulously.

"No, probably not. Not anymore," he answered, looking sadly at

Frank. And then he became fixated on the gifts under the tree. "How's your little black friend doing?" he asked while staring at the colorfully wrapped packages.

"He doesn't like you very much," Frank answered honestly.

Tom nodded his head as he looked at a roughly wrapped package, obviously wrapped by the boy.

"Yeah, well ..." Tom paused and turned to Frank, "Tell him I'm sorry about what I done."

Frank didn't know what to say, but he nodded his head at Tom.

"I'd best be going," said Tom, as he walked to the door. "I may stop by in a few days just to see if this place is a ghost town."

"Stop in any time you're in town, Tom," said Matthew. "I always keep a pot of coffee on the stove, except when I'm asleep, of course."

Tom shook his head slightly. "Sorry, Davies, I don't much like coffee. I'm a lemonade man, myself."

Tom turned to Luke before the pastor could respond.

"Say, Martin. How's your chicken supply? I heard that you sell em', sometimes. Maybe I could buy a dozen off of you."

"Chicks, or full grown?" Luke asked.

"Biggest and fattest."

"Yeah, we've got enough for that," said Luke. "I'll send Frank out to get you some crates. Go ahead and take what you need."

A mischievous smile came across Luke's face.

"I'll send a bill over with Zekiel in a few days. He can bring the crates back with him."

"Humph. Very funny," grumbled Tom. "But remember - the law says the baby always belongs to the mother. She's my slave, so I'd be gettin' another slave and there's nothing he could do about it, even if he is free."

"Zekiel's a Christian, and the pastor here's been teaching all of our people what God says about waiting til marriage. I don't think you'll be getting any free slaves outta this."

"You need to talk him out of this, Martin. If he keeps this up, it'll just be self-inflicted torture. Both of them will be miserable."

Luke smiled and held one finger up. "Or ..., you could set her free. Or you could sell her to me. Or you could let her marry a free man and still be your slave. Or...."

"Oh, for heaven's sake! You drive me insane!" Tom opened the door and stormed out. He slammed the door behind him as he left.

Luke walked to the window and watched Tom stomp off to the chicken house in a huff.

"Frank, would you run and get those crates for Tom, please?" asked Luke, "We'll wait until you get back."

"Sure, Pa," Frank answered as he ran for the door. "I'll be back in a second."

As the door slammed a second time, Luke turned to Pastor Davies and asked, "Do you think I overdid it?"

The pastor shrugged.

"With you, Luke, I'm never quite sure."

Chapter 52

After the woman and her two children had taken their morning time of refreshing and breakfast, Tal and Sadie helped them settle into their little hideaway. They were given extra food and candles and a stick of leftover Christmas candy for each of them. Tal asked the children to be extra quiet today because it was the morning after Christmas and there might be lots of white folk in the eating room, including the sheriff and a judge. They were told that they might not be able to come out for a while and if they had to relieve themselves, they would have to use the empty bucket. As Sadie closed up the opening in the wall she reminded them once again of the importance of being quiet.

"Try to sleep a lot, today," she said. She handed each of the children a slate and some chalk. "Maybe you could have some fun drawing pictures for each other."

Tal restacked the bags of onions and potatoes against the wall and then followed his wife into the cookhouse. It was still early, but Otis, Mabin, and Gideon were already gathered on a bench staring at their cups of coffee and taking a sip, once in a while. Tal took a tin cup off of a nail, went to the stove, and poured a cup for himself. Mahta's door opened and she stepped out and surveyed the group. As soon as she spotted Sadie, she motioned her over and invited her into her room to talk.

Tal wandered over to the table where the men were gathered and slid in next to Otis. After a short silence, he asked, "So, was yesterday a dream, or did Master Martin really say what I think he said?"

Mabin continued to stare at his cup as he let out a short chuckle. "Oh, he say it alright. Probly ain't a slave on d' place could sleep long enuf last night to dream much o' anythin'."

"Today, when all dem white folk come, we sign our names to d' papers," said Otis.

"Might surprise a few of them to see that we actually know how to spell our names," chuckled Tal.

"I practice some, last night," said Otis. "Don' wan' to look stupid."

The four men sat at the table thinking about what Otis said. They each felt a little stupid. They had no idea what all of the ramifications were to this freedom that they had dreamed of all of their lives. Now that they were to be freed, they were afraid.

Gideon finally spoke what they were all feeling.

"Feels like we all a bunch of chickens in a chicken pen. Someone open d' door to d' pen 'n set us free. Lots of grubs 'n bugs 'n good food out dere, and no fence, but we know dere's some foxes out dere somewhere. Mebbe it safer t' stay in d' pen."

"Hmm," Mabin nodded his head in agreement. "I'm thinkin' maybe I stay in d' pen awhile 'n get more learnin'. Might wander out a little to get used to it but I think I stay near d' gate. Massuh Luke's a good man to work for."

"Ain't no fox in *that* family, fo' sure," Tal added. "Sadie 'n I talked last night 'n decided it be best to stay here 'n have our baby grow up free, 'n some safe."

"We decided d' same," said Toby from the doorway.

The men hadn't noticed their arrival, but quickly stood and greeted the couple, scooting benches around to make room. The noise drew Mahta and Sadie out, and it was decided that breakfast could be made while they all discussed, together, this stunning event that had already changed their lives forever. Soon after Toby and Hope arrived, Ambrose and Dinah joined the discussion. As breakfast was being dished up, Washington, Zekiel, and Joshua arrived to complete what they thought was probably the largest gathering of freed slaves to ever eat a meal together in the history of the entire state of Georgia.

The day had already begun in an unprecedented fashion. On Christmas Day, Luke had declared that on the following day, as far as he was concerned, the Martin plantation had no employees and no slaves except Joshua, and Joshua was given the day off. It was unseasonably warm and the proceedings were to be held in the front yard. No negro had been called upon to set up the table and chairs, nor had they made any of the food or drinks.

The Martins and all of their guests, except the sheriff and the judge, had helped with the preparations. The Statler and Willis families brought drinks and snacks in honor of the occasion. Henry brought a wagon load of chairs from the church. Ted and Nathan Willis had volunteered to help Frank feed the animals until everyone had arrived.

A day of leisure, with not a chore to be done. It was a strange experience for the slaves huddled together in the cookhouse. Pastor Davies had wandered down to the cookhouse to see how they were all doing and be a comforting presence. They watched from the three windows facing the house, as the white people milled around on the great porch and in the yard.

"That's Judge Wilkins," said Pastor Davies, as he stood with his nervous black friends. "The only one who hasn't arrived is Sheriff Roily."

"A judge, a banker, a lawyer, 'n a sheriff," Mabin pondered the list. "I don' understan' how we 'come so important. I woulda chosen to stay unknown 'n of no consequence to other men."

Some of the others spoke in agreement.

"Unfortunately," Pastor Davies answered sadly, "the negro slave is becoming more and more the center of attention. Your best recourse is to place yourselves in the hands of the Almighty, and trust that he understands, and that he is good."

"Massuh Martin has placed his family in some discomfort, as well," Washington commented. "Is possible they will suffer some degree of retribution from men of their own race who fear opposing opinions."

"Retro... retro...what?" asked Toby

Pastor Davies smiled. "Retribution. It means revenge, or some sort of payback for doing something that displeases another person."

"Dere he is," said Zekiel. "Dat's d' sheriff man."

Everyone turned their attention to the window. Some instantly grew more nervous, but deep inside, no one wished this wasn't happening.

A short time after the sheriff's arrival, Luke and Sally strode hand in hand from the yard to the cookhouse. They seemed light on their feet and obviously excited. The pastor smiled as he watched everyone begin to brush off their skirts and tuck in their shirts. No one else was smiling, nor was anyone sitting. They were all standing and staring apprehensively at the door. The door did not open immediately because Luke and Sally had paused outside the door to say a quick prayer. When they entered the room, they each wore a smile that quickly faded as they looked around the group. Realization hit them both at once as they stood in the silent room.

"I think I've placed you all at a distinct disadvantage," said Luke. "We have given you very little time for all of this to sink in, while Sally and I have had weeks to become comfortable with the idea. I apologize. What can we do to help you before we go out to join our friends?"

"Well, suh, I guess Hope and me was wondering what be different tomorrow, or a week from tomorrow," said Toby. "We would like to stay here. Would life be d' same as it was before?"

Sally began looking around the room. Her eyes settled on the stack of Bibles that were sitting on the shelf. She let go of Luke's hand and went to get a Bible.

Ambrose nodded his head in agreement with Toby."

"Yes, suh. Me 'n Dinah bleve little Eli would be safer here. We would like to stay. But if we stay, why would you need to free us? What good would it be for you?"

Sally was busily thumbing through the pages of a Bible until she found the place in the book of Philemon that she was looking for. She quickly moved over to Tal, gave him a nudge, and handed him the Bible.

"When you learn to read better, over the months ahead, you

might want to read this letter from the apostle Paul to his friend who was a slave owner." Sal looked around the group and smiled. "If someone were to look at all of us a month from now, they might not see a difference. Everything might look the same as it always was to the outside observer, but to us, our relationship with you will never be the same again."

Sally leaned over and pointed to a place on the page.

"Tal, would you read from here to here for us, please? This is why we are doing what we're doing."

Tal cleared his throat and placed his finger below the first word and moved it along as he read each word.

"…..that you might have him back forever, no longer as a slave but more than a slave, as a beloved brother – especially to me, but how much more to you, both in the flesh and in the Lord."

There was silence in the room as Tal closed the book. Sadie began to tear up. Mahta smiled and uttered a long "hmmm'.

"Those who choose to stay," said Luke, "will work side by side with us as friends, brothers and sisters. Should anyone choose to leave and try a little adventure out on their own, we will still be friends, brothers and sisters. We will send you off with a little money, food and clothing, and a letter of recommendation to help get you started. If things don't work out, we hope you would come back to live here."

"And should you get into any kind of trouble," Sally added, "get word to us and we will come to help you."

"That's right. That's why we have all of these friendly witnesses here today. A white man's testimony is allowed in court and we would flood the courtroom with white men and women who are friendly to you. The sheriff is an exception of course. His reason for being here is so that he will understand that the law is behind what we're doing. Judge Wilkins and my dad grew up together. He would be a powerful witness, in any court."

Sally looked at Zekiel. "This also means that you are all free to come and go. There's no need to sneak around at night."

Mabin chuckled. Zekiel frowned at him.

"Just remember," Luke cautioned, "don't go trespassing on other people's property without permission. And don't go around assuming you will now be seen as equal with everyone else. It will pay you to be cautious and lawful."

Baby Eli began to fuss and Dinah moved to the back of the room to nurse him.

"I think Eli's saying we've talked enough," said Luke as he reached for Sally's hand. "Oh, and one more thing," Luke said, and rubbed his free hand through his hair. "If anyone is considering leaving in the next few weeks, let me know so I will know how to plan my projects. Okay?"

"We's been talkin dis over all mornin', suh," said Mabin. "Ain't none o' us plannin' on leavin any time soon." He smiled and added, "If you have us, suh, we would like to hire to work for you 'n Miz. Martin."

Her emotions came too fast for her to control and Sally began to cry. That, of course, set Hope off and, with eyes full of tears, she walked over and hugged Sally. They both sobbed unashamed.

Luke stood staring at the two women leaning over their swelling bellies. "Well," he said, "I guess that means you're all officially hired for employment on the Martin Plantation. After our guests leave this afternoon, I'd like you all to stick around and we'll discuss wages and housing. It's best to have all of our cards on the table and start this whole thing off knowing what's expected of each other.

Pastor Davies nodded his head and added with delight, "You're going to like what Luke has to say."

"We'll save that for later, Matthew." Luke nodded his head in the direction of the house, "Everyone is out there waiting for us."

He walked over and gently separated Sally and Hope.

"In an hour or so, you can pick up where you left off but right now, it's time to set some people free."

He took Sally's hand and they led their black friends out the door and up to meet their white friends, and the sheriff.

Most of the guests were familiar to Luke's workers, either from visits to town or the farm, but the slaves were noticeably uncomfortable, due to the newness of the circumstances. Pastor Davies was quick to begin introducing Judge Wilkins to each of them, and Ben followed his example by introducing his wife, Wilma, and his lawyer, to those he knew. Frank grabbed Joshua and called to the other children to follow them to the haystack to play while the adults were occupied with the ceremony. Sally and Mrs. Willis chatted with Dinah and Hope and soon they were comparing bellies and laughing.

Luke noticed Sheriff Roily standing off by himself, holding a cup of coffee and frowning. Luke wandered over and stood beside him, watching the mixing of colors.

"Afternoon, Sheriff."

"Afternoon," grunted the sheriff.

They both stood and quietly took in the sight of people shaking hands, talking, and even smiling once in a while when something was said.

Luke finally said, "We're looking at the finest bunch of people I've ever known."

"My job is to keep the peace, and what we're looking at, is big trouble," countered the sheriff.

Luke turned to the sheriff. "That looks real peaceful to me. Everybody's getting along."

"Black and white don't mix."

Luke looked back at his friends. "Who's happier right now, you or them? Who's more at peace?"

"Let's get this thing over with," said the sheriff, sounding as if he'd rather be anywhere else in the world than standing by Luke and talking. He walked away from Luke and sat down in a chair.

Luke called everyone together and asked them all to be seated. Old habits don't die easily and the slaves were hesitant. At Luke's gentle insistence, they finally complied but sat in a group, slightly apart from the white people.

Luke asked Pastor Davies to open with a prayer. Even those who were not necessarily believers bowed their heads politely as Matthew prayed. Everyone except Sheriff Roily. He sat, slumped in his chair with his arms folded, looking disgustedly around the group. Suddenly he perked up as his eyes landed on Mahta. He did not remember having seen her before. The chair creaked noisily as he sat up straight and studied her unfamiliar face. Judge Wilkins opened his eyes and glanced in the direction of the squeaking chair. His eyes moved from Roily, to Mahta, and then back to Roily. He then closed his eyes again until the pastor finished his prayer.

Luke stood and thanked his friends for taking time out of their day for what he hoped would never be needed. He reminded them that they had agreed to affix their signatures to each certificate of emancipation, as a witness that these men and women had been freed by Luke and Sally Martin and they could not be captured or sold as slaves to another person, for they belonged to God - and God only. They were now free to live and seek employment and conduct their own family business in their own names as they saw fit.

"I believe that the Lord has led Sally and me to do this," Luke concluded, "and in no way should it be thought to imply an opinion of others' choices regarding slavery. We intend to defend these friends of ours vigorously in the courts should the need arise, because the testimony of a black man holds no weight in our courts. As men and women of character and integrity, we expect that you will be willing to join us when necessary; and we pray that it will *never* be necessary."

Luke explained that when he read off each name, that particular slave was to come up and receive two certificates of emancipation and walk down the line acquiring signatures from each person, on both copies. (Luke would keep the second signed certificate in case the first got lost or stolen.) He then informed the gathering that each slave had been taught how to spell and write their signature, and Sally would be at the end of the line with pen and ink for them to sign the bottom of their papers with their own name. A few eyebrows raised but no one said anything.

Luke then asked all of his visitors to line up at the table and handed each one a pen. Ink bottles were on the table for their use.

Judge Wilkins nudged the sheriff. "Don't worry, Patrick, You're not signing that you approve. You're signing as a witness that this actually happened, that Luke set these people free, that's all."

The sheriff scowled. "I can't believe you're in on this, judge."

"A man has the right to do as he wishes with his own private property. It's the law, and you know it. You are sworn to uphold the law, just as I am. I'm not saying I approve or disapprove. I am signing my name as a witness that this was done legal."

"Well, I don't like it one bit!" pouted Roily.

"Most of Georgia won't like it," agreed the judge, "but that doesn't change what happens today." The judge looked at the group of slaves and added. "I have to admit, I have always had trouble placing them in the same category as cows, horses, and sheep. That just doesn't work for me."

The sheriff groaned.

"Come on now, Patrick," said the judge, with a smile, "Let's go do our duty."

The process went smoothly as each person gathered signatures and congratulations and then returned to his or her seat, clutching the precious new possession. The witnesses placed their pens on the table and returned to their seats, except for the sheriff, who focused his attention on Mahta and casually moved to a tree near her. Leaning against it, he lit a cigarette and kept his eyes on the back of her head.

All but two names had been called. Luke explained that Joshua would be freed in five years when he would be more capable of taking care of himself.

"And that brings me to my friend, Mahta," Luke said as he motioned in her direction with his hand.

The sheriff suddenly became keenly interested in what Luke had to say.

"I do not own her yet, so I cannot set her free."

The sheriff dropped his cigarette and stood away from the tree. A smile crossed his face. His bad day had just turned into a good day.

"We found her in our woods, barely alive, and she has been our guest during her recovery. She tells us that she had been left by the road to fend for herself. With the information Mahta gave me, my mother's lawyer in Savannah has been instructed to find her owners, and offer a fair price for her purchase. I have her freedom papers all written up and ready, should they agree to sell her to me and send me her papers. I thought it might add a sense of urgency by using the courthouse box number. Sally and I have been praying that the papers would be here by now, but I guess the Lord didn't think it was necessary."

Sheriff Roily immediately walked to Mahta's side and clamped his hand on her shoulder. "You'll have to come with me," he said with authority.

"Now hold on there a minute, Patrick," said the judge, as he stood to his feet. "You seem a might too anxious." He pulled an envelope from the inside pocket of his jacket and walked up to give it to Luke.

"This arrived in my office with a cover letter of explanation from a man claiming to be your mother's lawyer, two days before Christmas. I haven't seen you since then and I thought it might be fun to hand deliver it, right about now."

Everyone grew tense and quiet as Luke ripped the envelope open. They all watched the expression on his face for a clue to the letter's content. He did not oblige them. With a serious look on his face he raised his head and looked sadly at Mahta.

"I hope this doesn't hurt your feelings, Mahta, but the letter says that they don't want you back. I won't say why, but personally, I don't think you're all that old."

Everyone broke out in cheers and celebration. The coyote with the star on his chest looked extremely disappointed as he released Mahta. He glared bitterly at Luke and the judge but, for the moment, there was nothing he could do.

Chapter 53

Luke and Sally were both deeply moved that every freed man and woman had chosen to stay. That is what they had prayed for. And now that all of the visitors except Matthew had departed, it was time to deal with the details of freedom and employment. Sally invited everyone to gather on the porch to enjoy drinks and dessert together while they talked. There was some hesitation until Sally explained that this was a special moment for Luke and herself, as well as for them, and she wanted to do something tangible to mark the change in their relationships. Toby and Hope smiled at each other and took each other's hand, then nearly sprinted up the steps and plopped themselves down in a couple of padded chairs. The rest followed, and the uneasiness became only a memory as Frank, Joshua, and Sally handed out servings of pie. Certificates were admired and there was a bit of good-natured teasing about each other's signatures and penmanship.

After Luke finished his pie, he leaned against the porch railing and addressed his friends.

"I know Christmas was yesterday, but today is the day you have each received a gift from us. It was the Lord that kept urging us to do it."

Luke made eye contact with Ambrose.

"God has done miracles on this plantation and has proven he has no special love for the white man over the black man. We are of equal value in his eyes."

Luke turned to Dinah.

"What men have torn apart, God has brought back together. You know it was God, don't you, Dinah?"

Dinah looked at Ambrose as she nodded her head.

"Ambrose?"

"Yes, suh," Ambrose nodded at Luke. "I see him everywhere now, suh."

Luke continued, "Mahta should have bled to death. The fire could have destroyed our crops and buildings. Ambrose shouldn't be walking."

"Yessuh, that's right," said Mahta.

Luke continued. "When things get ugly, it's easy to forget the blessings. When I was young and my dad wasn't giving me my way, all of his past sacrifices, gifts and hugs didn't matter to me one bit. I had forgotten the past and was living for the moment. Well, I've done that to God, too, at times, and I don't want to do it again. So I intend to continually remind myself of all the love he's showered on all of us here at the farm. If I go to jail, things will change for all of us. And if God were to do nothing more, what he's done is enough. I will not turn away from Him."

"Amen! Never! That's right," said Washington enthusiastically.

Hope jumped in, "He giv' me Toby 'n a baby."

Toby laughed, "He giv' me Hope 'n a baby."

"He giv' me a family," Joshua chimed in.

"He dun giv' us Miz Martin's cherry pie," Gideon snickered.

Everyone laughed together, enjoying the moment. When things quieted down, Mabin stood up and walked over and placed his hand on Luke's shoulder.

"The Lord give me forgiveness, 'n from den on I need no more. But he keep givin' anyway. He give me a bes' friend." He looked at Luke and then at the others. "Den he give me lo's o' friends." He swept his hand in front of him indicating all of them. "Den he give me freedom. How kin I ever turn away from him?"

"Amen! Never!" Washington repeated.

"Tell them about Sid, Luke," said Sally with anticipation.

Luke looked at his feet and smiled, then raised his head and spoke.

"Many of you have never met Sid and Maggie Pennington," he began.

Tal and Sadie perked up.

"Sid is the reason you are all learning to read and write. He's the one that taught Tal and Sadie, and now Tal and Sadie are passing his gift on to you. God is blessing you, through someone you've never met. Isn't that amazing?"

Luke motioned to Pastor Davies.

"Matthew wrote the Penningtons a few months ago to tell them of our decision to teach all of you. He told them we intended to purchase more slaves and build more buildings and grow more crops. He also told Sid that I had often mentioned not liking slavery, and that he suspected that I would eventually set you all free."

"Looks as if I'm a prophet," chuckled Matthew.

Luke smiled, "Maybe so. We have recently received a package from California. In it, was a letter and some gold coins." Luke paused to let the murmuring die down. "Sid writes that the mine he and his brothers are working has produced far beyond what they had hoped for."

Luke pulled two gold coins from his pocket and held them up. He looked at Tal and Sadie.

"Sid says these are for you. He calls it teachers' pay, and he expects that you will do a good job teaching."

Sadie gasped as Luke stepped over to hand them the coins. Everyone else swarmed around them clamoring for a look at the coins, something they had all heard about, but never seen. Frank and Joshua jumped up and down, trying to see over the adults. It took some effort to regain everyone's attention.

"Remember, it's not legal to have school for blacks," Luke reminded them. "If you speak of learning, just talk as if you're picking up a little reading and writing from various places and incidents. Don't talk about being paid to teach or use the word, school."

They all nodded their heads in agreement.

"I would advise you not to flaunt your freedom or your education. Keep a low profile, but use it when you need it."

There was more nodding of heads.

Luke pulled a letter from his shirt pocket and held it up. "Sid and

Maggie have also sent Sally and myself ....." Luke began reading from the letter, "'... *a gift to help finance whatever this project is that the Lord seems to be doing through you, and for your Negroes. My pappy would be whippin' me right now if he could, but I think you know what the Lord wants you to do with the money.*

'Maggie sure does miss Sadie, so I've cheered her up by agreeing to visit you all, this coming summer. I expect there will be lots of changes by then.

Blessings on all of you; Sid and Maggie Pennington.'"

As Luke folded the letter and returned it to his pocket, not a word was spoken.

Luke smiled as he looked over the faces of his dark-skinned friends. He knew deep down, that he had been living for this moment for years. It had been God's plan, and God himself was now bringing all the pieces together. Luke felt as if his heart was about to burst. Apparently Sally felt it too, because she jumped up from her chair and slipped her arm around him.

"Tell them, Luke. I can't stand to wait any longer!"

"Yeah, me neither," Luke agreed. "Let's get this business meeting started.

He took her hand in his.

"Sid's gift was substantial," Luke began. "His brothers struck a large vein of gold prior to his arrival. God moved in a good man's heart and he has blessed all of us through a gold mine thousands of miles away. Our farm has also been profitable and we have had no crop loss for years. Sally and I have prayed hard for the last couple of weeks, and this is what we've come up with."

Luke picked up a folder from a small table beside him.

"We have gone back through our records and calculated how many weeks each of you have been with us. Each of you will be paid $1.00/week plus room and board for your labor on our farm starting from the day you arrived. And from this day forward, you will all be given a raise to $2.00 per week."

Luke paused as jaws dropped and eyes grew large. His audience was attempting mental calculations, which most of them were incapable of doing. Mabin locked eyes with Luke. He was dazed. He had no idea how much money it meant, but he knew it was a great deal. Luke just smiled and nodded his head.

"I will ask Tal to take charge of your bookkeeping and keep records of your pay," Luke continued. "He understands numbers and adding and subtracting. and he has my permission to teach you what he knows. At the end of each month, Tal and I will meet and compare records and I will make a deposit into the account I have set up at the bank. Your money will be available whenever you need it. You are free men and women and you are free to use your wages as you see fit."

Luke laid the folder on the table.

"I have one more thing to tell you. With much of the money Sid sent us, I have purchased the thirty acres directly across Town Road from this farm from Chester Haley. It's laid out pretty well for dividing into six, four-acre parcels, side by side, each with approximately three acres of trees and one acre of crop land. About six acres on the south end is swamp, but Chester said I had to buy that too, in order to get the other twenty-five. What this means to you is this: each person - or couple - will be given a four-acre piece of land from Sally and me to use, in any way you please, in exchange for five years of work on the Martin plantation. This is to be totally separate from the weekly wages."

With the exception of a couple exclamations of amazement, the ex-slaves were silent. They stared at Luke and Sally, wondering if they might have misunderstood. Some heads turned and looked in the direction of what they had known as 'Chester's field'. Otis, usually the quietest among them, felt the need to speak up and make sure he wasn't dreaming.

"Suh?"

"Yes, Otis?" Luke responded.

"Do you mean dat five years from now, I can actually stand on land I kin do wit as I please? Land o' my own?" Otis asked, hardly daring to believe it might be possible.

"Well, not exactly," Luke answered. "According to the slave codes, slaves are not allowed to own property. But you will be given one hundred percent say in what happens on the four acres, and if the day ever comes that you are allowed to own land, Sally and I will immediately sign the papers and you will own it."

"And, Otis," added Sally, "you've already put in your five years, and so have Gideon, Toby, and Mabin."

Hope gave a squeal.

"That's right, Otis," Luke assured him. "The order of choice will be according to length of stay and Gideon was here three months before you, so he gets to choose his parcel first, then you, and then Toby who, when we add Hope's few months to his, has only now reached his five years."

"Does this mean we can build our own place, suh?" Toby asked.

"That's what it means," Sally answered.

Hope's hands covered her face as she cried unashamedly while Toby held her close. He wore a huge smile, but his eyes were closed as he praised God.

Gideon stood there in shock and uttered a quiet, "Lordy!"

Tal's mouth was hanging open as he realized what had just been said.

"Suh, do you mean....dat.....?" He couldn't finish his sentence.

"That's right, Tal," Luke answered. "Add Sadie's time to yours, and you already have almost a year on the books. Two more years and you two will have your own parcel. Zekiel, you're half-way there."

Luke held his hand up. "One more thing. Should you choose to move on some time in the future, we will pay you for the land whether or not you have papers of ownership, because in our minds, we consider it your property."

"Suh?" asked Gideon, with a puzzled look on his face, "Mabin ben here longer den us. What bout him?"

Mabin had been quietly leaning against the porch railing, taking in all of this new information and trying to process what it all meant to the group as a whole. Everyone would now be relating to each other in a whole new context. When he went to visit Toby and Hope, it would be as a free man, and, in a sense, a black landowner, visiting other free black landowners, and some day maybe even with the actual papers. They would all be responsible for making more of their own decisions.

Mabin was aware of one thing above all else. Luke had always treated him well and Mabin loved him as a friend. But the last wall was finally being torn down and it would change everything forever. From this day forward, Mabin's best friend would no longer be his possessor, and Luke's best friend would no longer be his property. They could now, in a real sense, be just two men who are friends, two brothers in the Lord who love each other. They would be neighbors, and partners. They would be working together of their own free will. This was no small thing that the Lord had brought about and Mabin felt about ready to explode, he was so filled with gratitude and praise. Gideon's voice brought him back from his thoughts to what was being said.

Gideon nodded in agreement. "Yes, suh. What about him?"

Luke gave Mabin a half smile, combined with a slightly ornery look.

"I haven't forgotten Mabin." Luke kept his gaze fixed on his friend, "He's a large part of the decision-making team on this farm." Luke looked down at Sally. They smiled knowingly at each other and then back at Mabin. Then Luke continued, "We've got something special in mind for Mabin."

Chapter 54

The two men climbed down from the wagon and Mabin walked around to the back to grab an axe. He rubbed his thumb along the edge to check for sharpness, then walked over to the edge of the road and stood beside Luke as he gazed out from the rise, over the plantation.

"No coyotes or crows, dis time," Mabin eventually spoke up.

The two listened to the small trickling stream. A squirrel ran up a tall Georgia pine and out onto a branch where it was safe, to once again, show off his talent of scolding intruders.

"The last time we were up here, you said it was a good place for God to meet a man for a talk," said Luke.

"I do come up here some," Mabin responded. "We talk some, yes."

Luke and Mabin stood together watching the boys running toward the chicken house, as the sound of their voices drifted faintly above the trees.

"What tree should we cut first?" Mabin finally asked.

"It takes ten minutes or so to get here by wagon. Probably five, at the most, to walk straight down from here," said Luke, as he continued to watch the boys.

"Dat sounds right, yes," Mabin agreed. "Where should we start cutting?"

"I was trying to figure out how long it would take you to get to work in the mornings."

"You want me to come up here in the morning to cut wood?" Mabin asked.

"No. I figure we can cut some today, while we're here."

Mabin turned curiously to Luke. Luke pretended not to notice.

"Okay den, which of dese trees should we cut?" Mabin asked again.

"Oh, none of these; we'll cut up the road a ways." Luke spoke in a 'matter of fact' tone that confused Mabin.

"Den why do you have us stop here, suh?"

"Because I like scenery, and the view from your place is the best for miles around."

"Oh .....," Mabin started shaking his head as his mouth fell open. "No, suh!"

"Yes, suh," Luke retorted with a grin.

"Oh no, suh!"

"Oh, yes."

"But suh ......"

"You can argue all day, Mabin," Luke said, with pretend finality, "but we'll cut the trees up the road. I will not cut the trees on your land! From this day forward, by verbal agreement, this is your land to do with as you please. I pray that someday soon it will also be in writing, with our signatures on it."

"No, suh! Dat's not what I meant. I wasn't talkin' about not cuttin' trees."

"Come with me, Mabin. I want to show you something," Luke insisted, as he started walking back down the road from where they'd come. "And practice calling me Luke once in a while, okay?"

"But, suh.....!"

Luke ignored him and kept walking. Mabin finally followed Luke down the road. About two hundred fifty feet from where the stream crossed the road, they came to a small tree that had rocks piled around it. Luke pointed to the rocks.

"The surveyor piled those there. They are two hundred fifty feet from the stream."

Luke noticed that Mabin's eyes were flooded, but he continued to talk in a tone that challenged interruption. "This logging road is your northern border. The stream is your western border. Real easy to find - natural borders. The surveyor placed a large pile of rocks on the lower corners that can't be missed."

Luke waved his hand out over the slope in front of him.

"The surveyor has drawn everything up and registered these ten acres as a separate parcel."

"But......."

"If you refuse this," Luke quickly interrupted his friend, "you will break Sally's and my hearts. To be able to do this for you has brought us a joy that I can't even begin to describe."

Mabin couldn't help the tear that rolled down his cheek. Luke watched him anxiously as Mabin scanned the land before him.

"It feels like too much," Mabin finally said.

"It's not."

"Freedom would have been enuf," Mabin paused, and then added, "Luke."

"We couldn't just set someone free and then drop them off at the nearest street corner. That's what Mahta's owners did to her. And besides that, we've been together for so long, we are a part of each other. I want to share this land with you, Mabin. It's a part of both of us, a part of who we are."

Mabin watched Joshua and Frank walking to the house, each carrying a basket of eggs.

"I wouldn't tell this to no other," Mabin pulled his attention away from the boys and turned to Luke, "but, well, I never been alone before. Scares me a little."

Luke was surprised. "I'm not sure I understand, Mabin,"

Mabin shook his head and then added, " I don't want to be by myself," he said, letting all of the air out of his lungs as he spoke. "Always lived with other men in bunkhouses. I had someone to talk to, someone to cook for."

"So you *are* turning down our offer?"

"Maybe. Maybe not," Mabin's expression began to reflect a confidence that Luke had first seen on the day he had asked Mabin's advice about the changes; the day they had found Mahta.

"Dere's a boy down dere wit no daddy," Mabin continued. "I grown kinda fond of him 'n I'm askin' my friend, Luke Martin, if his young slave kin live up here wit me when I gits a place built. I kin help Joshua 'n he kin help me."

Luke relaxed and spoke in a tone of pretend doubt.

"Well, I don't know if that will work," he said. "I'm not sure Frank will agree to have his friend living so far away."

Mabin felt a little lighter. "So you sayin' I needs to get permission from a thirteen-year-old boy?"

"You might have to throw in a few overnight visits and your good cooking once in a while in order to bring him into your camp," Luke said, nodding his head with pretend seriousness.

Mabin smiled, and then looked out over the hillside once again. "A man never knows what d' good Lord got in mind in a day." He paused a moment, "When I's younger, maybe ten, twelve year ago, I's up here choppin' wood for you papa. I member tellin' d' Lord sure would be nice to live up here." Mabin chuckled, "Never mentioned it again. Never even thought I was askin'."

"I guess you were right," Luke said as he put a hand on his friend's shoulder. "When God meets a man here for a talk, He really *does* listen, doesn't He."

It finally began to sink in. Mabin turned to Luke with a big grin on his face and pounded the air with his fist. "Whoooeee! Ain't this sumthin'?"

Mabin turned back to gaze out over what was now, in a sense, his. He raised both arms to the sky, looked up and said boldly, "Ain't *YOU* sumthin'!" And then he started to laugh and shake his head in amazement. He leaned over and scooped up a handful of soil, continuing to chuckle as he moved the soil around with his thumb.

Luke was enjoying every minute of it. He had never seen this side of Mabin. He watched as Mabin threw the handful of dirt into the air.

"You're kind of a physical picture of how I felt when I got saved," Luke laughed. "Getting set free really does something to a person, doesn't it?"

Mabin looked at Luke, with a big grin on his face that he couldn't wipe off. He added a tone of seriousness into the mix, "D' revren say d' Bible say, 'In dis worl' you will have trouble', 'n more trouble to come. But you 'n me, Luke, we both free as we kin be now, while we're on this worl'."

Mabin took in a big breath of fresh air and then became serious again.

"I can't shake d' feelin' dat d' Lord done glue a white man to a black man, 'n now I gotta wonder jus' what he has in mind."

Luke chuckled as they walked back to the wagon. "Whatever it is," he said, "according to Sid Pennington, his pappy wouldn't like it."

"From what you tell me, his pappy wouldn' like what's hidin' in d' cellar neither," chuckled Mabin.

"No," Luke agreed, "he would not - which reminds me, we had better get started cutting the wood that the Quakers in Greensborough have ordered from us."

Chapter 55

There was a knock on the front door. Tom scooted his chair back from his roll-topped desk and took a moment to get his bearings. He rubbed his neck and looked at the clock on the hearth. It was four o'clock. He had spent the last three hours immersed in planning his crop for the coming year. Reading bank statements, checking prices and making orders had given him a slight headache. The knock came again; Tom groaned and stood to his feet. Rubbing his head, he strolled down the hall to the door. Etta had come from the kitchen but Tom arrived first. Opening the door, he forgot all about his headache. There, standing in the doorway was a large, young, nervous black man holding a handful of camellias that he had picked. He shoved the flowers toward Tom and said, "Good afternoon, sir. Dese is for you."

Tom's eyes looked down at the flowers, but he didn't move a muscle. Eventually he looked back up at Zekiel and then swiveled his head and glanced at Etta. Her eyes were on the flowers and looked as if they were about to pop out of her head. Tom returned his attention to Zekiel when the boy spoke.

"I was wonderin', suh, if I be allowed to call on your slave, Rena, suh."

Tom thought he heard a faint, high pitched sound come from Etta. Again his eyes bounced to the flowers and back to Zekiel. Only Tom could know what was going on in his head as they all stood for a moment in awkward silence.

"New at this, are ya, boy?"

"Suh?"

Tom let him suffer a moment and then grunted. "The master doesn't want flowers!" he said firmly, but then his voice softened a little. "The girl gets the flowers."

A look of shock came over Zekiel and he jerked the flowers around behind his back.

"No, suh," he said, as quickly as he could. "Dese flowers are ..... for Rena .....suh."

Tom grunted again. "They'd better be."

"Oh yes, suh. Mabin tol' me to bring flowers. Didn' say who dey was for."

"I see. So......," Tom paused, then toyed with him. "What did you bring for me?"

Etta groaned, then threw up her hands and went back to the kitchen.

"You, suh?" Zekiel asked in dismay.

"Yes, me, ... uh .... Zekiel, was it?"

"Yes, suh. I'm Zekiel, 'n .....," he searched for the right words but couldn't find them. "I didn' bring nothin' for you, suh."

Zekiel looked devastated.

Tom studied him for awhile, as if totally unaware of his suffering.

"Did Martin let you all loose?" he asked, seemingly out of nowhere.

"Yes, suh," Zekiel answered, puzzled.

"Big mistake," Tom said bluntly. "You people ain't ready for it. You hand a bunch of flowers to Billy Glenn, or Ellis, or Roily, and you'd be dead - or wishin' you was!"

"Din' mean no harm, suh."

"That is my point exactly, boy! Half you folks'll be dead before you figure out how to be free and fit in with the white folks. Shoot, I don't know, maybe you'll never fit in!"

"I be frightened to come to you, suh. I understand it dangerous to be free." Zekiel looked at the ground. "But it is also dangerous to be a slave."

"You were frightened to come here?"

"Mister Martin say I musn't dishonor you by sneakin' aroun'. He say I mus' come to your door."

"Luke said that?"

"He teachin us *how* to fit in, suh. You right, we needs to be teached," Zekiel replied humbly.

Tom couldn't help himself. "Taught."

"I ask your patience, suh."

Tom was surprised that he found himself kind of liking the guy. It flustered him a little. He fumbled for words.

"Yeah, well, I guess there wouldn't be much harm in letting you visit Rena for an hour or so."

Zekiel perked right up and stuck his hand out to shake Tom's hand.

"Thank you, suh. I won' cause no trouble, suh."

Tom looked at Zekiel's hand and became even more flustered.

"Okay, now wait a minute! There you go, not understanding again!" To Zekiel's surprise, Tom swatted his hand down.

"This thing goes both ways, you know. You were afraid to come talk to me? Well, I'm not all that comfortable either." Tom shifted his weight around and looked down the hall to see if Etta was listening.

"You see, boy, I ain't never actually shook hands with a nigra before."

"You ain't, suh?"

Tom was frustrated with himself for even talking like this, especially to a black man.

"No, I ain't. At least...., now don't take this wrong, but I don't remember ever seeing *anyone* do it. You nigras over there at Martin's better go into this thing with your eyes wide open. Don't you think everything will change over night. Truth is, it'll take a lifetime. People don't just wake up one day and know how to speak Spanish, or read, or be *free,* for that matter. "

"No, suh," Zekiel shook his head. "I don't. Thank you for helpin' me."

He held out his hand without thinking and Tom sputtered and swatted it away again.

"Get out of here before I'm the one that shoots you!" he said, with a raised voice.

"Yes, suh."

Zekiel backed away as the door slammed shut.

"Aaagh," Tom vocalized his frustration and Etta scurried down the hall to see if he was alright.

"Martin set them all free, Etta," said Tom as he leaned back against the door.

"His slaves, suh?"

"That's right, and I think they're going to be real sorry."

Etta walked past him to the drawing room window and pulled the curtains back. "Mebbe, mebbe not," she mumbled, half to him and half to herself. She watched Zekiel stick his nose in the flowers as he walked along. Tom joined her at the window as Zekiel approached the door and paused to brush off his clothes and straighten up his bouquet. They watched together as Zekiel knocked on the door, and then waited until Maybeth opened it. There was an exchange of words and Maybeth went back inside. Zekiel waited patiently until Rena came to the door and invited him inside.

"He's a nice enough boy, I suppose," said Tom, as he straightened himself up and returned to his desk, sat down, and scooted his chair in under it.

Etta kept watching the closed door of the shack. From where he sat, Tom couldn't see the smile on her face.

Chapter 56

A maximum of ten hours per day, six days a week: that was the agreement, with the exception of harvest time. During the cotton harvest, every able-bodied man, woman, and child would be required to work for the Martins from sunup to sundown, and sometimes more - but they would be paid extra.

By the middle of March, the air was warmer and the azaleas were beginning to bloom. Otis and Gideon were each behind a horse and plow, waking up the sod from its winter sleep. The rest of the men were clearing a ten acre parcel of trees and bushes to make room for a larger peanut crop, while Joshua and Frank kept the fire under control at the brush pile. Al Willis and his two sons had been hired to chop and pull stumps, using Al's four large horses and two mules from Addison the blacksmith.

It was about eight hours into the day on Friday, when a long line of weary-looking slaves in ragged clothing paraded down Town Road, heading toward Grantsville. Luke guessed there might be fifty or more, including the children. He knew that the nearest town from the direction they were coming was about twenty-five miles away. Even the white men riding horseback looked tired.

All work on the farm came to a halt as everyone watched them go by. About half of them were lighter-skinned Mulatto's, fathered by the white masters of their mothers. The adult slaves were tethered together with rope tied around their waists, and the children held onto the rope with one hand as they walked along. One young girl, who looked to be ten or twelve years old, was carrying a baby in a pack on her back. Even the children rarely glanced to the side at the onlookers. The faces were expressionless and the feet were bleeding; the group had an eerie resemblance to a herd of cattle being taken to market to be sold.

Luke was swept with emotion when he turned and walked over to where Mabin was standing with an axe in his hand, watching along with the rest. He felt dejected and hopeless. "It'll never end, Mabin. There will always be an endless supply as long as it's legal."

Mabin nodded in agreement, "The ocean gots a whole lot more fish den one man can catch. But d' man still goes fishin'." He pointed up his axe, "Dere's a school of fish swimmin' by."

"Hmm. Fishers of men," said Luke thoughtfully.

"Was our readin' lesson las' night," said Mabin.

They both watched as the procession moved silently along. One of the horses snorted, and a rider coughed. That, and the dragging of feet and hoofs against the dirt road, were the only sounds that accompanied the travelers.

"Mebbe we could pick up d' glass for my two windows tomorrow mornin'," suggested Mabin.

"Yes, and I could stop in at Addison's to get him started on the peanut wagon, and pick up a couple more axe heads," Luke agreed. "You, Toby, Gideon, and Otis all clearing trees puts me a little short of axes. Who knows? Wally might have your woodstove ready."

Mabin finally pulled his gaze away from the lifeless parade heading down the road. He spit on his hands and adjusted his grip on the axe handle. He stepped up to the tree he had been working on and took a swing at it with the axe, then another and another. He paused, took a deep breath, and smiled at Luke, "Who knows? Mebbe dere be time for a little fishin'."

Luke turned and motioned to the rest of the onlookers. "All right, everyone," he said, raising his voice so all could hear. "Let's get back to work. Peanuts don't grow on trees, you know!"

"Kinda handy, you bein' short 'n me bein' tall."

"Not so much," said Joshua. "You don' git mud dropped on *your* head."

Mabin chuckled, "You could move down a ways, you know."

"Wanna work wit *you*. Don' much like workin' alone."

"Me, too," Mabin agreed. "Chinking cabin logs is more fun when I has someone to drop mud on." He stuffed some of the mud in a crack between the logs and then purposefully let a huge glob of mud land right in front of Joshua.

"Oops! Sorry." Mabin joked with a smile.

"Hey!" Joshua jumped back and accidentally stomped on Mabin's big toe.

"Ow!" Mabin jerked his foot from under Joshua's foot and the next blob that landed on Joshua's head actually *was* an accident. Mabin tried to wipe the mud off of Joshua, then started laughing when all he managed to accomplish was spreading the red tinted goop all over the boy's head and face. Joshua couldn't see the results.

"Dere, dat better," said Mabin with a grin. "You lookin' fine, now."

Joshua looked at Mabin's red hands and grew suspicious.

"Do my head look like your hands?" he asked, squinting accusingly.

Mabin frowned and studied Joshua's head. "Yeah, s'pose it kinda does."

"Aargh!!" Joshua stomped off to the stream to wash off the mud.

Mabin joined him, and after they were both soaked from splashing each other, they sat and watched the sunset.

"So, whatcha think 'bout your own room?" Mabin asked.

"Do I have to sleep in it?"

Mabin looked down at the boy beside him and thought a minute.

"Nope. Sleep in my room if you want, but d' room is still yours. It be dere whenever you ready. You kin put your stuff in it."

"Stuff? What stuff?"

"You frog collection, you chalk 'n slate board, you shoes, I don' know - stuff."

"Don' have a frog collection."

"Start a butterfly collection. Won't smell so bad as a frog collection."

They both laughed together and then became silent.

"Mabin?" Joshua finally asked. "Dem kids dat went by today, dey won' never have their own room, will dey." It was more a statement than a question.

Mabin looked out over the plantation, to the road where the slaves had walked. After giving it some thought, he answered.

"Mos' of 'em, probly not - not in dis worl', anyway. But rooms in dis worl' don' count for much, no how. What counts is d' great big, beautiful room Jesus is makin for each of dem that bleve. Some of dem tired folks bleves, or will bleve in Jesus, so dey end up jus' fine. Dey's jus' passin' through, headin' for glory jus' like us."

Joshua sat quietly, thinking.

"You really bleve dat?" he finally asked.

"I know it!"

Joshua reflected on the confidence he heard in Mabin's words.

"Well den," he concluded. "I know it, too."

As they stood and headed down the hill to the farm, Mabin put his hand on Joshua's shoulder and said, "I spose it might cheer 'em up a little if someone tol' 'em bout Jesus 'n d' rooms. I think dat's what I'll pray for 'em, tonight."

"Me, too."

Chapter 57

Two nice new blankets, four glazed pottery plates, and a mirror; that was the shopping list Sadie had sent along with Mabin; the first purchases Tal and Sadie had ever made with their own money. The change from the gold coin weighed in Mabin's left pocket as he carefully wrapped the mirror in the two blankets and placed it in the back of the wagon. It was the first time that Mabin had walked right in and made a purchase independently of Luke. Luke had filled Wally in on the new happenings at the Martin plantation the month before, when he had placed the order for the two panes of window glass, the woodstove, and stove pipe for Mabin's new cabin.

Satisfied that the mirror was secure, Mabin reentered Wally's store to make his own personal purchases. Two women were standing at the counter and Wally was busy bagging their groceries. Mabin stepped up behind them and quietly waited his turn. The older of the women turned and frowned at him. He smiled back at her. She grunted and turned her attention back to Wally and her friend. When Wally handed her the change, she deposited the coins in her handbag while glancing uncomfortably over her shoulder at Mabin. He smiled back at her. The lady and her friend gathered up their bags, and as they left, the older woman sniffed and said to her friend, "Apparently someone has failed to teach their slaves to keep a respectable distance."

"That's why they mustn't be set free," agreed the other, "They don't know how to act in civilized society!"

They both turned and glared at Mabin. He tipped his hat and

gave them his best 'humble servant' look and said, "Have a good day, ladies," as they walked out.

Wally turned his attention from the door back to Mabin.

"Did you get the things loaded?" he asked.

"Yes, suh, I did," Mabin said as he stepped up to the counter. "I'd like t' purchase two blankets t' wrap aroun' d' glass dat Massuh Martin order for me."

While Mabin was speaking, the bell on the door tinkled as it opened and Luke, Frank, and Joshua entered the store. The boys bumped Mabin as they squeezed in front of him to gaze at the colorful candies in the display case below him.

"How's your cabin coming along?" Wally asked, ignoring the interruption. "Luke here says the glass is for the windows in the cabin you're building for yourself."

"Hope to start the roof tonight, suh."

"This is all very interesting, you know," said Wally. "It's not exactly common in these parts for a black man to have enough of his own money to buy his own things for his own house."

Luke stepped up beside Mabin. "Would you do us a favor, Wall, and not talk about it to your customers?" asked Luke.

Wally nodded thoughtfully. "Yeah, I suppose what you've done will get out soon enough as it is. The sheriff's more than likely already gone and told everyone he knows."

"You're probably right," Luke agreed. "I ran into Billy Glenn and Lenny. Billy asked me why I can't leave well enough alone and then spit near my boots. And Lenny.....? Well, he thinks Billy's funny."

"You've got a lot of friends, Luke. Don't let those guys get to you." Wally walked around the counter and motioned for the two men to follow. He led them into a side room and pointed to two crates.

"The big one's the woodstove, and the other's the glass. If you're careful with the glass, you should be able to stay warm inside, while you enjoy the view outside."

"Tank you, suh," said Mabin, "While Massuh Martin 'n I put dese in d' wagon, I like to add two lamps, extra wicks, 'n three cans of whale oil to my buyin', if dat's okay wit you, suh."

Wally laughed, "It's okay with me if you buy everything in my store. Wouldn't hurt my feelings one bit. I'll get the things together and we'll all rendezvous at the front counter."

Luke and Mabin carried the stove first, and then the glass wrapped in the blankets out to the wagon. While Mabin settled up with Wally, Luke loaded the stovepipe and lamp supplies. Shortly, Mabin came out of the store carrying the whale oil, followed by two boys with candy sticks sticking out of their mouths.

"How much did those cost, Mabin?" asked Luke, looking a little surprised.

"Two for a penny, suh."

A look of shock came across Luke's face.

"For them!? You paid way too much, Mabin."

"I thought so, too," answered Mabin, "but when Missuh Matkin threw in d' candy I decide go ahead and buy 'em."

"Hey!" protested Joshua, looking offended.

"Don't pay 'em no mind," said Frank as he climbed into the wagon. "That's called guff, and it's worth gettin' a little guff to get a little candy."

When all four were on the wagon, Luke turned the horses in the direction of the church.

"Well, Mabin," he said, "what say we drop the boys off at the church to help Matthew clean up for the Sunday service, while we go fishing?"

As they sat in the back of the wagon, riding away from Wally's Market, Joshua asked, "Guff? What's guff?"

Chapter 58

The auction had already been going for an hour when Luke pulled the wagon up beside a group of four men that were talking amongst themselves and comparing notes that some of them had written on sheets of paper.

"Excuse me, gentlemen," Luke interrupted. He recognized the barber, as the men looked up at him. "Oh, hello, George."

"Back for another pretty girl for your boy, are ya, Luke?" George joked.

Luke smiled, then quickly turned around and said. "That, Mabin, is guff!"

Turning back to George, he motioned his head toward the auctioneer.

"Where'd these come from?"

"They brought sixty-five of them down from up north," George answered.

One of the men standing next to George added, "They say some of 'em's runaways, and some of 'em's resales from other planters. A few of m' can't speak a lick of the King's English."

"You buying, George?" Luke asked.

"I'm looking for a young lad to clean up around the barber shop, and run errands. He doesn't need to speak English. I can teach him what little he needs to know. I can make a barber out of him too."

"Yeah? Well, good luck, George. We'll let you get back to what you were doing. I just might make a few purchases myself."

Mabin stayed on the wagon seat as Luke climbed down and

worked his way through the bidders and over to the inspection area that the auctioneers had set up for their potential customers. Around each slaves neck was a card attached to a string. The card contained basic information about the slave, such as approximate age, origin, and skills. Luke spent the next half hour reading the cards and looking over the bidders, studying the demeanor of those who would soon own these human properties.

"Remember, we ain't savin' d' whole worl'," Mabin had reminded him.

Luke kept reminding himself of those words as he read the cards and prayed.

"Age – 35, no English, fieldworker" said the writing on the card Luke was reading. He looked up at the face of the man. He looked intelligent enough to figure out a way to survive what was ahead of him.

Luke noticed Jerry Ellis and his driver, Del, looking over a couple of young black men. He would keep an eye on them. Luke knew about half of the white men who were gathered today. He was not concerned with those he knew would be kind, or even rough, on their slaves. It was those who were known to be cruel, that bothered him. He watched as a man and woman he did not know, inspected the little girl with the baby strapped to her back. He remembered noticing her as the procession had passed by his farm.

"Good," he thought to himself, "This woman will take them under her wing and they will be okay." He looked around at the other slaves. None seemed to take notice of the two children, so he assumed they were without family. His good feeling was quickly dashed, however, as the woman grabbed the girl's upper and lower lips and roughly jerked her mouth open to inspect her teeth. The girl yelped and the woman instantly slapped her.

"Silence!" the woman insisted in a firm whisper.

The young child's eyes began to water, but she stood silently while the woman excessively stretched her upper and lower lips, taking her own sweet time checking the teeth.

Luke felt the gold coins in his pocket that only he and Sally knew about.

A second package had arrived from Sid only the week before.

As his fingers played with the coins, Luke thought back to the stage driver's comment about how heavy the package was, when he had handed the box to Luke. Luke had joked with the man about it being as heavy as a solid block of gold. He remembered opening the package later that evening after Frank had gone to bed. He and Sally had stared, speechless, into the box of thirty gold coins, each worth a hundred dollars. It was probably a full minute before either of them had noticed the letter. The letter no longer existed, but Luke remembered it, almost word for word.

"Luke and Sally,
I can picture your faces as you look inside this box. It's okay. You can close your mouths now, and yes, the money is real.

I was not completely forthright with you when I left for California. My brothers and Maggie and I have been secretly involved with the abolitionist movement for many years. Yes, we did own slaves while we lived in Grantsville. It was a necessary cover while we helped set up the railroad in Georgia.

When I said I was going to try my luck at mining out here with Tom and Lloyd, our mine had already been helping to finance the movement since '52'. When Tom and Lloyd struck another vein, they asked me to come out and manage things. We now have about twenty miners working for us, and eleven of them are freed slaves. I told you the truth about Thaddeus. I did set him free and he really does have an exceptional gift with numbers.

You can probably imagine how thrilled we were to get the letters from Matthew telling us of your intentions to expand your farm operation and begin focused 'slave shopping'. Matthew is aware of our project out here; however, for his safety we have kept him ignorant of places and names to which we send financial assistance. Matthew is not a stupid man and, should you be as successful as we hope, he may deduce the situation between us. He may even have hoped for this when he sent the letters; I do not know. However, we must insist you never confirm his suspicions in any way, should he confront you.

By the way, it was I who slipped your name to Hackquakmithston. They slipped it to Henry to feel you out. He has no idea that I was involved.

You will eventually have to come up with a cover story for Ben Statler, explaining your income. Your mother might be a possibility.

Expect another package in a couple of months. Burn this letter for the safety of all.

Pappy is not happy with how his sons turned out. Of that I am sure!"

Post Script: "As you can see, The Almighty has a good supply of miracles still available."

Post Script: "Remember, burn this letter. Observe its total destruction!"

Luke fingered the coins again. When the couple moved on from the girl, to inspect other slaves, Luke walked over to her and read the card that was hanging from her neck: "Age – 9 or 10 yrs., no English, father died of sickness at sea, mother died walking to Grantsville, baby boy, 1 yr."

That was all that was written.

At the end of the day, Frank sat by his father on the wagon seat as they traveled home. Mabin and Joshua sat on the back end of the wagon bed flanking a young man named Richard, who had a card that said, "27 yrs - captured runaway-resale-carpenter", and a very tall man named Sondabay, whose card read, "30 yrs - captured runaway-resale-mill worker". The four sat scrunched tightly together, with their legs dangling off the back of the wagon. Behind the three men sat a thirty-year-old woman named Clara, who Luke had bid away from Jerry and Del, simply because he didn't like the way the two were studying her. Clara had even thanked him, as he filled out the papers for her purchase.

Luke was feeling good. As the fisherman rolled down the road, he couldn't help telling the story to his passengers of how the man had to restrain his wife when Luke outbid them for the girl and baby.

"There is no doubt she would have clawed my eyes out if she could have," Luke said. "Her last words to me were, "God has a place for people like you!"

"He sho' do, suh. He sho' do," Mabin laughed loudly. "But it a dif'rent place den she was meanin'!"

The young girl and her baby brother sat quietly next to Clara, listening to the words, but not understanding any of what was being said.

As was to become the normal pattern after the purchase of any slaves, Luke and Sally sat the adults down and briefed them as to the situation that they had been bought into. Mabin was introduced as the foreman in charge of employees, which always seemed to bring curious looks from those who understood the difference between the words 'slave' and 'employee'. The Martins grew to love this moment, because it opened the door to a huge opportunity to explain that God wanted each of them to experience a taste of what he will do for them, forever, in heaven, if they repent and turn their lives over to him.

"At this moment," Luke told them, "you are our property to do with as we choose. But, even here in Georgia, we can legally choose to set you free. And it is our intention to do so within the week, just as soon as I get your papers filed in court."

Clara sat up and leaned forward, looking intensely into Luke's eyes, wondering if she had heard correctly. Richard's and Sondabay's heads swiveled to look at each other and then turned back to Luke and Sally.

"It is our sincere hope," Sally continued, "that you choose to stay with us and work for wages, room, and board, but, as goes with freedom, you will be free to leave if you wish."

"As I said," Luke reminded them, "being set free here is merely a taste of what God will do for us in heaven."

Mabin smiled and chuckled.

"It is becoming a common saying around here that, 'This is just a glimpse, it's not heaven. Heaven comes later.'"

"Massuh?" said Sondabay after a short silence, "I am not a runaway. I am a free man. I was kidnapped at night by four black men as I lef my work at the cotton mill in Boston. They destroyed my papers and sell me to the slavers."

Luke stared thoughtfully at Sondabay as he digested this new information.

"Well, except for a short time in-between," Luke raised his eyebrows and smiled, "I'd guess the Lord wants you to remain free, but this time your papers will be witnessed, registered with the court, and I will keep a copy with me."

"If you choose to return to Boston," Sally added, "we will help with your fare, providing you work for us for two months before you leave. Do you have family there?"

"No, ma'am."

"Den, if I was you," Mabin advised, "I stick aroun 'n serve d' ones dat sets you free. Dey paid a good price fo' you."

"Yes, suh."

"Maybe this would be a good time to let you in on our plans," Luke interjected. "We are in the process of expanding crop production and need more workers. This will include some construction projects, and I think you could be quite helpful, Richard. We will also be needing a larger and more efficient ginning system, which I had in mind when I chose you, Sondabay."

Luke paused for a moment, and then smiled at Clara. "You haven't seen everyone yet, but we've got three women who are due to have babies shortly - my wife here, being the soonest. I'm sure you've noticed her condition; it's kinda hard to miss."

Sally cleared her throat as a mock warning that Luke should tread carefully.

"Another woman here gave birth a few months ago," Luke continued, "and now, I have acquired two young children with no parents. We have an older woman who is a wonderful nurse for the little ones, but there's too much for her to do alone." Luke gave her a pleading look. "So, I am really hoping you will choose to stay here and help us, Clara."

Mabin leaned back against the wall and chuckled again. "He fraid o' changin' diapers."

Luke frowned at Mabin, but didn't deny the accusation.

Sally and Hope had instantly taken to the children. Sally named the girl Deanna, after her grandmother, and the boy, Russell. Both children had very little energy when they arrived, and were noticeably underweight. Their hair had a reddish tint, which is often a sign of malnutrition. A few days of special attention and a good diet seemed to restore some energy and bring some life back to the glazed-over eyes.

Clara happily shared Hope and Mahta's ex-residence with Deanna and Russell and in time, began to feel as if they were actually her children. She clucked over them like a mother hen as she went about her work assignments. Russell was strapped in a pack on Clara's back as she worked her way down row after row, hoeing the site of the primary vegetable garden of the plantation. With Deanna at her side, Clara carried on a continual, one-sided conversation as if she thought Deanna could understand every word, but every once in a while, Clara would stop and give a lesson. She would point to her hoe and say, "hoe." Deanna understood what was expected of her and would point to the hoe and repeat, "hoe".

"Seed," Clara would say as she handed each seed to Deanna for her to plant. Deanna was always ready to repeat, "Seed".

In only a few days, Deanna learned almost everyone's names. She could also say phrases like 'Food, please', or 'Water, please', or 'Rest, please', and words like 'happy', 'sad', 'brother', 'yes', 'no', and 'thank you'.

Hope was always faithful to fetch Clara and Deanna for the lessons at the cook house. She was convinced that the young girl was a genius and would pass up all of the others in her learning. It was at these sessions that Deanna became more comfortable with Frank and Joshua.

By the end of March, she had begun to venture farther from Clara's side until, one day, she even spent some time after her work learning how to fish with the boys. From then on, they were a threesome. During their times together, the boys didn't just teach Deanna how to fish. They also took it upon themselves to teach her how to speak in sentences. As they made hay tunnels, climbed trees, and built secret hideouts, the two boys continually drilled Deanna on the sentences they were teaching her.

One day when everyone was in the cook house for their lessons, Luke and Sally dropped in for a visit. Sadie urged various individuals to stand up in front of the group and give a sample of what they had learned. Otis was very willing to jump up and proudly open the Bible and read John 3:16 perfectly. Mabin wrote on his slate, "I am forgiven. I am free." He held it up for all to see and everyone applauded. Dinah and Ambrose stood up together and quizzed each other on addition and subtraction. Clara eagerly stood up and wrote her name on the slate. She held it up for all to see, and cheers erupted. Then Clara gently urged Deanna to come stand beside her and speak some of the English that she had learned.

With slight hesitation, Deanna stepped up and stood tightly against Clara. Clara patted her head and said, "It's okay, child." And then Clara spoke slowly and clearly, "Speak.... English....words."

Deanna looked around the room and then stood straight and looked at the back wall of the room.

"Joshua...." she said, "is d'...smartest....man... in d'...world."

All heads suddenly turned in Joshua's direction. Most everyone looked as if they'd just caught him with his hand in the cookie jar. Joshua smiled and puffed out his chest and said, "Bout time someone figure dat out."

Mabin and Toby started laughing, and Toby asked Deanna, "What else doze boys teach you, girl?"

When all eyes were once again on her she said slowly, "I.... do... not... understand."

Clara reworded the request.

"Speak.... more... English...words."

By now, everyone was smiling in anticipation of what else a couple of boys might have taught her to say.

"Frank....is stronger....den...Toby."

"Hey!" Toby protested loudly, as the room burst out in laughter. The two boys jumped up and ran out the side door with Toby hot on their trail.

Deanna began to tear up, confused about the turmoil she seemed to have caused. Hope was the first to notice, and she went to Deanna and knelt down and gave her a hug. Clara caught on also and pulled up a chair to sit down beside Hope.

"Good....not bad," said Clara when Deanna looked at her.

"I do not....understand," sniffled Deanna.

"Neither do we," agreed Hope, with a smile, "Men are strange."
Deanna stared at her blankly.

"Men... are...goofy!" Hope tried again.

Deanna didn't get it.

"Men...happy. Men good," said Clara, "We'll leave it at that for now."

As the two women smiled at her, a smile returned to Deanna's face. Hope stood up and smiled at Clara.

"We have to teach her a bunch more words 'fore we be able to teach her how to understand men," Hope said.

"Honey," declared Clara, "I don't know that many words!"

Chapter 59

On April eighteenth, William Mance and his wife Holly arrived from their home in Alabama, as requested. The Martins had contracted with Mr. Mance to come and supervise the construction of a newer and larger gin and ginning house that was to be built next to the river. Henry Blackstone at the 'Feed n Seed', had recommended William because of his experience in building six of these bigger and more efficient gins in Alabama and Tennessee. The project was expected to take from six to eight weeks and Mr. and Mrs. Mance would be living in the Martin's guest room during their stay.

Along with their luggage, their wagon had come heavily loaded with all of the preformed iron parts that would be needed for the construction of the largest, most modern gin in eastern Georgia. Luke had seen a similar one being constructed in Savannah when he was visiting his mother in the winter. As soon as he laid eyes on it, he knew it would be the answer for the unused land he had been purchasing lately. The river would now have the responsibility of turning the crank, freeing one or two people for other work. The smaller gin would be moved to the new gin house so, if necessary, both could be in operation at the same time.

The engineer was no slacker, and he was anxious to get to work. The morning after their arrival, as the Martins and the Mances sat at breakfast, William slammed a plateful of food down and gulped two cups of coffee in record time. Frank watched in fascination, but it was hard for Sally. She was certain that he had tasted none of it.

Holly, however, was obviously comfortable living in other people's houses and meeting new friends. As she ate her breakfast at a proper pace, she filled Luke and Sally in on a few of their adventures while building the latest water wheel-powered gins. She also asked them a few questions about life on the Martin plantation and seemed keenly interested when told that most of the black workers were free men, working for a wage.

"It will be truly interesting to see if they'll be willing to work hard enough for William," said Holly. "We absolutely cannot stay longer than eight weeks. My daughter is expecting our first grandbaby in the middle of June and we simply must be there."

William spoke with his mouth full of eggs.

Sally winced at the sight.

"How do you keep them motivated?" he asked.

"Along with their wages, we bury them in love, faith, and kindness," Luke answered. "It works real well. I recommend it to everyone."

"Yeah, well, we'll see," said William. "In my experience, a few cracks of the whip do pretty good, too." He opened his mouth wide and shoved in too many potatoes.

Luke frowned. "If you brought a whip with you, keep it in your wagon. We've never used one here and don't intend to start now."

William smiled and gulped down a large cup of coffee without pausing to breathe.

Sally looked away.

As William scooted his chair back and stood up, he said, "Motivation's not *my* problem, it's yours. If your way works, I'll live with it for a few weeks. As my wife said, we can stay no longer than eight weeks and, finished or not, we expect the full price."

"Agreed," Luke said as he hurriedly tried to finish his meal, "I have six men whose only assignment will be this project until it's up and running."

Sally winced again as Luke took a bite that was way too large.

"The tall one named Sondabay is a mill worker," Luke said, as he took another large bite. "He's very bright and I plan on having him take charge of the ginning portion of my cotton project. I expect you to teach him, and myself, how it all works and how to fix whatever breaks."

"Very good," nodded William. "Let's get started."

Luke took one more big bite of food and a quick gulp of coffee, then stood up and grabbed his hat off the hook by the door. Frank jumped to his feet also.

"Sit down, Frank," Sally insisted. "Finish your breakfast."

"But Pa didn't!" Frank protested.

"Do you have a gin house to build?" asked his mother.

"No, ma'am."

"Well then?" she asked.

Frank sat back down to finish his meal. William chuckled as he opened the door to leave.

Luke turned to Frank, "Sorry, buddy, but you'll do better at school on a full stomach."

"I wish I was Joshua. He doesn't have to go to school all day," Frank pouted.

"Believe it or not, you'll thank me later, Frank," Luke said as he threw a wink Sally's way and followed William out the door.

The two men stopped at the head of the porch steps and Luke pointed out the three men who were putting the finishing touches on an eighty-foot-long stone wall and chute at the edge of the river. "That's where I want it. We've built the wall according to the design you sent me, and it should be all ready to go. Virtually every available man I have has been working on it for the last two weeks."

Luke pointed next to the stacks of lumber. "I think I have everything that you asked for on the list."

William Mance nodded his head with approval. "Very well, then," he said, "you fetch this 'Sandy' fellow and I'll show him how we will proceed. We will put two of your men on building the wheel, and the others will work on the building."

"It's Sondabay," Luke said. "His name is Sondabay."

"Strange name, but very well, I'll try to get it right."

"I would appreciate it. Some people don't have much they can call their own. All he came here with was what he was wearing and his native name. It would be best to, at the very least, let him keep his name."

"Then 'Sondabay' it is."

William smiled at Luke. "If you would please gather…. *Sondabay*… and the others, I shall proceed to build for you the best, most modern, cotton ginning establishment that can be had.

Sondabay and Richard were instructed by William Mance on how to, somewhat, understand the drawings that he had brought with him and they, in turn, guided the others. Richard proved to be a highly-skilled carpenter and, a few days into the project, was assigned the position of foreman over the framing crew by Mr. Mance. Ted and Nathan Willis worked alongside Zekiel and Richard as they raised a large 'post and beam' skeleton into the sky. Sondabay and Toby built the wheel and connected the axle and mounts. Then, with the help of the other workers, a mule, and a large tripod in the river, the wheel was set in the chute and made ready for the moment when the large metal plate would be cranked up to allow the water to run into the chute and turn the wheel. Once the wheel was finished, all six men focused their attention on completing the huge building that was designed to house both the new and older gin, and to store more bags of cotton than Luke's farm had ever before produced.

The month of May arrived on a dry and sunny, eighty-degree day. It was four o'clock in the afternoon and work on the plantation was finished for the day. William and Holly Mance walked arm in arm along the driveway out to Town Road. As they walked along, Zekiel and Washington rode past them on a spotted, grey mare. They waved and howdy'd as they bounced by, and the Mances returned their greeting. The couple watched the horse clip-clopping on down Town Road toward Grantsville.

"This is quite the place," remarked William, as they resumed their walk.

"The fellow in the saddle is named Washington," said Holly. "Sally says he has hired himself out for pay to the blacksmith in town two evenings a week to help build the Martin's peanut wagon, and also wagons for other planters."

"No place quite like this place," said her husband. "Sometimes religious people do strange things, but this idea of Martin's appears to be working. Luke only has them working from sunup to three or four, and surprisingly enough, my project is still on schedule. On our last project we had slaves working sunup to sundown to get it done on time."

Holly smiled. "Guess where that big guy on the back is going."

"Zekiel?"

"Sally says he gets off at the bridge down the road. It seems he has a gal slave he's interested in on the farm across the river."

"Last week, just after sundown, I saw a girl walk him down to the river bank. They talked for a minute or two and then he went into the river and waded back over to this side."

"Yes," said Holly knowingly, "Sally says that they have made offers to her owner but he refuses to sell. It seems he's using the girl to try to get Zekiel away from the Martins."

"Can't blame him. That Zekiel's a hard worker," said William, as the couple arrived at the end of the drive. They stood and watched as a large tree came crashing to the ground across Town Road. Five men with axes, saws, and a hooked knife immediately went to work limbing the tree and removing the bark. Almost before the tree hit the ground, Gideon was chopping away at another tree. The Martin's son, Frank, and a young black boy and girl were dragging branches to a pile for burning. This week, the focus was on Gideon's new home. Next week the men would all spend their free time working on Toby and Hope's house. The previous week, Otis's house had received the finishing touches on the roof.

Teamwork seemed to be the answer, and Luke had instilled in his people the idea that each individual has a stake in the success of the others. This went against the anthem of the slave industry, which was that 'fear motivates' and the power to inflict pain is the road to productivity and prosperity.

"Will you look at those men?" said William, shaking his head. "Look at all the energy they still have at the end of a work day. If Martin would keep them working on the gin we could have it finished a week, or more, early!"

Holly shook her head.

"No, William," she said, "you're missing the point. All energy isn't physical. The Martins seem to have found a source of mental and spiritual energy that also translates into quality physical labor."

"Yeah? Like what?"

A carriage rounded the bend on the road from Grantsville, headed north.

"Oh ...," mused Holly, pretending thoughtfulness, "like things called hope, self worth, love, respect, minor little things like that."

"You left out the God part, preacher lady," said William jokingly.

"Yes, they would say Him, too."

The Mances watched as the carriage slowed from a trot to a slow walk. The man and his two women passengers ignored them as they stared at the hard-working black men and the three partially completed log homes a hundred yards across the road. They frowned and rudely pointed at the black men as they whispered to each other and shook their heads in disgust. The horse continued to, slowly, draw the carriage along. Eventually, the man spit toward the cabins and said something that must have been funny, because they all broke out in laughter. The man then urged the horse back to a trot and they moved on up the road until they were out of sight.

"Hmmm," said William, "It would seem that not quite everyone is fond of what's going on here."

"I want to go back to the house, William."

Holly sounded disturbed and her husband glanced down at her. Her eyes were glued to the children hauling branches to the pile. Her look was a mixture of sadness and worry.

"Are you okay, dear?" William asked.

"I feel like something bad is going to happen here," she finally answered.

Chapter 60

It was not exactly as Luke had first pictured it in his mind, but he still found humor in it. The women were not sitting in a line on the porch; they were sitting in a half circle in the shade of the pecan tree. But they *were* knitting baby clothes, with the three bellies being used as tables to hold the partially finished apparel. Dinah was not present because she had taken over the cooking and cleaning chores in the house, but Mahta was sitting next to Hope, completing the half circle, as she peeled potatoes. Dinah's baby, Eli, was attempting to do push-ups on a blanket.

"Shore is sumthin', ain't it?"

Luke hadn't seen Mabin approaching from behind.

"It sure is," answered Luke. "It's been so long; I didn't think we'd have any more children.

"Them three shore is big, ain't dey?"

Luke smiled and nodded, "Big and beautiful."

"Big n' slow."

"Yeah," Luke agreed, "especially the last few days. Sally says the baby is riding lower. She thinks it could be any day now."

Luke and Mabin stood watching and contemplating that possibility for a while.

"Sure is sumthin', ain't it?" Mabin finally said again.

"It sure is."

Luke glanced in the direction of the vegetable garden where Holly Mance was visiting with Clara and playing with baby Russell, relieving Clara of her burden while she hoed the ground.

"Joshua says he and you had some dinner guests up at your place last night." Luke looked mischievously at Mabin, "How did it go?"

"Fine," Mabin replied bluntly.

The two men stood watching the half circle of women as the sound of hammers drifted up from the river.

"Deanna seems to be learning English quickly."

Mabin knew Luke too well. "Smart girl," was all he said.

For a short time, only the sound of hammers broke the silence.

"Clara seems very nice," said Luke, feigning disinterest as he looked back over at Clara and Holly.

"She is," said Mabin.

Luke recognized the tone of finality in his friend's voice. He had known him long enough to know that it was time to change the subject.

Luke pretended to clear his throat. "Otis should be bringing the peanut wagon home tonight, along with the hundred-and-fifty fryers I ordered from Bill Benning."

Mabin visibly relaxed at the change of subject. "Dat's a lot of chicken, suh," he said.

"You'll never believe this, Mabin, but Tom liked our Christmas chickens so much he said he'd buy another dozen when it was time to butcher and Al Willis ordered a half-dozen, like he did last year."

"That's still a lot of chickens."

"It is," Luke agreed. "Toby and Ambrose paid me for seventy-five chicks. They want to try selling them in Grantsville for extra income."

"Now, how dey gonna do that?" asked a surprised Mabin. "Dey ain't never sold nothin' before in their lives."

"They've got ambition, and mouths to feed. Do you remember when they took that half-day off last week in trade for a couple of longer days? They went into town and got a commitment from Pastor Davies to buy thirty chickens for the church picnic. The Methodists have committed to twenty-five chickens for *their* picnic, Wally bought two, and the Browns bought two. It takes some pretty good salesmen to sell fifty-nine chickens before they even have any!"

"My, oh my," said Mabin, shaking his head, "You best be real careful, or dem two might sell dis farm right out from under you nose."

"No problem," Luke responded confidently, "we'd all come up and live with you!"

Luke's response didn't register with Mabin. He had suddenly become concerned with what he was watching.

"Suh?" he asked. "Is Miz Sally alright?"

Luke focused in on his wife. Her face was red and she was clutching her stomach as she nodded her head and said something in response to the other women's apparent concern. Luke took a few steps toward her but relaxed when *she* noticeably relaxed. He watched as she took a deep breath and blew the air out. She then took up her knitting needles and resumed her knitting as she chatted with the others.

"I think she's okay," Luke assured Mabin. "It's the third or forth time that's happened in the last couple of days. It's like the body is firing warning shots, warning everyone that something's about to happen."

Mabin looked around warily. "What about to happen, suh?" he asked.

Luke glanced back at Mabin, incredulous.

"Oh!" Mabin suddenly got it. "Dat!"

Luke broke out in laughter. "Yes, that."

Mabin grew concerned again. "Shouldn't we get her up to d' house 'n into bed? Miz Dinah done passed out on the ground."

Luke was still snickering. "This could go on for days. When it's time, Sally will let us know. And most women don't pass out on the ground, Mabin."

Mabin finally began to shake his head slowly and a smile crossed his face.

"I think it time for me to go check on d' fields or sumthin'. I don' wants to give you any more stories to tell den I already have."

"What did you cook last night for Clara and the kids?"

"Now dere you go, diggin' for more stories."

"Joshua will tell me."

Mabin laughed. "I think I hear Joshua and Tal calling. Dey sayin' dey need help fencin' d' cow pasture."

As Mabin walked away, he heard Gideon calling for Luke. He turned back to Luke and pointed to the road.

"Better go find out what d' man want; could be important."

Luke sighed and nodded his head, then both men went in different directions.

Gideon met Luke on the road. He seemed nervous and looked back over his shoulder up toward his half-finished house.

"I think summun in dere, suh," said Gideon. "I'z goin over to do a little work on d' roof 'n I seen a dark figure move across d' window. I sneak up to d' window but couldn't see nobody. Den I hear a draggin' soun' in d' corner near d' door. I pushed a little on d' door but sumthin's holdin' it closed."

Luke studied the cabin in the distance across the road. "You stay here and watch the place while I go get some help," he instructed. "Stay behind that tree over there in case someone decides to take a shot at you."

"Yes, suh," Gideon said, and hurried over to the tree.

When Luke returned, he had his loaded pistol in his hand. Richard and Ambrose were carrying axes and Toby had Luke's Enfield rifle pointed toward Gideon's house. The hammer was pulled back and ready.

"There's no window or door in back, so whoever or whatever it is, will have to deal with all of us. Keep some space between us; let's find out what's in there."

The five men crossed the road and carefully walked the field toward the cabin, all eyes fixed on the window. They stopped about fifteen feet from the building and Luke motioned Gideon and Richard toward the left side of the window, in case someone decided to jump out and make a run for it. He whispered for Toby to stay where he was and keep the rifle pointed at the window. Luke signaled for Ambrose to follow him to the door. A faint sound of something moving came from the cabin and the two men flattened themselves against the wall beside the door. Luke reached out with his free hand and pushed, but the door didn't budge. When he pulled his hand back, there was trace of blood on his fingers. Looking closer, he saw a small amount of blood on both the door and the jamb. Luke held his hand up for the others to see and mouthed the word 'blood'. Toby nodded and raised the rifle butt to his shoulder.

"Whoever is inside, come out," Luke commanded loudly. Thinking he heard someone whisper, he motioned to the others that there was more than one person inside.

"You need to come out now. If you don't cause us any trouble, you will not get hurt, but you need to come out right now." Luke was sure he heard more whispering.

He motioned for Ambrose to move to the door and push hard. Luke held his pistol firmly and prepared to move in and protect Ambrose. There was a dragging sound from behind the door and Luke signaled Ambrose to wait.

"Thatchu? Mistah Luke Martin?" asked a cautious voice from inside.

Luke didn't recognize the voice but answered, "Yes, I'm Luke Martin."

"I'm commin' out, suh. I don't mean no trouble. We need yo' help."

"All of you come out slow," Luke called back."

"Yessuh," the man answered. The door slowly opened and out stepped Henry Blackstone's slave, Gabriel. He had blood on his shirt and pants but didn't look injured.

"I have a man here das been badly beat, suh," said Gabriel. "Massuh Henry foun' him in his woodshed. Massuh Henry say you live up dis' road. Been commin' for two whol' nights. Hidin' in the day."

"Who is it? And why didn't Henry bring him?" Luke asked.

"Don' rightly know who he is, suh. Massuh can't come. Say he bein' watched. Say he thinks mebbe it sumthin' called a 'setup', suh."

Luke pointed to the slave's shirt.

"That his blood?"

"Yes, suh."

"Can he come out?" Luke asked.

"No, suh. His legs is broke. That's why Massuh Henry thinks it was someone else who put him in his woodshed. We move him when it so dark we couldn't see nothin'. Had to feel our way along. Massuh help me carry him out o' town. Din' want no blood found on his wagons. Say to ask you for other clothes and tell you to burn these."

Luke looked around cautiously, suddenly feeling very paranoid.

"You need to get back inside out of sight," he instructed Gabriel. "Ambrose, you and I will go in and check this fellow out. Gideon, take Ambrose's ax and you and Richard start clearing whatever you're still wanting cleared."

Luke scanned the area again, just in case. Anyone could be in the trees and not be visible.

"Toby," Luke lowered his voice a notch. "I need you to go back and let the ladies know that we have a passenger for the railroad. Tell them there are injuries. They'll know what to do. Act casual and even sing to yourself or something, as you walk back. Pick up a rock and throw it at a squirrel, or something. Just another 'day in the sun'. Know what I mean?"

"Yes, suh. Nice day for a walk."

The three men entered Gideon's house, with Gabriel in the lead. Sitting propped against the wall behind the door was a thin black man who had obviously received a vicious beating. His entire face was swollen and bloodied, his shirt had been shredded by a bull whip, and his legs were clearly broken.

Luke looked from the man to Gabriel. "How on earth did you carry him this far, and in the dark?"

Henry Blackstone's slave began to tear up, and his shoulders slumped. He looked wearily into Luke's eyes, "Don't know if I did. Don't remember most of it."

Luke put his hand on his shoulder and nodded. "Maybe you had some help."

"Yes, suh, maybe I did."

Ambrose had been studying the man on the floor. Suddenly he groaned and knelt down beside him. He lifted the man's hand and shook it side to side.

"You still wif us, my friend?" he asked. "Kin you hear me?"

The man's head bobbed and he made a slight noise.

"Is me. Ambrose. You safe now, Idiot."

Luke perked right up and looked closely. "Might be," he thought to himself. "Too much damage to be sure."

At the sound of his name, one eye opened slightly. "Amb...." Idiot lifted his hand slightly. "Ambro...... dat you?"

Ambrose squeezed his hand and nodded his head. "It's me. Nobody gonna hurt you ever again, Idiot. We get you fixed up."

"No......" The man peered out from his swollen face. "Done."

Ambrose didn't argue.

"What I tol' you before, at d' plantation. I was sooo.... wrong," he said. "I was d' idiot, not you. I hope you din't bleve me. I foun out God is real. Jesus is real. And even do' you went through this, I knows for a fact God is good 'n he loves you. You gotta bleve me, man!"

Ambrose was still holding his hand and felt the shudder that went through Idiot's body. He watched the man closely, hoping for a response.

"He lets me find Dinah, and he give me a son. I was a mess, but Jesus forgive me."

Ambrose watched his friend's eyes close. He shook his hand vigorously and patted his cheek.

"Listen to me, Idiot! You needs to ask him; he forgive *you*," Ambrose paused and watched as Idiot's eyes slowly reopened. "You need him!" Ambrose stressed desperately. "We all, really *do*, need him."

The cabin fell quiet. All eyes were on the dying slave. Silent prayers were flying out through the unfinished cabin roof, filling the universe. After what seemed like an eternity, a faint and barely discernable smile appeared on the swollen face. They were all sure of it. The body shuddered. The smile faded, the eyes closed, and Ambrose wondered.

All of a sudden he felt the hand that he was holding begin to squeeze his own hand. It was a surprisingly firm grip. Ambrose stopped wondering; he knew everything was fine now. The hand went limp and the body sagged. Ambrose was sure that in the place where that life had just gone, he would never be called 'Idiot' again.

From outside the cabin came the sound of a tree cracking and then crashing to the ground, then all was quiet.

Chapter 61

Hope was washing the cut on Otis's forehead when she spoke, "I say we don' give dem d' satisfaction o' seeing a body. Let 'em forever wonder if he got away."

"I'll dig a hole in d' woods out back my place in d' morning," said Gideon, "den I cuts a tree 'n let it lay on d' grave for a week or two. Dem partic'lar white folks is too lazy t' move a whol' tree."

"I helps you dig," said Ambrose.

The small group was gathered around a table in the cook house. The two lamps on the table were the only lights burning. Luke and Sally had spent the evening entertaining the Mances to distract them from the other events on the farm. They had retired early, as had most of the others.

"You shun't a tried to stop dem from dumpin' the baby chicks, Otis," said Toby, "We could always get more chicks, but dey' ain' no store dat sells more Otis's."

"Dat Mistuh Ellis fella say I'z sneakin' a runaway Negro outta town. He say I'z hidin' him under dem boxes o' chickens."

Otis winced as Hope dabbed the cut with a rag.

"I tol' 'em I don' know nothin' 'bout no runaway Negro, but dey push me back 'n start throwin' boxes."

"What dey hit you with?" asked Hope.

"I'z bent over chasing baby chicks 'n met d' heel of a boot. Next ting I knows dey's all gone 'n chicks is runnin' roun' ever'where." Otis looked over at Toby, "I think I catched all but five 'r six. Sorry, but it gots too dark to find d' rest."

"I'd say you done real good, Otis," smiled Toby. "I'll ask Massuh Martin to look for 'em when he sneaks Gabriel back into town tomorrow. Who knows? Maybe dere be a line o' little chickens waitin' for him on d' side of d' road!"

The latch clicked as it lifted, and Washington entered the room. As heads turned, he said, "Seen the light an' was hopin' I might find sumthin' to nibble on ...." Washington noticed the cut and lump on Otis's head.

"Hooowee! What happened to you, Otis?" he asked. "You didn' have no lump when you left Mr. Addison's place wit d' wagon."

"Din't see no baby chicks in d' road when you come home, did you?"

"Stayed late at Addison's makin' horseshoes. Too dark to see much. Dem chickens beat you up 'n run away?"

"Dem chickens had help," Hope explained. "Dem white men where Ambrose come from was lookin' for one of dere Negroes."

"Dey ain' gonna fin' 'im," added Ambrose.

"Is he in the root cellar here?" asked Washington.

"Nope," Ambrose answered with confidence. "He done gone to heaven!"

"Oh," said Washington thoughtfully. "I see." He paused and then asked hesitantly, "Is any o' us in trouble for dis?"

"Dey done it to him, demselves," Hope said with disgust. "He made it dis far afore he die in Gideon's cabin. I think we should bury him here 'n let 'em think he escaped."

"I guess this is it, isn't it," Washington stated flatly. "Free to make our own decisions that could maybe get us in trouble."

"Wouldn't be on d' Martins, dis way," said Toby. "Dey wouldn't never need to know where he wound up. Dat way dey got no cause to lie."

"If he asks us where we put him, we kin tell him dat we'd rather not say, and leave it at dat," Gideon agreed.

"I guess 'at decide it den," said Ambrose. "I meets you at your place wid two shovels at d' firs' sign o' light."

The next evening, Mabin and Clara stood on the porch that Mabin had finished building two days before. It was the fourth time Clara had shared a meal with Mabin and the first time that it was only the two of them; the three children were eating with the rest of the group at the cook house. They watched Gideon and Otis walk across the road from the plantation to Gideon's cabin. Ambrose stepped out of the cook house, stretched, and also headed the same direction. It had been agreed that, after the evening meal and a short rest, the men would all gather to help Gideon put the finishing touches on the roof and clear a few more logs. Then Gideon would be on his own at his place, and the focus would switch to finishing Toby's house.

"We're standing on what is probably the highest point for a hundred mile in any direction, maybe farther; seventy, eighty feet above d' rest o' d' world." Mabin shook his head in wonder. "Ten acres and a cabin on top o' d' worl'," he paused thoughtfully, "an Massuh Martin done give it to me!"

"I only knowed two other freedmen afore I come here," said Clara, "They didn't have nothin'. They was hungry and 'bout starvin'."

"You a free woman, Clara. What *you* thinkin' to do?" Mabin asked, still looking out over the land below him.

"Them two chillen ain't free, an' they don' have no mama."

There was a sad tone in Clara's voice that caused Mabin to glance down at the woman who was standing a foot away from him.

"No, dey don'," he said as he looked away.

"I grown fond of 'em, you know," she said.

"You ain't hid it very well," Mabin smiled.

Clara's sadness suddenly left her and she turned to Mabin with a smile. He looked at her curiously, wondering about this quick change of attitude.

"I *am* a free woman!" she stated, as if she had just realized it for the first time. "I have a place t' live, food t' eat, 'n I earn a wage! Think of it, Mabin. I earn money!"

"So, what you thinkin' to do?" Mabin pressed.

"I'm thinkin' to stay 'n earn enuf money to buy 'em two young'uns!"

Clara looked at Mabin, wondering if he thought she had lost her mind. But he didn't; instead, he looked relieved. That surprised her a little.

"Tal says I have earned eighteen dollars already," Clara added.

"Dat so?" Mabin feigned surprise. "Seems I knowed you longer 'n dat."

Clara's smile gave way to mild surprise.

"Yes," she agreed, "it does."

There was a quiet pause and then Mabin said, with some regret in his voice, "Well, I s'pose it's time to go help Gideon."

"Yes," she agreed with a sigh. "I s'pose it is."

"Church!? You want to take her to church?" Tom Grant asked incredulously.

Zekiel shifted nervously, and then locked his fingers together in front of his chest and nodded.

"Yessuh. I do, suh."

"Now, just where around here would you find a church for nigras? It ain't legal for colored people to teach religion."

"At d' Baptist church, dey lets us sit in d' balcony, now. But Massuh Martin say we kin meet early this Saturday morning in d' cook house 'n hear Preacher Davies preachin' - he gots a license to do it."

Tom raised his left eyebrow and studied Zekiel.

"That so?" he asked. He continued to study Zekiel, taking full pleasure in making him uncomfortable.

Zekiel stuffed his hands in his pockets and nervously bounced up and down on the balls of his feet. He wished he was anywhere but where he was.

"Is it working?" Tom finally asked.

Zekiel stopped bouncing. "Suh?"

"Is religion fixin' ya?" There was a trace of sarcasm in the tone of his voice.

"Suh?"

Tom rolled his eyes in frustration. "I mean, is it doing ya any good?" His voice was raised slightly.

Zekiel gave the question some thought.

"Well, suh, not so's you'd prob'ly notice. But inside, it feels like some things is gettin' fixed."

"That so." Tom said thoughtfully as he processed Zekiel's request for a moment.

"Martin had better be careful. He gets careless and he could spend a few months settin' in a jail cell," he thought to himself.

"I suppose you can take Rena across the river for the morning, but just this once. Do you hear me?" said Tom, continuing attempting to look stern.

A big smile spread across Zekiel's face as he reached out to shake Tom's hand.

"Oh, yes, I hear you, suh. Thank you, suh."

Tom swatted the hand away in frustration.

"I told you not to do that! Can't you learn nothin'?!"

"Oh no, suh! I mean, yes, suh."

Zekiel became frustrated; his shoulders dropped and his hands hung at his sides.

"Thank you, suh." He stood facing Tom and, for a moment, showed no emotion. But soon a smile crept slowly back onto his face.

"Thank you, suh," Zekiel repeated.

"Just git going!" Tom kept up the act. "You better remember to have her back by noon!"

"Yes, suh. I will, suh."

Tom turned in a huff to go back into his house and crashed right into Etta, knocking her to the floor, flat on her back.

"Wha...!" Tom exclaimed in total surprise. "I had no idea you were there, Etta. Honest!"

He looked back to Zekiel as if hoping for affirmation.

Zekiel stood there with his mouth open, and said nothing.

Tom turned back to Etta, "I didn't see you. Are you okay?" He leaned down and reached his hand out and helped her to a sitting position.

Etta sat up, half dazed for a moment. Then, with her eyes staring at Tom's knees, she asked, "Kin I go too, Massuh?"

Tom was concerned she had hit her head and might not be thinking clearly.

"Where do you want to go, Etta?"

She slowly raised her eyes to meet his. "To d' meetin', Massuh." Then Etta smiled and added, "I jus' fine, suh."

Tom stood up and pursed his lips and squinted his eyes in suspicion. He glanced back at Zekiel. Zekiel's mouth was now shut but his eyebrows were raised high. Tom began to suck air in through his nose and Zekiel saw his chest expand, giving the impression of an imminent explosion.

Suddenly, Tom threw his hands up in exasperation, then slapped his thighs and exhaled. "I must be going crazy!"

"Sure!" he said loudly, "Why not? Why don't you all go to church?" Tom stepped around Etta and moved on down the hall. "Why doesn't the whole world go to church? Why try to accomplish something around here when you could be settin' around singin' and doing nothing! Why don't we all just earn our keep in our spare time.......?" He continued to grumble to himself as he disappeared into his study and slammed the door, leaving Zekiel staring down at Etta.

"You jus' gonna' stand dere, or is yo' gonna' help an ol' woman to her feet?"

Zekiel burst into action and pulled her to her feet. Before he turned to leave, he looked over her shoulder down the hall and then back at Etta.

"Did I hear dat white man say dat all you can come tomorrow?" he asked with a grin.

Etta glanced over her shoulder to make sure the door to the study was still closed.

"Same ting I hear him say, so he musta say it," she said quietly. "You go tell everyone at Rena's house, and I spread d' word to d' others."

Etta took a couple of steps back and started to close the door. She paused.

"I hope ya'll haf enuf room ober dere."

She smiled and closed the door.

The idea was received with some skepticism on the part of Tom's slaves. They gathered Friday evening after dark in the eatin' house to discuss what was said by Zekiel and Etta. A year ago something like this would not have even been considered, but every slave was keenly aware of every instance over the past couple of months that seemed to indicate changes in 'Massuh' Grant.

It was brought up that Del and Glenn were no longer making their lives miserable. They now had new pants, shirts, and dresses, and the shacks were all being replaced with nicer buildings.

Big Joe and Maybeth remembered that the massuh had treated them with more kindness since Joe lost his eye, and Rena added that, even though he said he would work her extra hard as punishment for running away, the work had not been excessively difficult.

The item that received the most attention was the mysterious conversation between Massuh Grant and Massuh Martin that resulted in the joint effort to harvest the rest of the cotton.

"Strangest thing I ever see," chuckled Big Joe. "Firs' Massuh talkin', den yellin', den layin' on d' groun' holdin' a flower, den talkin', den yellin', den ridin' way, den turnin roun' 'n goin' back n' talking sum more."

Others nodded as they remembered watching the two white men, pretending not to be staring as they worked.

"Don' it beat all dat Massuh Martin sho up wif his niggers 'n hep us?" remarked a slave named Tuck.

"Sumthin' happen' dat day," Belle agreed. "I'd almos' give up my nice new shack to know what dey wuz sayin' up dere."

There was a murmur of agreement and more snickers. But everyone fell silent when Etta began to speak to them.

"It be goin' on longer 'n dat." Etta spoke in a serious tone, "Sumthin' been happnin' to Massuh since he took it to me. His gram-mammy 'n me, we raise a goo' boy. Now d' Lor' bin pullin' it out im'."

"Pull what out im'"?

"D' good part o' im'," Etta said with a smile. "D' debil don' wan us to see dat part."

The room fell silent as everyone thought on what Etta said.

"Lots o' us knows what a good beatin' feels like," offered the slave named Jackson. Heads nodded in agreement. "I figure I stays put 'n does my chores."

"Think Massuh beat us, Etta?" asked Tuck.

"No, I doesn't. I think d' debil gon' lose out."

Then she turned to Jackson and looked as if she was reconsidering. "It be better if sum stays put 'n keep up wit d' chores. Massuh Tom don' need no problems fum us jus' cuz he say yes."

Etta's words eased some of the nervousness in the room. The seventeen slaves who had been the most nervous about going volunteered to stay and work the farm. The rest also felt better because the massuh would have less reason to give out whippins. Most of Tom's slaves felt it was worth the risk.

Chapter 62

Saturday morning, the crossing began at dawn. Rena, Maybeth and Big Joe, and their children showed up first. Zekiel met them at the river and helped Joe bring the children through the waist-deep water. Soon, others began to appear from the trees and walked into the river without any hesitation. Some of the men had small children riding on their shoulders, while a couple of the larger children raced each other from the trees to the water and swam to the other side. As they reached dry ground, they gathered to wait for the others. About fifteen to twenty people were in various stages of crossing when Zekiel noticed Etta emerging from the woods with Belle.

"You wait here, Rena. I be right back."

Zekiel hurried across the river, picked Etta up and carried her to the other side. As they crossed, they attracted some light-hearted banter from those still arriving at the river's edge. A couple of the men asked if Zekiel would come back and carry them across. Reaching dry ground, Zekiel gently set Etta on her feet and apologized for not keeping her totally dry.

"Lan' sakes!" Etta chuckled, "If I go to church dry, I won' fit in wit d' rest o' d' herd. When we walks into dat place, ain't none o' us gonna need no baptizin', thas fo' sho." This time she laughed loudly, obviously very pleased with her own humor.

The crossing continued until, to the surprise of some, Abel walked hesitantly out of the woods and into the water. He was the last one. He was greeted on the other side by nearly fifty curious faces, although Etta wore a smile. There were a few raised eyebrows and, for a minute, there was an awkward silence.

"Thought I'd come see whats all d' fuss about," Abel finally remarked, with a straight face. "Sides, I don' gits many chances to git away from dat place."

"No, we don't, do we?" said the big man with the patch over his eye.

Abel and the others looked at Joe as he reached out his hand to Abel. Abel looked at the outstretched hand and hesitated for a moment, then slowly responded in kind. That was all it took; the weeks of tension were over.

Zekiel smiled and said a soft "Praise d' Lord" as he took Rena's hand and turned to lead the soggy group to the cook house. Most of the group walked thoughtfully, as they mulled over what had just happened. Occasionally, someone would glance at Big Joe and Abel who walked silently, side by side.

"Good things is hapnin' *fore* we gets to church," Etta told Belle, shaking her head as they walked along. "Kin you magine what gonna happen *at* church?"

Belle looked confused. "No. What gonna happen?"

"Land sakes, child!" Etta looked excitedly at Belle. "I gots no idea, but kin you magine? Could be anything. Could be wonderful!"

Belle walked along silently, trying to figure out what it was that Etta was imagining.

Pastor Davies had spent the night at the Martin home because Luke had agreed to his idea of holding a special 'one time' service Saturday morning for his slaves that might encourage more of them to attend church in town with the Martins on Sundays.

It was still early when Otis finished up with the milking. No one else had come out of their houses yet; he was getting paid extra for taking care of the animals on this particular Saturday morning. Otis forked some hay to each of the three cows and stuck the milking stool in a corner, then carried the two full milk cans out of the barn into the early morning sun. He froze in place, the milk cans still in his hands.

"Lawd, have mercy!" he exclaimed, as he caught sight of Zekiel leading a mass migration of Negroes up from the river toward the cook house.

Richard and Sondabay were laughing and teasing Washington about how his snoring was better than his singing, as the three of them walked together to the cook house for an early breakfast.

"I'll put on some coffee while you two great sinnin' singers set up the tables and benches for the service," Washington instructed. "And mebbe' you could fry me up a couple of eggs while I go out back to warm up my singin' voice and say a few prayers for you."

Sondabay nodded his head in agreement. "Richard, he do need a few extra prayers to get him through and ...., well, look at that! Somebody already done start breakfast for us," exclaimed Sondabay, as he spotted smoke rising out of the chimney.

"It's startin' out to be a real nice day, after all," Washington commented as he looked at the chimney, then added, "just so long as you two leave off bout my singin'."

"Do d' Bible say to 'make a joyful noise to d Lord,' or 'make a mournful noise'?!" Richard continued to press.

"I honestly don't know how I continue to put up with ...."

Washington glanced in the window as he walked by. "What.....? What's going on in there?"

Washington quickened his pace to the door. Richard and Sondabay squeezed in around him as he stood in the doorway, staring at the large room full of people, black people, most of them strangers.

The benches and tables had been arranged, and Zekiel and Rena were already sitting in the center of the front row, looking as if they expected the service to start any minute. All of the benches and chairs were filled, and children were sitting on the tables. Toby and Otis were handing out coffee and tea, and Hope was visiting quietly with Big Joe and Maybeth.

Toby looked past Washington toward the door, and said in a loud voice, "Joshua, go fetch more tea pots and cups from wherever you can find them!"

Washington hadn't even noticed that anyone had slipped in behind them. He turned and saw that Mabin and Joshua had followed them from the men's shack.

"What's going on, Mabin?" he asked.

"Don' know," Mabin answered without taking his eyes off of the scene before him.

"Looks as if word o' your singin' ability is spreadin' like wildfire," Mabin chuckled as he looked down at Joshua.

"Better git movin'," Mabin said, nudging the boy. "Don't know as there's enuf cups on d' whole plantation, but go see what you can find. Go to Clara's place firs'. Maybe Deanna can help you get 'em ."

Mabin focused in on Mahta as she stood at the stove pouring tea into the few remaining empty tin cups for their many guests.

Next, Mabin pulled Sondabay aside. "Not so sure dis a good thing hapnin'," he said in a lower voice. "At least *some* of dem is from Mistuh Grant's place. Maybe you could fetch d' sack o' coffee from d' root cellar whilst Richard greets some of dese people. I think I bes' go tell Massuh Luke 'bout dis."

As Mabin closed the door behind him and headed for the big house, Ambrose and Dinah, with little Eli snuggled in her arms, wandered sleepily into the room and became instantly wide alert.

Tom wandered around his large house holding the cup of coffee in his hand, taking a sip once in a while. He had found the coffee pot on the stove next to a pan of hot muffins and sausages on a warming rack, and assumed he would stumble upon Etta somewhere in the house, doing some early cleaning.

Eventually, Tom wound up back in the kitchen, grabbing a muffin as he passed by on his way to the front porch. He took a large bite as he stood against the railing and scanned the farm for any sign of human life. Finally he noticed Nate and Gus working with pitch forks, out in the east field spreading out the hay to dry. Taking a final gulp from his cup, Tom tossed what was left of the coffee over the railing and set his empty cup down. He took a bite of the muffin and moved down the porch steps. The muffin was finished by the time he walked into the carriage house. There was nobody there. He checked the barn and found young Niles in the process of milking, and Adam pitching hay into the horse stalls.

"Mawnin, Massuh," greeted Niles, without turning away from his work.

"Morning."

Tom returned the greeting half-heartedly as he scanned the rest of the barn. He shook his head thoughtfully and turned to leave but then he paused and asked, "Kinda quiet around here this morning. Are the rest up at the eatin' house eating breakfast?"

"Sum iz, 'n sum iz hoein' d' corn," Niles offered, still not looking at Tom.

Tom looked in the window of the eating house and, sure enough, four men and three women were sitting at a table finishing up their breakfast. It seemed odd to him that nearly forty of his slaves would be hoeing the cornfield. It suddenly dawned on him that there were no children around.

He began checking the slave shacks, one at a time. First he would knock, and when there was no answer, he would check inside. Nobody there. The story was the same in every shack.

A strange feeling coursed through him as he approached the next to the last shack. As he reached out to knock on the door, he took a deep breath to regain his composure.

"What on earth is the matter with me?" he asked himself. *"I'm the master of this plantation! I'm the boss. Why would they all go out there without getting my instructions?"*

Tom rapped on the door. He heard a thump inside the shack and then the door made a loud squeak as it began to open slowly. He took a step backward as old Bud stuck his head out of the opening. Thirty years ago, Tom had thought Bud was one hundred years old, but now he wondered if it might be true. Now Bud was useless, slow and toothless, and very slow. Tom had often considered getting rid of him, but he never quite got around to it. He was never so glad to see him as at this moment.

"What on earth is going on around here, Bud?" Tom asked, somewhat irritated. "Where is everybody?"

Bud stared at him. Bud was also hard of hearing.

"This place is like a ghost town!" Tom yelled, "Did every man, woman, and child go out to the cornfield?"

Bud shook his head. "Shursh," he toothlessly replied. Then he smiled a big gummy smile.

"Shum o 'em at shursh, jush like you shay."

Tom stared at him blankly.

"Shursh," Tom repeated, in a flat, emotionless tone.

Bud nodded his head, assuring Tom that he had gotten it just right and then, without the master's permission, Bud withdrew and closed the door.

Tom turned and walked away, reminding himself again that it was time to get rid of Bud. But he knew he would never quite get around to it.

Once he was back in the house, Tom poured another cup of coffee, helped himself to another muffin and a sausage link, then walked out to the porch and sat down in his chair, racking his mind as he tried to put the pieces together.

"Could they have all run away at once? That would have taken a lot of planning to pull off."

He looked out over the farm and saw the two women he had seen in the eating house, heading to the vegetable garden, each with a hoe in hand. He replayed the tapes of recent memories in his head. Eventually, Tom came to his conversation with Zekiel. Suddenly it dawned on him.

"Shursh!" Tom spoke the word out loud. He sat up straight in his chair.

"That's where Rena and Etta are! I told the boy he could take them to church at the Martin's!"

He sat back in his chair thoughtfully. "Would the others have gone there, too?" he asked himself. Then he remembered speaking some careless words as he stormed off to his study.

Tom stood to his feet and walked purposely down the steps,

heading directly for the river. When he arrived, his suspicions were confirmed. Footprints were everywhere, on both sides of the river.

"I don't believe this!" Tom said in amazement. "They thought I was serious!"

The sound of a man's voice, coming from the direction of the new eating house, grabbed his attention. It was too far away for him to understand what was being said, but the man was clearly speaking with authority and excitement.

"I do not believe this!" Tom repeated to himself."

He spun himself around and walked as fast as he could, back to the barn. He would have Niles saddle his horse, and he would go pay the 'church' a visit.

Chapter 63

Pastor Davies had been lobbying for a long time to allow blacks to attend services. The congregational vote was unanimous, as long as certain conditions were met. The blacks must enter through the side door, and they must sit in the balcony at the back of the church, and they must not be rambunctious.

Luke, Ben, and Henry had expressed their disappointment to Matthew about the restrictions. Their friend agreed that it was disappointing, but reminded them the vote was unanimous and therefore, no division.

"One step at a time," he had said, "and that first step was huge. The whole town is talking. Some people in town approve, though most do not. But the whole congregation voted on the same side, so there's no room for outsiders to slip in and divide us according to our votes. That's almost miraculous!"

Luke and Frank walked together down to the cook house to inform those who might be eating an early breakfast that, during their meeting with Pastor Davies, the Martins and the Mances would be eating breakfast with the Statlers at the Stelman Hotel in Grantsville and should be back around noontime. They were halfway there when Mabin exited the building and headed toward them. His look of concern slowed them to a stop as he walked up to them.

"Guess I didn' hear we was havin guests dis mornin', suh." Mabin spoke hesitantly.

"I'm sorry, Mabin," Luke nodded. "I forgot to tell you that Zekiel asked for permission to bring Rena to the meeting."

"Well, yessuh. Rena, she here." Mabin fumbled around, not knowing quite how to tell Luke the full extent of what had happened. "Uh, maybe you should come see for youself."

He motioned for them to follow as he turned and walked to the cook house.

Luke entered the cook house expecting to see a few of his friends beginning to cook breakfast. What he found instead was standing room only - and not much of that.

"Wow!" Frank exclaimed. "Pa, can I stay here today? This is great. Where did all of these people come from?"

"I'm not sure, Frank," Luke said in amazement, "there's not much room for you. It'd probably be best if you come with us today."

"Hey, Frank, over here!" they heard Joshua shout. "We can squeeze you in, here on this table."

"Excuse me, suh."

Luke turned around to see Tal standing in the doorway carrying the two chairs from his house.

"I had to fetch these chairs for Dinah and Sadie," said Tal. "All the seats were already taken when we got here for breakfast. S'pose there won't be no breakfast today."

Frank and Luke moved aside.

"Can I stay, Pa?"

Luke hesitated.

A man standing nearby chuckled, "No one would step on him, suh. He be kinda like a firefly floatin' thru the night - easy to see. Kinda like glowin' in the dark."

Luke turned to the speaker and was surprised to see Abel, Tom's former driver. Luke slowly stuck out his hand. "It's good to see you, Abel," he said half heartedly, his head still filled with confusion.

Abel shook his hand.

"Are the rest of these folks from Tom's farm?" asked Luke.

"Don't know some of dem, suh. But mos' of us come over early. Massuh Grant say's okay."

Luke's eyebrows raised in unison.

"Was this Tom Grant's idea?"

"Uh, no, suh. I hear was Zekiel's idea."

Luke scanned the crowded room until he found Zekiel sitting next to Rena. They were in the center of the front row. Best seats in the place. Luke wanted to ask Zekiel how he had pulled all of this off. How had he managed to get Tom Grant, of all people, to agree to this? He began to work his way through the crowd when he heard his son's voice.

"Can I stay with Joshua and Mabin, Pa?"

Luke turned and looked behind him. "I guess you can, but you'd better do whatever Mabin tells you. You hear?"

"I will. I promise."

With a whoop, Frank began to work his way to the table that Joshua was sitting on. Luke turned back to find Zekiel but Matthew had come in and found his way to the front and begun to thank everyone for coming. Luke decided not to interrupt. He quietly apologized to those who had to scrunch up to make room for him to leave.

Friday evening, Sally had invited the Mances to accompany them to Grantsville for breakfast the next morning. The gin house project was only a few days from being finished, and she wanted to do something special for them before they left.

"I'm kind of jealous of your son," Holly Mance commented as the two couples traveled to Grantsville. "I think it would be simply fascinating to be a bug on the wall at your Negro gathering."

Luke nodded in agreement as he gently urged the two horses down the road.

"Yeah, me too, especially this one. Somehow, the Lord figured out how to fill that whole room!"

"They do love to sing," said William. "Holly and I have listened to them from the porch. Sometimes they hooted and hollered between songs, though I have no idea why."

"But they sure had a great time of it; that was obvious," Holly added.

"I'll give you that," William agreed with a nod. "They do enjoy themselves."

The carriage moved on down the road and into town with Luke and the Mances conversing non-stop. It wasn't until he pulled the carriage up to the Hotel to let his passengers off that Luke realized Sally had barely said a word the entire trip. As the Mances stepped down from the carriage, Sally remained seated.

"Are you alright?" Luke asked, as he noticed the strained look on her face.

It was quite a few seconds before she began to relax.

"I don't wish to ruin everyone's Saturday morning," she finally responded in a soft whisper.

Luke stiffened and his eyes grew large, "Do you mean it's time, Sal? Why didn't you say something earlier?"

"I think I should go home to my bed. I'm so sorry, Luke. I shouldn't have come." She began to weep.

Ben Statler approached the carriage and offered to help Sally step down. She turned to him with a weak smile and shook her head.

Ben noticed the tears and looked past her to Luke, "Is there anything I can do to help, Luke?" He motioned to his wife, who was standing on the steps, to come join them.

William and Holly had been standing back, trying not to interfere with whatever was going on. Now Holly, suddenly understanding, stepped forward. "Do we need to go on back home, Sally, or should we find the doctor and stay in town?"

"I would like to have my child in my own bed," she said weakly. "I'm sure there is time if we leave now."

Luke nodded his head and looked at William, "I believe that would be best. We do apologize."

Luke turned to Ben, as the Mances climbed back into the carriage. "Would you and Wilma find the doctor and send him out to the farm?"

Then Luke smiled, "It looks as if there might be some labor being done this morning."

Ben chuckled, "I believe that's labor that a woman can't have someone else do *for* her while she stays and eats breakfast."

"I don't believe this is the time to joke around!" Wilma Statler said urgently. "The doctor lives at the other end of town, and we should hurry to catch him before he gets called somewhere else." She pulled on the sleeve of Ben's jacket. "Come on, Ben. You men don't seem to get the picture!"

Ben looked back at Luke and Sally as he was dragged away. "Believe me," he half shouted, "If I don't get the picture yet, you can be sure she'll have it all painted for me before we find the good doctor!"

Luke turned serious again and looked up the road. He turned the horses and headed toward home. Sally was weeping and apologizing to William and Holly, while Holly tried to reassure her that they were not being inconvenienced. As for Luke, he was trying to contain his excitement as he anticipated meeting the new life that God had prepared for his family.

Chapter 64

Tom dismounted and tied his horse to the post in front of Luke's house.

First he knocked, then pounded, on the front door. He hadn't expected an answer but it was polite to start at the owner's house before searching around.

"I wonder if Martin has any idea what's happening here today? He's getting way too lax," Tom thought to himself as he walked across the yard toward the cook house where all of the noise was coming from.

His curiosity began to overshadow his irritation. *"There's no way they could all fit in there, is there?"* he wondered.

Tom walked up to a window and peeked inside. All of the windows were open, but Tom could only see the backs of two or three black men. He had no way of telling if they were his people or Luke's. Moving to the window near the corner, he stood on his tiptoes, only to see a sea of black heads.

"My word!" He whispered.

He recognized a faint smell of alcohol in the air. "So that's why they're so happy and singing so loud," Tom thought with disgust.

"We can help you git your nigras' back for ya, Tom."

Tom nearly jumped out of his skin. He had been so intent on finding out what was going on inside, he hadn't even noticed Jerry Ellis and his younger son, Gregory, come around the corner of the building. Tom spun around and slammed himself against the building, his heart pounding wildly.

Gregory began to giggle in a way that told Tom where the smell of alcohol was coming from. He became disgusted.

"Don't you ever do that again, Jerry! I can see you two done got yourselves stone drunk on stupid, before you even had breakfast. Now get yourselves out of here before you do something we'll all regret!"

Jerry began to giggle stupidly, along with his son. "Now Tom, we were just riding by, minding our own business."

He giggled some more.

"We heard all this noise inside there," he said, pointing to the building. "We got curious, just like you did."

"The difference is," Tom interrupted as he put his hands on his hips, "I ain't drunk! Now, leave, before you do something really dumb."

Jerry acted as if he hadn't heard.

"Let's go in there and get your nigras back."

Suddenly, Tom grew concerned. He turned his attention to Gregory.

"Where's your brother?" Tom asked.

"Rascal and Del are out back, guarding the back door so's no one can slip out."

Fear swept through Tom. He tried to act calm.

"Are they as drunk as you are?" he asked.

"Don't know for sure." Gregory snickered and his body swayed. "They might be."

"Oh, for .....!" Tom grumbled in frustration.

"I'll go get them all out for you." Jerry interrupted Tom, and headed for the door. He braced himself and then kicked the door in. Drawing his pistol from its holster, Jerry went inside.

"Whoa!! What an entrance!" Gregory exclaimed as Tom raced for the door. Just as Tom reached the doorway and ran inside, Jerry fired a shot at the ceiling to get everyone's attention. The response was not quite what Jerry had anticipated.

Because the room was so crowded, almost everyone thought they were being shot at and the room exploded into action. Like a net full of fish, people instinctively tried to run in every direction but there was no room to run. Panic became the rule of the moment. Many fled in the direction of the door, carrying Jerry along with them. Jerry had no idea what had gone wrong or what was happening to him. He panicked and fired his gun into the crowd. The shot intensified the mayhem as both he and Tom were overrun by the black sea of mankind intent on fleeing the building.

Rascal and Del, upon hearing the shots coming from inside, drew their weapons and looked nervously at the back door. Suddenly the door flew open and people started pouring out of the building running in all directions. In their confused, drunken state, the two men opened fire. Gideon and Big Joe watched Otis drop to the ground like lead. Joe instantly pushed Maybeth to the ground and joined Gideon as he chased after the shooters. Del turned and fired as he ran, and Big Joe dropped. Rascal Ellis fully intended to kill Gideon as he turned to shoot, but he tripped on a stone and rolled. The gun fired as he rolled and Jerry Ellis' oldest son lay dead from his own hand. Gideon tore the gun from Rascal's hand and fired two shots at Del as he disappeared into the trees. He pulled the trigger a third time and the hammer merely clicked.

Gregory felt almost giddy, as he heard the shots and watched men, women, and children pour out of the building. Terrified 'nigra's' were a funny sight to him. He fired a shot into the air and the fleeing crowd turned away from him and ran for the protection of the new gin house. Gregory howled with laughter as he stumbled after them with a colt pistol in each hand. He shot directly into what he called the 'herd of black cows', and a woman fell. He fired again and a young boy dropped.

Inside the cook house, Tom pulled himself up to his hands and knees and looked around. People were still trying to get out. His head felt as if someone had jumped on it. He heard shots fired outside and a feeling of dread swept over him. He watched as Jerry pulled himself to his feet by hanging on to a support post. Jerry looked groggy, as he searched the floor for his pistol. Tom saw the pistol before Jerry did. It was lying next to a woman who was laying face down and not moving. He quickly crawled over and grabbed it. Jerry smiled and stumbled in his direction.

"Thanks, Tom," Jerry said as he reached out to take the gun.

Tom pulled the trigger. Splinters from the ceiling above Jerry's head sprinkled down and Jerry froze in place. Another shot sounded outside from somewhere near the gin house.

"Hear that, Tom?" Jerry spoke carefully. "I need my gun to defend myself."

"These people ain't got no guns, Jerry. You'll be just fine. The only guns around here are yours." Tom stared coldly and aimed directly at Jerry's chest. He pulled the hammer back until it clicked in place.

"I'm just going to borrow this one for a couple of seconds," Tom said coldly.

Jerry quickly backed away until he stumbled and fell backwards.

"That's okay, Tom. Keep it as long as you like." Jerry said as he turned and scrambled out the door as fast as he could.

Tom released the hammer and set the gun down. He looked at the woman lying beside him. Blood was trickling out from under her head. He drew in a large breath of air and let it out. He shook his head and rolled the woman over.

"Etta!" he gasped.

When Jerry had busted the door down and fired his first shot, Zekiel had not wasted his time trying to piece together what was happening. Before Rena could look to see what the commotion was about, she felt herself being half dragged, half carried, across the floor to Mahta's room.

"Get behind d' bed 'n stay dere!" Zekiel commanded roughly as he shoved her into the room and slammed the door shut.

Zekiel then turned to see a swarming mass of people pushing in all directions, desperate to find an exit to safety. He heard glass breaking and then a second shot which instantly intensified the action. Mahta get shoved backward against the hot stove, putting one hand back on the hot stove top as she tried to balance herself. Zekiel dove into the terrorized crowd and threaded his way to Mahta. When he reached her, she was bent backward with her back flat on the stove. Her dress seemed to be steaming as he lifted her up and threw her over his shoulder. With another surge of adrenaline, Zekiel somehow managed to make his way back through the crowd to Mahta's room. He carried her in and closed the door, then laid her carefully on her stomach on her bed. Rena's head slowly rose from behind the bed.

"She burnt her hand, fo' sure. Don' know 'bout her back, but her dress come close to burning. It's *still* smokin'!"

Zekiel was so wound up he didn't wait for Rena to respond. He hurried out of the room and closed the door behind him. The eating hall was half-empty now. Only a minute or so had gone by. He saw a half-dozen people strewn about on the floor, groaning and trying to get up. He was about to help a young man when a shot was fired outside the front door. Zekiel headed toward the sound but many at the front door turned and fled to the other door. He fought against the current, reaching the door just as another shot rang out - but from inside the building. Zekiel glanced back inside and saw Tom Grant pointing a gun at another white man. He had no idea what that was all about, but turned his attention to the yard as he heard another gunshot outside and saw a young boy fall to the ground.

A white man was laughing loudly as he waved his guns in the air and staggered around the pantry building, toward the new gin house. The man glanced back behind him and saw Deanna, with baby Russell in her arms, trying to run. She was in total panic and crying as she ran. Gregory thought that was pretty funny. He laughed as he took aim. Clara was on the ground with a bullet in her leg. She screamed just as Gregory pulled the trigger. The clapboard siding right above Deanna exploded in woodchips and the girl fell down in fear. This made Gregory think his shot was successful, so he turned his attention to those fleeing into the nearly-finished gin house.

"Trapped like rats!" he shouted angrily into the building, as he stumbled up to the loading dock.

Mabin had forced his way out of the building in time to see Deanna stand up and run around the corner of the meeting house carrying her brother. He ran to Clara who was trying in vain to stand up and go after the children.

"I be alright, Mabin. You hurry n' go hide dem chillins. Please, Mabin!"

The pleading in her voice convinced him.

"Okay, Clara, but you lay back down 'n play dead for a while till I gets back, ya hear?"

"I will. Hurry!" She urged him.

"Don' move!" he reminded her.

As he stood to run, Mabin spotted Gregory standing by the corner of the pantry and raising the gun in his left hand to shoot toward the gin house. Mabin knew what he had to do. He ran and tackled Gregory just as the man pulled the trigger. Gregory lost hold of one of his pistols as the two men rolled around on the ground. Unfortunately, Jerry Ellis arrived just in time to pick it up. He raised his arm in the air and brought the gun handle down on Mabin's head. Jerry kicked the black man's body off of his son and Gregory struggled to his feet.

"Let's go find your brother and get out of here!" Jerry seemed on the verge of panic.

Gregory was now very angry, as well as drunk. He pushed his dad away. "Not yet! I'm sick of things always goin' so good for Martin."

Gregory focused on the gin house, his voice now steely and cold, "Them niggers in there ain't free now! They's all penned up!"

"Son, this has gotten out of hand. Let's get out of here!" The urgency was growing in Jerry's voice.

This time Gregory pushed his father off of his feet. He turned, ran to the building, jumped up onto the loading dock and grabbed a lantern that was hanging on the wall. He threw it inside. Next, he took his whiskey bottle from his pocket and took a swig before pouring the rest of its contents onto the floor. Gregory looked around and suddenly began to giggle again. He had spotted the torch mounted on the wall just inside the opening. Taking the torch down, he felt around in his pocket until he found a match. Gregory lit the torch and touched it to the mix of whale oil and whiskey. Flames shot across the floor lighting up the gin house. He looked around and smiled.

"Trapped like the rats they are," he said smugly, and then tossed the torch onto a large stack of cotton sacks, which quickly began to burn.

Satisfied, Gregory walked out onto the dock. He turned around for one last look, just as Ambrose and Dinah, carrying little Eli, ran out from behind the burning pile of sacks, followed by Frank and Joshua, headed for the opening to another room. Gregory pulled his pistol from his right holster and emptied his gun in their direction. Before he had a chance to return his gun to its holster, his face was being slammed into the wooden floor and Zekiel was pummeling him with both fists. Jerry raised his pistol to protect his son but the shot went high as Toby made a running tackle into his side.

The whole event, up to this point, had taken less than four minutes.

Chapter 65

Sally was in a deep sweat as she leaned her head on Luke's shoulder. Luke was working his jaw muscles hard as he ground his teeth and silently prayed. William and Holly sat quietly in the back seat, once in a while giving each other a glance of concern as the carriage wheeled down the road. Sally suddenly groaned loudly.

"I can't make it, Luke," she whimpered. "I'm going to have the baby."

"Only a few more seconds, Sal. The drive is just past these trees. We're as good as home."

As Luke finished speaking, he and the Mances heard three distinct shots come from the farm. He looked at Sally but she obviously hadn't heard them. He turned to William.

"Did you hear anything just now?"

"Sounded like shooting," said William with a nod indicating the tree tops. "Is that smoke coming from your place?"

Luke snapped the reins until the horses broke into a run.

As the carriage entered the plantation drive, it became obvious their concern was justified. Two pregnant black women were running across the yard to the main house and a man resembling Tal was running close behind, urging them forward as he repeatedly glanced over his shoulder. As the carriage raced to the house, William noticed some people behind the gin house running to the woods. Suddenly they all heard more shots as a black man ran into a tall white man and they both rolled around on the loading dock swinging fists at each other.

"My God! What on earth is going on?!" Luke asked with alarm, as he urged the horses to a stop in front of the house.

Four or five adults and a child ran out of the barn, heading to the river as fast as they could go.

Luke began shouting orders to his passengers.

"William, you and I will carry Sal into the house. Holly, I guess it's up to you to help Sally deliver. William and I will lock the doors on our way out. I think I saw Sadie and Hope run inside. If they're in there, they can help you, but if not, you are on your own! Do not unlock the doors for anyone you don't know!"

Luke leaped from the carriage.

"Okay, let's go, William!"

The men sprang into action, lifting Sally out of the carriage and carrying her up the steps as if she weighed almost nothing at all. Holly held the doors open as they carried her through the kitchen and up the stairs to her bed. Sally half screamed and half groaned as another hard contraction grabbed hold of her. Luke immediately turned and left the room with William following behind.

"Hope! Sadie! Are you in here?" Luke yelled, as he ran down the stairs. "Hope! Sadie! Tal?"

The door to the small pantry off the kitchen opened. Tal and the two women came out.

"Oh, thank you, Lord! Thank you, thank you, thank you!" Luke exclaimed, as he stepped into the kitchen. "Sally's upstairs having a baby! Holly needs both of you to help."

"What's going on out there, Tal?" he asked desperately.

"We were listening to Pastor Davies preaching when the door opened and a white man come in and started shootin'. Don't know who, or why, suh."

Luke snapped into action, motioning for Tal and William to follow. "Come with me, fellas. We've got to get out there and stop this!"

As the three went out, Luke stopped long enough to lock the door.

"Help us, Lord. Please, help us," Luke prayed desperately, then turned and ran down the steps. Luke had his pistol drawn and was scanning the area carefully. He saw a black woman crying over a young boy who did not appear to be conscious, and Clara, dragging herself over to Mabin, who was rolling over and groaning as his world began to come back into focus. Then the three men froze momentarily in their tracks; flames were shooting out of the large doorway of the gin house.

Toby was jerking Jerry Ellis to his feet when Luke ran up to them. Then he looked toward the burning barn just in time to see Zekiel kick someone with a bloodied face off the loading dock to the ground.

"You're gonna' hang, nigger!" Jerry yelled angrily at Zekiel. "You killed my boy!"

For some reason, without giving it any thought, Luke's left hand flew through the air and he backhanded Jerry. Toby took a couple of steps back as Jerry spun totally around and landed, sitting, at Toby's feet. Luke stepped up to Jerry and looked down on him.

"If my son is hurt in any way, Ellis, *you're* the one who'll be swinging from a tree."

Luke didn't wait for a response. Calling over to Zekiel, he asked, "Where's Frank, Zekiel?"

"Some is in dere suh," he nodded as he was forced off of the dock due to the heat. He landed on his feet and looked sadly at Luke, "Don't know how many."

Jerry tried to stand up but Toby put him on his back with his foot.

"I didn't know your boy was here, Martin," Jerry said in a strained voice.

Luke ignored him. He looked up at the smoke pouring out of the loft's double doors.

Zekiel cleared his throat nervously, clearly worried. "I think I seen dem two boys in dere, suh, 'long with Ambrose n' Dinah and d' baby."

He kicked Gregory. "This'n was shootin' at em!" Zekiel added with great emotion.

"That's a filthy lie, nigger!" Jerry tried again to get up, but Toby pushed down hard with his foot.

"He was shootin' in there, suh. I didn't see who at," Toby said, in support of Zekiel.

Luke was slowly coming to a boil. He whirled around to William who was standing off to the side with Tal.

"What's the easiest way to bust in there, on the back side? Maybe the fire hasn't reached that far yet!" Luke asked him, frantically.

William smiled weakly at Luke, glad to be able to help. "That's one of the few things we had left to wrap up, Luke. If everyone ran to that part of the building, then they're probably not even in there. There were no boards on the back of that room. Richard was supposed to finish that, tomorrow. They could have run in here at the front and right back out again from that corner room."

William stopped smiling, "I guess the unknown is the shooting."

Luke looked to the sky and said a quick, "Please, Lord. Please!" and then bolted for the back of the building. Some of the others followed him. Smoke and flames were pouring out of the gaping opening of the back room. No one was behind the barn. Luke looked around frantically and then yelled his son's name at the building.

Suddenly, William remembered what he had seen when they had arrived in the carriage. He scanned the edge of the forest.

"Tal, let's go check the woods over there. I think I remember seeing some people go in there."

Tal and a couple of Tom's slaves followed William to search the woods.

Luke yelled Frank's name as loud as he could. Suddenly there was some pounding from inside the building, up in the loft. Someone inside was apparently trying to break open an escape route. The banging was steady for a while and then it became more infrequent. It looked as if the boards were loosening. At the sound of the next crash, smoke began to flow out through the new gaps in the siding. Then there was coughing, and then silence. Luke could hardly stand it.

"Frank! Try again! You're almost out!" he shouted.

There was more coughing and then more silence.

"Hit the wall again!" Luke yelled, as loud as he could.

Luke began to pace back and forth.

"Hit the wall again!" he shouted.

More coughing; then suddenly the upper wall exploded into splinters and chunks of siding. Everything appeared to shift into slow motion as a man flew out of the gin house loft. The smoke seemed to be chasing him out as he flew through the air with his flailing arms and legs engulfed in splinters of wood. When the man hit the ground, it seemed to Luke that he bounced two feet up again before coming to rest, motionless and unconscious.

"Please, Lord. No more!" Luke prayed as he ran to the crumpled body on the ground. "We need miracles now! Please!"

He immediately recognized Abel and assumed he was dead. The right arm was broken at a ninety degree angle between the shoulder and the elbow. The left shoulder was obviously totally out of its socket.

Luke heard a higher pitched groan and then a cough come from the loft. His hopes soared.

"Frank!" he said, as he turned and looked up. He saw a woman on her knees, smoke pouring out around her.

Zekiel and Toby came running around the building.

"We got them two tied to a wagon wheel, suh," said Toby, all out of breath. "Zekiel didn't quite kill his fella after all."

Luke pointed up to where the woman was now in a sitting position with her legs dangling out over the edge.

"Belle!" Zekiel exclaimed. He ran to stand under her.

"We'll get a ladder, Belle," Zekiel called up as Toby joined him.

Suddenly Belle started coughing and leaned forward a little too far. The two young black men instinctively threw up their hands to break the fall and the three of them landed in a heap.

Belle rolled over coughing and gagging, and trying to suck in the fresh air. The sound of the building collapsing in on itself caused Zekiel and Toby to forgo counting their bruises and scramble to their feet to drag Belle away from the building.

It was over in seconds.

Luke stared at the flames and cried.

Chapter 66

"The Lord giveth, and the Lord taketh away," Luke told himself, as he fought the tears.

A quick tally had revealed that Otis was dead, as was the son of one of Tom's slaves and, of course, Jerry's son, Rascal. Big Joe had taken a bullet in his left side and was once again being held by his wife. Clara had been shot in the leg, and Mabin had a huge knot on his head. Abel was in very bad shape but not dead. He had broken both arms and badly injured his shoulder.

Belle said that while they were in the gin house loft, Abel had told her to tell Big Joe one more time that he was sorry about the eye. He said he was going to make a way for her and a couple of others to escape but that he probably wouldn't live to tell Joe himself. Then he had stood up and run with all his might across the loft and through the wall.

"Who were the others?" Luke asked her, halfheartedly.

"Don't know em', suh. They mus' live here, at your place."

Belle went into a fit of coughing. Luke's heart sank.

Suddenly, Jerry was screaming and yelling at Luke, "Your niggers murdered my son, Rascal!" He had overheard someone saying that his son was dead. "They tried to kill Gregory! You're finished, Martin! I'll see to it there's a whole lot of slaves hangin' from your trees!" He fought furiously at the ropes that held him to the wheel.

"No, suh! We din' kill no one!" Gideon and the others protested. "Dem white men, dey was shootin' at us."

"It don't matter what they say, Martin. Ain't no colored folks get to testify in any court. Me and my son, and Tom Grant, will testify that what I'm sayin' is the truth." Jerry spit at Toby, but it fell short.

"Tom Grant will be testifying to no such thing!"

All heads turned at the sound of Tom's voice as he slowly walked out of the meeting house with Jerry's gun in his right hand. Luke took a couple of steps toward him, but Tom walked right past, straight to Jerry. He leaned down until his face was about six inches from Jerry's face.

"And I doubt that pastor fella that's inside helpin' folks will be much help to ya, neither!" But I'll tell you what Tom Grant *will* testify to, Jerry. I'll tell the judge that you shot my cook in the head while she was visiting some friends! You grazed her right above her ear, and if she dies, you die!"

Tom shoved the gun up against Jerry's nose. With his left hand, he pulled a flask of whiskey from Jerry's jacket.

"There are white men here, who will testify that me 'n the good pastor were the only *sober* white people that saw all of it happen."

Keeping his eyes locked on Jerry, Tom stood up, still pointing the gun at his face. He pulled the hammer back, and the clicking sound clearly affected Jerry, who was in a deep sweat, his eyes completely focused on his own gun.

"Tom Grant will testify that Jerry Ellis shot into a crowd of innocent men, women, and children while they were minding their own business, praying and singing. You and Del and your boys were the only ones who had guns. Even I didn't have one."

Luke looked around. "Del?"

"He run off when young Mistah Ellis falls down and shoots his self," said Gideon, stepping forward.

"Liar!" Jerry yelled, "You shot my boy!"

"No, suh," answered Gideon, calmly. "I din't have no gun. D' gun go off when he fall."

Luke stepped up to Jerry, leaned down and grabbed him by the hair. "Not one more word from you!" Luke jerked his hair. "My son was in that building. If he doesn't show up ....," Luke searched for words. "Well, you might as well be saying your goodbyes to little Gregory here, and to your slaves, and to your farm, and all your friends, because you won't be seeing the outside of a prison ever again."

Luke let go of his hair and stood up. He instructed Gideon to ride to town and make sure the doctor was coming, "but not the sheriff!" he stated firmly. He also instructed him to find Ben Statler, and the Judge, telling them what happened, and to hurry back out to the farm.

Tom set the women to taking care of the wounded as best they could. He then divided up all of the able-bodied men and boys, except the one he called Willy, and sent them out to search the woods for those who were missing.

"Zekiel and Rena and the preacher are inside, along with an old woman with a burned hand," Tom said to Luke. "The three of them are taking care of Etta as best they can. I think I'll go check on them and send the preacher out here to help."

Turning to Willy, Tom handed him the gun and nodded toward Jerry and his son.

"If they cause you any trouble whatsoever, shoot them!"

Tom headed to the cook house, not thinking of what Luke might be going through. Toby and Tal had gone ahead of him and were already at the porch steps as Hope stepped outside. Luke glanced back and saw William standing and staring at what was left of the burning gin house. He had come back from searching the woods without Frank or the others.

"William?" Luke called out, dreading the answer.

William turned his face to Luke, his eyes filled with compassion, and slowly shook his head.

Zekiel's words echoed in Luke's head.

"I think I seen dem two boys in dere, suh......"

His body trembled and the tears came, as Luke imagined Frank's body in the rubble. He dropped to his knees and wept.

William Mance felt completely worthless. He had no idea how to help. His feet felt rooted to the ground. Eventually he turned away, and once again stared at the fire and tried to make sense of it all.

It wasn't long before Luke remembered the bigger picture. He had a wife who was, at this very moment, bringing forth another child. He took a deep breath and stood to his feet. He asked the Lord to give him strength and to, for now, focus on what God was doing inside his house.

As Toby filled Hope in on what had transpired, she looked sadly over his shoulder to Luke. Her eyes began to water and tears ran down her cheek. Stepping around Toby, her mouth trembled as she watched Luke force his heavy feet up the steps.

"Oh, suh," she said, as Luke raised his head to his three former slaves. When he reached the porch, Hope unashamedly stepped forward and wrapped her arms around him and cried. The two black men looked down at their feet. Luke put his arms around the young girl and tried to comfort her as he also wept.

"I don't understand, suh," she finally said.

"I don't understand either," Luke agreed through his tears. "I guess that's what keeps us in our rightful place."

"Suh?" she asked, after a moment of thought.

"When we don't understand why he's allowed something, our place as Christians is to trust him. We have to take a step back, and let him be God."

Hope stood back and wiped her eyes. "Then what?" she asked, as she stared blankly at his chest.

He lifted her chin with his finger. Their eyes met, and he smiled.

"Then .....," He paused in thought for a moment. He realized that her question was also his question. And then the Holy Spirit answered them both.

"Then we give a sigh of relief that he is a good God. And we move on. Sometimes we're sad. Sometimes we're weary. But there's always this underlying knowledge that God is good." Luke paused, "And that's how we make it."

"Amen."

Somehow, Tal's voice reminded Luke once again, that his wife was having a baby. He rubbed his eyes with both hands and asked Hope. "How's Sally doing?"

"She workin' hard, suh, but no baby yet. Miss Holly 'n Sadie tol' me t' can go see if everybody is okay."

"Is she alright?"

"Yes, suh. I bleve so."

"Okay, then," Luke looked at the three of them. "She is not to be told about Frank or any of the deaths until she's had the baby and we are sure they are both okay."

Luke pointed to himself, "I'll decide when to tell her."

Suddenly Luke noticed Ambrose peek around the corner of the house. When Ambrose saw that he had been seen, he hesitantly stepped out into full view.

"Ambrose?" Luke asked as he took a few steps toward him, "Where have you been? Where are Dinah and the baby?"

Luke was afraid to ask the question that flashed in his mind.

"Ain't been no shootin for a while, suh. Is everythin' safe now?"

"Yeah, it's safe now. Things didn't turn out very good, but it's all over." Luke paused and then asked, "Where have you been?"

"We run out d' back of d' gin house an' I took 'em through d' woods to Mabin's house."

Luke stiffened and took a deep breath, "Who did you take to the cabin, Ambrose?"

"My Dinah, Eli, 'n d' boys, suh. I tol' em t' stay put til I comes back for 'em."

Luke suddenly felt weak all over. He stared at Ambrose while he took time to process what he had just heard.

"The boys?" he asked. "Do you mean Frank and Joshua?"

"Yessuh, d' boys." His white teeth began to show as a slow grin crept across his face.

Luke let out a whoop, Frank-style, and gave Ambrose a big bear hug.

"Praise the Lord, Ambrose! Praise the Lord!"

"Yes, suh. I do, suh." Ambrose still had a smile on his face, but he wasn't quite sure how to handle Luke's excitement – or the bear hug.

Luke released him and gave him an energetic swat on the shoulder. Luke couldn't help it. The tears broke loose again.

"Let's go get em', Ambrose. Let's go!"

"Yes, suh. We go git em."

The two men disappeared around the corner of the house.

Those left standing on the porch could hear Luke shouting, "Thank you, thank you, thank you, Jesus!" as he ran up the hill.

The screen door squeaked as Holly Mance pushed it open and looked around. Disappointment crossed her face. "I was going to tell Mr. Martin that he is the father of another son."

Hope squealed and ran to the door, squeezing in behind Holly.

"He be right back, ma'am," Toby assured Mrs. Mance. "He be right back."

Chapter 67

Early the following afternoon, the carriages and wagons from Grantsville began to arrive at the Martin plantation for the funeral service. Henry brought Gabriel along with him. Ben and his family arrived close behind the Judge, the doctor, and one of his nurses, who had traveled out together.

Pastor Davies had skipped his lunch and come straight from the church service. He was helping to set up chairs and benches as he thought on all that had transpired. Two men were headed to prison; three, if Del was ever captured. Many were battered, broken, and sad. Four men and a boy had died. Along with Otis, and the young boy, Richard and Sondabay had died in the gin house. It was they who had been hiding in the loft with Belle and Abel.

The sound of distant singing reached Matthew's ears. The song was, 'Swing Low, Sweet Chariot'. The preacher turned to see three wagons coming up the drive, completely packed with Negroes, except for Tom Grant, who was driving the lead wagon. A fourth wagon soon came into view loaded with the Willis family.

Luke came out of the house and greeted Tom as the wagons came to a halt. "Thanks for bringing them, Tom. This means a lot to all of us."

Tom grunted. "Course Big Joe, Abel, and Etta didn't exactly feel up to coming," he explained. "Maybeth asked to stay with Joe and Etta, and Belle was pretty determined to stay with Abel."

Luke's eyebrows rose, "Belle, huh?"

"Yeah, interesting, ain't it?" said Tom, with a straight face.

"Well, I guess he *did* save her life, didn't he?"

"Yeah, I suppose he did, at that," Tom shrugged and, without another word, moved on to where the service would be held. As the others climbed off the wagon, Zekiel helped Rena down from the back. Luke returned to the house to gather his family.

The mood was somber as the mourners gathered around. Matthew watched Tom Grant find a seat near Henry Blackstone in the back row. He saw Mahta sitting in a rocking chair, one hand wrapped in clean white bandages, holding the baby, Russell. Ambrose stood in the shade of an oak tree, holding his young son, Eli. Sadie and Hope sat side by side, both with their hands folded on their bellies. Luke helped Sally walk slowly down the stairs of the house and over to join their friends. Frank followed along behind, proudly but carefully cradling his day-old brother, Warren, in his arms.

When the Martins were settled in the front row, the pastor looked out over the black and white faces. He turned to his left and observed the four wooden boxes to be buried. (The smallest of the four boxes would be buried this afternoon, across the river.)

As he was about to speak, Eli began to fuss. It took Ambrose a moment to quiet him. The pastor waited with a smile. When all was quiet again, Matthew took a breath to speak just as baby Warren began to squeak. Frank flushed beet red. He put his brother on his shoulder and gently patted him on his back, but in his nervousness he did it too hard and Warren squawked all the louder and then spit up. Deanna giggled and others chuckled as Luke reached over and took the baby. Soon all was silent again.

"A time to laugh, and a time to mourn," the pastor said, and gave a quick, fleeting smile. "The Lord giveth, and the Lord taketh away."

Matthew looked back at the boxes. "Yesterday, we had a total of five departures."

He looked at the two young expectant mothers and smiled again. "And recently, the Lord has begun to bless this place with what will soon be a total of five new babies."

Pastor Davies looked at his listeners and shook his head, "I don't pretend to understand it all."

Hope nodded her head and spoke softly as she looked down and rubbed her stomach. "All we kin do is take a step back, 'n let Him be God."

Chapter 68

Two weeks after the incident at the farm, the Martin family sat in their pew at church. The greetings and announcements had been made and Pastor Davies was giving the opening prayer. Among other things, Matthew prayed once again for all of those who were involved, both mentally and physically in helping after the attack. He finished his prayer by asking the Lord to "some way, some how, work out this event for the good of the kingdom."

The double doors at the main entrance to the sanctuary squeaked slightly as they opened. Even with their heads bowed and eyes closed, everyone could tell by the sound of the shuffling feet that someone was coming in slowly.

A young child in the row in front of the Martins whispered, "Look, Mama!"

His mother shushed him, but then with head still bowed and pretending to still be praying, she turned and looked over her shoulder. Luke and Sally heard a quiet gasp and then the sound of whispering.

"In the name of the Lord Jesus Christ, our Savior, we thank Thee. Amen."

Matthew finished his prayer and raised his head along with the rest of the congregation. He looked to the rear of the room and a slight smile appeared. A few heads turned and there were faint whispers. A battered old black woman with a bandage around her head was holding Tom Grant's arm for support as they entered the sanctuary.

As more and more attention was focused behind them, Luke, Sally, and Frank also turned to look. Sally let out a whimper, as she fought back tears of happiness.

"Do you see that, Frank?" Luke whispered to his son. "God answered Pastor Davies' prayer before he even finished it!"

"Hello, Reverend," Tom greeted with a straight face and some volume, "We thought we'd visit you' all this morning and do a little worshipin'."

"It's good to have you, Tom, and you too, Etta," smiled the 'Reverend'.

There was more whispering and an usher pointed Tom and Etta toward the stairs to the balcony. Tom misunderstood the usher and thought he was pointing to an empty space on the far end of the back row. He led Etta toward the balcony stairs but, instead of going up, he slid into the back row tight up against big Mrs. Millhouse. Etta sat down next to him. Mrs. Millhouse scrunched up as close to her husband as she could and sat stiffly staring at the front. Her face had turned dark red.

The sanctuary quieted. A child giggled. Luke nodded to Tom and smiled and Tom returned the nod. Henry whispered to his wife. They stood up and walked down the middle aisle to go to the back and greet Tom and Etta.

Big Mrs. Millhouse misunderstood and assumed that was her cue. She whispered to her husband and nudged him until he motioned to his four children that they were leaving, to join Henry in his supposed protest. When the Millhouses began to move, Eleanor Toffee also misunderstood Henry's actions and led her two daughters up the aisle behind Henry. She was puzzled when Henry turned left and she hesitated, but she had committed herself. She followed the Millhouses out of the building.

Jack Woodruff, who was sitting three rows up, glanced up from staring at Etta and saw a whole line of black heads peeking curiously over the balcony at the happenings below. He knew that if this was allowed, all of the others would try it. And in his mind, that would be a disaster. He stood up to join the other protestors. His wife remained seated. Jack took her arm and tried to pull her to her feet.

"You sit right back down, Jack! We aren't going anywhere!"

The man quietly sat down in submission, as Henry and his wife returned to their seats.

Luke was praying hard during all of the commotion. Suddenly he slapped his hands down on both legs and stood up.

"Come on, Sally. We're gonna go sit with Tom and Etta."

He said it loud enough to be heard and not be misunderstood. Sally shifted the baby to her shoulder and joined the rest of her family as they stood up and quietly walked to the now, almost empty, back pew. Luke slid in next to Tom. Sally and Frank followed.

"Sorry about all of this, Tom."

"I used to be just like em'," Tom answered, but not all that softly. He made no effort to lower his voice as he turned to Luke and added, "And it wasn't all that long ago."

Matthew gave a signal and the pump organ began to play.

"Let's all stand and join together in singing 'A Mighty Fortress Is Our God'."

The congregation returned their attention to the front of the room, and stood to their feet.

Tom stood when Luke did, but Etta remained seated and smiling.

"You know something, Luke?" Tom spoke loudly so as to be heard above the organ as the organist played the introduction. "I've decided to give Rena to Zekiel for a weddin' present."

Heads began to turn but most caught themselves and looked back at the pastor.

Luke was surprised to hear Etta laugh. And then he heard her say, "Dat's him, suh."

Luke stole a glance at Tom. Tom was frowning at Etta.

Luke joined in with everyone else as they sang the first verse but his mind wasn't on it. He was tossing something else around in his head. Finally he leaned over to Sally and said, "I think I know who got the slice of pie."

"*A mighty fortress is our God, A bulwark never failing. Our helper He, amid the flood of mortal ills prevailing.*

For still our ancient foe doth seek to work us woe. His craft and power are great.........."

Tom didn't know the song and he didn't know how to read music, so he was content to watch and listen. He looked at the faces, and most of the people seemed quite normal. They looked as if they meant what they were saying.

"Did we in our own strength confide, our striving would be losing, were not the right man on our side, the man of God's own choosing.

Dost ask who that may be? Christ Jesus, it is he; Lord Sabaoth His name, from age to age the same. And He must win the battle."

As he listened to the words, he suddenly realized how tired he was. His life really had been a battle, and the enemy was indeed, very strong. When the last verse was sung, he was surprised by its effect on him. The enemy wasn't going to win after all. The idea was very interesting, if it was true.

Tom hoped it was.
"Let goods and kindred go, this mortal life also.
The body they may kill: God's truth abideth still.
His kingdom is forever."

The song ended and everyone sat down.

He folded his arms across his chest and let his eyes wander around the room. The large cross at the front and the stained glass window behind it were impressive but not overpowering. Flowers in vases were sitting on the front edge of the raised platform. The high ceiling caught his eye and for some reason he leaned his head back and looked straight up. He jerked in surprise at all of the black faces looking down at him and Etta.

Tom regained his composure and watched as Matthew opened his Bible to preach. Then he looked around one more time and nodded his head.

"So this is it, huh?" he asked Luke while looking back at Matthew.

Luke thought about what had transpired in the last few minutes.

"No, Tom, this isn't it."

He paused.

"That comes later," Luke said, quietly.

Epilogue

"A lull in the fighting is not the end of the war."

Luke sat through the rest of the service not hearing a word of Matthew Davies' sermon. He could not stop thinking of Tom's question: "So this is it, huh?"

How could he tell Tom that life just might get a whole lot messier as the devil cranks up his efforts to keep him from coming to Jesus? Tom would need a friend. Frankly, Luke didn't feel up to the job.

"How on earth did it come to this?" Luke asked himself. "Me sitting in church next to Tom Grant, of all people, and an old, beat up, black angel (at least according to Tom)."

Luke began piecing together what had probably been the craziest year in his entire life. He remembered Tom's murder of Joshua's father, Mahta being left to die in the woods, the grass fire, and the fear on Hope's face after the fire. He pictured the scars on Toby's neck after Tom whipped him, and Big Joe's empty eye socket. It went on and on. A woman and her two children fleeing for their lives, a broken man called Idiot being carried for days only to die on the floor of an empty cabin, the gin house fire and the five deaths that resulted. Luke shook his head.

All of that time, effort and money, wasted. Mance said he was willing to come back next summer and rebuild, but Luke knew the money would have to come from somewhere else. Not a big problem for the Lord, he supposed. But it was certainly out of Luke's realm of control.

But there also had been miracles. He leaned slightly forward and looked past Tom to Etta. The bandage around her head and the obviously damaged face told a hard story. And yet, there she was with her hands folded in her lap, sitting next to her former attacker, the one she called 'Massuh'.

Luke leaned back in his seat. He could swear she was still smiling.

"It seems so peaceful right now," he thought, yet he had an underlying sense that this was all just a warm-up. Slavery was an accepted way of life here in the South, but a man from up north named Lincoln was campaigning for the presidency of the Union on the platform of limiting slavery to its present borders. Some northerners wanted him to promise that he would eliminate slavery altogether if he was elected. All through the South, there was talk of secession if Lincoln became president. Neighbors were eyeing neighbors suspiciously, trying to discern which side the other was on. Even among true Christians, opinions about owning slaves varied widely.

There would be no peace until heaven, of that Luke was sure. At such a precarious time as this, why would God plant him, of all people, at Tom's side? Suddenly he was revisiting his conversation with the Lord by the river, under the bridge. The congregation laughed at something Pastor Matthew said, but Luke heard none of it.

"You need each other," Luke heard the Lord saying. *"There is still some refining to do."*

"But Tom can be so irritating!" Luke responded in his thoughts.

He got no response.

He waited and listened, giving the Lord every chance to think of something to say, but still got nothing.

Luke leaned forward again and peeked at Etta. The woman had obviously learned how to suffer *well*. She was nodding her head and listening intently to the sermon, still smiling.

Settling back, Luke looked thoughtfully at the cross behind Matthew.

"I want to be like that little old black woman, Lord."

He nodded his head and closed his eyes in prayer.

"Yep," he nodded again, "I want to be just like you and her."

Finally, Luke smiled too.